I0617691

Divine Intervention

Book Six in the Just Call Me Angel Series

By

S.R. Claridge

Global Publishing Group

Global Publishing Group

Printed in the United States of America

First trade edition: February 2011

10 9 8 7 6 5 4 3 2 1

ISBN 978-0-9864223-0-0

The author would like to offer special thanks to her personal and brilliant team of editors: Cash, Jerrye, Gary, Matt and Beth

She would also like to thank the editing team at Global Publishing Group for their diligence to detail.

S.R.Claridge thanks her family for their love and support, and God for every blessing He has bestowed.

~

DIVINE INTERVENTION is the sixth book in the Just Call Me Angel series. A complete list of books by S.R.Claridge is located at the back of this book.

For previews and information about the author, visit www.SusanClaridge.com or find her on Facebook, Twitter, Instagram, LinkedIn

For information on other Global Publishing Group Authors, please visit: www.GlobalPublishingGroupLLC.com

KEY CHARACTERS IN THE JUST CALL ME ANGEL SERIES:

Giovanni Maratinzano: Angel's Grandfather and the Capo Di Tutti Capi

Angel Maratinzano: Head of the Maratinzano Family

Lucia Maratinzano (aka "Olga"): Giovanni's sister and Angel's Aunt who raised her.

Sophia Buscetta: Angel's mother and Salvatore's daughter.

Salvatore Buscetta: Head of the Cosa Nostra in Sicily

Carl Cusanelli: Giovanni's Compare

Andrew Venturini: Boss of the Venturini Family; Ex-Special Detective on the Chicago Police Force

Tony Andriachini: Angel's Ex-Fiancé and son of the Andriachini Boss.

Sean Shepherd (aka "The Snake"): Made Member of the Maratinzano family.

Big Mike: Made Member of the Maratinzano family.

Monahan: Messaggero, the liaison between the Italian Crime Families and those in the States.

Chito: Head of the Chicago street gang, The Cobras

Trig: Made member of the Maratinzano family

Chase: Made member of the Maratinzano family;
computer genius; weapons specialist

CHAPTER 1

Detta stepped from the shower, wrapped herself in a towel and then wiped the steam from the bathroom mirror. The kids were off to school and she could finally relax. Towel drying her long, dark hair and slipping her arms into an ivory colored, fleece robe, she trudged down the narrow hallway of her mobile home and into the kitchen for a cup of coffee.

"Where is it?" Came his voice from the adjoining living room, startling her. "It wasn't in the fruit bowl as promised."

Detta's eyes quickly scanned the lime green speckled, linoleum countertop and landed on the white bowl of fruit at the end. "That's where I placed it," she said, lurching toward the bowl and then emptying its contents onto the countertop.

He joined her in the kitchen, shaking his head in a display of obvious disappointment. "I don't have to tell you what betraying me means, do I?"

Detta shook her head. "I didn't betray you. I placed it in the fruit bowl this morning." Panic began to set in as she opened and closed every drawer beneath the countertop, thinking...hoping it had somehow fallen inside. She turned toward him, pleading. "I swear to you. I put it there this morning."

She could feel his eyes burning through her. "This is problematic, Detta," he gritted.

"I know," she whispered.

"Can you make another?"

Detta shook her head. "I could only hack into their system once. It would be impossible for me to do it again undetected. It's heavily guarded."

He drew a knife from the block near the sink and then turning quickly toward her, ran the tip of it down her cheek until the blade rested against her throat. "Let's make one thing clear," he hissed, slithering behind her so his lips lay close to her ear lobe. "I trusted you to give me what I asked for and in return you and your disorderly rug rats would be left alone, even protected..." He abruptly stopped, as if a thought had entered his mind and then lowered the knife and spun Detta to face him. "Is it conceivable that one of the children took it?"

Detta gasped. "No! Nicholas, NO!" She threw herself to her knees and gripped his legs, begging. "Please leave them out of this. They know nothing about it."

"They may know nothing about it and yet they may possess the very item I am seeking," he said, kicking her from his legs. "Get dressed. We are leaving immediately."

"Where are we going?" She hesitantly stood.

"I think it's time we paid a visit to East Side Junior High, don't you?"

Detta's eyes widened. "No, Nicholas! You can't. I refuse to help you hurt children."

The words had barely left her lips when he backhanded her across the face with such force that she lost her balance and struck her head against the countertop. The last thing she remembered before slipping into unconsciousness was the cool linoleum against her cheek and a wave of nausea.

"Sorry, love," Nicholas sneered.

Within moments Detta's ankles and wrists were bound by duct tape and her eyes and mouth taped shut. He then dragged her outside and threw her into the trunk of his car.

"We have a problem," he hissed into his cell phone as he crawled behind the wheel and started the ignition. "Get a delivery truck and meet me at the warehouse in one hour. We're heading to East Side Junior High."

CHAPTER 2

"What do we do once we get inside the school?" Thomas asked as he climbed into the passenger seat of the delivery truck and then slicked back his hair with a comb retrieved from the pocket of his black, leather jacket. "I mean, how do we find what we're looking for?"

"We use any means necessary," Nicholas seethed, tightening his grip on the steering wheel.

"We gonna shoot kids, boss?" Thomas narrowed his brow. "I don't wanna shoot no kids." Thomas was a Nicholas wannabe but he lacked the guts to do what needed to be done. He wanted to appear powerful and have everyone believe that he and Nicholas were tight, but the truth was he was weak and Nicholas knew it. There was only one way to motivate Thomas.

Pulling a Glock from his jacket, Nicholas took aim at Thomas. "You will kill whoever I tell you to kill. Capisce?"

"Yeah, I got it," he cowered.

"It's kill or be killed. You understand?" Nicholas gritted.

Thomas held up his hands. "Yeah. Yeah. I got it."

"Good," Nicholas snipped, lowering the gun and feeling satisfied. "Besides, I don't think we'll need to kill any kids. We'll take out a few teachers if we have to and that will scare the kids into telling us everything we need to know." A sadistic grin filled Nicholas's face. "And I know who is going to die first."

"Who?" Thomas asked, wide-eyed.

"We need to teach Detta a lesson," he sneered. "I want to make sure she knows that mistakes are costly."

"You gonna kill Detta?" Thomas gasped. "I thought you and Detta were a thing. Like you loved each other."

Nicholas's eyes darkened. "First rule of business: Love only yourself. Be loyal to yourself. Trust no one, especially not a woman you're bedding down with. They're good for a fuck but if you hang around too long they'll fuck you over." Nicholas gave Thomas a sideways glance. "That's wisdom right there. Remember that."

Thomas nodded. "So, how are you gonna teach Detta a lesson?"

"Her sister works at the school and you're going to kill her," Nicholas said nonchalantly.

Thomas squirmed uncomfortably. "Why do I have to kill her? Why don't you kill her?"

Nicholas made a clicking sound with his tongue. "Thomas, Thomas, Thomas. You're going to create a diversion by killing Detta's sister, while I sneak into the building and find the rug rats that stole what rightfully belongs to me."

Looking at a copy of a school schedule he had pulled from the front of Detta's refrigerator, Nicholas checked his watch and noted which classroom he would visit first. "Ms. Schneider, Room 206," he muttered. "It's your lucky day."

CHAPTER 3

The Snake pulled the tank to the front of Chicago's East Side Junior High School and turned to face Angel. "Ms. Maratinzano, I don't think this is a wise course of action," he said, his grimace a display of disapproval.

"I know," she sighed, "which is exactly why Giovanni can never find out. Agreeing to do it was the only way to shut Olga up."

The Snake's half-grin told Angel that he understood her dilemma. It was no secret to anyone in the Maratinzano family that Olga's relentless demands could drive a person over the edge. If Olga hadn't been Giovanni's sister someone would have certainly taken her out by now.

"I think I should accompany you inside," he said, killing the ignition and then checking the clip on his .45 and slipping it back into his waistband.

"Yeah, because my arriving with an armed body guard won't look weird," Angel uttered sarcastically, lowering the visor mirror and checking her reflection. "I have to appear to be a regular business woman, coming in to talk to the kids on career day." Angel raised the visor. "I just don't know what in the world I'm going to say to a group of thirteen year olds to hold their attention."

"Thirteen. Hormones raging. I can tell you what Chase would say," the Snake smirked.

"I don't think the teacher will appreciate me talking about sex." Angel laughed. "Wish me luck."

"You don't need luck," he said and held up her 9mm. "She's loaded and the safety's on."

"I'm pretty sure guns aren't allowed in schools." Angel pushed the gun away.

"With all due respect Ms. Maratinzano, you either take the gun or I tag along; the choice is yours."

She hated when he formally addressed her instead of using her first name; and he knew it. Narrowing her eyes, Angel cocked her head slightly to the side. "Do you honestly think someone is going to try and take me out in a middle school?" She pursed her lips and glared at him as if to imply he was paranoid. "No one, except you and Olga even know I'm here."

"Me or the gun," the Snake stated matter-of-factly.

As she opened the door and slid from the seat, Angel carefully placed the gun into the back of her waistband and smoothed her black pencil skirt, to be sure her black suit jacket covered it. "Fine, I'll take it," she said. "Happy now?"

"I'd be happier if you let me come inside."

Angel rolled her eyes. "You worry too much."

"It's my job."

"Over-achiever," she teased.

He was right, it was his job to protect her and a certain amount of worrying came with that occupation. After all, if anything happened to her on his watch he would have to answer to Giovanni; a body guard's worst nightmare and some would say a fate scarier than even death.

Angel leaned her head inside the car. "Relax. This is a middle school, filled with pre-teens who are more interested in each other than anything I have to say. I'll be back in twenty."

After closing the Tank door, Angel headed briskly up the sidewalk toward the school; her black pumps clicking noisily against the pavement. *Sometimes body guards can be a pain in the ass,* she thought; but she couldn't blame the Snake for being cautious. They had been through a lot together and he had worked for Giovanni for a long time. He knew, better than anyone, the importance of protecting Giovanni's assets, of which Angel was considered his greatest.

The closer she came to the front doors, the more nervous she grew, silently berating herself for not taking the time to prepare a formal speech or at the very least, jot down a few ideas on note cards. She was a planner by nature so winging it didn't come easily. Stopping momentarily Angel inhaled and then exhaled quickly. It was silly to be nervous she told herself. After all, she had looked down the barrel of a grenade launcher, been hurled from an airplane and exploded off of a dock; surely she could face a classroom of eighth graders. The truth was, she didn't want to be here. She wasn't even sure why or how she had let Olga convince her to do this. It was just like Olga, though, to volunteer Angel without her consent.

During Olga's recent visit to her favorite hair salon, she promised Elsa, the salon owner, that Angel would talk to her granddaughter, Ruby's, eighth grade class about being a successful business woman in a working man's world. Somewhere amid the babbling about Elsa's newly remodeled salon, her incessant ranting over her new and improved hairdo, which looked just like her old one; and her rambling on and on about how thrilled she was to receive a Fitbit from Elsa, even though she didn't know what it was or how to use it, Angel heard herself agreeing to go just to shut Olga up.

"I can't talk to kids about being a Mafia boss," Angel had initially objected.

"Merciful Heavens, child!" Olga had exclaimed, gripping her chest in over-dramatized fashion. "Why, you'd scare the living daylights out of those kids. No, no, no. You need to tell them

13

what it's like to own a pub in Chicago. Except,
leave out all the sex parts, you know, with you and
Grayson and then you and Andrew and you and
Tony and did you ever sleep with your old chef,
Anthony? Oh, that Anthony, what a hunk-a-hunk-
a-burnin' love he was."

They had had this conversation at breakfast
and Angel picked up a piece of toast and chucked
it across the table at Olga.

"It's disrespectful to throw things at your old
aunt," she said, taking a bite out of the toast.
"Your sex life is nothing to be ashamed of, dear. I
just don't think you should tell children about it."

"I wasn't going to talk to them about my sex
life!" Angel rolled her eyes. How Olga could rabbit
trail a conversation into an entirely different topic
was amazing.

"Oh," she shrugged. "Well, then why'd you
bring it up?"

"YOU brought it up!"

Angel had stormed from the room,
flabbergasted; while Olga mumbled something
about how she'd consider owning a pub if it meant
she would get to have sex with hot Italian men.
"Don't look a gift horse in the mouth, missy," Olga
called after her.

Olga had won, as usual, and here she was,
entering East Side Junior High School to talk to
the kids about anything BUT sex. Through the
double glass doors, Angel made an immediate right
turn into the front office. As she approached the
desk, a bright eyed, red head looked up and
smiled. "Can I help you?"

Angel cleared her throat. "I'm here to speak to
an eighth grade class for career day," she said.

"Okay, we'll need to get you a badge." The red
head stood and pointed to a clipboard which was

on the counter in front of her. "Sign in here and then I'll need to see your driver's license."

"My driver's license?" Angel puzzled.

"District policy," the red head said with a smile.

Angel bit her bottom lip. "I don't have my driver's license with me." Mafia Bosses didn't run around with identification on their person, neither did most of the Made members of the family. It wasn't wise.

The red head sighed with obvious exasperation. "What is your full name?"

"Angel Maratin..." she began and then stopped abruptly and cleared her throat. "Angel Martin," she corrected herself. There was no sense in using the family name on the off chance that someone might recognize it. Better to be safe than sorry.

"In which classroom will you be speaking?"

Angel stared blankly. She didn't know. Olga never gave her the teacher's name and, come to think of it, she didn't even know Ruby's last name. All she knew was that Ruby was Elsa's granddaughter and she was going to be speaking to her class. This was embarrassing. With a slow blink and a deep breath, Angel began to explain the story, but mid-way through the red-head interrupted her.

"Excuse me," she said, holding her finger up to indicate that she needed a moment. Then she turned to a dark-haired, heavy-set woman sitting next to her. "Sandy, can you facilitate this delivery?"

Sandy looked up from her computer screen. "What delivery?"

"The Wholesome Goodness truck that just pulled up outside," the red-head said, pointing to the window. "He'll need clearance through to the cafeteria and, since Ms. Martin came with absolutely no information, it's going to take me a while to figure out where she is supposed to be."

Angel found the woman's snide sarcasm unnecessary, not to mention disrespectful. Her jaw tightened and the hair on the back of her neck bristled, as she struggled to remind herself that this woman didn't know her. Had she known that the Capo di Tutti Capi's granddaughter was standing before her, she probably would have refrained from using such a sardonic tone.

"I don't see a delivery scheduled for today," Sandy said, leaning closer to her computer screen and squinting at the data. "I'm showing a cafeteria delivery for next Tuesday."

The red head displayed her annoyance with an eye roll. "Just handle it," she snipped.

Angel watched as the delivery man entered the office and spoke momentarily with Sandy, who then led him out of the office and down the hallway toward the cafeteria. "Now," said the red head, redirecting her attention back to Angel, "you said you were speaking to an eighth grade classroom?"

"Yes."

"I'll have to contact each teacher to find out which one is expecting you," she muttered condescendingly as she plunked down into her chair. People who were mean for no reason infuriated Angel and she silently envisioned ramming her 9mm into the woman's face and giving her one last chance to improve her countenance. The thought made her smile. She was still fantasizing about it when all of a sudden a gunshot rang out like a cannon. The red-head shrieked and dove beneath the counter and even Angel, who was accustomed to the sound of gunshots, flinched and instinctively squatted down.

Quickly crawling around the counter to where the red-head lay hunched into a ball, Angel pulled out her gun and put her fingers to her lips, indicating that the woman should be quiet. Her eyes widened in terror when she saw Angel's gun.

Just then a woman with short black hair and round glasses darted into the office. "Shooter!" She screamed. "Go to lockdown!" "Go to lockdown!" The black haired woman hollered and then dove toward the red head's desk, pushing a button that was located on the underside of the counter. An automated voice boomed over the speaker system throughout the school: THIS IS AN EMERGENCY LOCKDOWN. THIS IS NOT A DRILL. THIS IS AN EMERGENCY LOCKDOWN. THIS IS NOT A DRILL.

The black haired woman glared frantically at Angel. This was every teacher's nightmare. This was every parent's worst fear. "Who are you?" She blurted, glancing at Angel's gun. "What do you want?"

"I'm not with the shooter," Angel blurted.

"Are you a cop?" The black haired woman asked.

"No."

"Then why do you have a gun?" The woman's eyes darted from Angel to the gun and back to Angel. "I can't explain right now but I'm here to help. Who are you? Do you have any weapons here? Is there a security guard?" Angel's questions came rapid fire as she glanced nervously toward the office doors.

"I'm Principal Radley," the woman uttered breathlessly. "There are no weapons on the premises and no funding for a security guard. Our only defense is to pray that everyone remembers the proper lockdown protocol."

17

Another gunshot rang out and Principal Radley's body trembled uncontrollably.

"Did you call the police?" Angel whispered.

"The minute we press the lockdown button the police are notified," she answered, her voice shaking.

"Then they are on their way," Angel muttered more to herself than to the women next to her. Checking the clip on her 9mm, she clamped it back into place and took a deep breath, grateful that the Snake had insisted on her bringing her gun.

"I'm going after the shooter. You two stay under the counter. I have a guy outside who can help. His name is the Snake."

"The Snake?" The red-head looked up and her eyes widened. "Who are you?"

"It doesn't matter. When the Snake comes rushing toward the door, which should be any second now, you need to buzz him in. Do you understand?"

The women nodded slowly.

"Tell him I think the shooter was disguised as the delivery guy and I'm headed toward the cafeteria." Angel took a deep breath. "Did you get that?" Principal Radley nodded. "Which way is the cafeteria?"

The Principal pointed and leaving the two women huddled beneath the counter, Angel crept through the doorway and down the hall. The school was silent; so quiet it felt surreal. Sliding out of her heels so not to make clacking sounds against the tile floor, Angel moved quickly, noticing that every door she passed was shut and the lights were out. It was obvious that the students and teachers had practiced this lockdown drill more than once. Fear hung so thickly in the air that it was almost palatable. Anger churned inside of her.

*How dare anyone come into a school and terrorize
children like this.* As rage and fear fought for top
billing in her gut, Angel gripped the 9mm a little
tighter.

As she peered around a corner and down the
next hallway, she saw a sign indicating that the
door to the cafeteria was to her right. Quickly
crossing to the other side of the hallway, she
positioned herself to peek into the cafeteria. Sandy
and a woman, whom Angel guessed to be the gym
teacher because she wore white tennis shoes and
clutched a whistle in her hand, were lying face
down on the floor next to each other in a pool of
blood. They had been shot execution style but
there was no sign of the executioner. A wave of
nausea hit Angel's stomach, followed by a fierce
anger.

Moving passed the cafeteria doorway; she
quickly raced down the hall with her gun
outstretched. There had only been two shots fired
and Angel was determined to find the shooter
before he could kill again. East Side Junior High
School was connected to the East Side Elementary
School so external alarms were now sounding in
both buildings. *The police should be here soon,* she
told herself. There was no sign of the delivery man
on the first floor so Angel started up the staircase
at the end of the hall. At the top of the stairs she
heard a whimper coming from the boy's restroom
to her right. Using her gun, Angel slowly nudged
the bathroom door open. Then immediately
ducked down and began checking beneath the
stalls for feet. Under the sink she found a blonde
haired boy, curled into a fetal position, trembling
and crying. Angel rushed toward him, bent down
and extended her hand. "Come with me," she
whispered, but the boy covered his face with his
arms and wept harder. Kneeling in front of him,

Angel pleaded, "I'm not going to hurt you. We need to get out of here."

He shook his head and wrapped his arms tighter around himself.

"What are you doing in here?" Angel asked, trying to spark conversation so she could coax him out of hiding. "Why aren't you locked in a classroom with the rest of the kids?"

Peering out from between his arms, he gave Angel a quick once over and she caught a glimpse of his terrified, teary, blue eyes. "I was trying to give this to my brother," he sniveled, opening his right fist and displaying a small, black jump drive. "He needs it for his science project otherwise he'll get a bad grade and Mrs. Palumbo said if he gets one more bad grade, he won't be allowed to play soccer anymore."

Angel could tell by his size, his facial features and his voice that he was not a junior high student. She surmised that he must be a student from the adjoining elementary school.

"My brother loves soccer more than anything in the world. So, when I saw the drive in Mrs. Palumbo's fruit bowl this morning I knew that Jack forgot it so I snatched it," he continued.

"Who's Mrs. Palumbo?" Angel asked, hoping that keeping him talking would garner trust and enable her to lure him out from under the sink.

"The lady I live with." He lowered his teary eyes to the floor. "I'm a foster kid."

"What's your name?" Angel asked.

"Caleb," he answered quietly, peering cautiously up at her. "Are we gonna die?" The question caught Angel by surprise. It was so forthright, so raw and honest that it gripped her heart. "I don't want to die," he cried. "I don't want to die. I want my mommy!" He broke into sobs.

Angel had no experience with children but she could remember the feeling of growing up missing her mom and she definitely knew what it felt like to not want to die. Reaching down, she gently wiped a tear from Caleb's cheek. "Sshh," she said and glanced over her shoulder toward the bathroom door. If the shooter came in, they were sitting ducks. Somehow she needed to convince Caleb to follow her and fast. Angel leaned in closer and whispered, "I know you don't want to die. I don't want to die either. That's why we've got to get out of here. Come with me and I'll get you somewhere safe. I promise."

His terror-stricken eyes stared back at her and she could only imagine what was running through his little mind. How could he trust her when she was a complete stranger and he, like most children, had probably been taught to never trust a stranger? What's more, she was holding a gun, which probably intensified his fear. Despite that possibility, she couldn't put her gun away on the off chance that the shooter might come barreling through the door.

"What's your name?" Caleb asked.

"Angel," she said softly. "How old are you, Caleb?"

"Eight... and a half," he uttered.

"Well, that's old enough to be my helper," Angel said and felt a tiny glimmer of hope as Caleb's eyebrows raised slightly with interest.

"My teacher says I'm one of the best classroom helpers."

"That's great, because I'm going to need a good helper," Angel said softly. "We've got to get out of here."

"But I can just hide under the sink until the police come," he whispered.

Angel shook her head slowly side to side. "Listen, Caleb, there's a man with a gun somewhere in the school building and you can't stay here because he might find you just like I did. So, I need you to come with me. Can you do that?"

"What if we run into the man with the gun?" Caleb asked.

"That's what my gun is for," Angel answered bluntly, setting the 9mm on the floor next to her knees and reaching for his hands. There was no sense in lying to him or trying to soften the situation. She needed to get him to safety and in order to do that, he had to trust her. Lying to him wouldn't earn his trust. This she knew firsthand.

"You mean, you'll shoot him?" The innocence of youth glistened in his eyes.

Angel swallowed hard. This was not a conversation she ever envisioned having with a child. "Yes, I'll shoot him."

Caleb's face contorted into a grimace and his brows narrowed. "Good," he said sharply and crawled out from under the sink. "I hope you kill him. I'll help you." His innocent glare was suddenly laced in anger, an anger Angel knew all too well.

With Caleb tucked behind her, Angel made her way out of the bathroom and started back toward the staircase. She wanted to get Caleb to the office where the police would find him and get him safely out of the building; only then would she go back and find the shooter. Nearing the stairs, Angel heard a noise from behind a classroom door located across from the boy's restroom. She pushed Caleb against a row of lockers and stood in front of him, then twisted her neck ever so slightly so she could peer through the glass window in the door. Most of the classroom windows were covered, but the cover on this one was crooked, leaving a gap just large enough for Angel to look through. Inside the classroom stood a man waving a gun and barking instructions, but it was not the delivery man Angel had seen earlier in the front office. Her pulse quickened as the realization that there might be two shooters in the building hit her.

"How did he get in there?" Angel whispered more to herself than to Caleb. "I thought the doors were all locked."

"That's Ms. Schneider's room," Caleb whispered. "She probably forgot to move the magnet from the door jam. Jack's in that class."

"Your brother?" Angel's pulse quickened as she watched the shooter dig through backpack after backpack, hurling them across the room. What was he doing? *What is he looking for?*

"Uh-huh. Well, he's not my real brother. He's a foster kid too and we've been at the last two homes together so I call him my brother. He's my best friend too, even though he's a lot older than me," Caleb explained.

Angel watched in horror as the shooter pulled a woman, presumably Ms. Schneider, to the front of the classroom and pushed her to her knees. He was going to kill Ms. Schneider execution style in front of the students. Angel's options were limited and she was running out of time. Her eyes darted from the window down to Caleb. She took him by the shoulders, leaned in close enough to put her lips next to his ear, and whispered, "I'm going to keep the shooter here and I need you to run to the front office as fast as you can. Tell the police where they can find us. Can you do that for me?"

Caleb nodded his head up and down and then leaned his lips next to her ear. "Angel?" Caleb said softly. "Don't let him hurt Ms. Schneider. Jack says she's the nicest teacher in the whole school." He opened his right fist, displaying the black jump drive. "Oh, and will you give this to Jack for me?"

Angel took the jump drive and slid it into her jacket pocket. "I promise. Now go. Run as fast as you can."

Caleb took off down the staircase, while Angel turned her attention back to the window.

This killing spree stops here, she said to herself, glaring at the shooter through the tiny strip of glass in the door. Two people were dead and if a third body hit the floor Angel determined it was going to be his. Her heart pounded wildly as she took a deep breath and clutched the 9mm. Her shot had to be precise. It would have been ideal to remove the students from the room before she blew him away, but, as Angel could attest, they were not living in an ideal world. The students were going to be traumatized either by watching him kill Ms. Schneider or by seeing Angel kill him. The second option was more palatable.

Time was ticking. *A clean shot through the head or a straight shot through the heart?* The heart gave a greater margin for error, but the head lowered the chances of him getting off a shot. She'd have to open the door with one hand and fire almost simultaneously with the other, hoping she could do it before he fired back. After all, she wasn't wearing a vest; a fact that would upset Andrew if he ever found out. *I wish Tony were here.* She thought. *He could take this asshole out with his eyes closed.*

Angel watched the shooter step toward Ms. Schneider and place the barrel of the gun against the back of her head. Time was up. One deep breath and then Angel yanked the door open and fired. The first shot sailed into his neck, knocking him backwards and splattering blood across the whiteboard behind him, but not before his gun fired, lodging a bullet into Angel's left shoulder. She cried out as the bullet ripped into her flesh, but she was not going to lose this fight. Too many lives were at stake. Cries erupted from the students huddled in the back of the room as Ms. Schneider wailed and curled into a ball. Angel's next shot found the center of his forehead and he hit the floor like a sack.

"Nice shootin'," the Snake's voice came from behind her and Angel whirled around with her gun ready. "Whoa," the Snake blurted. "It's me."

"Thanks for showing up," she mumbled, but the Snake strode passed her, toward the shooter's body. He pulled out his phone and snapped several pictures and then turned toward Angel.

"We need to get out of here before the police get upstairs."

Angel gave a nod, starting to feel woozy from the gunshot wound. The Snake was right, they didn't need to be front and center of a police investigation or have it plastered all over the headlines that a Mob Boss engaged in a school shootout. Giovanni would be unhappy with that type of publicity; in fact, he had made it very clear that no publicity was the best kind.

Ms. Schneider was in an obvious state of shock as the Snake lifted her to her feet and directed her toward the back of the classroom. The students enveloped her into their huddle; everyone's arms wrapped tightly around the person next to them. Cliques didn't matter today. Geeks. Jocks. Nerds. Cheerleaders. Goth kids. Tom boys. Whether you were rich or poor, black or white, gay or straight; it didn't matter. Today there were no labels, no defining lines. Today, there was no discrimination. In this darkest hour, they needed and clung to each other for life and life was all that mattered.

Angel started following the Snake down the hallway but then stopped at the top of the staircase and clutched her wounded arm. "Sean..." her voice tapered off. She was losing blood quickly. "There are two men..." her voice faded as the darkness engulfed her.

Looking back over his shoulder, the Snake noticed her wound for the first time and swore aloud. "I knew I should have escorted you," he spewed.

Racing upward, he caught Angel just as she lost consciousness, lifted her over his shoulder and dashed down the remaining stairs. He needed to get her out of the building without running into the police and his only hope was to go out the same way he had come in, through the back doors located in the cafeteria.

A combination of raw instinct and keen military eye for detail had enabled him to stealthily get into the school unnoticed and would hopefully help them escape unnoticed now.

After Angel had entered the building, the Snake watched as the delivery truck pulled up to the front door and the man in the passenger seat got out and walked inside. Something about the truck bothered him although he couldn't put his finger on what it was; so when the driver pulled around to the back of the school, the Snake followed. He watched closely as the driver got out of the truck and stood outside of the steel double doors, as if he were waiting for something. Moments later, someone pushed open one of the doors and the driver quickly propped it open and went inside. When the building alarm began to sound, the Snake leapt from the Tank, gun in hand, and headed toward the propped open door. Peering inside, he saw two women, face down in a puddle of blood. He had quickly explored the first floor, searching for Angel, when a little blonde boy came dashing around a corner and ran right into him. The boy bounced off of him and landed on the floor, staring up at the Snake with terrified eyes. "I'm not going to hurt you," the Snake told him. "My name is Sean and I'm looking for my friend, Angel. Have you seen her?" The boy pointed toward the stairs and the Snake took off in a sprint. All he could think about was the fact that he had to get to Angel before the shooters did. Now, with her limp body dangling over his shoulder and her blood soaking into his shirt, he realized he had failed.

The outside alarm continued to wail as he raced across the cafeteria and darted out through the propped open door, moving toward the Tank. He couldn't help noticing that the delivery truck was no longer parked outside. Then gently placing Angel into the backseat, he jumped into the driver's seat and sped out of the lot, across the field directly behind the school, over several medians and onto a subdivision street. Sirens filled the air as police, fire trucks and ambulances descended upon the school.

The Snake pounded his fist against the steering wheel and cursed aloud. He was in big trouble. Not only had Angel been shot, but there was a very good chance they had been caught by the school's security cameras. Giovanni was not going to be happy about the publicity nor about the fact that he had failed to protect his granddaughter.

CHAPTER 4

By the time the Snake pulled the Tank up to the Emergency entrance at Northwestern Memorial Hospital, Angel's skin was a gaunt shade of grayish green.

Leaping from the Tank, he carried her inside and helped two male emergency technicians place her securely onto a gurney. "We'll need you to wait outside, sir," the lady behind the desk told him. "You'll need to fill out some paperwork." She shoved a clipboard into the Snake's hand but his eyes remained glued to the gurney and the two men wheeling Angel down the hall and through the double doors.

What had he done? At Angel's request, he had sneaked behind Giovanni's back and taken her to the school against his better judgment. On top of that, he failed to protect her. He never should have allowed her to enter the school unaccompanied. He knew better. Mafia Bosses were not to be left alone, anywhere, at any time with the exception of when they were secure in their own home with the exterior perimeter guarded. What the hell was he going to tell Giovanni?

Pulling his cell phone from his pant pocket, he dialed. "Don Venturini," he spoke into the phone. "This is the Snake."

"Knock that crap off, Sean. I may have a new title, but to you I'm still just Andrew," Andrew retorted. "We've been through too much to get wrapped up in formalities now. What's going on?"

"There was a school shooting a little while ago at East Side Junior High," the Snake began.

"Yeah, I heard," Andrew said. "Two dead plus the shooter. It's terrible. It makes you wonder what this world is coming to, people going into schools and threatening kids."

"That's just it," the Snake said. "I don't think it was random."

"I'm not following."

The Snake took a deep breath. "I don't think it was random because Angel was there. She took out the shooter but she was hit in the process. We're at Northwestern Memorial and I haven't told Gio..."

"What the hell was she doing there?" Andrew hollered.

"It's a long story..."

"Who knows she was there?"

"Just me, Olga, whoever she talked to inside the building and now you."

"Don't tell anyone anything until I get there," Andrew blurted. "I'm on my way."

CHAPTER 5

Storming into the emergency waiting area, Andrew was hard to miss. He looked like an angry bull with flared nostrils and his dark, brooding eyes. Two body guards, dressed head to toe in all black, escorted him in and took flanking positions in the doorway. The Snake leapt to his feet when he saw him.

"Where is she?" Andrew blurted.

"In surgery." The Snake shook his head and sank back into one of the chairs. "It's my fault. I deserve what's coming to me. I didn't get to her in time."

"Did the bullet clear?" Andrew asked and the Snake shook his head.

"I don't know. Sirens were blaring, she was unconscious and all I could think about was getting her to safety. I didn't stop to check if the bullet came out of the other side or not."

"What was she even doing there?" Andrew barked. "What the hell happened?"

Andrew paced in front of him as the Snake recounted the events of the morning. His detective mind churned over the facts and he interrupted the Snake with questions, most of which went unanswered. Why did Olga promise Angel would speak at the school? Why did Angel agree to go? Why didn't the Snake accompany her inside?

"She wouldn't allow me to go with her!" The Snake blurted defensively. "I even had to force her to take her gun." He exhaled, leaning forward on his knees and dropped his head into his hands. "She's so stubborn!"

"Well, I can't argue with that," Andrew uttered, sinking into an adjacent chair. "I'm guessing she wasn't wearing a vest either."

The Snake shook his head. "But the vest wouldn't have saved her from this shot."

"It's the principal of it," Andrew chided. "She has GOT to start wearing one everywhere she goes."

"She's got to stop going places!" The Snake blurted.

Their conversation was cut short when a doctor emerged from behind the double doors and they both leapt to their feet. The doctor explained that the bullet had gone through, missing the bone entirely. "She was lucky," he said. "She lost a lot of blood but I see no reason why she won't recover fully."

"When can we see her?" Andrew asked.

"She'll be in recovery for the next forty-five minutes or so and then we'll move her to a room where we can keep an eye on her overnight. She's going to be weak and sore for a while. You'll be able to see her then."

The Snake sank back down into his chair and put his head in his hands. "What am I going to tell Giovanni?"

Placing a hand on his shoulder, Andrew uttered, "Nothing. You and my men will stay here for the night to guard Angel. I'll take care of Giovanni but I will need something from you in return."

"What?" The Snake looked up to see what could only be described as sadness etched on Andrew's face.

"Let's just say I've got to hit one out of the park and I might need you to lob me the ball."

Without further explanation Andrew turned and made a beeline for the exit, stopping only momentarily to give instructions to his men. "When will you be back?" The Snake hollered after him. "What should I tell Angel?"

"Tell her she should have been wearing a vest."

CHAPTER 6

The Snake led the Venturini men to Angel's hospital room, then stopped several feet from the door, turning to face them. "I don't want you leaving this room unattended for any reason. Got it? Not to get a bite or take a piss."

One guy nodded and the other just stared, chomping obnoxiously on a piece of gum.

"What are your names?" The Snake asked.

"Lenny," the man to his left said, while stretching out his hand and giving the Snake a firm shake. "Lenny Getgher."

Lenny looked familiar with his dark, bushy eyebrows, droopy brown eyes and thick wavy black hair. "You have a brother named Danny Getgher?" The Snake asked.

"Yep, but he's an asshole. Don't judge me based on my brother's less than appealing lifestyle." Lenny smoothed his hair. "I'm aces."

The man next to him guffawed loudly, shook his head and resumed chomping his gum. "You don't agree that he's aces?" The Snake asked.

"He's green, a newbie. He don't know what it means to be aces yet."

"How did you get guard detail for the Venturini Boss if you're a newbie?" The Snake began to wonder whether assigning Lenny to guard Angel was a wise choice.

"Me and Andrew...I mean, Don Venturini, go way back. He saved my ass a few times when he was a cop and I owe him."

"More like he owes you, you snitch," the gum chewer sneered.

"I ain't no snitch," Lenny retorted and then turned his attention back to the Snake. "I was an informant." He puffed out his shoulders and cracked his neck to the side.

"Informant. Snitch. There ain't no difference," the other guy clucked and maneuvered his gum across the front of his teeth to the other side of his mouth. He was several inches taller than Lenny, cleaner shaven and all around better looking.

Lenny bumped his chest into the other guy. "A snitch is a rat. An informant is a carrier of information. I was an informant. You got a problem with dat?"

"I don't trust snitches and I don't like informants."

The Snake immediately stepped between the two men and pushed them apart.

"And your name?" The Snake asked the gum chewer.

"Jacob," he retorted with a deliberate glare.

"Jacob what?"

"Denalli."

"How long have you been with the Venturini family?"

"Long enough..." he quipped and the Snake grabbed him by the collar of his black silk shirt and slammed him backwards against the wall with such force that it knocked the gum right out of his mouth. "Long enough to see that somethin' ain't right," he sputtered and the Snake released him. Jacob adjusted his collar and smoothed his shirt.

"What do mean something isn't right?" The Snake asked.

"Why don't you tell me?" Jacob growled. "You're the one who's working for the Capo."

The Snake shook his head. "What does Giovanni have to do with this?"

Jacob shrugged. "I don't know, man, but something's wrong. Way wrong. I can smell it."

The Snake stared at him, a sour pit churning deep in his gut. He, too, had sensed that something wasn't right but he couldn't determine what it was. Giovanni had appeared distracted the past several weeks, as if he sensed it too. It was the feeling that a storm was brewing despite sunny skies.

"We're all a little jumpy lately," Lenny said. "It's the boss," he leaned closer and whispered. "He's been acting all funny-like; all jacked up and nervous and edgy and shit."

"Why?" The Snake asked.

"We should be asking you that question," Jacob chided. "Whatever is going on is coming straight from the Capo."

"What makes you think that?" The Snake asked.

"Don Venturini has been having a lot of private meetings and private phone calls," Lenny explained.

The Snake shrugged. This wasn't unusual for a Boss. Much of what they did was in secrecy. Still, the Snake couldn't shake the feeling that Jacob and Lenny were onto something.

"Yeah," Jacob agreed.

"And he's been moving our guys around. I heard that he's been talking to the Capo A LOT." Lenny's eyes were wide as he emphasized the phrase A LOT.

Though this wasn't cause for concern, as it was not out of the question for a Boss to meet with the Capo; it was, however, unusual for one particular Boss to have regular meetings with the Capo. Typically, all five Bosses would come together to discuss business. Then again, Andrew had a unique relationship with the Capo's granddaughter, which could explain more frequent conversations.

"I heard he has a girlfriend from another family and it ain't Angel," Jacob sneered. The Snake listened with skepticism. He knew how

Andrew felt about Angel and couldn't imagine him with any other woman.

"I heard that the Venturini family was no longer going to exist; that we're so weak after the death of the last Don and his sons that we're going to be shut down," Lenny whispered.

Narrowing his eyebrows, the Snake found Lenny's perspective over-dramatized. Families weren't just shut down and they didn't cease to exist. There had been cases where feuding had rendered a particular family dormant and quiet, but they always came back. The Maratinzanos were a perfect example. After Angel's father had been murdered and the majority of the Maratinzano members killed or driven out of the city, it took years for them to flourish again. In fact, Angel was still re-building the family.

"Yeah, I heard something similar," Jacob admitted. "And that's why the Boss has been relocating our members. They say he's been hooking them up with the other families so they have some place to go."

"What?" The Snake uttered more to himself than to them. Andrew hadn't mentioned anything, then again, since the CoBroGas attack, when his father and brothers were killed; the Snake hadn't spent any time with Andrew. Was it possible that he had plans to get rid of the Venturini family once and for all?

"We worry about one thing now!" The Snake blurted. "For the next twenty-four hours your job is to guard Ms. Maratinzano with your life. Capisce?"

"Capisce," they said in unison.

"Nobody comes in this room," the Snake gritted. "Nobody."

"What...what about the doctors and nurses?" Lenny stuttered.

"Nobody goes in until I get back."

Lenny and Jacob took flanking positions on either side of Angel's hospital room door while the Snake headed down the hall to make a phone call. He dialed Andrew but the call went straight to voicemail. He felt uneasy about Lenny and Jacob. Jacob had a defiant nature that would undoubtedly hinder his ability to follow instructions and Lenny seemed emotional, like he could get rattled too easily. Not only that, but they were quick to spill their guts to him, which made the Snake doubt their loyalty to Andrew. If they couldn't be loyal to their own Boss, how could he trust them with the safety and well-being of another Boss? These men were not exactly Boss level security and the Snake found it hard to believe that Andrew, now head of the Venturini family, had placed them as his personal guards. Of one thing he was certain, something wasn't right. He thought to dial Chase and ask him to begin erasing any surveillance footage from the school, but Andrew's order to talk to no one pressed powerfully at the forefront of his mind.

With nerves churning his stomach, the Snake made a quick jaunt to the men's restroom, where he splashed cold water on his face and tried to force himself to breathe easier. Leaning both hands on the sink and staring at his reflection in the mirror, he mulled over the facts. Fact one: Angel was alive and she was going to fully recover. Fact two: Giovanni didn't know anything had happened to his granddaughter on the Snake's watch so technically he wasn't in trouble...yet. Fact three: The school shooting wasn't random and it was no coincidence that Angel was in the building at the time. He couldn't prove it, but he knew it and his instincts were rarely wrong. Fact four: He had until Giovanni heard about Angel being shot to figure out what was going on, because after that he would be anxiously looking over his shoulder and running for his life. Despite years of loyalty, Giovanni would see only the fact that he disobeyed an order and failed to protect Angel; and that was a crime punishable by death. There would be no escaping the power, anger or vengefulness of the Capo di Tutti Capi.

CHAPTER 7

"I need to talk directly to Giovanni," Andrew barked into the phone. "Tell him it's Andrew Venturini. Yes, DON Venturini." Andrew couldn't get used to the fact that he was now Boss of the Venturini family. Though he took the position out of respect for his father, God rest his soul, a part of him, a very big part of him, longed to go back to being Special Detective Andrew Venturini, one of Chicago's finest. He had loved being a cop but was torn between the contradiction of his oath to the force and the Omerta to his family. When his father and brothers were murdered, Andrew felt he had no choice but to fill his father's shoes and carry on the family legacy.

"Don Venturini," Giovanni's gruff tone came through the phone.

"With all due respect, sir, please call me Andrew."

"Ah, you are still struggling with the nature of your identity within the family and your moral obligation to uphold the laws of the city you have served for so long. I understand. You will realize in time that the city will have forgotten you but su familia, your family, is a legacy that will never forget and will never die." Giovanni took a deep breath. "But you did not phone to hear my lecture. What can I do for you?"

"I'm calling about Angel."

"Ah, Michelangela, si. Am I to believe you have considered my offer?"

"Yes, sir. I have." He took a deep breath. Lying to the Capo di Tutti Capi was no easy task. "But before I accept, I would like to take her away..."

"Take her away?" Giovanni interrupted.

"For the weekend," Andrew clarified. "I'd like to take her to a small lake house for a couple of days, get her out of the city into some fresh air, with your permission, of course."

"Ah, a farewell weekend," Giovanni uttered beneath his breath and then sat in silence; a silence that as it lingered became so haunting that a part of Andrew wanted to hang up and pretend he never made the call.

Finally, Giovanni spoke. "I do not want to see Michelangela hurt. She will not understand that it is best for her in the long run, for you and for the families. Under the circumstances I will allow this trip, assuming of course that you will take proper security measures at this lake house."

"Yes, sir. I will take several of my men..."

"You will take the Snake also," Giovanni interrupted, "to ensure that Michelangela returns from this get-away."

This was working out better than planned. He could take Angel away long enough to give her a few days to heal and for them to come up with a believable story about how she had been wounded; thereby saving the Snake from the potential risk of Giovanni's wrath. At the same time, he and the Snake could corroborate on what happened at the school and hopefully find out who was behind the shooting. Most importantly, the Snake could be there for Angel after Andrew dropped the bomb. He didn't want her to be alone.

"She will return safely," Andrew promised. "Grazie Giovan..." he began but was interrupted mid-sentence.

"And upon your return you will officially accept my offer?" Giovanni said it more as a statement of fact than a question. "We will make it public then."

"Yes, sir," Andrew answered with a deep pit in his stomach. For Giovanni's offer was one he could not refuse despite the fact that it would change his relationship with Angel forever.

"Very good. I will make the proper arrangements," Giovanni uttered and then disconnected the call.

CHAPTER 8

Thomas pulled the delivery truck into the warehouse and closed the door. Then, using a crowbar, he pried open the trunk of Nicholas' car and found Detta, still taped and bound. Hoisting her out, he pulled the tape from her eyes and lips. "Don't scream," he whispered.

"Where's Nicholas?" Detta blurted in breathless panic, squinting while her eyes adjusted to the light.

"Dead."

Detta's eyes widened. "The boys? Where are Caleb and Jack?"

Thomas shrugged. "All I know is that Nicholas went into the school and he never came out. I think the kids are fine."

"Did the police kill him?"

"No. I think it was the Maratinzanos," Thomas seethed. "I knew that lady in the office looked familiar."

"What were they doing there?" Detta shook her head. "We were guaranteed that no one would learn of our plan." Using a pocket knife, Thomas cut through the duct tape around Detta's wrists and ankles; and then she ripped off the tape and rubbed her sore skin. "Did Nicholas find the jump drive?"

Thomas shook his head. "I got a call from one of our guys on the inside. They said that some little kid is telling the cops and the news stations that an angel saved him." Thomas narrowed his eyes. "And get a load of this. My informant says that he told one news lady that he gave this angel a jump drive to give to his brother."

Detta gasped. It had to be Caleb. "Caleb must have thought the drive belonged to Jack," Detta muttered to herself. "That's why he took it."

She stared at Thomas. "But how would Angel Maratinzano have known about the drive and how would she have known that it was at the middle school?" Panic rose in Detta's voice. "Have they been watching us the whole time?"

"It don't matter," Thomas quipped.

"It DOES matter!" Detta's eyes widened with fear. "If they have been watching us then we are all in danger. We have to leave town NOW!"

Thomas grabbed Detta by the shoulders and shook her. "Calm down!" He barked. "Even if Angel has the drive, she don't know what's on it. It's encrypted, right?"

Detta nodded.

"So they don't know what they got and alls we need to do is get it back," Thomas released Detta and leaned against the car.

"You can't just walk up to a mob Boss and demand the jump drive." Detta leaned against the car next to him. "Angel Maratinzano is the granddaughter to the Capo di Tutti Capi, the most powerful man in the mafia world. He will have you killed for merely looking at his granddaughter."

"My guy says that Angel arrived at Northwestern Memorial about an hour ago, and that she was shot."

"How reliable is this source?" Detta asked.

"He's straight up. A no bullshit guy," Thomas retorted with the slight tilt of his head. "I figure if she was taken straight from the school to the hospital then she still has the drive in her possession, so I sent some guys to retrieve it."

"You know that she will be heavily guarded..." Detta began but Thomas interrupted her.

"Stop worrying," he groaned. "I've got it covered." He draped his arm around Detta's shoulders. "My boys will get the drive and we'll be back in business."

Detta bit her lip.

"Now, I'm gonna take you home so you can get in your car and hurry to the school. They've set up a special lot for parents to pick up their kids." Thomas took her face between his palms. "Everything has to appear normal."

They walked across the warehouse, toward Thomas's red Mustang. "There's one more thing you should know," Thomas said as they climbed in the car. "Nicholas killed your sister. He said it was a reminder to you that complications were unacceptable."

Sandy! Detta's heart stalled, though she showed no outward emotion. There was no point. Showing weakness to Thomas could get her killed and wouldn't bring her sister back. Detta tensed her jaw and swallowed hard. "Then there will be no more complications," she uttered.

"Good," Thomas said and started the ignition. "I'll take over Nicholas' role and we'll get Leo to fill my shoes."

CHAPTER 9

Tapping lightly on Angel's door, the Snake pushed it open and stuck his head inside. She motioned him in with a slight nod and a half smile.

"Don't say it," she moaned.

The Snake pulled a chair next to her bed and sat down. "Ms. Maratinzano, I let you down today and I'm sorry."

Angel shook her head slowly. "You saved countless lives today by forcing me to take my gun..." her voice faded groggily. "It was my fault I got shot." Angel drew in a deep breath and winced from the pain. "Besides, this was a fluke."

"With all due respect, Ms. Maratinzano, there are no flukes." His face flushed and the Snake gritted his teeth, as he rose from the chair and turned toward the window. It was obvious that he was angry. "You are the granddaughter of the Capo di Tutti Capi, granddaughter to the Head of the Cosa Nostra and Boss of the Maratinzano Crime Family..." his voice tapered off as he shook his head. "There are no flukes!" He hollered.

Angel didn't know how to respond. The Snake had never yelled at her before and that, coupled with the intense pain radiating down her arm, left her speechless.

Lenny stuck his head inside the room. "Sorry to interrupt but you gotta see this." Grabbing the television remote, he turned on the local news to coverage of the school shooting. "It ain't just local news either." He flipped the channel to CNN, where the reporter was talking about what took place at East Side Junior High School and showing footage of students being evacuated. "Some kid ID'ed Angel."

"What?!" The Snake whirled around.

45

Angel tried to sit up straighter in bed. "Caleb?" She whispered.

"I don't know his name, ma'am, but he's telling the press about how he was saved by an angel. Andrew...I mean, Don Venturini, ain't happy. He says you guys gotta get ready to go. NOW!"

"Go where?" Angel mumbled.

"He's got somethin' lined up, but told me to tell you to get ready 'cuz after the Capo sees the news, the Snake's ass is grass, man." The Snake glared at Lenny and he scurried from the room.

"This isn't your fault," Angel uttered. "I'll talk to Giovanni and tell him that you were against the idea from the start."

"I don't think that's gonna help," the Snake said. "My job is to protect you and I... I dropped the ball today."

"There's Caleb!" Angel blurted, pointing toward the TV. "That's the little boy I found under the bathroom sink."

"That's the same kid who almost ran me over in the hallway," the Snake added.

They intently watched as a reporter leaned down and talked with Caleb. "You told the police that an angel rescued you?" The reporter asked.

"Uh-huh," Caleb uttered. "I was hiding in the bathroom and she found me. She was really nice."

"What were you doing in the bathroom during a lockdown?" The reporter asked.

"My brother forgot his jump drive for his science project and I came to give it to him when the sirens started blaring. I got scared and hid in the bathroom. That's where I met Angel and she got me out of there. I was her helper." Caleb's eyes lit up when he explained that Angel had made him her special helper.

"Do you remember what this angel looked like?" The reporter asked.

"Sure. She had dark brown hair and brown eyes and white, straight teeth. Her eyes were friendly and she was wearing a black coat and a silver cross necklace. Oh, and she had a really big gun."

"A gun?" The reporter gawked.

"Uh-huh, a black one. She said she was going to use it to kill the bad guy."

Angel was amazed at how well he was able to describe her, even down to the silver necklace. Under such stressful circumstances she couldn't have told you what Caleb was wearing. Only his terrified blue eyes were burned into her memory.

"If you could see this angel again, what would you say to her?"

"Thanks for saving me and my brother and Ms. Schneider and for giving Jack his jump drive." Caleb waved at the camera as if he were waving directly to Angel. "Oh, and tell Mr. Snake I said hi."

The Snake muted the TV. "Jump drive?"

For obvious reasons Angel had completely forgotten about the jump drive. "It's in my jacket pocket. Where are my clothes?" She tried to sit up and winced from the pain.

"You had surgery. Your clothes are in here." The Snake pulled a bag from the closet and handed it to Angel.

Just then Lenny burst into the room. "We got company and they ain't here to deliver no flowers!"

"In the building?" The Snake raced back to the window and looked down onto the parking lot and out over the streets.

"Our sources say we got visitors coming in from the front and the back. Two men. Heavily armed."

Jacob stuck his head in. "Don Venturini says you need to get her to the roof on the double."

The Snake turned his panicked gaze to Angel
and she could tell he was sizing up the best way to
get her out of the hospital. "He must be sending a
chopper if he wants us to get to the roof," he
muttered. "Ms. Maratinzano, I'm going to have to
disconnect your IV."

"Just do it," she blurted and the Snake ripped
the tape from her skin and pulled the needle out in
one fluid motion. She was still groggy and
lightheaded from the effects of the anesthetic and
the morphine she had been given for pain, so when
she tried to stand up, she fell sideways into the
heart monitor. "I don't know if I can run," she
admitted.

"You won't have to," the Snake retorted, lifting
her into his arms. She clutched the bag of clothing
to her chest and buried her face in his shoulder.
Then, telling Lenny and Jacob to maintain their
positions, the Snake and Angel made their way out
of the room and toward the stairwell.

"Shouldn't they have come with us?" Angel
asked, dangling limp-like in the Snake's arms.

"No," he panted. "They can buy us some time.
Create a diversion. If these men, whoever they are,
see guards outside of your room they'll assume
you're still in it."

"Why do you think they're after me?"

"Because I don't think what happened in the
school was random or that it was a coincidence
that you were there," he explained.

"It just doesn't make sense," she sighed. "No
one even knew I was going to be there."

"I knew. Olga knew. Olga's hair salon friend
knew and her granddaughter..."

"Ruby," Angel interjected.

"The point is we don't know who else Olga
talked to or who else her friend or granddaughter

may have talked to..." his voice tapered off as he panted.

Once in the stairwell, the Snake set Angel down for a brief moment and dialed Andrew. It went straight to voicemail. Spewing obscenities he scooped Angel back into his arms and barreled upward, toward the rooftop door.

"I think we're jumping to conclusions," she said, as he set her down on the top landing. "If I was the target the delivery man would have taken me out right there in the office when he came in. And why kill those two women if they were after me?" None of it made sense.

The Snake pasted his ear against the steel roof top door. "I hear a chopper," he said. "I'm going out. As soon as I know it's clear, I'll come back for you. Stay right here."

He was gone before she could open her mouth to object. *Where am I gonna go?* She mumbled sarcastically and then was suddenly startled to hear a door below her open and noisily slam shut. She could hear footsteps, but they sounded more like someone pacing than approaching. Still, the reality was that she had no weapon and no strength to get away should they confront her. Lowering herself quietly to the floor, Angel slid her hand into the bag that held her clothing and, using her good arm, searched for her cell phone. Her mouth was dry with panic, as she retrieved the phone from her suit jacket pocket and tried to maneuver to her favorite's menu and select the Snake's number. She was just about to place the call when the shuffling sound grew louder. Through her morphine haze she couldn't tell if the footsteps were growing closer or just louder and her heart began to race. The faster it raced the more her shoulder throbbed and the dizzier she felt.

"We got trouble," a man's voice filled the air and Angel froze. Was he talking to her? Did he know she was there? "Somebody took out Mikey," he said. "Nah, it wasn't the guys guarding Angel. We didn't even get to her room when he hit Mikey. It was somebody else and he was waiting for us, like he knew we were coming." Realizing now that he was talking on his phone, Angel strained to listen. "Don't worry 'bout it. I'll find her and the drive and..." The whizzing sound of a silenced gunshot filled the stairwell and stopped the man mid-sentence. Hearing the thud of a limp body hitting concrete, Angel gasped, louder than she intended; and then she froze. Everything grew quiet. Too quiet. She knew that whoever had shot the man on the phone had heard her gasp and was coming for her. Each step he took was intentionally quiet and though she could barely hear his footsteps, she could feel his presence. With her good arm gripped tightly on the railing, she tried to pull herself to her feet, but she was fighting against the effects of blood loss and strong medication. Even if she could keep her balance long enough to walk to the rooftop door, she would never be able to push it open. The footsteps neared and Angel lunged toward the steel door, smacking her cheek against it and dropping her phone in the process. Sliding down the door, she cried out in pain and braced for the worst. There was no escape.

Just as she caught a glimpse of the top of a man's head and his two eyes peering up at her from the staircase below, the rooftop door burst open and the Snake hoisted her up and out into the evening air.

Within seconds they were in the chopper and Trig was lifting them into the gray, cloud-filled sky, hovering above the city.

"Good to see you, Boss lady," Trig grinned, flipping his long dreadlocks over his shoulder. "Sit back, relax, this cat's got your back."

Angel tried to keep her eyes open but the pain medication was too strong. The last thing she heard was the whirring of chopper blades as she drifted into unconsciousness.

CHAPTER 10

When Angel awakened she was in a king-sized canopy bed with cocoa brown satin sheets and a goose down comforter that felt cool and soothing against her skin. The room was dark, but she could see tiny rays of light around the edges of the curtains which were drawn closed over a window to her right. On a nightstand to the left of the bed sat a prescription bottle and a glass of water. She had no idea where she was and she laid there momentarily, trying to recall the last thing she could remember. The staircase. The rooftop. The helicopter. They were tiny flashes of awareness. She remembered Trig greeting her and the chopper lifting into the air, then nothing.

Taking in her surroundings, she couldn't complain. Wherever she was and whoever her host, they were taking good care of her. Adjusting her neck a little higher on the pillow, Angel glanced down and suddenly noticed that she was completely naked. This was alarming! Who had undressed her? Where were her clothes? Why had they undressed her? No sooner had she started to panic than the door opened a crack and she saw a familiar face.

"Knock, knock," Andrew said with a smile.

"Where are my clothes?" Angel demanded.

Andrew carried in a tray of food and set it down on the end of the bed. "Now, calm down, Sweetheart..."

"I will not calm down. Why am I naked?" Angel scowled at him. It wasn't that she was opposed to being naked in front of Andrew. In fact, quite the opposite; but there was a principle at stake here. She should get to decide when and where, how and why she gets naked.

"Take it easy. Nothing happened." He sat down on the side of the bed and took her fingertips in his hand. "In all of the jostling around to get you here, your wound bled through, so we stripped off your hospital gown, cleaned you up and put you to bed."

"We?"

The edges of Andrew's lips curled into a smirk. "Don't worry, Sweetheart, nobody peeked but me."

Angel blushed. "You have a very bad habit of seeing me naked while I'm unconscious."

"I need to stop that," he teased. "The unconscious part, I mean, not the seeing you naked part."

Andrew moved the tray of food so Angel could reach it. There was buttery toast, a cup of coffee and scrambled eggs. "Did I sleep through the night?" She asked.

"No, only a few hours. The doctor said your diet should be bland for a while and I don't know anything blander than plain scrambled eggs."

"Where are we? Does Giovanni know I'm here?" She shoveled in a bite of eggs. It felt good to eat. She hadn't realized how hungry she was until she smelled the food.

"You are a guest at one of the many Venturini estates just outside of the city," he explained. "And, no, Giovanni doesn't know exactly where you are, but he knows you are with me."

"Do you know anything more about the school shooting?"

Andrew's smile faded quickly at the mention of the school, and Angel knew what was coming next...the vest lecture. She should have worn a Kevlar vest, blah, blah, blah. The fact of the matter was, the vest was bulky and heavy and

she didn't like the feel of it. Besides, how was she
supposed to wear the vest without it being seen?
Was she supposed to tell the students that a
woman business owner in Chicago should wear a
bullet proof vest? Not a bad idea, actually, but not
exactly the message she wanted to convey. Her
arguments and her reasoning wouldn't matter to
Andrew. She had argued her case a hundred times
before. He believed she shouldn't step out of her
home without a vest. In fact, if he had his way she
wouldn't step out of her home at all.

"We'll talk after you eat and get dressed," he
said, rising from the bed and heading for the door.

"Andrew?" Her voice stopped him in the
doorway.

"Thank you."

He turned as if to say something and then
obviously decided against it, spun back around
and abruptly closed the door behind him.

When she had finished eating, she gently
scooted herself to the side of the bed, planted both
feet on the floor and slowly stood up. She felt
surprisingly good, not nearly as dizzy as she had
felt earlier. Carefully making her way to the
bathroom, Angel found her clothes hanging neatly
on the back of the bathroom door and a
toothbrush and toothpaste on the counter by the
sink. *Typical Andrew, thinks of everything.* Her
sleeve was putting too much pressure on her
wound so she decided to rip it off. It took some
doing, and she had to stop every few seconds
because of the pain, but she finally managed to rip
off the left sleeve of her blouse and slide her arm
through the hole. When she was finally dressed
and her teeth were brushed, she left the bedroom
and slowly made her way down the hallway toward
the voices she heard coming from up ahead.

Entering a family room area, Angel saw the Snake and Trig, sitting on a brown leather couch to her right and Andrew sitting on a brown leather couch adjacent to them. A built in entertainment center housed six television screens and Angel knew right away they were for watching surveillance feed. To the left was a beautiful bar with leather stools and detailed stone work. Upon seeing her, the men grew unnaturally quiet and Andrew leapt to his feet. "I'd offer you a drink but you're on pain meds."

"I just need to sit down," she uttered, beginning to feel woozy again.

The Snake was drinking a beer in a tall, chilled glass and Trig was having a Coke. Everyone knew Trig didn't drink alcohol if there was any chance he would be needed to fly the chopper. "Drinking and flying ain't like drinking and driving, man," he had previously explained. "You have a fender bender in the air and you dead. You dead." Angel remembered how he had comically flipped his dreadlocks behind his head and shook his finger for dramatic effect. Chase, on the other hand, wasn't opposed to throwing back a few before flying. He said it made the ride more thrilling, for him and his passengers.

Slowly sinking onto the couch next to Andrew, who was sipping a glass of Cabernet, Angel asked, "Do you have my phone? It wasn't with my clothes." She was worried she might have lost it when she dropped it in the stairwell.

Andrew retrieved her cell phone from his pant pocket and set it on the coffee table. "We couldn't have you waking up, calling someone and jeopardizing our position."

"So, we're in hiding?"

"You are for now," Andrew said, patting her knee. "Until we get a gauge on how Giovanni is going to respond to everything."

"We might all be up shit's creek," Trig added and pointed at Angel. "You, for going to the school in the first place." He then pointed at the Snake. "You for taking her to the school and letting her get shot." The Snake wasn't amused. "And my sorry ass for flying your sorry asses here."

"And you for hiding us," Angel said to Andrew.

"Yeah, well, I was only able to buy us the weekend so we've got two days to come up with a plan," Andrew said.

They sat in silence for a moment and Angel imagined they were each pondering possible scenarios. "I'd feel more comfortable if we could bring Chase into our discussions," Angel broke the silence.

"I second that," the Snake added. "We should also see if he can erase any school surveillance feed that may have visual recognition of Angel or me." He took a large swig of his beer and returned the empty glass to the coffee table.

"I've got Sal working on it," Andrew said. "He's erasing you two from the surveillance feed and then we'll get copies of the real version and the edited one. That should give us some insight into why those men were there," Andrew explained.

Sal was Andrew's longtime friend in the FBI. Angel didn't know if he was a Mafia sympathizer or if his loyalty was only to Andrew, but he had been influential in helping her and her family on more than one occasion. He was smart and had "ins" in certain circles but he lacked the technical savvy of Chase.

"We know why they were there. To hit their mark," the Snake uttered while staring at Angel.

Angel shook her head. "They weren't there for me. They were looking for something. Something specific." The Snake huffed in obvious disagreement, crossed his arms over his chest and leaned backwards on the couch. "I'd like to see if Chase can pull up footage from the cafeteria and the classroom where I killed him…"

"And where you got shot," the Snake interrupted.

"Dude, I could have Chase meet me somewhere and then kidnap him and bring him here," Trig said.

"No," Andrew barked defensively. "Sal can get us everything we need. Besides, we need Chase to be our eyes and ears on the inside. If or when Giovanni finds out that Angel was at the school and took a bullet, we're going to need to know his plans so we can stay one step ahead of him."

"I think you're making too much of this," Angel sighed, trying to lean back on the couch without bumping her left shoulder. "The reality is that no one even knew I was there."

Andrew met eyes with the Snake and gave a slight nod, at which time the Snake let out a grunt of frustration. "Stop saying that," He sneered at Angel. "It was no coincidence that the shooters were in the building the same time you were. SOMEONE knew you were going to be there." He rose from the couch, huffed across the room toward the bar and retrieved another beer. Angel had never seen him like this. If the Snake was anything, he was calm and cool, even if a bomb was strapped to his chest or he was leaping from an exploding jet wearing a chute with a hole in it. He didn't lose his head. Angel studied him, completely taken aback by his outburst.

"Sean, what's going on?" She asked, but he didn't respond. He left his beer bottle on the bar and stormed down the hallway. As if on cue, Trig immediately jumped up and followed him.

Turning to Andrew, Angel said, "No one knew I was going to be there. I don't understand why he's so obsessed with this." Andrew met her gaze and for a brief moment she saw a certain softness in his eyes, like a sense of sadness washed over him. Just as she reached her hand toward him, he cleared his throat and clenched his jaw.

"Maybe he's tired of putting his life on the line for someone who doesn't take it seriously." Andrew's eyes grew dark and a somber expression shadowed his face. "It gets maddening trying to protect someone who runs around as if they are untouchable."

"I don't think I'm untouchable," Angel objected.

"Do you have a death wish then?" Andrew spewed sarcastically.

"The fact that a shooter was at the school the same time as me was a fluke. He wasn't after me. He was looking for something. Maybe the fact that I was there was some kind of Divine intervention."

Andrew grimaced. "Divine intervention? Really, Sweetheart, that's a stretch even for you." He removed himself from the couch and walked toward the bar.

"I believe in Divine intervention," Angel blurted.

"I'm sure you do," Andrew sneered.

"Don't you?"

Andrew didn't answer. He emptied his wine glass in one swig and then refilled it.

"If I hadn't been there, and if the Snake hadn't forced me to take my gun, Lord knows how many people might have died...how many kids might have died." She added emphasis to the fact that the lives at stake were those of innocent children.

"All I'm saying is that maybe I was supposed to be there for that very reason."

Andrew whirled around to face her. "Yes, because God uses so many mob Bosses to save lives," he sarcastically spewed. He emptied his wine glass a second time and then turned his back toward her and shook his head.

Slowly pulling herself from the couch and making her way toward Andrew, Angel asked, "Why are you so mad at me?"

He turned to face her and at first it appeared as if her question amused him, but then his smile faded and his eyes darkened. "How many people have died because of you?"

His words sliced into her like a dagger. The answer was too many. Too many people had died and he, of all people, knew it was a fact that she didn't take lightly. Why was he throwing it in her face now?

Glaring at her, he licked his lips and then pursed them together as if a part of him were trying to prevent the verbal lashing that was begging to roll from his tongue. "It's one thing for a man to lose his life while protecting his family, but it's quite another thing for him to be gunned down because of carelessness or a disregard for one's own safety."

"I don't have a disregard for safety!" Angel hollered.

Andrew burst into sardonic laughter. "You have no regard for your own safety and yet you prance around expecting others to provide security by putting their lives on the line, risking their wellbeing for your every whim."

Angel couldn't believe what he was saying. More than that was the depth of anger and hatefulness in his tone. She took a step back from him but he pursued. "What's the matter,

Sweetheart? Truth hurt?" Angel had never seen this side of Andrew and she didn't like it. She turned to go away from him but Andrew caught her good arm and yanked her around to face him. She cried out from the pain in her shoulder. "Don't walk away. We've just begun. You're the one who always wants to know the truth, right? You're the one who seeks out truth no matter how painful it may be. No matter who or how many wind up dead. So, here's some truth for you..." he drank in a deep breath. "Your presence at that school didn't save lives; it cost two women their lives and endangered the lives of children. Children!" He yelled so loudly that it made her muscles instinctively tense. "You'd like to believe you were used as some Divine tool of protection, but here's a reality check, Sweetheart, the only thing you did today was endanger yourself, the Snake and a bunch of teachers and students, who otherwise would have had a peaceful morning."

She didn't know what to say and as she started to pull away, Andrew's grip tightened.

"You want to know why the Snake is so upset? Because you've almost gotten him killed several times! And the problem is you don't seem to learn from your mistakes. You don't seem to care that people are dying on your behalf." Andrew seethed. "And this time... THIS time the Snake might not live through it!"

Angel gasped but Andrew kept going.

"You want to know why I'm upset?" He yelled.

Angel stared into his eyes, tears welling within her own.

"Forget it!" He spewed, forcefully releasing her arm. Andrew turned his back toward her, placed both palms on the bar and hunched over it.

"Don't stop now," she taunted. "Tell me." Andrew didn't respond. "Then let me guess. It's

60

because I've put your life in danger, too...because I don't wear a vest everywhere I go...because I don't listen and because you think I'm stubborn and because..."

"Because you can't see beyond yourself." Andrew exhaled loudly. "You don't care how your actions affect the people around you. In fact, you don't even think about how people will be affected. My father and brothers are dead!" He whirled around to face her. "You're selfish, Angel. What YOU want is the only thing that matters and in that regard you are exactly like your grandfather."

She opened her mouth to retort, "that's not true," but emotion robbed her of sound.

"And I'm tired of it," Andrew continued with a surreal calm. "I'm tired of worrying about you. I'm tired of cleaning up after you and of the collateral damage you consistently cause." He placed his hands on his hips and tightened his jaw. "I'm done, Angel."

"Done?" She repeated softly.

"With you. I'm done with you."

His words hit her heart like a grenade and Angel turned in tears and rushed from the room, her throbbing shoulder was nothing compared to her crushed soul.

When two of Andrew's men appeared in the doorway, he motioned for them to go. "Stay outside of her door. She doesn't leave this place," he gritted. "Capisce?"

"Si, Don Venturini, she won't go nowhere," one of the men replied.

"You want us to confiscate her cell phone, Boss?"

"No, I've put a block on it. She won't be able to reach anybody," Andrew explained.

"Won't that make her suspicious?"

Andrew shook his head. "It'll appear like her calls are going through. She won't know the difference." They nodded and disappeared into the hallway just as the Snake appeared and stepped into the family room. "You heard?" Andrew asked.

"Every word," the Snake replied.

"Thanks for lobbing me the ball," Andrew uttered, filling his glass and emptying it in one gulp.

"Are you sure you want to go through with this?" The Snake asked, seeing the obvious sadness in Andrew's eyes.

"What choice do I have?" He rebutted. "It'll be better for everyone."

"You didn't have to be that hard on her," the Snake gritted.

"Yeah, I did," Andrew muttered softly. "It's the only way."

CHAPTER 11

Angel fumbled with the lid on the morphine bottle, finally getting it open and swallowing a pill to relieve her aching shoulder. If only it could have the same effect on heartache. Tears streamed down her cheeks as she tried to understand what had just happened. Despite the fact that she was willing them to stop, Andrew's words replayed over and over in her mind. He hated her, of that she was certain, though she didn't understand why. Earlier he had been his sweet and charming self. What had changed? Why did he suddenly despise her? How could he say such hateful things to her? Right now more than anything she wanted to get as far away from Andrew as possible.

Opening the bedroom door, Angel eyed the two guards. "I'd like to leave," she said.

"Sorry, Ms. Maratinzano, but Don Venturini has made it clear that he would like for you to remain his guest," the shorter man to the left answered.

"I don't care what he wants," Angel chided. "I'm leaving."

"Sorry, ma'am," the man to the right replied. "But we have our orders."

"Do you know who you're talking to?" Angel blurted, rage beginning to surge through her.

Both men stared wide-eyed. "If you'd like us to get Don Venturini for you, we can do that," the man to the right responded.

"Yeah, we can do that, but that's all we can do," the other man reiterated.

Angel slammed the door in their faces, whirled around and made a beeline for her phone, which she had left on the nightstand when she took the morphine. She dialed the Snake but it rang empty; no voicemail. She then dialed Chase but the call

rang and rang and rang. She tried Olga, Sophia
and finally Giovanni but each call rang endlessly,
never forwarding her to a voicemail. She might not
be the sharpest, most technologically inclined
individual, but her gut told her that someone had
tampered with her phone and she believed that
that someone was Andrew. The question was why?
Why would he hold her prisoner? Why would he
disallow her to contact her own family? After all
they had shared, why would he treat her so badly?

Angel was fuming. She paced back and forth
across the bedroom floor, gnawing angrily on her
index fingernail, trying to make sense of what was
happening. All that Andrew had said to her,
painful as it was, had been said deliberately and
Angel wanted to know why. What game was he
playing? Regardless of whether or not he meant
what he said, she would not play into his hands
and would never give him a chance to explain.
"You think I'm like my grandfather now," she
mumbled to herself, "just wait until you see how
long I can hold a grudge." Sitting down on the bed,
she opened the back of her phone so she could
remove the tracking device Chase had installed. It
was an ultra-sensitive mechanism that allowed her
to be tracked not only to a specific location, but to
the exact spot where she stood. It was Giovanni's
way of protecting her, though there were times
when it made her feel more like a prisoner than an
adored granddaughter. Right now, she was
determined to escape and she wasn't going to take
a chance on Andrew being able to use the tracking
device to find her. When she pulled out the
battery, Angel was amazed to find that the tracking
device was gone. Someone had already removed it.

Quickly reassembling her phone, Angel opened
her email account. She wasn't certain an email
would get through the block, but decided to try to

send a message to the one person she knew would come to her rescue.

CHAPTER 12

Tony had seen the news about the school shooting and was in route to the Towers to question Angel when his phone beeped. Part of him thought it highly unlikely that the angel the little boy on TV had described could be Angel Maratinzano; but another part of him saw it as too much of a coincidence to let it go unanswered. Besides, if she had been at that school, he knew Giovanni would be none too happy about it and thought Angel might need a little moral support. If nothing else, it was a good excuse to pay her a visit. He hadn't seen much of her since the CoBroGas attack, when he learned about her and Andrew's elevator indiscretion. The thought of it made his pulse quicken and his lips curl into a snarl. He was jealous, yes, but there was more to it than that. He still wasn't convinced that Andrew hadn't somehow orchestrated the nerve gas attack so that all of the Bosses would be killed, he could take over the Venturini family, re-write the rules and marry Angel. Angel had scoffed at his theory, calling him paranoid; but if Tony knew anything about love it was that there were no limits to what a man would do for it.

At the next stop light Tony opened his email and saw a note from Angel that read: COME A LITTLE CLOSER BABY. His heart leapt alive in that moment as he maneuvered a quick U-turn, and stomped the gas pedal to the floor, heading immediately out of the city. He estimated it would take him thirty minutes to get to the location encoded in Angel's message. It was a cryptic message only he would know. "I'm comin' Babe," he whispered into the night. "I'm comin'."

CHAPTER 13

Angel wasn't certain Tony would receive her
message, but she had to work under the
assumption that he would, that he would
remember what it meant and where to go. Because
of the strange way both Andrew and the Snake
were behaving, she didn't know who else to trust.
Slowly maneuvering her left arm into her suit
jacket, Angel slid the morphine bottle and her cell
phone into her right pocket and then left her black
pumps by the sink. There was no sense
attempting an escape in heels. She'd been there,
tried that. Glancing around the room, she scanned
the room for her 9mm, which was nowhere to be
found. This was further confirmation that
something was fishy. Why would Andrew take her
gun away from her? Andrew was an advocate of
her always carrying a gun and always wearing a
vest.

Drawing open the curtains Angel looked
outside and realized that the light she had seen
coming through the window was a security light,
not sunlight. She glanced at the time on her
phone. 10:15pm. It also became quickly clear that
escaping through the window would be impossible.
Even if she could unlock it and push it open with
one arm, it was two stories off the ground. If she
tried to jump, she'd end up severely injured or
worse. Angel grunted in frustration as she pulled
the curtains closed. Plan B. She'd have to
incapacitate Andrew's guards and escape through
the door.

Crawling into bed, Angel lay down and began
to mentally prepare for her academy award debut.
Her performance had to be good, no, great. It had
to rival that of Meryl Streep if she had any chance
of succeeding. She started out with small, tiny

whimpers that grew into wails of pain. "Help me," she moaned and then threw herself onto the floor with as loud a crash as she could create. She gripped her shoulder and this time, cried out for real. "Help me, please!" Angel wailed over and over until she heard the door creak open and saw one of the men peer inside.

"Ms. Maratinzano, are you okay?" He gasped and rushed toward her, bending over to try to lift her back into the bed. In one fluid motion she swept her legs around knocking his legs out from under him and sending him crashing to the floor. Then, grasping the gun from his waistband, Angel scurried to her feet and took aim at his head.

"One sound...one move...and your dead," she uttered. "Interlock your fingers behind your head and work your way to your knees." He did as he was told. "Now face the wall and keep quiet."

"Please ma'am, you don't gotta do this," he began but Angel shut him up by pressing the nose of the gun into the back of his head.

"Now, calmly call your buddy and tell him to come in here and help you," she instructed.

"With all due respect, why would I need his help? This ain't a believable scenario."

Angel pushed the gun harder against his head. "It looks to me like you could use a little help," she chided.

"Louie. Louie! Come help me lift her back into the bed. She rolled out," he hollered.

Louie approached the door snickering. "You mean you can't lift that little thing into be..." His voice abruptly stopped when Angel met him at the door with the barrel of his buddy's .45.

"Don't speak," she ordered, taking the .45 from his hand and instructing him to place his palms atop his head and get down on his knees, facing the wall. She then pulled a .22 from the back of Louie's pants. "Do you have any other weapons?"

"Maybe you should search us," Louie teased and the other man glared at him.

"Nice and slow," Louie continued. "I got a big weapon right between my legs..."

Angel took the handle of the .45 and clubbed Louie over the head. His body fell sideways with a thud. "I mean no disrespect Ms. Maratinzano," the other man blurted. "Truly."

"What's your name?" Angel asked, pacing directly behind him.

"Leo. They call me the Lion."

"Have we met before?" Angel narrowed her eyes. "You look familiar?"

Leo shook his head. "I would remember."

"Do you have a silencer handy, Leo?"

"A silenc..." Angel could see Leo's body tense as the reality of her question sank in. "No, ma'am, I ain't got a silencer."

"Okay, here's what we're going to do. You're going to help me tie up your friend and put him in the bed. Then, you're going to escort me out of here. Capisce?"

"You're puttin' me in a bad spot lady," Leo shuttered. "You know what happens if I go against Don Venturini's orders?"

Angel guffawed. He's afraid of Andrew? Sure he was a Boss now, but hardly someone to be feared, or was he? Had becoming the Venturini Boss somehow changed Andrew? Angel shook the thoughts from her mind and re-focused on Leo. "You do know who I am, don't you?"

Leo nodded his head quickly up and down.

"Who do you fear more, Don Venturini or Giovanni?" She leaned down over him. "Help me and Giovanni rewards you. Obey Don Venturini's orders, which are clearly in violation of the Capo's trust, and, well, I don't have to tell you what Giovanni will do to you."

It didn't take long for Leo to tape Louie's ankles and wrists tightly together and lift him into the bed. Angel instructed Leo to put a piece of duct tape over Louie's eyes and then, after shoving three morphine tablets down his throat, she whispered, "Say nighty night," as Leo taped his mouth and covered him up with the goose down comforter. She hoped the pills would sedate him so that if anyone looked into the room, they'd see a lump under the covers and naturally assume it to be Angel asleep in bed. She was hopeful that it would buy her some time.

With a .45 wedged in her waistband, a .22 in her right suit pocket and the other .45 gripped tightly in her right hand, she instructed Leo to lead the way out. "The fastest, most quiet way out," she told him, warning that she planned to fire on anyone who tried to stop them and would not hesitate to use him as a human shield. Angel didn't like pulling rank or resorting to violence, but Andrew had left her no choice.

At the end of the hall opposite the family room, was a small kitchen with a wooden table that sat four, a stainless steel refrigerator and stone countertops. A window to her left showed that they were still too far above the ground to jump. "This is a dead end!" Angel spat and took aim at Leo's head.

"No, ma'am," Leo gasped. "The old Don had a dog." Angel let her eyes follow Leo's arm as he pointed to a doggie door that was built into the right side of the room.

"Do you think I'm stupid? We're up two stories. If I crawl through there I'll plummet to my death." Angel gritted her teeth and placed the gun against Leo's forehead. "My grandfather would kill you right here and now for deceiving me," she snarled.

Leo held up trembling hands. "Ms. Maratinzano, I'm not lying." Leo knelt slowly onto all fours and poked his head through the doggie door. "It's like a little ramp, like an indoor dog slide that drops to ground level. I swear."

"You go down first," Angel sneered.

Much to her surprise Leo hadn't been lying. The ramp led straight to the ground level with another doggie door that took them out into the night air. Angel was a cat person but made a mental note that if she ever got a dog she'd build it something cool like this. Once outside Angel instructed Leo to take her to one of the garages and outfit her with a vehicle. He was hesitant but obedient and once they were inside a black Town & Country, he drove while Angel kept the .45 aimed steadily at his head.

"As soon as I am safe, I'll release you to return to the Venturini's," Angel told him.

"No!" Leo blurted. "I mean, please don't make me go back."

Shocked by this outburst, Angel studied him. He was short compared to most body guards, but muscular. It appeared as if his olive skin hadn't seen the sun in a while and his eyes, a milk chocolate in color, looked sunken with exhaustion. He had dark brown hair that was cut into a short crew and wore a silver band on his left hand. Something about him felt familiar, but she couldn't put her finger on it.

"Are you married?" Angel asked, nodding toward the ring.

"No, ma'am, not anymore." His voice was laced with sadness and Angel knew there was a story behind the ring and the girl it represented.

"Is that a wedding band?" She pried.

He nodded. "But she's gone. She couldn't handle my lifestyle, my work. I came home one night and she had moved out."

"I'm sorry," Angel said quietly. "It's not an easy line of work."

His lip tightened. "She gave me an ultimatum and she didn't get that I couldn't pick her because if I did I'd be dead."

"What do you mean?" Angel puzzled.

"I was ordered to hit a mark. If I didn't, I'd have been labeled disloyal and I'd become the next mark. You get that, right?"

"I understand what you're saying..." She answered softly, a part of her also aware of how difficult it was for an outsider to understand. Not long ago the mafia world had been new to her as well.

"Margo, that's my wife, said if I killed someone in cold blood, she'd leave me. She's a good Catholic girl. She said she couldn't love a killer." Leo's face reddened and his grip on the steering wheel tightened. "I tried to tell her I didn't have a choice. I didn't have a choice!" He screamed in a loud, raspy tone. "It was either kill or be killed."

Angel could see Leo fighting back tears. She was shocked to see this big, bad mobster named Leo the Lion pour out his feelings like a child. *It just goes to show that no matter how strong we appear, love can break us,* Angel thought. "Let me ask you a question. Do you not want to go back to the Venturini's or do you want out of mafia life forever?"

Leo pulled the Town & Country to the side of the road and threw it into park. Turning to face Angel, his eyes were pleading. "Please, Ms. Maratinzano, I'm begging you. Don't send me back to the Venturini family. I'll serve the Maratinzano family. I'll be loyal, but I can't go back to the Venturini's."

Angel was completely taken aback not only by his request but by the fear etched on his face. What was wrong with the Venturini family? Did it involve Andrew? "Why?" She asked.

"Don't you know? You must know or why else would you have been at that school?" There was a mixture of fear and confusion on Leo's face. "I want no part of what is going to happen. As God is my witness, I want no part of this."

"No part of what?" Angel asked. "I'll talk to Andrew for you and..."

"NO!" He yelled. "Please, don't." Leo shook his head back and forth. "The Venturini's are somehow involved."

"I'll talk to Giovanni then," she promised and Leo put the gear shift into drive and pulled back onto the road.

"I might sound crazy sayin' this, but I think you kidnapping me is one of those acts of Divine intervention." He glanced over at her and smiled. It was the first time Angel had seen him smile and she noted how the dimples on each cheek gave his appearance a certain gentleness. He didn't look like a mobster worthy of the nickname Lion. "Because I've been prayin' for a way out...prayin' real hard...and here you came. You could've shoved me in the bed and left with Louie instead but you didn't. You picked me and for what it's worth I just want you to know I'm grateful."

Divine intervention. Maybe, she thought. *Maybe.*

CHAPTER 14

Chase turned off the local news and leaned back in his chair, rapidly spinning a pencil between his fingers. Two things bothered him. First, the fact that Andrew had taken Angel on a spontaneous weekend getaway with the Snake on precisely the same day as the school shooting. And secondly, that an eye witness claimed to have been rescued by an angel who fit his Boss's description right down to the silver cross that hung around her neck. It was a little too coincidental. So far, Giovanni either hadn't seen the news or hadn't made the connection and Chase was determined to keep it that way; at least until he could do a little more digging.

He quickly pulled up the satellite feed to the Towers, intending to block the reception into Giovanni's apartment but was surprised to find that it had already been blocked. "The plot thickens," he uttered to himself. "Someone else doesn't want Giovanni to know about the shooting," he mumbled to himself. "But who and why?" Even more puzzling was the fact that whoever had done it encoded it so that their identity and the origination of code couldn't be traced. Simple curiosity now morphed into a personal challenge and Chase was determined to figure out who was behind this and why.

"What kind of funky-ass mess did you get yourself into this time, Boss lady," he mumbled beneath his breath as he placed the pencil between his teeth and let his fingers pound the computer keyboard. "First, let's see where you really are." Chase pulled up the tracking device and pinpointed the Venturini estate, which was located just outside the city. "That checks out," he muttered. She was with Andrew, just as Giovanni had said; but the fact that he could have taken her out of the city after the school shooting was forefront in Chase's mind. "What would she be doing at a school in the first place?" He drummed the pencil against the table. There was only one person who might have insight into that answer. Olga. Olga kept a pulse on everything happening in Angel's life, particularly her personal life. She was queen of the family gossip, taking particular interest in anything that was kept from Giovanni. Claiming to know more than Giovanni was a subtle sibling dig in a great, ongoing rivalry. If Angel was at East Side Junior High that morning, Olga surely knew about it; and if she knew about it, it wouldn't take long for Chase to schmooze the information out of her. The fact was Olga could make a mean Cannoli but she couldn't keep a secret to save her life.

Looping his laptop beneath his arm and clenching the pencil between his teeth, Chase headed upstairs to the Penthouse.

CHAPTER 15

Tony pulled in front of the farmhouse and killed the lights. There was no sign of Angel. The clock on the dashboard read 11:20pm and he decided to give her until midnight before breaking the rule and attempting contact. He opened her email and read the words again: COME A LITTLE CLOSER BABY   A surge of adrenaline flowed through him as he recalled the night they had decided to make this song title their secret code.

Though it hadn't been that long ago, it seemed like another lifetime entirely. Angel and Tony had recently become engaged but Angel's aunt, Olga, protested, saying Angel should not marry Tony. Olga made Angel's life miserable and one night when she called Tony in tears, he had picked her up and brought her here. It wasn't the most romantic spot in the world, but it was off the beaten path, out of the city, and a place where no one could find them. The old farmhouse became their hideaway from the pressures of the world. That night, as they lay in each other's arms a song by Dierks Bentley came on the radio. It was titled, Come A Little Closer Baby, and it was then and there that they designated that phrase their secret code. They made a pact that if either of them sent this phrase, the other would drop everything and come to the farmhouse. No questions asked. No preemptive explanations needed. No expectations. The agreement was simply to show up.

Tony hadn't thought about that night or that particular song in a long time, but the memories were flowing now. Her touch, her tears, her dreams for the future, and all that they shared were now foremost in his mind and clouded with a sense of regret. If he could go back in time, instead of leaving her, he would have found a way to leave the family and take her with him.

So much had happened since that night. So much had changed. When his father had found out who Angel was, Tony was forced to vanish from Angel's life without explanation. An Andriachini could never marry a Maratinzano. But he watched from a distance and when her identity was finally revealed to her, he could no longer stay away. Despite the fact that he could never have her as his own, Tony couldn't stop loving Angel and made a promise to himself to protect her.

He pulled up the Dierks Bentley song on iTunes, closed his eyes and leaned his head against the back of the seat; allowing the melody to carry his thoughts back to another time. If his Angel was returning he would not mess it up again.

CHAPTER 16

Angel winced from the sharp pains darting through her shoulder and instructed Leo to pull into a gas station. The morphine had little effect on the pain but was making her nauseated. "I need food," she told Leo. "Do you have any money?"

Leo retrieved a money clip from his pocket. "I have forty bucks," he said, holding up two twenty dollar bills.

"Will you buy me something to eat? Crackers, bread, anything. And a Diet Coke?" She grimaced with a wave of nausea. "I promise I'll pay you back."

Leo smiled. "It's on me," he said and leapt from the car, scurrying inside.

As soon as he entered the gas station Angel slid into the driver's seat, put the gear in drive and sped off. She didn't like deceiving Leo, but she couldn't let him learn the whereabouts of the farmhouse, and if she sent him off in the Venturini's stolen vehicle, he would surely end up dead. His only chance for survival was on his own.

With the .45 lying on the seat next to her, Angel let her left hand rest limply on her lap and steered with her right. She really was feeling nauseated and a little dizzy from the medication. Food would have helped. Narrowing her eyes, she forced herself to focus on the road, praying that she would remember how to get to the farmhouse and that Tony would be there waiting.

CHAPTER 17

When Tony saw headlights approaching, he readied his .45 and ducked lower in the front seat. It had to be Angel, as no one else, other than his father, knew about the farmhouse; but better safe than sorry. As soon as he saw that it was Angel behind the wheel, he leapt from the car and rushed toward her. Angel killed the ignition and reached across her body for the door handle, but Tony beat her to it, yanking open the driver's door. "Babe!" He exclaimed, immediately noticing the wound to her shoulder. "What happened?"

"I was shot," she mumbled as a wave of nausea swept over her.

"You tell me who did this and I swear I'll..." Tony clenched. Heads were gonna roll for this. He would see to it.

Lifting her from the car, he then carried her up the steps to the farmhouse porch, unlocked the door and once inside, placed her gently on the couch. She was clammy and pale and he rushed to the sink to get a cold compress for her forehead and a glass of water.

He hadn't been back to the farmhouse since that last night with Angel, but it was exactly as he had remembered. One big open room with a small kitchen to the right and a king sized bed in the back left corner. A small bathroom jetted off from the bedroom area and the rest of the room was filled with furniture that dated back to his great, great grandfather's era. A wood-burning brick fireplace filled the wall to the right with a mantel that bore framed photographs of Tony's ancestors. An oval shaped, multi-colored shag rug in the center of the room, covered most of the now scuffed wooden floorboards. Atop the rug sat a burgundy floral couch, matching arm chair and a large coffee table made out of fossilized wood. His great grandfather had left the farmhouse to him and only him, and though Tony didn't know why he was chosen above all of the other family members, he was grateful.

Gently laying the cold, dampened compress across Angel's forehead, he covered her with a quilt and sat down next to her. "You remembered the song," she uttered, sliding the compress upward so it wasn't covering her eyes.

"How could I forget?" He grinned. "Best night of my life, Babe." Tony gave her a wink. "How are you feeling?"

"Nauseous," she moaned. "The morphine makes me sick to my stomach."

"You need food," he stated matter of fact.

"I know, but there was no time to stop and I don't have any money." She closed her eyes, inhaled sharply and then exhaled, as if she were fighting a wave of nausea. "Lucky for you, I do have money and did stop." Tony went to the car and retrieved several bags of groceries. "How about I make us something to eat while you tell me what you were doing at East Side Junior High today."

"How did you know I was at the school?"

"Little boy describes being saved by an angel with a silver cross necklace and you show up with a gunshot wound..." Tony raised an eyebrow. "Doesn't take a brain surgeon, Babe." He opened up a loaf of bread and began making sandwiches. "Besides, I'm the one who gave you the necklace, remember?" He asked with a wink.

Angel smiled. She did remember.

"So, why were you at that school?" He repeated.

"Does Giovanni know?" Angel tried to sit up and then sank back down again.

80

"I don't know. I was on my way to see you when I got your email, but if he's seen the news, I'm sure he knows. You don't get to be Capo by being stupid."

Tony carried two plates to the couch, helped Angel sit up and then set one of the plates on her lap. "Your favorite," he beamed. "Pastrami and Swiss on pumpernickel rye with mustard, relish and a dash of kraut."

A smile spread across her face. "We ate this last time we were here," she said softly.

"Yep." Tony sat on the coffee table facing her and took a big bite of his sandwich.

"I can't believe you remembered what we ate last time we were here," she mumbled quietly.

"Babe, I remember everything about that night." Setting his sandwich down, he tenderly stroked the side of her face with the back of his hand. "I remember what you were wearing, the smell of your perfume, the way your eyes glistened in the candlelight, the way we..." He stopped talking and cleared his throat. "I remember everything." Picking up his plate and taking another bite, he looked at Angel. "Eat. You need your strength."

"You sound like Olga," she teased.

"Just this once I'm going to take that as a compliment."

When they had finished eating, Tony poured them each a glass of red wine and joined her on the couch. He could see by the color returning to her cheeks that she was beginning to feel better. She sipped the wine and told him the whole story, beginning the moment she had walked into the school up to the moment she had abandoned Leo at the gas station.

"I understand why you don't want Giovanni to know you were at the school, and I understand the Snake being afraid Giovanni will blame him for your getting shot, but what I don't understand is Andrew's involvement." Tony stood up and walked toward the fireplace. "Did you call him after you were shot?"

"No. I passed out and when I woke up after surgery the Snake and Andrew had coordinated our escape from the hospital."

"And you don't know who was pursuing you at the hospital?" He asked.

Angel shook her head.

Her story was disjointed at best with too many questions and not enough answers. It was like staring at a thousand puzzle pieces, none of which seemed to fit. Tony sank onto the couch next to her. "It's late and I don't think we're going to figure out anything tonight. Let's get some sleep and we'll come up with a plan tomorrow." He helped Angel to the bed and then, taking a pillow, headed toward the couch. As much as he wanted to crawl into bed beside her, he didn't. He didn't know where they stood. He didn't know what she expected. He didn't know what or rather, who she wanted. Turning off the lights, Tony lay down on the couch and exhaled quietly. For a few moments silence filled the space between them.

"Come a little closer, baby," Angel sang softly. "I feel like lettin' go..." She drank in a labored breath. "Of everything that stands between us..." her voice tapered off.

Tony's heart raced. She was singing the lyrics to the song. Their song. Did this mean what he hoped it did? Was this a sign that she was choosing him?

"And the love we used to know," she continued. Her every breathy word tugging at his heart.

He scooted upward on the couch and took a breath. "I wanna touch you like a cleansing rain," Tony sang softly and he could hear Angel quickly inhale as if startled by the fact that he knew the next line.

"Let it wash all the hurt away," they sang softly in unison. "So come a little closer baby, I feel like lettin' go."

You could hear a pin drop as Tony left the couch and made his way to the foot of her bed. There, standing in the dark, he was at a loss for words.

"Tony," Angel whispered and then broke into quiet sobs.

Crawling into bed beside her, Tony tenderly lifted her onto his chest and stroked her hair. "Sshh, Babe," he said. "It's gonna be okay."

"I don't know what's happening," she cried. "I don't know who to trust, not even in my own family. I'm constantly afraid, either for my safety or someone else's and I'm so tired," she sobbed. "I'm just so tired."

"Come a little closer babe, if there's still a chance," he sang softly, stroking her hair. "Then take my hand and we'll steal away, off into the night... 'til we make things right."

Angel leaned upward. "Do you think I'm selfish?"

He knew by the question that criticism from Andrew was causing her the most pain. "No, Babe, you're not selfish. I don't know why Andrew said those things to you. He's always been an elitist dick but since becoming Boss of the Venturini family, his ego has grown to ultra-dick proportions." Angel smiled as he tucked a piece of her hair behind her ear.

"Ultra-dick proportions?" She repeated.

"Yeah."

"Is that the technical term?" She teased.

"Are you gonna harass me even when I'm trying to cheer you up?" Forgetting about her shoulder, he playfully flipped her over and climbed on top of her. Angel cried out in pain and Tony quickly leapt off. "Sorry, Babe, I forgot about your arm."

Sitting up, she gripped his left shoulder with her right hand and pulled him closer. "It's okay. I'm okay." She leaned upward toward his lips and whispered, "Come a little closer baby..."

His lips brushed against hers and a tiny moan escaped him. Every fiber of his being ached for her. Sliding his hand behind her neck, he drew her into a deep kiss, carefully maneuvering her lower onto the bed. "I don't want to hurt you," he said quietly, unbuttoning her blouse. "But I want you."

Angel put her fingers to his lips as if to say don't talk, just touch. "Take me," she whispered and Tony obeyed. He fulfilled every carnal urge, relishing in her body and in the fact that his Angel had returned.

CHAPTER 18

Olga was futzing around in the kitchen when Chase entered the Penthouse and asked to speak with her. Since Sophia and Salvatore were still in hiding from the Stidda somewhere in Sicily and Angel was with Andrew, Olga had the Penthouse all to herself. She appeared happy to see him, immediately pouring two cups of coffee and carrying them to the dining room table with a plate of Cannoli. "Talking is more fun with a snack," she explained and then plunked her rounded hips into the chair across from Chase. "So, what can I do for you?" Olga asked.

"You being the eyes and ears of the family..." Chase began and Olga cut him off.

"Well, I can't argue with that," she chuckled.

"I was hoping you could help me out with something."

"I'd be happy to help," Olga beamed, shoveling in a bite of Cannoli and then washing it down with a gulp of coffee. "What's on your mind?"

"It will go faster if I show you." Chase spun his laptop around to face Olga and hit play on the newsfeed he had ready to go. As soon as the reporter announced that there was a shooting at East Side Junior High, Olga dropped her Cannoli. "Oh, keep watching," Chase said. "It gets better." By the time Olga saw the interview with little Caleb and heard his description of Angel, her hands were trembling and tears welled up in her eyes.

"Merciful Heavens!" She gasped.

"Any wild-ass information you'd like to share with me?" Chase widened his eyes, raised his eyebrows and took an over-dramatized bite of his Cannoli.

"Is … is she all right?" Olga's voice trembled.

"Is who all right?" Chase mused.

"Angel!" Olga blurted. "My Angel! Is she all right? Oh, Merciful Heavens, what have I done?" Olga wailed and buried her face in her hands.

Chase moved to a chair beside Olga and pulled her hands from her face. "Yes, she's fine. She's with Andrew and the Snake at one of the Venturini estates."

"Thank the Lord!" Olga uttered, making the sign of the cross over her body.

"What did you mean when you said, 'what have I done?'" Chase narrowed his eyes to tiny slits. "That's an odd-ass thing to say…" his voice fading. "Unless you had something to do with her being at the school?"

"Why on earth would you think I had something to do with her being there?" She blurted, feigning offense.

Chase raised one eyebrow. "You may be one feisty ass broad, but don't play dumb with me. I know you. I know all about your crazy-ass, matchmaking schemes for Angel, and I'm willing to bet you were the one who sent her to the school. You probably sent her there to meet some hot guy you met the other day at the supermarket."

Olga's eyes widened and she gasped. "How did you know I met a man at the supermarket? Is Giovanni having me followed?" She narrowed her eyes and growled.

"I'm Giovanni's eyes and ears. I'm watching everything, all of the time. No one in this family can take a shit without me knowing about it," Chase quipped. "So, speaking of shit, let's cut through it and get to the wild-ass truth."

Olga took a deep breath. "I asked her to go to the school, but not to meet any man. I asked her to talk to one of the classes about how hard it is to be a career woman in a man's world." Olga wrung her hands together. "It's hard for her, you know, being surrounded by men all of the time. She has no girlfriends. Why, there's so much testosterone in the room at any given moment that it's a wonder we women haven't started growing beards and sprouting penises."

Chase's stern exterior cracked at the visual Olga had painted and he chuckled aloud. "Now, THAT would be something to see."

Olga's face drew grim with concern. "Why hasn't Angel come home? Why is she with Andrew and the Snake?"

"I don't know," Chase shrugged. "That's been bouncing around in my brain too." He got up and moved back to his original seat, spun his computer to face him and took a gulp of coffee. "Giovanni tells me that Andrew called and asked his permission to take Angel away for the weekend and that he ordered the Snake to tag along."

"Merciful Heavens!" Olga gasped. "Does Giovanni know she was at the school?"

"I don't think so," Chase said and fidgeted in his seat.

Olga leaned forward and whispered, "We need to keep it that way."

"Yeah, no shit," Chase agreed.

Just as Olga began explaining how Elsa had asked if Angel would mind speaking to Ruby's classroom on career day, Big Mike burst through the front door. "We got a problem!" He belted. "Two men were gunned down at Northwestern Memorial hospital."

"Were they our men?" Chase asked.

"No," Big Mike uttered.

"Then how is that our problem?" Chase shrugged.

"Their bodies were found in the stairwell."

"Again, how is that OUR problem?" Chase quipped.

Big Mike handed Chase a photograph and the moment he looked at it, he knew how it concerned them. The shirts had been removed from both men and they were lying on their backs. An upside down cross with the number 266 below it was drawn on each man's chest, and spray painted on the wall above the bodies was one word: ANGEL

CHAPTER 19

Angel and Tony awakened to the sound of banging on the farmhouse front door, followed by Andrew's voice. "You have until the count of three to open the door or I open it for you," Andrew hollered. "One...two...three!"

Tony leapt from the bed but only in time to see the door frame crack beneath the weight of the sledge hammer swung by Andrew's body guard, who looked like he could have starred on WWF.

"What the hell are you doing?" Tony barked, wrapping a sheet around his waist and grabbing his .45 from the nightstand.

Stepping through the doorway, Andrew's jaw tightened and he glared at Angel, who was sitting up in bed with the sheet draped around her. She couldn't tell if it was anger or hurt etched across his face.

"You broke my door!" Tony yelled.

"Somehow, I think we're even," Andrew seethed, his eyes darting from Tony to Angel and then back to Tony.

"What do you want?" Angel asked.

"What belongs to me," Andrew retorted.

"I don't belong to you," Angel snapped.

"Well, this is awkward..." Tony chided.

Andrew shifted his weight and pursed his lips together. "Actually, I was referring to the vehicle you stole from me last night. See, it does belong to me and I'd like it back."

Angel dropped her head, embarrassed, as Tony walked to the coffee table, grabbed the keys and tossed them to Andrew. "You can see yourself out, Ace."

Andrew nodded slowly and then turned and tossed the keys to his body guard. "Take the car back to the house. I'll meet you there later."

"But, with all due respect sir, I can't provide protection if I'm not with you," the body guard replied.

"I won't need protection here," Andrew answered.

"I wouldn't be too sure of that, Ace," Tony sneered.

"You have your orders," Andrew said to his guard.

When the body guard left, Andrew took off his black trench coat, hung it over the side of the couch and sat down. "As soon as you two are dressed, we need to head out," he said, matter-of-factly.

"I don't know what kind of delusion you're living under, Ace, but we're not going anywhere with you," Tony retorted, pointing his gun at Andrew. "Now, why don't you take your ultra-Don-Boss-of-the-world-ego and get your ass out of my house before I do something I'm going to regret."

A smirk spread across Andrew's face. "Put the gun down, Tony. You and I both know you're not going to shoot me."

"Like I said before, I wouldn't bank on that, Ace," Tony quipped.

Reaching into his front pocket, Andrew retrieved a photograph of the men found dead at the hospital. He handed it to Tony, who cursed aloud and then lowered his gun and sank onto the couch.

"What is it?" Angel asked, trying to maneuver her way off of the bed without being exposed. She finally managed to wrap the bedspread around her, grab her clothes and move into the bathroom to get dressed. She tried to eavesdrop through the door but they were speaking too low. A part of Angel wanted to stay in the bathroom forever, while a larger part wanted to

storm out and give Andrew a piece of her mind.
Yet, deep inside she just wanted to throw a pity
party and cry. Her shoulder throbbed and her
heart was more confused than ever. Not to
mention the humiliation of having Andrew walk in
on her and Tony in bed. A sour pit formed in her
stomach. What had she done? Had she pushed
Andrew away forever? Then again, he made it very
clear that he was finished with her. *So, I have
nothing to feel guilty about,* she told herself, but she
wasn't buying it.

By the time she emerged from the
bathroom, Tony and Andrew had moved to the
kitchen table and were drinking coffee. Tony had
set a plate of pastries in the center of the table and
was shoveling a cheese Danish into his mouth.
"Babe," Tony said, jumping up when he saw her.
"I'll get your coffee." He pulled out a kitchen chair
and motioned for Angel to sit down. Then he
quickly filled a cup with coffee and set it in front of
her. She couldn't have felt more awkward, seated
there between the two men in her life.

Andrew slid the picture toward her and,
upon seeing her name written on the wall above
the bodies, the pit in Angel's stomach churned.
"Why is my name written above them?"

"It's a sign. They're sending a message,
which is what we've got to figure out," Tony
uttered.

"Speaking of figuring things out," Angel
chided. "How did you find me here? I mean, since
you removed the tracking device from my phone."

Andrew disregarded her sarcasm. "There's
a tracking device in the vehicle you stole. We
located it right after we found poor Louie taped and
drugged in your bed." Andrew appeared
unamused.

"Taped and drugged? A little kinky, but I like it, Babe," Tony grinned.

"If you hadn't turned me into a prisoner, I could have asked to borrow the car, but you left me no choice," Angel retorted.

"I was protecting you..." Andrew began but Angel cut him off.

"I don't need protection!"

"Yes, I can see that by your stream of recent bad choices!" Andrew barked, and Tony scowled at him.

Clearing his throat in an awkward gesture, Andrew pointed to the photograph. "Your name is written above the bodies to indicate that the message is meant specifically for you," he explained to Angel.

Angel brought the picture closer and analyzed it. "Where is this? I've seen this place."

Andrew nodded. "Yes, it's in the stairwell at Northwestern Memorial hospital."

Her eyes widened. "And your men? Are they all right?"

Shrugging his shoulders, Andrew exhaled. "They're gone."

"I'm sorry," Angel uttered.

"They're not dead. That is to say, we haven't found their bodies yet." Andrew quickly ran his fingers through his hair. "But they haven't checked back in."

Tony narrowed his gaze. "That's not cool," he mumbled.

"No, it's not," Andrew agreed and Angel didn't have to ask why. Every member knew the rules. Check in was mandatory and expected. If a member stopped checking in they were considered rogue and untrustworthy, in other words, as good as dead.

"What does the message mean?" Angel changed the subject. "And why is it directed at me?

"The upside down cross is a sign of the devil, right?" Tony posed. "But I don't know what 266 means."

"I've got Sal working on deciphering it now, but I think you might want to consider bringing Chase into the mix," Andrew said.

Angel gawked at him. She had recommended bringing Chase in yesterday but Andrew shot down the idea. "Why the change of heart?" She asked, as he rose from the table and lifted his black coat from the chair.

"I was trying to protect you, but I'm done with that. We need answers and Chase can get them faster than anyone else."

"Seems you're done with a lot of things lately," Angel muttered.

Andrew met her gaze for a moment and it felt as if he wanted to say something, but then he turned his back and left. A part of her wanted to chase after him, to demand an explanation, to learn the reasons for his behavior; but all she could do was sit there, frozen in silence and watch him drive away.

CHAPTER 20

It had been a long night. After viewing the photograph, Chase had immediately jumped on his laptop and began cross-referencing the symbol of an upside down cross with the number 266 and the Maratinzano family, but came up with no results.

Olga waddled into the dining room. "Have you been up all night?" She asked Chase, who looked haggard.

"Just most of it," he said with a yawn.

Big Mike joined them shortly thereafter and Olga carried in a fresh pot of coffee and a tray of homemade biscuits and gravy and crispy bacon.

"When did you make all of this?" Chase asked.

"I didn't sleep much either," Olga replied.

As they sat at the table, Olga picked up the picture from the hospital and analyzed it again. "What does this mean?" She asked. "Why is my Angel's name associated with these men?"

"That's what we need to find out," Big Mike answered.

"The big-ass bonus question of the day is how is all of this linked to East Side Junior High School?" Chase added.

"You lost me," Big Mike said and Chase and Olga filled him in on the fact that Angel had been at the middle school the morning of the shooting. "Does Giovanni know?" Big Mike grimaced.

"I don't think so and I wasn't about to waltz my carefree ass downstairs and tell him," Chase quipped. "If you think he should know, feel free, but I don't have a death wish."

"No thanks," Big Mike said.

Right then, Chase's cell phone rang, startling him. "It's Tony," he announced to Olga and Big Mike. "Chase man, go," he answered.

"It's me," Angel's voice came through the phone. "I need your help."

"Well, if that ain't a big-ass understatement," Chase chided. "Where are you?"

"I'm with Tony and I'm safe," she responded.

"I thought you were with Andrew?"

"It's a long story," she sighed. "My phone is dead so I'm using Tony's. I'm going to send you a photograph and I need you to..."

"If it's a pic of your name above two half-naked men with the number 266 on their chests, I've already got it and running a search," he cut her sentence short.

"How?" Angel asked.

"It was dropped off anonymously at the Towers. Listen, boss lady, I don't know how long we can keep this under wraps from Giovanni, so you and the Snake better high tail your wild asses home. We're gonna need damage control."

Angel explained that the Snake was hiding out at the Venturini estate, anticipating Giovanni's wrath when he finds out that the Snake allowed her to go into the school alone and almost get killed.

"I'm gonna need a little more context on the phrase 'almost get killed,'" Chase muttered.

"I took a bullet in the left shoulder, but I'm fine, just a little sore."

Chase cursed aloud and then told Big Mike what she had said. Big Mike grabbed the phone from Chase and put it on speaker. "Angel, this is Big Mike, where are you? I'll come and get you."

"She's with me, Ace," came Tony's voice through the phone. "As soon as she's ready to come home, I'll bring her."

"Merciful Heavens! Are you losing a lot of blood?" Olga yelped. "Are you going to be alright? Oh, this is my fault," she wailed. "This is all my fault."

Angel explained that the Snake had taken her to the hospital where the bullet was removed and that Andrew had used Trig to evacuate them from the hospital to escape the shooters. "So, they weren't just leaving a random-ass message for you, you were their target," Chase said.

"But, why?" Big Mike interjected.

"That's what we need you to find out, Ace," Tony responded. "Somehow the school and the message are connected."

"There's more," Angel said.

"There always is," Chase uttered sarcastically.

"Something is going on in the Venturini family. I can't explain it but I need you to send some men to find a man named Leo. They call him the Lion."

"No disrespect, boss lady, but can't the internal affairs of the Venturini family wait until after we find out who shot you and what this message means?" Chase rolled his eyes.

"Leo knows something. I could tell he wanted to tell me but he was too afraid. He helped me escape from the Venturini estate..."

"Escape?" Big Mike blurted.

"Oh, merciful heavens!" Olga threw her hands into the air. "Just come home, my Angel, come home."

"It's a long story," Angel sighed. "Just pick up Leo the Lion and bring him in. I'll be there in a little while."

Angel disconnected the call and Olga, Chase and Big Mike stared blankly at one another. "If all of these things are connected..." Big Mike began. "If the whole plan to shoot Angel was contingent on her going to East Side Junior High, then we need to find out who sent her there."

"We already know who sent her there," Chase answered and glared at Olga. "We just don't know why."

"I told you I didn't know she would be in any danger," Olga sputtered and Big Mike drew his gun.

"You better start talking, old lady," Big Mike seethed.

"Cool your ass down," Chase interjected, taking a step closer to him and pushing his arms down so that the gun was no longer in Olga's face. "She didn't do it, or at least not on purpose."

"You know if Giovanni finds out you were the one to send her to the school, sister or not, you're as good as dead," Big Mike warned.

"Yes, and if he finds out you just pulled a gun on his sister, you can kiss your sweet cheeks goodbye as well," Olga rebutted with a humph.

"Everybody chillax," Chase blurted.

"I didn't know she would be in any danger," Olga reiterated. "I swear. I was just doing a favor for a friend." She shook her head back and forth. "I would never put my Angel in any danger. Never." Olga waddled into the kitchen making the sign of the cross over her body.

As soon as she left the room, Big Mike turned to Chase. "You know what Giovanni will do to her when he finds out she was the reason Angel went to the school."

"Which is why he can't find out," Chase added. "I'll keep trying to decipher the message. You find Leo and then go to this salon and pick up a woman named Elsa." Chase scribbled an address on a piece of paper and handed it to Big Mike. "She's the one who asked Olga if Angel would speak at the school. She's the one that can tell us why."

Big Mike hurried out the front door of the Penthouse while Chase sat in front of his laptop, fidgeting in his seat, twirling a pencil between his fingers and bouncing his right knee spastically up and down. Too many unanswered questions made for an overly anxious Chase. Why was Angel sent to the school? If someone wanted to take her out, why do it at a school? Had she been followed to the hospital or was someone tipped off? Who left the message and what does it mean? Who blocked the satellite signal into Giovanni's apartment? Sooner or later someone was going to leak what happened at the school to Giovanni and then all hell was going to break loose. The only thing Chase was certain of was they were running out of time.

CHAPTER 21

Olga slid the Taser from her handbag and slipped it into the right pocket of her tan trench coat. She hoped she wouldn't have to use it, but knew she was willing to do whatever was necessary. Elsa was not just her hairdresser, she was a friend; or at least Olga thought she was. Now, it appeared that Elsa had betrayed her trust and Olga wanted to know why.

Lurking in the hallway just outside her bedroom door, Olga waited patiently until she heard Chase close his laptop and leave the Penthouse, presumably heading to the secret meeting room where all of his equipment was set up. Then, she made a beeline for the door. Zapping the guard at the Penthouse door was easy. She knew him well and he had no reason to distrust her. His name was Harry, though she called him Dirty Harry because he reminded her of Clint Eastwood.

"Sorry, Dirty Harry," she muttered as she stepped over his twitching body. "It'll stop hurting in a few minutes."

A twinge of guilt tugged at her as she entered the elevator and hit the ground floor button. "A girl's gotta do what a girl's gotta do," she mumbled, exiting at the garage level.

"May I be of service, ma'am?" A large body guard asked as she stepped from the elevator.

"I'm in a terrible hurry, son," Olga said in her most desperate old lady voice. "Can you take me on a quick errand?"

"I'd be happy to call upstairs and have a driver sent down for you," he said.

"Can't you take me?" Olga smiled. "You do have keys to the vehicles, don't you?" Olga's eyes dropped to the key ring attached to his belt. On it hung one key and she was certain it was the one used to open the lock box that held the keys to all of the Maratinzano vehicles.

"Yes, ma'am, I have keys but I'm stationed to guard this level so I'll have to call someone to..." As he turned to make the call, Olga zapped him with her Taser causing him to fall forward, hitting the ground with a loud thud.

"Sorry," she whispered. "It's nothing personal." It took some doing but she was finally able to roll him over and remove the key from his belt, open the lock box and select a set of car keys. When he started to get up, Olga zapped him once more and then hurried toward the vehicles, which were parked all in the same row. There were six black Town & Country SUV's, two black stretch limousines and several black Hummers. Depressing the open button on the key remote told her which vehicle was hers and she hurriedly climbed in, tossing her handbag on the seat next to her.

Seconds later Olga pulled the SUV out of the Towers and into traffic. Though she would have loved to get behind the wheel of one of those Hummers, she knew the Town & Country was car enough for her. Olga let out an excited shriek as the passenger side tires climbed up and over a curb and then slammed back onto the pavement. It had been a while since she had driven and this SUV was a far cry from her older-than-old Oldsmobile which she had affectionately named Big Brown Bessie. Bessie had been her trusted steed for the greater part of twenty years and she missed her. More than that, she missed the freedom that came from being behind the wheel.

CHAPTER 22

Giovanni stormed into the secret meeting room with such force that Chase leapt to his feet. "What the hell is going on?!" Giovanni huffed.

"Let me explain..." Chase stuttered, holding his palms up.

"My sister commandeered a vehicle and Tasered two of my men?" He hollered.

"What?!" Chase exclaimed. He had been so consumed with trying to track the block on the satellite signal and decipher the message from the hospital that he hadn't bothered to monitor internal security channels.

"Am I to believe that you know nothing about this?" Giovanni growled.

Chase plunked down in front of his computer and began pulling up the internal security feed. "I'll be damned," he uttered, as he watched Olga Taser Harry at the Penthouse door and get on the elevator. Switching the feed to the ground level cameras, he saw her zap the guard twice and steal the car. "Damn!" Chase blurted when he saw her speed out of the garage and into the street. "That's a wild-ass woman on a mission, right there." He shook his head.

"And you have no idea where she is going?" Giovanni questioned.

Chase momentarily froze. His gut told him she had probably overheard him instruct Big Mike to pick up Elsa and she was trying to get to Elsa first; but why? He was caught in a quandary. If he told Giovanni about Elsa, it meant telling him about Angel being at the school. If he didn't tell him, then he was, essentially and for all intents and purposes, lying to the Capo Di Tutti Capi; a crime punishable by death. Chase nervously licked his lips. By the same token, if he brought up what happened at the school now, Giovanni might kill him for not telling him about it sooner. This was definitely a lose-lose situation.

Giovanni's eyes burned through him. "I do not like to be kept waiting," he warned, motioning for his body guards to block the doorway. Chase swallowed hard, realizing he was in deep trouble.

"I don't know where she's going," Chase said, his voice cracking with fear. "But I can track the vehicle and send some men to escort her home."

"Do it now."

He didn't need to be told twice. Chase's fingers flew across the keys as he pulled up the GPS tracking screen, located the vehicle Olga was driving and monitored her progress.

"Put the feed on the large screen," Giovanni ordered and Chase did as told.

It appeared as if his suspicion had been correct and she was heading for Elsa's hair salon. When the vehicle stopped outside of the salon, Chase turned to Giovanni. "It looks like she's going to get her hair done, sir."

Giovanni's guards snickered and he whirled around with an intense glare that instantly shut them up. "Why would she Taser two of my men just to get her hair done?" He seethed.

"No disrespect, sir, her being your sister and all, but Olga can be a fly-by-the-seat-of-her-pants kind of lady," Chase said, hoping he was going to accept that as a rational explanation.

Giovanni shook his head.

"Not to bring up a touchy subject, but..." Chase lowered his voice to a whisper, "...she did Taser you once."

Giovanni pound his fist against the table and Chase jumped. "I want to see her the moment she returns!" He left the room as forcefully as he had entered and it was only after Giovanni had gone that Chase realized beads of sweat had formed across his forehead.

His cell phone buzzed and Chase quickly wrapped the ear piece around his left ear and answered. It was Big Mike telling him what he already knew. Olga was at the salon. "What is she doing here?" Big Mike barked. "How am I supposed to bring in Elsa with Olga in the way?"

"Bring them both in," Chase quipped. "But, be careful, Olga's already dropped two of Giovanni's men with her Taser and he's pissed. In fact, bring her in and you'll be a hero around here."

"Great," Big Mike groaned. "I'm gonna need back up."

"Your big-ass can't handle two little old ladies, man?" Chase laughed. "Seriously?"

"What am I supposed to do? I can't hit 'em and Olga knows I'm not gonna shoot her. I have no leverage."

Chase moved to where he had three laptop screens in front of him and attempted to pull up live surveillance for the salon building. All he could see was from the front of the hair salon. Either there were no cameras in the back of the building or their signal had been blocked. It would take too long to try and figure it out and Chase wanted to get back to deciphering the message. "Sit tight and wait until Olga comes out of the salon. Don't let her see you and then when she leaves, you go in and get Elsa."

He disconnected the call with Big Mike and tossed his blue tooth atop the table. Then, returning to his main laptop, he continued cross-referencing the upside down cross with the number 266 and the Maratinzano family, Chase rubbed his eyes. Unless he could somehow narrow the parameters, this search would take forever.

Just then the idea to call Sal hit him. Sal could help with the search. Putting his ear piece back on, Chase dialed Sal and was dumbfounded to discover that he was the one who, per Andrew's instructions, had blocked the satellite signal into Giovanni's room and several other areas of the Towers. "Why did you hide your identity?" Chase asked him. "Why didn't you just call me and have me block the feed in the first place?"

"I was told to keep it confidential. That's all I know," Sal responded.

Chase was also surprised to find out that Andrew had already sent him a picture of the bodies and he was currently running a system wide search using similar parameters. "How did Andrew get a picture?" Chase asked.

"One of cops knew of his relationship with Angel and sent it to him," Sal explained.

"Let me know what you find," Chase said.

"Ditto."

Chase disconnected the call to Sal and immediately dialed Andrew. Just as he finished leaving a voicemail, Tony stepped into the secret meeting room and informed him that Angel was in the Penthouse and requesting a meeting with him. Tony helped Chase gather up several laptops and they both hurried upstairs.

By the time Chase set up the computers atop the dining room table, Angel had showered and dressed and emerged from her bedroom wearing a make-shift sling formed from a pillow case.

"Boss lady, you got some 'splaining to do," Chase uttered.

"I know," Angel sighed. "But first, I need you to look at this." She slid the jump drive Caleb had given her across the table.

"What is it?" He asked.

"It's probably a kid's science project, but I thought we better take a look before I return it."

Chase plugged it into the USB port on his laptop and watched as the file began to load and then stopped. It was encrypted. "How many junior high science projects are encoded?" Chase mumbled and then cursed aloud. "I shouldn't be surprised, nothing is easy today."

"You seem extra-stressed," Angel noted. "Everything okay?"

Chase smirked and bobbed his blonde, spikey-haired head up and down. "Oh, yeah, I forgot that you weren't around for the wild-ass activities of the morning." He started the decoding program and then leaned back in his chair, twirling a pencil between his fingers. "Let's see...where should I start?"

Tony and Angel exchanged confused glances and then directed their attention back to Chase.

"Well, your crazed-ass old aunt went on a Tasering spree, took out two of Giovanni's men, and then stole a car..."

"What?!" Angel exclaimed, wide-eyed.

"Yeah, that was pretty much my reaction too," Chase quipped. "That is, until your grandfather demanded I track her, which I did and it showed that she went to Elsa's salon."

"Why would she Taser Giovanni's men and steal a car just to go to a salon?" Tony asked.

"Because it was Elsa who asked Olga to get me to speak at the school," Angel muttered, mentally trying to connect the dots.

"Ding, ding, ding, we have a winner," Chase chided, pointing to Angel. "But I couldn't tell that to Giovanni because he doesn't know about the school thing yet."

"How is that possible?" Tony snorted. "It's been all over the news."

"Andrew had Sal block the feed into certain areas of the Towers to keep Giovanni from finding out," Chase quipped. "I don't know why he didn't just call me and ask me to do it, since I'm sitting right here in the building with access to everything." It was obvious that Chase was pissed about Andrew going to Sal.

Angel sank lower into her seat. "So, what is Olga doing with Elsa?"

Chase shrugged. "Who the hell knows. Zapping her? Killing her? Hiding her? There is no telling what's going on in that crazy-ass brain of hers."

He explained that there was a possibility that Olga had overheard him telling Big Mike to bring Elsa in.

"So, she's protecting her," Angel surmised aloud. "Tell Big Mike to leave the salon and go pick up Leo. I'll go get Olga."

Chase made an alarm sound with his mouth and then said, "That's the wrong answer, Boss lady, but thanks for playing."

"Sorry, Babe," Tony added, "but your butt is staying here."

"Olga will listen to me. I can get her to come home faster than anyone else can."

"Not gonna happen, Babe," Tony quipped. "End of discussion."

Angel abruptly stood up. "Do you know who you're talking to?" She barked, glaring at Tony, who nonchalantly sat down next to Chase, crossed his arms over his chest and grinned.

106

"Yeah, Babe. In fact, I know you in the Biblical sense, so let's not pull rank," Tony said with a smirk.

"Damn! This day just keeps getting more crazy-ass entertaining by the minute!" Chase whooped.

Phoning Big Mike, Chase instructed him to leave the salon and retrieve Leo the Lion. "I'll babysit Olga via surveillance," he said and then disconnected the call. Turning to Angel he asked, "What info do you think this Leo guy has?"

"I don't know," she shrugged, "but he told me there was something going down that he didn't want to be a part of." She shook her head. "He was terrified of what was going to happen. All I know is that it has something to do with the Venturini family."

The three of them sat in silence as each tried to make sense out of all that had happened. Then Chase did a double take at his computer screen and blurted, "Holy, Mary, Mother of..."

"What?" Tony and Angel said in unison.

Chase sat motionless, which was a rarity, and color drained from his face. Without answering, he reached for his phone and dialed Sal. "I'm uploading a file to you now. Please tell me I'm not looking at what I think I'm looking at."

Tony and Angel raced to the other side of the computer so they could see the screen. "That doesn't look like a science project," Tony remarked.

"What is it?" Angel asked.

Chase disconnected his call with Sal and shook his head. "What did Sal say?" Tony asked.

"He's going to run the file through his system and get back to me," Chase answered.

"What do you think we're looking at here?" Tony questioned, leaning closer to the screen.

"Blueprints," Chase said.

"Of what?" Angel posed.
"The Vatican," Chase answered.

CHAPTER 23

Olga approached Elsa's hair salon with her Taser clutched tightly in her right hand and an angry scowl on her face. She was a woman on a mission, though she wasn't exactly sure how it was all going to go down. In asking her to have Angel address her granddaughter's classroom, Elsa had put Angel's life in danger; and Olga wanted to know why. Was it intentional or had it been a strange coincidence? Had someone instructed Elsa to ask Olga for this favor? And if so, who was behind it?

Storming into the salon she immediately spotted Elsa in the back by the waxing room and made a beeline for her. "Elsa!" Olga's voice bellowed through the salon and everyone grew quiet.

"Olga, why on earth are you hollering?" Elsa muttered, eyeing the Taser. "What's wrong, dear?"

"Did you see what happened at East Side Junior High?" Olga barked. Elsa's dyed orange hair flipped up and down as she nodded her head, closed her eyes, bit her overly glossed bottom lip and put her hand to her chest.

"I spoke to Ruby's mother. It was just awful."

"And it never dawned on you to call me and check on Angel?" Olga narrowed her eyes and glared at Elsa.

"Angel?" Elsa appeared alarmed. "What happened to Angel?"

"Merciful Heavens! She was shot at the school!" Olga belted and Elsa grabbed her chest and gasped.

"What?! Ruby said Angel never showed up, so I just assumed..." her voice tapered off as Olga waved the Taser in her face.

"If you're lying to me, Elsa, I swear I'll Taser your ass until you can't remember your own name and leave you brain dead in a pile of your own drool," Olga seethed.

"Olga!" Elsa gasped. "What a terrible thing to say, and even worse to imply that I would do anything to hurt your niece." She crossed her arms over her chest and stuck her pointy chin into the air. "And then to come in here and threaten me. Why, I just don't know what to say, except I'd like you to leave."

At that moment Olga glanced up and saw a large, unfriendly looking man approaching the front door. He was dressed in black from head to toe and there was no mistaking the bulge of a weapon beneath his jacket. She didn't recognize him as one of Giovanni's men, but she would have bet her life that he was mafia. "Uh-oh," she winced. "We've got trouble." Grabbing Elsa by the arm, she dragged her into the waxing room. "We're gonna have to sneak out the back," she whispered.

"Why? Who are we hiding from?"

Olga shushed her.

"Don't shush me! I demand to know what is going on." Elsa crossed her arms again and gave a defiant stomp.

Elsa's uncooperative attitude was problematic and Olga's mind was swimming with possibilities. If the man was from another family and had anything to do with Elsa convincing Olga to send Angel to the school, then Elsa's life was in danger because the plan had failed and Angel was alive. If, however, he was one of Giovanni's men, a new member Olga had yet to meet, then Elsa and Olga's lives could both be on the line. Olga knew

110

her brother well, and if Giovanni had discovered what happened to Angel and thought that Olga was the one responsible for it, she was as good as dead. Giovanni would see her actions as a betrayal and she wouldn't live to see daylight. Even brotherly love did not accept betrayal. Elsa was her only chance to prove her innocence; her only alibi in Giovanni's eyes.

"You and I are sneaking out the back door and then I'll explain it to you," Olga whispered and nudged her toward the doorway.

"I'm not going anywhere until you tell me what's going on," Elsa rebutted and with that Olga snapped. She placed the Taser against Elsa's stomach and zapped her. Elsa fell forward into Olga's arms, almost knocking Olga off of her feet.

"Good thing you're a skinny little wench," Olga muttered as she dragged Elsa from the waxing room to the back door and out into the alley. Wedging her behind a dumpster, Olga knelt down next to her. "Sorry, sweetie," she said, "but if Giovanni finds out you were the one who asked me to send Angel to that school, we'll both be maggot food." Elsa was still unconscious but Olga felt the need to explain nonetheless. "We'll hide here until that man leaves and then we'll take your car to a safe location."

Reaching inside her handbag, Olga retrieved her cell phone, pulled open the back and removed the tracking device Chase had installed. It was originally meant for her protection because she had been kidnapped in the past; but now, under the current circumstances, it was a liability. "Sorry Chase," Olga muttered to herself as she tossed the tracking device into the dumpster along with her phone.

When Elsa began to awaken, Olga placed the Taser against her throat. "If you scream, I'll zap you," she promised and Elsa's eyes widened. "Now, where's your car?"

CHAPTER 24

Thomas crawled out of bed, zipped up his jeans, pulled his black t-shirt over his head and gave Detta a light pat on her bottom. "I like filling Nicholas' shoes," he said with a grin. "I'll be back tonight to fill them again." Looping his arm around her waist, he pulled Detta close and whispered in her ear. "I like our new arrangement. Don't you?"

Detta nodded but didn't say anything.

"Tonight, I'm going to take you from behind and make you lose your mind," he slurred into her ear, leaving a residue of spit against her lobe.

Detta forced a smile. "I can't wait," she lied.

Once Thomas stumbled out of the front door, Detta lit a cigarette and smoked it down to the butt, then she lit another and another, all the while pacing the length of the cramped mobile home living room. What was she going to do? This whole thing had been a big mistake and she wanted out, but it was too late. She was trapped. Nicholas was dead, which wasn't a cause for mourning. The whims of youth had once made her love him, but those days were long gone. His abusive behavior had destroyed any feelings she had ever felt for him, other than fear. In fact, her fear of him was the reason she was in this mess. If she had only had the courage to say "no." Now, despite the fact that he repulsed her, she was stuck with Thomas, and if she wanted to stay alive she had no choice but to play along, both in and out of the bedroom.

Sex with Thomas might have been bearable if it weren't for the fact that he was a slobbering drunk and dumber than a concrete block. He wasn't bad looking and had a powerful, muscular physique, but that was the sum of his good parts.

Beyond that he was stupid and arrogant; a lethal combination. So, when Detta learned that Thomas' plan to retrieve the jump drive had failed, she wasn't surprised. Not only had the men he sent to the hospital been killed, but the killer had left behind a clue for Angel Maratinzano; one Detta feared the Maratinzano family would have little trouble deciphering.

Earlier that evening when Thomas had arrived at her trailer, stumbling drunk and beside himself with rage, she hurriedly sent Caleb and Jack to their room. Thomas was vowing to do unspeakable things to whoever killed his men and left the clue behind and Detta feared that, in his inebriated frame of mind, he might release his anger on the children. Despite her disgust, Detta knew of only one way to calm him and it worked. She tried to escape the entire sexual act by mentally analyzing who might have discovered their plan and how. Was there a contingency plan should something like this happen? Or did Nicholas believe there would be no errors?

What weighed most heavily on her heart and mind was the fact that her younger sister, Sandy, was dead. Innocent Sandy, who knew nothing of their plan, had paid the price for Detta's error. If only she had put the jump drive in a place where Caleb wouldn't have found it, Sandy would still be alive and none of this would be happening. If she would have known something like this could happen, she would have never allowed Nicholas to talk her into it. She only did it for the money, and at the time didn't realize that her part of the plan could become dangerous. Her job seemed simple. Hack into the Vatican security system and provide Nicholas with the schematic designs and codes he sought. In return, he would provide protection for

her and her foster kids and put $50,000 in her
bank account.

Fifty thousand dollars would give her a new
start on life. She could pay off her debts and get
ahead for once. Now, Sandy was gone and her
bank balance was still in the red. Detta pressed
her cigarette butt into the overcrowded, plastic ash
tray on the coffee table and immediately lit up
another smoke. Turning on the television proved
to be a mistake because when the local news
announced Sandy's death and mentioned that the
school was planning a memorial service, it was all
Detta could do to keep from breaking down. She
collapsed onto the couch and sobbed, inadvertently
dropping her cigarette and burning a small hole in
the carpet.

"Ms. Palumbo?" Caleb spoke softly as he
poked his head from the bedroom and crept toward
the couch. "Ms. Palumbo, are you all right?"

Detta looked up at him and feeling an
unspeakable rage, screamed obscenities. Caleb
took a step backwards. "This is YOUR fault! YOU
killed her! YOU stole the jump drive! YOU should
be dead instead of her!"

Caleb burst into sobs and dashed from the
room. Detta wasn't his real mother, of course, but
she was the only mother he'd ever known and her
sudden rejection broke his heart. He raced out of
the front door, tripping on the first step and falling
face first to the ground. "I HATE YOU!" She
screamed as he scrambled to his feet and rushed
down the street, into the brisk night air.

CHAPTER 25

It was the middle of the night and Chase couldn't sleep. Big Mike had been unable to find Leo the Lion. Andrew wasn't returning phone calls and Olga and Elsa were MIA. Nothing was adding up and he sensed that they were running out of time.

The good news was that Giovanni had yet to learn about Angel being shot at the school. Chase viewed this as a tiny miracle of technology. Giovanni was so focused on Olga's recent antics that he hadn't realized Angel was even back in the Penthouse. He thought she was still on her romantic get-away with Andrew. Chase knew that eventually he was going to find out, and then all hell would break loose; but until then the goal was to acquire all of the answers before Giovanni could start asking questions.

The secret meeting room door crept open, startling Chase. "Can't sleep?" Angel asked, tightening the black, silk robe around her waist and dropping into a chair next to him.

"Too many unknowns," he answered with a sigh.

"Me too," she muttered.

"Boss Lady, can I ask you something?" Chase said.

"If you stop calling me 'boss lady,'" Angel teased.

"How is it that you went away with Andrew and ended up returning with Tony?" Chase raised his eyebrows. "I mean, I've met girls who get around, and don't get me wrong, I LIKE girls that get around; but you don't fit the bill."

Angel exhaled. It was hard to explain, or was it? Actually, it should have been hard to explain but Andrew had made it very simple. "He doesn't want me," Angel uttered, her voice catching on a lump of wedged emotion. "Andrew doesn't want me."

Chase blew out air through his lips. "Yeah, right, and the Pope is a wild-ass Protestant."

"No, really, he told me that he is done with me. He said he doesn't love me." It felt surreal to verbalize. "In fact, I think he actually hates me."

"What?" Chase scrunched up his face in disbelief. "That cat adores your stubborn ass. No disrespect, Boss Lady, but I've never seen a guy so weak-ass smitten. He'll do anything for you."

Angel shook her head. "Well, if it was that way once, it isn't that way anymore."

"So, you're giving up and settling for Tony?" Chase said it with a hint of sarcasm.

"I wouldn't say being with Tony is 'settling!'" She responded with indignation. "He loves me."

"Yeah, but he's not goo-goo-gah-gah-ass smitten. That's all I'm sayin'." Chase shifted in his chair and twirled a pencil as he continued. "I think Tony wants you but more than that he doesn't want Andrew to have you; whereas Andrew wants what's best for you even if he knows it can't be him." Chase raised his eyebrows. "Love is a wild ride."

Angel stared at him, his words piercing her heart. Was it possible that Andrew had deliberately pushed her away because he thought it was best for her? Had she jumped into Tony's arms too quickly? A nauseating wave of confusion swept over her.

The subject was then dropped for the rest of the night and Angel was grateful. She was certain her heart couldn't bear anymore and focusing on finding ways to locate Olga took priority.

Together they watched surveillance feed from every camera angle available, but after Olga and Elsa exited through the back door of the salon, they vanished into thin air. The SUV she had stolen from the garage remained parked outside the salon, but Olga was nowhere to be found.

"She had to have commandeered another vehicle," Chase blurted with obvious frustration. Angel could tell that being unable to locate Olga unnerved him.

"Have you traced her phone?"

Chase's answer came in the form of a facial expression that read "duh."

"Okay, let's think." Angel got up and began to pace in front of the table. "If you were Olga and you felt the need to hide out, where would you go?"

Chase guffawed. "There's no telling with that crazy-ass broad." His fingers danced across the keyboard. "An all-night male strip club," Chase joked and Angel smiled. The thought wasn't too far-fetched.

"Maybe she stole Elsa's car?" Angel posed.

"It's worth a look," Chase answered. "If I can pull up DMV registration information on Elsa, I might be able to figure out where they went." Chase shook his head. "How do two old ladies vanish and why?" Bouncing his knee up and down, he put a pencil between his teeth and clicked the keys. "I really thought she would bring Elsa home with her, to prove to Giovanni that she had nothing to do with your being at the school," he muttered, maneuvering his lips around the pencil.

"But she knows that if Giovanni doesn't believe her, he will have Elsa killed," Angel interjected.

"Do you think it's possible that Elsa could have wanted you to be at that school for a reason?

That she was helping someone orchestrate a hit on you?"

Angel shook her head. "Not a chance. I don't think Olga has told Elsa who I am, or even that we are a mafia family."

"All of these questions will be answered if we can just find her!" Chase barked, spitting the pencil from his lips. "Otherwise, it's my head that's gonna roll. Giovanni isn't the most patient cat in the world."

Angel gazed out the window, overlooking the city. "She's out there somewhere and we have to trust that she knows what she's doing."

"Not making me feel better, Boss Lady," Chase quipped.

"I'll handle my grandfather. You just find Olga."

CHAPTER 26

Angel was awakened early by a loud banging sound on the Penthouse door. "Ms. Maratinzano, my apologies," Harry said when she ripped open the door with a scowl on her face.

"It's 4:30 in the morning!" She barked. "I just went to bed at 3:00am!"

"My apologies, ma'am, but there's an urgent call for you. It's from Don Venturini," he explained, holding up a cell phone for Angel to take.

Angel took the phone, thanked Harry and walked into the living room. "Andrew?"

"Don't speak, just listen. You need to meet me at the pub now. Bring Harry with you for protection, but trust no one else. Leave your cell phone in your room. Trust no one, Angel." Before she could respond Andrew disconnected the call.

Rushing to her bedroom, Angel threw on a pair of jeans, a black cashmere sweater and her black Converse tennis shoes. Her aching shoulder made her move slower than normal, but she pushed through the pain. Pulling her hair into a low pony tail, Angel brushed her teeth and then popped three Ibuprofen into her mouth and washed them down with water. She slowly lowered a Kevlar vest over her head and checked the clip on her gun, clamping it back into place and sliding the gun into her waistband. Her gut told her to trust Andrew, but her mind and her heart felt leery of him. He was different and until she could understand how and why he had changed, she would not completely trust him.

Opening the Penthouse door, Angel met eyes with Harry, who appeared to already have an exit plan in place. Without a word, he motioned for Angel to follow him and then led her into the stairwell. Several flights down, they cut into the hallway and took a service elevator to the street level near the rear entrance of the building. Just outside the entrance Harry opened the passenger side of a black Hummer with dark tinted glass, and Angel climbed inside.

He handed her a cell phone and instructed her to listen to the voicemail message that was on the phone. Angel selected the message and put the phone to her ear. "You don't have reason to trust me and I know I have hurt you, but please believe me when I tell you that I am trying to protect you. Things are not as they appear and unfortunately, neither are people. I need you to trust me one last time, Angel."

Angel lowered the phone into her lap and stared out the window.

"Ms. Maratinzano, my instructions are to take you to meet Don Venturini, but only if you agree to go," Harry explained. "Do you agree?"

Despite her apprehension, Angel gave a nod and Harry pulled the Hummer from the curb and sped down the street. In the message, Andrew's voice had sounded almost desperate and Angel knew that she would never be at peace until she got to the bottom of whatever was going on.

"Why didn't he call me on my cell phone?" Angel asked Harry.

"There can be no trail of communication, nothing traceable," Harry answered. "Don Venturini will explain everything you need to know."

They rode in awkward silence for a few minutes and then Angel broke the ice. "I heard about my aunt Tasering you," she said. "I'm sorry about that."

The corners of Harry's mouth curled slightly upward, as if he were somewhat amused.

"I must confess, I didn't see that coming," he replied, keeping his eyes on the road. "I've never been dropped by an old lady." He shook his head side to side. "She's a crafty one."

"If it makes you feel better, she Tasered Giovanni once. He didn't see it coming either. None of us did."

A chuckle escaped Harry's serious exterior. "I'm surprised your aunt is still among the living."

Angel smiled. "I guess there are perks to being the sister of the Capo di Tutti Capi."

"I would imagine there are perks to being his granddaughter, as well." Harry glanced sideways at Angel and then quickly redirected his gaze to the road.

They rode in silence the rest of the way and upon arriving at Tetterbaum's Pub; Harry escorted Angel to the back door where two men stood guard. Once inside, Angel followed Harry to the secret entrance behind the bar, wherein he ushered her inside and told her to wait for Don Venturini. Moments later, Andrew stepped inside and closed the door behind him. He looked different. Weary. Stressed.

"Thank you for coming," he said.

"Why are we meeting here? You know that Chase can monitor everything in this building..." she began but Andrew put his fingers to her lips.

"I've taken care of that," he uttered. "We're not being watched or recorded."

Angel put her hands on her hips. "Are you going to tell me what's going on?" She snipped. "Why you've dragged me out of bed in the middle of the night?" She paced back and forth. "Why you've been a jerk?" Her voice rose and the anger in her gut grew.

Andrew stepped toward her, placing both palms on her cheeks, gently cupping her face in his hands. "I love you," he said softly, never taking his eyes from hers. "I want you to know that and to remember that forever."

Angel pushed his hands away. "Then why did you say all of those things?" She demanded. "Why were you heartless and cold and hateful?"

His eyes glassed over and Angel could tell he was fighting back emotion. "I didn't mean what I said." Andrew grunted with obvious frustration. "You are a stubborn woman and you don't think things through, and that ultimately endangers you and those around you, but I didn't mean..."

"Oh, and you're Mr. Perfect," she interrupted, rolling her eyes and crossing her arms over her chest. "You become a Don and suddenly you think you're God's gift to the rest of us?" Angel pushed past him, heading toward the opening. Was Tony right? Had becoming a Boss turned Andrew into an ego-maniac?

"Sweetheart," Andrew called after her, catching her fingers and tugging her toward him. "This is bigger than you or me or us."

"What's bigger?" Angel searched his face for revelation. "What's bigger, Andrew?" She squirmed, freeing her hand from his. "You speak in code and then expect me to understand. You won't tell me what's going on, but you ask me to blindly trust you; and in the same breath you tell me not to trust anyone." Angel threw her good arm into the air. "I don't get it."

Andrew grabbed her by the shoulders, but when Angel winced from the pain he immediately released her. "I forgot," he said. "How are you feeling?"

"I feel like I've been shot," Angel quipped.

"I'm sorry."

Exhaling and leaning against the shelving, Angel shook her head. "I thought we were on a

good path, you and me. I thought we
were...together. What happened?"

Andrew lowered his gaze to the floor. "I
can't tell you."

"What does that mean?" She stood up
straighter and narrowed her eyes. "You think I
don't deserve an explanation?"

"No!" He barked. "You do deserve an
explanation, but I can't give you one." Andrew's
voice cracked with emotion. "Not now. Not yet."

"Ever?"

"I don't know," Andrew said with a sigh.

Angel was seething. "Well, I don't know if
I'm going to wait around for you to suddenly decide
to stop being cryptic..."

"You made that crystal clear when you
jumped into bed with Tony," he interrupted and
she felt her face flush.

"You said you were done with me!"

"So you immediately climb into Tony's
bed?"

"Tony loves me!" She hollered.

"NO!" Andrew yelled so loudly that every
muscle in Angel's body immediately tensed.
"Loving someone means you do what is right for
them above all else." He huffed. "Loving someone
is hard and it hurts like hell sometimes." Andrew
turned his back on Angel and ran his hand
through his hair. "Loving a person means you
protect them even when you know they will hate
you for it, and you'll lose them forever." His voice
faded as he spoke.

Angel moved closer and placed her hand on
his shoulder. "Andrew," she whispered. "You
asked me to trust you one last time and here I am.
Now I'm asking you to trust me enough to tell me
what is going on. Please?"

There were tears in his eyes as he turned to face her. "I can't, Sweetheart," he said softly. Then in one swift motion he sank the syringe into Angel's neck and she fell forward into his arms.

A moment later the Snake stepped through the secret entrance that led to the underground tunnels. "It's about time," he said as he lifted Angel from Andrew's arms. "I was beginning to think you didn't have the kahunas to go through with it."

"You know where to take her," Andrew said. "And this time, let's make sure she doesn't escape."

CHAPTER 27

Chase was in a tizzy. Olga and Elsa were still missing. The Snake and Trig had been missing since the morning of the school shooting and now Angel and Harry were gone. Giovanni was fit to be tied, demanding answers that Chase couldn't give.

"I've called all of them, multiple times," Chase told Giovanni. "No one is answering or returning my calls."

"Track them!" Giovanni barked.

"I did!" Chase hollered back and then quickly softened his tone to one of respect. "I did, sir. Angel left her phone in the Penthouse. Harry's phone was found downstairs in the parking garage. Trig and the Snake must have destroyed their tracking devices because they're not even registering on my system."

"What about Lucia?" Giovanni growled. Everyone else in the family called her Olga, but Giovanni always referred to her by her birth name.

"I found her phone and tracking device in the dumpster outside the hair salon," Big Mike said as he entered the secret meeting room.

"Unacceptable!" Giovanni raged, throwing his fist into the air. "This is unacceptable! People do not disappear!" Giovanni paced across the room with his hands held tightly behind his back. "Get me Andrew!"

Chase rolled his eyes. "You're not going to want to hear this, sir, but Andrew's not responding either."

Giovanni's eyes widened. "Is this a plot against me? Against my authority? Has he stolen away with Michelangela and Lucia and my men are helping them escape my reach?"

Big Mike stared at Chase with wide-eyes. That was a scenario that hadn't crossed his mind. "We need to tell him everything," he mouthed and Chase frantically shook his head no.

"He'll kill us," Chase mouthed to Big Mike while Giovanni was staring out of the windows overlooking the city.

"If you don't, I will," Big Mike threatened.

Just then the door to the secret meeting room burst open and one of Giovanni's men paraded in, making a beeline for the Capo. He whispered into Giovanni's ear and Giovanni responded in Italian. "Fissarli in una stanza e aspettare per le mie istruzioni."

"What did he say?" Chase whispered to Big Mike.

"Someone must be here," Big Mike explained. "He said to secure them in a room and wait for his instructions."

Chase let his fingers fly across the keyboard, pulling up surveillance feed from the security cameras located around the building. He was hoping to catch a glimpse of whoever it was, but there was no time to sort through that much feed. During his quick search he realized that the rear entrance camera had been tampered with, replacing the real feed with a stagnant image of the street. Chase cursed aloud, drawing Big Mike's attention.

"What?" Big Mike asked, leaning over Chase's shoulder to view the monitor.

"Someone re-set the rear entrance security camera to render a fake-ass image," Chase explained. "Only they went one step further and created multiple images to rotate according to time of day." Chase placed his pencil between his teeth and let his fingers dance rapidly across the keyboard.

"Isn't the surveillance system encoded for security purposes? Who would be able to do that?" Big Mike questioned.

Chase shook his head. "Me. I'm the only one with the security codes." Bouncing his knee spastically up and down, Chase worked to un-do what had been done to the camera and re-set it. "Son of a...."

"What?" Big Mike interrupted.

"Whoever did this put a password on it so that I can't easily un-do it." He exhaled loudly. "I'm going to have to run it through the decoding program and that will take time," he huffed. "Time I don't have."

Big Mike stood up straight and exhaled. "Well, that answers the question of how did Angel and Harry get out of the Towers unnoticed."

Moments later, when Giovanni's man had left the room, he turned his attention to Chase and Big Mike. His eyes burned with a fiery rage that Chase felt certain would melt his head right off of his neck. "Gentleman," he began. "I will ask you one time and only one time." Giovanni pulled out the chair at the head of the table and lowered himself into it, folding his fingers together and resting his arms on the table. "Is there something you are not telling me?"

Chase swallowed hard, his eyes protruding from their sockets. Where to begin?

CHAPTER 28

"Merciful Heavens! Quit your whining," Olga spat at Elsa, as she peered through the motel room curtains.

"How long are you going to hold me prisoner here?" Elsa demanded.

"Until I know it's safe to let you go."

Elsa was sitting in a wooden chair with her ankles duct taped together and her knees and thighs taped to the base of the chair. Olga had gone around the chair several times and she was pretty sure, judging by Elsa's frail bone structure, that she was unable to break free and pull herself up.

"Who carries duct tape in their handbag?" Elsa spat.

"Lots of people," Olga retorted.

"That's not normal, Olga, dear. Normal people don't walk around with duct tape."

Olga leaned down into Elsa's face. "I carry it when I know I'm going to confront a traitorous friend," she growled.

"I told you I had nothing to do with Angel getting shot," Elsa reiterated. "No one instructed me to ask you to invite Angel to the school. I just thought it would be fun for Ruby to have a guest speaker that she knew."

"Ruby doesn't know Angel. They've never met. That makes no sense," Olga barked. "You're lying!"

Elsa threw her hands into the air and let them fall into her lap. "I think you're paranoid, Olga. I think you need medical attention. The psychiatric kind."

"Maybe I do, but being paranoid has kept me alive for the past thirty years," Olga defended.

"Do you hear yourself?" Elsa gasped. "It's like you've made up a bunch of bad guys in your mind. They're not real, sweetie. They're not real."

"Oh, they're real all right, and they'll kill you in a moment's notice if they think you've betrayed them."

"Betrayed who?"

"The family."

CHAPTER 29

By the time Chase finished giving a detailed account of what had transpired over the past several days, Giovanni's face was the color of blood. He pounded his fists on the table and made threats that rendered Chase motionless with fear. After numerous tirades in Italian, wherein he paced angrily across the room, Giovanni finally stood still in front of the windows and peered out at the city.

"Situata a Capo di Tutti Capi non è un reato punibile con la pena di morte," he uttered in a hushed town. "Di morte!" He screamed, turning to face Chase and Big Mike.

"Uh-oh," Big Mike uttered.

"What?" Chase gasped. "What's uh-oh mean? What did he say?"

"You don't want to know," Big Mike whispered.

"Silencio!" Giovanni growled. "I said lying to me is a sin punishable by death," he explained as he neared the table where Big Mike and Chase sat in wide-eyed panic. "But I am not going to kill you." Chase breathed a sigh of relief. "Yet," Giovanni added and slid into a chair. "If you meet my demands I will allow you to live, despite your treachery."

"Yes, sir," Chase muttered. "What do you need us to do?"

Giovanni held up his index finger. "First, you will find Michelangela and return her safely to me." Both Big Mike and Chase nodded. "Second, you will locate Lucia and Elsa and bring them to me. I will see fit to punish them for their crime."

Clearing his throat, Chase raised his hand to speak, like a child in school. "Sir?"

Giovanni scowled at him and Chase quickly lowered his arm.

"Third," Giovanni continued. "You will work with this Sal person from the FBI to decipher the message left for us, at which time you will bring the information to me and only to me; making certain that Sal understands that one word uttered to anyone else will result in his death and that of his family," he seethed. "I may kill him anyway for tampering with my surveillance equipment and blocking my satellite feed."

Chase nodded his head spastically up and down.

"And YOU," Giovanni yelled, pointing at Big Mike. "You will bring me Don Venturini, the Snake, Trig and Harry. I will deal with them."

"Yes, sir," Big Mike said quietly. As Giovanni stormed from the room, Big Mike turned to Chase. "How the hell am I supposed to do that when we can't find any of them?"

Chase's fingers were flying across the keys. "Even if we do find them, you can't bring them in," Chase said. "He'll kill 'em. All of 'em."

"And if I don't comply, he kills me!"

"There's another option and it appears to be the one everyone is taking," Chase whispered, glancing up from his computer screen and meeting eyes with Big Mike.

"What's that?"

"Disappear."

CHAPTER 30

Angel awakened in a dark room. It wasn't pitch black, as a trail of light shown from beneath the door, but dark enough to prove hazardous to one's mobility. She was lying on her back on a double bed. The Kevlar vest was heavy on her chest and she sat up, removed it and inhaled a much needed deep breath. She didn't know where she was and the last thing she remembered was talking to Andrew at the pub. Slowly making her way toward the crack of light beneath the door, Angel reached for the knob. She was locked in.

She ran her hands along the wall until she came to another door; this one opened. Finding a light switch, she turned it on and saw that it was a small bathroom with a sink and a toilet. She left the light on and the door cracked open.

Voices were coming from somewhere below, so she lowered herself to the floor in search of a vent. Finally finding one in the far corner of the room, she laid down and pressed her ear against it.

She could make out three distinct voices, one was the Snake and another was Harry, but the third voice was unfamiliar.

"You have your instructions," Harry said. "All you have to do is keep Ms. Maratinzano hidden until all of this is over."

"I'd take those orders seriously," the Snake quipped. "She's not going to make your job easy."

"Oh, please," the third man sighed. "I've been a cop longer than you've been alive. I've seen shit that would make your head spin. I think I can handle that little thing."

"That little thing, as you call her, is the granddaughter to the Capo. Anything happens to her and..." Harry began but was interrupted.

"I said I got it," the man sneered. "And I'm not afraid of the Capo."

"Then you're stupid," the Snake chided. "And it's been my experience that stupid usually gets people dead."

Angel was about to holler down the vent for the Snake but just as she opened her mouth, Harry said, "Let's review the plan one more time so we all know what to do." She heard what sounded like chairs being moved and the shuffling of papers and envisioned them sitting around a table.

"I don't know why I gotta be the babysitter when I'm the one that brought Andrew the big tip in the first place," the man spat.

"You're lucky to be alive, Lisben!" The Snake barked. "If I were Andrew I'd have killed you after you betrayed me."

Lisben! Angel gasped silently. She thought that he was dead. Everyone assumed it. After he had attempted to become an inside informant for Stidda and then responsible for spreading rumors among the police force that claimed Andrew had murdered his own family and Police Captain Senalli, Angel couldn't imagine why Andrew had allowed him to live. In fact, she recalled that Tony had offered to kill him and Andrew said that it would be his first line of business as the new Don. Why hadn't he done it?

"Andrew and I go way back," Lisben snipped.

"Friendship without loyalty is nothing more than a liability," the Snake sneered. "He may not have had the strength to kill you, but I do."

"Nobody is killing anybody," Andrew said as he entered the room. Angel heard his footsteps and a door close behind him. "We each have a role to play if we're going to pull this off. And we can't afford not to pull it off."

CHAPTER 31

Detta paced nervously. She had phoned her brother at least twenty times since Sandy's death. Now his voicemail was full and he still wasn't answering. She didn't know what to do. They needed to plan a funeral and she didn't have any money for one. She tried to call her sister-in-law, Margo, but the line was disconnected. She had no other family. To add to her stress, Caleb was still missing and it was her fault. She thought he would have come home last night, but he didn't. She had searched the trailer park and the adjoining neighborhood. Caleb didn't have many friends so she half-way expected to find him curled up under a tree, shivering. Despite Jack's begging to help her search, Detta made him stay at home, promising that Caleb would return. Though she uttered the words, she had the distinct feeling that it was a promise she would not be able to keep.

CHAPTER 32

Several more men joined the Snake, Harry, Andrew and Lisben in the room below her, and Angel kept her ear to the vent, absorbing every word.

"Gentlemen," Andrew began in a formal fashion, "I want to thank you for coming. I know your time is valuable so I will make this brief."

Why is he addressing them so formally? Angel wondered and then it hit her. There must be other Bosses in the room. Was Andrew coordinating something against the Maratinzano family? *No, he wouldn't do that... Or would he?*

"Why have we been blindfolded and brought to a non-disclosed location?" Don Andriachini demanded.

"I know my tactics may seem unorthodox, but this is for your protection," Andrew answered. "You cannot be questioned or coerced to lead someone to a location you don't know about."

"Why isn't the Capo here?" Don Andriachini questioned. "Your father, God rest his soul, would never have met behind the Capo's back."

"I understand," Andrew replied. "I mean no disrespect, but I have a valid reason for not wanting the Capo present. If you will hear me out, I believe you will understand." Angel could almost feel the tension in the room even from a floor above.

CHAPTER 33

Leo sat on the couch next to Caleb, trying to convince himself that coming here was the right decision. When Caleb had shown up on his doorstep in the middle of the night, he didn't know where else to go. Caleb was crying out for the angel that had saved him at the school. He believed that the angel could keep him safe and make all of his fears go away. Leo tried to comfort him, but nothing would soothe his little heart. Detta's words had scarred Caleb deeply and Leo knew of no other way to right the wrong than to stop it; even if it cost him his life.

When Giovanni entered the room, Leo bowed his head as a gesture of respect and Caleb stared at him with the innocence of youth. "I have been informed that you have information about my granddaughter?"

"Yes, sir," Leo answered.

"Is there anything that you require?" Giovanni began. "A glass of water?"

"Nothing for me, sir," Leo uttered, his voice trembling. "But the boy hasn't eaten anything since yesterday."

Giovanni motioned for one of his body guards, who stepped forward and bent his ear down toward the Capo's lips. "Portare loro cibo e acqua. Qualcosa per un bambino," Giovanni uttered and the man nodded and left the room.

"Grazie," Leo said.

"You speak Italian?" Giovanni asked.

"Si, um, yes, sir," Leo stuttered.

"That is a good start," Giovanni replied. "Now, why have you come to see me?"

"I want the angel who saved me," Caleb spoke outright. "Uncle Leo said she lives here in

this tall building." Caleb's lip quivered. "Please,
can I see her?"

"This is your nephew?" Giovanni asked
Leo.

"My sister takes care of foster kids. Caleb
here is one of them," he explained.

Giovanni nodded and then turned his focus
to Caleb. "Michelangela..." he began and then
caught himself... "Angel is not home at the moment
but she will be returning shortly. You may eat
some lunch and wait for her. Would you like that?"

Caleb nodded and once the food arrived,
Giovanni escorted Caleb and Leo to the secret
meeting room where Chase was working earnestly
on deciphering the message left for Angel at the
hospital. Giovanni made the necessary
introductions and Chase gave Caleb a knuckle
bump. "Hey, little dude, I saw you on television.
You're like famous now," Chase said and Caleb's
face lit up.

Giovanni took a seat at the head of the
table and Caleb sat next to Chase, while Leo sat
across from him. Caleb quickly devoured his
entire cheeseburger as if he were starving.

"My sister's on food stamps," Leo said
between bites. "I don't know how much the kid
gets to eat at home."

"I get a piece of fruit in the morning," Caleb
said, shoving in a French fry. "And then I get hot
lunch at school and it's pretty good." He took a sip
of chocolate milk through the straw. "My stomach
growls a lot on weekends, but not as loud as
Jack's. His sounds like a lion." Caleb bit another
fry. "Sometimes our neighbor sneaks me and Jack
some table scraps." Caleb chewed and swallowed
and then held up a fry and offered it to Chase and
then to Giovanni. Both of them declined so he
shoved it into his mouth with a grin. "This is good.

Thank you," he said and Giovanni felt a tug at his heart.

Clearing his throat and directing his attention to Leo, Giovanni asked, "Do you feel it will be appropriate for us to discuss business in front of your nephew?" He asked and Leo explained that he believed Caleb might prove helpful in lending insight into what had transpired.

"And I assume you want something in return for the information you appear so willing to give?" Giovanni chided.

"Si," Leo acknowledged. "I need your help." He set his cheeseburger down on the plate and wiped his mouth with the back of his hand. "I'm a Made member of the Venturini family. Your granddaughter was held captive at the Venturini estate after the school incident. She forced me to help her flee."

"She was held captive?" Giovanni blurted.

"She forced you?" Chase blurted at the same time as Giovanni.

Leo nodded. "I tried to tell her that something was going on but at that time I thought it was an exclusive, Venturini family issue. She tricked me and stole the car, leaving me stranded."

Giovanni leaned back in his chair, listening intently. "Continue."

Leo leaned forward. "Do you believe in Divine intervention?"

"I know a lot of funky-ass stuff happens with no explanation, if that's what you mean," Chase retorted.

"I believe we cannot question that which is Divine," Giovanni answered. "What relevance is this to your story?"

Excitement shone on Leo's face. "See, I believe your granddaughter kidnapping me was an act of Divine intervention. She could have just as easily taken Louie, but she chose me. Maybe that choice wasn't random. Then, she decided to leave me at a gas station in the middle of nowhere. Had she not done that, I wouldn't have overheard the cops talking ..."

"What were they talking about?" Chase interrupted.

"About having certain policeman assigned on a high profile security detail here in Chicago." Leo shook his head. "When I heard this, it was confirmation."

"What security detail?" Chase asked. "Confirmation of what?"

Leo shook his head. "See, I worried that you didn't get my message and that you wouldn't figure it out in time, and I was right to worry. You don't know what I'm talking about because it hasn't been released yet."

"You lost me," Chase quipped. "What message?"

"The one I left for you at the hospital."

Chase almost leapt from his seat. "YOU did that?!"

Giovanni rose from his chair and called one of his men into the room. "Escort the boy to the Penthouse to wait for Michelangela."

"But, sir..."

Giovanni glared at him. "Is there a problem?"

The man leaned closer to Giovanni's ear. "I ain't so good with kids."

"Then turn on the television," Giovanni retorted.

Chase quickly turned to Caleb. "You're one lucky little dude. You get to go to Angel's house and watch cartoons while you wait for her," he said and Caleb smiled. "Do you like cats?" Chase asked and Caleb nodded. "Angel's got two big 'ole cats upstairs. You'll love 'em. Their names are Midnight and Mo."

Caleb got up and followed Giovanni's man toward the door. "Are you going to come too?" He asked Chase.

"Nah, I gotta work but I'll come up in a little bit. Check the fridge. There's probably some Cannoli in there."

When they had gone, Giovanni turned his attention back to Leo. "Continue," he ordered.

"Wait a second," Chase blurted. "YOU took out those men at the hospital?"

Leo nodded.

"Why?" Giovanni demanded.

"They were going to kill your granddaughter," Leo answered. "They went there to find the jump drive and they were going to kill Angel in the process."

"How did you acquire this information?" Giovanni asked.

"When I saw Caleb on the news talking about an angel and a jump drive, I put it all together. Then, when I heard she was shot I knew Nicholas would target her at the hospital." Leo exhaled loudly and then took a deep breath.

"Who's Nicholas?" Chase asked.

"It's a long story," Leo muttered.

"You have my fullest attention," Giovanni rebutted, extending his arms.

"A couple of months ago I was commissioned to hit a mark." Leo dropped his head and shook it slowly side to side. "When I found out who it was, I couldn't do it."

"Why?" Giovanni questioned, disapproval in his tone. "Were you doubting the authority by which you received the commission?"

"Oh, no, sir, it wasn't that," Leo uttered. "I came to learn that this man was involved with my sister."

"Bah!" Giovanni huffed. "That's no excuse."

Leo lowered his gaze to the table, his shoulders slumping forward. "Probably not, sir, but I felt conflicted and I made the mistake of telling my wife about it."

"I bet that went over like a lead-ass balloon," Chase chided.

"Yeah, worse," Leo acknowledged. "Margo, that's my wife, told me that she couldn't love a man who would kill a person on purpose." He threw his hands into the air. "I tried to tell her it was my job, but she wouldn't listen. She left me."

Giovanni appeared more than unsympathetic to Leo's plight. "You were wrong to disobey your commission and ignorant for telling your wife." He ran his hands over his jowls. "I would have killed you for it. Now, what does this have to do with my granddaughter and the message you left at the hospital."

Leo shifted in his seat. "The man I was supposed to hit was Nicholas Diaglio. His family is from Italy."

Giovanni narrowed his gaze, lowering his eyebrows and studying Leo. "I am well aware of the Diaglio family," he uttered.

"To make a long story short," Leo continued. "My sister pleaded for his life and made a deal to cut me in on the payout she was due to receive from Nicholas."

"What kind of a payout?" Giovanni asked.

"Fifty thousand dollars. Tax free," Leo said. "I was gonna get half."

"Twenty-five thousand bones to let the guy live," Chase added. "I can see why you'd be tempted." Giovanni swung his head quickly and glared at Chase. "I mean, but that's no reason to disobey an order or anything crazy-ass like that," Chase quickly back-peddled. "I would never do that..." Chase's voice faded and Giovanni turned his scowl back toward Leo.

"Continue," Giovanni ordered.

"With twenty-five G's I'd be able to get Margo back and run away from the Venturini family. I could hide out in a small town somewhere and never have to look back." Leo shook his head. "The thing was I didn't know at the time what Nicholas was plotting. I guess I assumed it had something to do with selling drugs and laundering money because that's why he was on the hit list to begin with; but when I accidentally saw Detta's computer..." his voice faded.

"Detta?" Giovanni asked.

"That's my sister."

"What was on her computer?" Chase questioned and Leo's face grew pale.

He swallowed hard and then licked his lips. "It was a blueprint, like a schematic design with numeric codes."

Chase pulled up the image from the jump drive and spun his laptop around to face Leo. "Like this?"

"Yes!" Leo gasped. "Yes, that's exactly it! So, Caleb was telling the truth about giving the jump drive to an angel. I knew it!"

"What the hell is it?" Chase asked. "I know it came from the database at the Vatican, but it doesn't match the layout of the Vatican City, so I'm not sure what I'm looking at. All I know is that these numbers aren't longitude or latitude coordinates."

"You're right, it came from the Vatican. Detta hacked into their system," Leo uttered.

143

"Damn," Chase spat. "Your sister must have mad skills because that's virtually impossible to do undetected."

"What you're looking at is the Holy Name Cathedral," Leo whispered and made the sign of the cross over his body. "The street images and the image of the church are overlaid. You need a multi-imaging software to remove the layers so that you can decipher it."

"The Holy Name Cathedral? OUR Holy Name Cathedral?" Chase gasped. "Right here in Chicago?"

Leo nodded.

Chase spun his laptop around to face him and loaded the image into a software program. "Holy, Mary, Mother of..." he stopped. "You're right, here's North State Street and..."

"What does this mean?" Giovanni interrupted.

Leo went on to explain that Detta was a skilled hacker with a criminal history of using her technological talents for unethical purposes. "To put it bluntly, she's a thief," he stated. Asking Chase to put the information from the jump drive onto the large screen in front of the table, Leo stood up and explained every detail of the design, periodically pointing at the image.

"What the media doesn't know and hasn't released yet is the fact that the Pope is planning a visit to Chicago," Leo said.

"Rubbish!" Giovanni blurted. "His Eminence has not come to this city since 1979. Why would he come here now?"

"To beseech the constituents of the city to work together toward peace and to minimize violence," Leo answered. "See this blue line, here?" Leo pointed at the screen. "According to the cops I overheard at the gas station, that's the entry route.

They're going to bring him down Chicago Avenue to State Street to the Cathedral here, on the corner of State and Superior." Leo took a breath. "My guess is that he's never going to make it to the Cathedral."

"Why would anyone want to take out the Pope?" Chase quipped in disbelief. "I mean, don't most people, even non-Catholics, think he's an okay guy?"

"He said some stuff that pissed off some people," Leo explained.

"Giovanni pisses off people all of the time but nobody's plotting his death," Chase quipped and then looked at Giovanni. "No disrespect."

"This new Pope took it upon himself to stop all of the money laundering that has gone on in the Vatican for years. Basically, he doesn't want dirty money. He feels it taints the whole good, Catholic vibe," Leo explained.

"I remember his speech," Giovanni interjected. "I had conversations with families in Italia and Sicily at the time. None of them were offended enough to plot against His Eminence."

"That's because you got the watered-down, media version," Leo murmured. "The truth is, the Pope not only cut out their money, he cut them out. 'No absolution for the Mob,' were his words." Leo's eyes grew wide. "They're not allowed to make confession, to attend mass or to step foot in the Vatican."

"Rubbish!" Giovanni howled. "I would have been informed if this were the case."

"Maybe not," Chase added, thoughtfully. "Why inform the Capo di Tutti Capi of a plot you intend to carry out on his soil?" Chase raised his eyebrows. "When you can let the Capo take the fall for it."

"Exactly," Leo gritted. "Assassinate the Pope on American soil and the Mob families here take the blame."

"While the world focuses on the shock and tragedy of what happened in Chicago, the state with the highest crime rate, the families across the pond use their power to muscle in a Pope who is more understanding of their lifestyle," Chase spat out rapidly. "It makes perfect sense. In fact, it's wild-ass brilliant!"

Giovanni's face reddened. "Who is behind this?" He demanded.

Shaking his head, Leo sank back into his seat. "All I know is Nicholas got my sister involved..."

Giovanni pound his fist against the table, startling Leo into silence. "Bring me this Nicholas!"

"He...he's dead, sir," Leo stuttered.

"I thought you said you were unable to hit your mark?" Giovanni raged.

"I was, but I'm pretty sure your granddaughter killed him at the school."

It was obvious that Giovanni's blood was boiling and that he did not like to be the last one to know, nor to feel as if the wool had been pulled over his eyes. Leo took a step back from him.

"See, sir, what I can't figure out is how Angel knew about the jump drive or about Nicholas' plan. Somehow she must have known, right? Why else would she have gone to the school that morning?" Leo asked.

"Why indeed," Giovanni huffed.

"But then when she forced me to help her escape, she didn't seem to know anything about it. I told her that something big was happening in the Venturini family and I didn't want to be a part of it, but..."

146

"Why do you think this is linked to the Venturini family?" Chase piped in.

"Because I believe Don Venturini knows."

Giovanni abruptly rose from his chair and pointed his finger at Leo. "You are making accusations against a Boss, YOUR Boss. That is a crime punishable by death," he seethed.

"With all due respect, sir, it's only punishable by death if I'm wrong," Leo rebutted. "And I'm not wrong."

"How do you know Andrew..." Chase stopped. "How do you know Don Venturini knows about the plot to kill the Pope?"

Leo took a deep breath. "After I saw what was on Detta's computer, I questioned her about it, but she didn't know much. She kept saying that Nicholas had all of the contacts and that her job was merely to hack into the Vatican security system and supply him with travel information, parade routes, dates, schematics of the city streets, the church and the security clearance codes." Leo pointed to the screen. "I'm guessing that all of that information is on the jump drive." He paced back and forth. "Overhearing the cops at the gas station confirmed the Pope's visit, so all I needed to do was put the pieces together. I started snooping around, paying more attention everywhere I went. It was like all of my senses were heightened. I kept thinking that assassinating the Pope wasn't something one man could pull off, right?"

Chase nodded. "Impossible for one man."

"I overheard Don Venturini and a couple of our men discussing something, and they referred to it as 'something big.'" Leo made quotation marks around the words for effect. "I also heard Don Venturini on the phone one night and I heard him say the name 'Diaglio.'" Leo stopped pacing and stood perfectly still. "I couldn't believe it. Why

would Don Venturini be involved with someone like
Nicholas Diaglio unless he was in on the plot to kill
the Pope?" Leo shook his head. "After that, I
couldn't help noticing he started acting weird;
nervous-like. He was making more and more
secret calls and refusing to allow his body guards
to remain with him. He got rid of his regular
bodyguards and assigned two men who I wouldn't
trust if my life depended on it; one is even a
newbie." Leo's eyes widened, emphasizing the fact
that everyone knew a new recruit, or a "newbie"
was never placed in the position of guarding a
Boss. Even the Under Bosses were guarded by
Made members with a long and trusted history.
"The way he treated your granddaughter was..."
Leo paused as if he were searching for the correct
words. "It was..."

"It was what!" Giovanni demanded.

"It was mean and I've never seen Don
Venturini be purposefully mean."

"Behaving in a mean way doesn't prove that
he knows about an assassination attempt on the
Pope," Chase noted.

"I can prove he's been in touch with
Nicholas Diaglio," Leo blurted.

Reaching into his pants pocket, Leo
retrieved his keys and handed them to Chase.
Attached to the key ring was a small flash drive. "I
recorded his conversation," Leo said. "It's only one
sided, so you can't hear who he is talking to but
you can hear Don Venturini mention the name
Diaglio two times."

Chase looked to Giovanni, who nodded
giving his permission to proceed. Chase then
loaded the flash drive, plugged it into the USB port
on his laptop, and retrieved the information. They
all listened as the recording of Andrew's voice filled
the room.

"Nicholas Diaglio," Andrew said the name and Giovanni's scowl deepened. "This is big and I appreciate you bringing it to my attention. You've been very helpful. I will get with Diaglio and see what I can find out. This runs deeper than I thought and the fall-out will be extensive. I'll be in touch. Thank you." The recording ended and Giovanni was seething.

"Bring Andrew to me immediately!" He barked at Chase, who jumped in his seat. "I want an explanation for this!"

"I've been trying like crazy to reach him, but he's not responding to my calls. None of them are," Chase retorted with a certain frustration. "The Snake, Trig, Harry, Andrew, Angel..." his voice faded and he threw his hands in the air. "It's like they all just fell off the face of the planet." Chase shook his head. "I thought for sure Tony would know where Angel was, but he's as stumped as I am."

"He has them," Leo uttered.

"Who has them?" Giovanni growled.

"Don Venturini. He has them all."

CHAPTER 34

Thomas paced across Detta's living room, huffing and puffing like an angry bull. "We have to find that boy!" He yelled, startling Detta. "We don't know how much he has overheard and God only knows what he'll tell people! The whole plan could go up in smoke!"

"What does it matter?" Detta muttered through the cigarette that was barely hanging from her bottom lip.

"It matters because we don't get paid unless we finish the job," Thomas seethed. He came to a halt in front of the arm chair in which she was curled up, and towered powerfully over her. "Don't you want your money?"

Removing the cigarette from her lip, Detta looked up at Thomas. "There is no money, you idiot. Nicholas was the one with the connections. He was the one that was going to get the pay out and then pay us. I don't even know who his contact is."

A slow grin spread across Thomas' face as he leaned down toward Detta. "I do," he whispered. "Who's the idiot now?"

CHAPTER 35

Angel listened intently through the vent, as Andrew explained what was going to transpire to the other Bosses. "We have Intel that the Pope is coming to our city and that there are plans to assassinate him while he is here."

The Bosses were immediately up in arms. At first they didn't believe Andrew, arguing that His Eminence had not visited Chicago since 1979 and had there been plans on the books to do so, they would have been informed well in advance. Andrew couldn't refute that point and agreed that the manner in which the Pope's visit to the States had been planned was unorthodox. "Be that as it may, gentlemen," Andrew continued, "He is nonetheless arriving in less than seventy-two hours."

Angel could hear gasps of disbelief.

"Why have we been kept in the dark?" The Galante Underboss burst, and then it sounded as if he slammed his fist atop a table.

"Yes," Don Cullato agreed. "How did you know this and we did not know? Why was this kept from us?" The volume of his voice rose angrily.

"Part of the information was brought to me by an old colleague on the force, and the rest I stumbled upon while investigating another matter," Andrew explained.

"Are we to infer from the Maratinzano lack of representation that they are involved in the plot against His Eminence?" Don Cullato seethed.

"I am representing the Maratinzano's," the Snake interjected.

"Yes," Andrew added. "The Snake will be stepping into an Underboss role for the

151

Maratinzano family. I want that made clear to all of your men."

"Where is Michelangela?" Don Andriachini asked with a tone of skepticism.

"That is of no concern," Andrew answered flatly.

Angel didn't know what to think. Why would they strip her of authority in the eyes of the Bosses? She couldn't believe that Andrew was working against her and that the Snake was helping him; though it sure appeared that way. Had Tony been right about Andrew being untrustworthy? It didn't make sense.

"Does Giovanni know that the Snake has taken over for his granddaughter?" Don Andriachini asked.

"That is of no concern to you right now," the Snake quipped and Angel could only imagine the tense glares being exchanged.

"Not to appear insensitive, but, other than it being a tragedy, of what concern is it to us if His Eminence is assassinated?" Don Cullato posed. "Pope's are replaceable and so are Capo's, are they not?"

Angel couldn't believe what he had just said. How could a God-fearing Catholic man utter such blasphemous words? And why was he talking about the Capo di Tutti Capi being replaceable? *No wonder Giovanni never trusted the Cullatos,* she mused.

"I would urge you to choose your words carefully, Don Cullato, as you would hate to appear a sympathizer," Andrew warned. There were grumblings around the table and Andrew continued. "If the Pope dies on American soil at the hand of the American mafia, what do you think will become of our families?" He paused as if waiting for someone to speak, but the room

remained silent. "Every Boss will pay with his life.
Our families will be annihilated. We will have no
protection and the Capo will be ..."

"I think what Don Venturini is trying to say
is that our families will pay the price for what will
be considered, by the rest of the world and by our
own government, to be an act of terrorism," the
Snake interjected. "They will seek to blame and to
punish someone and that someone will begin with
the Capo and trickle down to the rest of us."

Angel could only imagine the expressions
on their faces. Her throat felt completely dry and
she could feel her heart beating wildly in her chest.
This is bad. This is really bad.

"So, if Giovanni's head is first on the line,
then why is he not included in this meeting?" Don
Andriachini asked.

Andrew exhaled. "Because I have reason to
believe that he knows about the plot against the
Pope and is either helping to facilitate it or is
willing to turn a blind eye to it."

Gasps filled the room and Angel felt as if
she had just been kicked in the stomach. *What?!*
How could Andrew say that? Giovanni would
never sit back and allow the Pope to be murdered.
Never! He had a temper and could be ruthless in
his business dealings, but he was nonetheless a
God-fearing, devout Catholic.

"That is a sizeable accusation," Don Cullato
sneered. "Do you have evidence to support it?"

Angel heard a chair scoot against the floor
and then Andrew's voice got a little louder. She
surmised he must have stood up and was pacing
around the room.

"Several weeks ago the Capo met with me
privately and made me an offer," he began and
then stopped and cleared his throat. Angel could
tell in his tone of voice that he was not comfortable

with what he was about to say. "It was an offer I could not refuse."

"What was it?" Don Andriachini demanded.

"In short, he said I was to become the next Capo di Tutti Capi," Andrew stated and an uproar of voices filled the room. It was obvious that the other Bosses were furious by this news. They ranted in Italian and Angel could only imagine the horrible things that were being said.

When they quieted down, Andrew continued. "It is not news to any of you that since my father's murder, the Venturini family has been weak. Many of my men have requested permission to seek membership with your families. Don Galante and Don Cullato, you have taken on several Venturini men." There was clearing of throats and grumblings. "I mean no disrespect in pointing this out, as I have granted them permission to leave."

"Your father would be ashamed!" Don Andriachini blurted.

"I imagine he would be," Andrew responded quietly. "Giovanni learned of the family disintegration and presented me with an opportunity not only to save the Venturini legacy but reaffirm it as a family of power and strength. I do not have to tell you what choice my father would have made if given this same opportunity." The room grew quiet and Andrew continued. "Giovanni arranged for me to marry a woman from the Brioschi family in Italy. The merging of the Venturinis and Brioschis will give both families a bi-continental presence and the revitalization they need."

"And you accepted his offer?" Don Cullato asked.

"It was an offer I could not refuse," Andrew uttered. "To not accept would not only have been

considered a personal insult to the Capo, but it
would have resulted in the forthright annihilation
of the Venturini name."

"Bah!" The Galante Underboss belted. "He
does not have the authority to promise the Capo
position to you. It must be a majority vote."

Everyone seemed to ignore the Galante
Underboss because no one responded to his
outburst. "So, if you marry the Brioschi woman
and strengthen the Venturini name, you will then
be offered the Capo position?" Don Andriachini
summed up.

"That is the deal," Andrew remarked.

"When are you to wed?" Don Andriachini
asked.

"Madeline Brioschi will arrive in the States
tomorrow and we are due to be wed on Tuesday
morning."

Tuesday! That's two days from now! Angel
gasped and the pit in her stomach grew deeper.
When was he going to tell her? Was this why he
had been treating her so badly? She suddenly felt
as if she might vomit from a heartache that was so
deep it was indescribable. Had she lost Andrew
forever? *No. Please, God, no. I can't lose him.*

"Though the offer is offensive to the rest of
us, it does not prove that the Capo knows about
the plot against the Pope," Don Andriachini
argued.

"In researching my wife-to-be, I learned that
she has been formerly wed and widowed to a man
named Adam Brioschi."

"So, she is not of Brioschi bloodline?" Don
Galante blurted.

"No," Andrew responded. "Her maiden
name is Diaglio and she is the biological sister of
the man who was recently gunned down at East
Side Junior High here in Chicago."

155

"I still do not see the connection between the Pope and Giovanni," Don Andriachini uttered.

"Nicholas Diaglio went to East Side Junior High looking for a jump drive that contained detailed information about the Pope's upcoming visit to Chicago," the Snake interjected. "That drive was inadvertently and ironically intercepted by Giovanni's granddaughter."

"Michelangela was at the junior high school?" Don Cullato narrowed his eyes.

"She was the one who killed Nicholas Diaglio," Andrew confided, "and somehow managed to get her hands on the jump drive, as if she already knew who had it..." Andrew's voice tapered off.

"So, you believe that Michelangela was working under Giovanni's orders to confiscate the jump drive for the purpose of assisting in the assassination attempt on the Pope? Don Andriachini questioned.

"I don't know," Andrew said with a sigh. "Maybe. Maybe not. Maybe she was following instructions but not aware of the bigger picture? Maybe she was simply in the wrong place at the wrong time."

Angel swallowed a lump that was rising in her throat. How could Andrew even think for a moment that she would do something like plot against the Pope? Sure, she shot the Mayor but that was an accident. She didn't plot to kill people. She wasn't a murderer and he knew it. At least, the old Andrew knew it. The tears that had been welling up in her eyes now spilled down her cheeks. *Maybe I was in the right place at the right time,* she thought. *Why can't he see the good?*

"All we know is that Olga sent Angel to the school that morning," the Snake added. "And as much as I pleaded with her not to go, she insisted."

"Giovanni used his sister and granddaughter to help in a plan to assassinate His Eminence!" The Galante Underboss shouted. "I say we take a vote right now. All in favor of removing the Capo from power and taking out Lucia and Angel..."

Angel could picture the Galante Underboss gallantly throwing his hand into the air as he spoke.

"Put your hands down!" Andrew barked.

People raised their hands?! Angel leaned against the wall in disbelief. It was mutiny. It was conspiracy. The Bosses were riling against her family without evidence of wrongdoing. Then again, they weren't dealing with the United States judicial system, they were living by the code of the Mafioso; a code that states if one looks guilty, he is presumed guilty and therefore killed.

"We cannot make false accusations. At the same time, we cannot overlook the fact that by arranging the marriage between myself and Madeline Diaglio Brioschi, Giovanni is aiding the Diaglio family; in what capacity we don't know and that's what we need to figure out." Andrew explained and Angel could hear a sense of disappointment in his voice. "We are attempting to locate Olga for questioning. We have Angel secured and until we have solid evidence to bring against Giovanni, this information must stay in this room."

Andrew went on to explain that they had copied the jump drive that Angel had confiscated from the child at East Side Junior High, and unbeknownst to her, they had men working to decipher it. Once they had deciphered the encoded file from the jump drive, he would send the information to each Boss. "At that time, we will be requesting manpower to help us stop the attack," he said.

"What about the police?" Don Andriachini posed. "Every family has brotherhood on the inside."

"Contacting them ain't such a good idea," Lisben muttered. "Unless you want 'em dead. We've got evidence that twelve officers have been assigned to a secret security team, beginning the date of the Pope's arrival to the States. Each of them has been offered a lump sum of money to participate. We're still running the pay-out numbers and trying to trace where the money is coming from."

"Just out of curiosity," the Galante Underboss hissed, "how much does one make to help murder the Pope?"

"Twenty-five G's," Lisben answered.

"Are you interested in helping them?" Don Cullato sneered at the Galante Underboss.

"If we know who these men are, why have we not eliminated them?" Don Andriachini posed.

"We're tailing them and monitoring their calls and emails, but right now they're more valuable to us alive," Andrew stated. "We don't know if they are a part of the assassination plot or if they are added security requested by the Vatican. We'll know more as soon as we are able to trace the money."

"What do you want from us?" Don Venturini asked.

"Your eyes and ears and any information you have on the Diaglio family and their connections in the States," Andrew answered. "You gentlemen have relationships with some of the families in Italia. We need to know the truth about the Diaglios and we need to know if they are indeed behind the attack on His Eminence." It sounded as if Andrew were pacing around the room as he spoke because his voice grew louder and softer at random intervals. "We need to know how many men are working with the Diaglios in Chicago. Who arranged for the Pope to come to the city and why has it been kept quiet?"

"We need to know how to stop the attack," the Snake interjected. "That's our first priority."

Don Andriachini cleared his throat. "It seems to me that a phone call to the Vatican, informing them of a threat, would be enough to change the Pope's itinerary."

"We've tried this already," Andrew responded. "Our contact at the FBI has reported the threat to the Vatican. Unfortunately, they receive thousands of threats against His Eminence every week. We have no reason to believe they will take this one seriously."

What about Salvatore? Angel thought. *He might know someone who could get a message to the Pope.* Salvatore Buscetta was old-school, Sicilian mob. His connections ran deep and Angel thought if anyone could reach the Pope, Salvatore could. She made a mental note to tell the Snake or Andrew to contact Salvatore, that is, if they ever had the courage to come upstairs and talk to her in person.

When everyone had finally left the room, the Snake turned to Andrew. "What are you going to do with Angel?"

"Keep her hidden," Andrew quipped.

"For how long?"

"Until this is all over," Andrew said. "That's all I can do."

"What happens when your fiancée arrives?" The Snake asked.

"I'll find out what she knows and then..." his voice faded.

"And then?"

"I don't know," Andrew muttered. "Either marry her or kill her. Those are the only two options, right?"

"Listen, man," the Snake said. "If Giovanni knows about the plan to kill the Pope, and I'm not saying he does, then he knows he's going to be the one to take the fall for it. So, either he's setting you up as the new Capo so that YOU'LL take the fall, or he's planning on sacrificing himself and leaving the leadership role to the only guy he trusts to be able to handle it." Their voices were growing quieter and Angel assumed they were moving toward the door. "Or, there's still the possibility that he doesn't know anything about the Pope and he's tired of you begging for permission to marry Angel, so he's forcing you to marry someone else."

What?! Angel gasped silently and put her hand over her mouth. Had Andrew asked Giovanni to marry her and was denied permission?

Andrew exhaled. "Yeah, I'd buy that scenario if it weren't for the fact that my fiancée is related to Nicholas Diaglio. That's a little too coincidental."

"True," the Snake uttered. "Do you think you'll ever tell Angel about Giovanni's offer?"

Angel leaned in closer to the vent in anticipation of Andrew's response. The silence felt as if it would last forever, and then Andrew said quietly, "No."

"You're going to let her believe you wanted to marry the Diaglio woman?" The Snake's tone indicated that he didn't agree with this approach.

"She's moved on," Andrew said. "And it's for the best."

"For her or for you?" The Snake rebutted and Andrew didn't comment or if he did, Angel couldn't hear him.

If they were still talking Angel could no longer hear them and she was almost grateful. All of the information was overwhelming and she needed time to process it. She didn't want to believe the accusations about her grandfather, but at the same time, she couldn't come up with a logical reason for Andrew to lie. On the other hand, Giovanni would never sit back and allow an attack on the Pope. It was against everything in which he believed. With her stomach churning into tight knots of anxiety, Angel sat on the floor by the vent and pressed her back against the wall. If Andrew believed she was guilty of conspiring with Giovanni and Olga in a plot against the Pope, why wouldn't he just ask her about it? Why all of this secrecy? Why kidnap her and hold her prisoner? *Is he punishing me for being with Tony?* She wondered, but more than that, she wondered if he even cared that she was with him. Was his pride bruised more than his heart?

Pulling her knees to her chest, Angel wrapped her arms around them. If only she had listened to the Snake and never entered East Side Junior High, then Andrew wouldn't be doubting her. He wouldn't have said those horrible things to her... or would he? Would he still have pushed her away? Angel felt helpless and completely alone. She had no phone. No gun. No idea where she was and she could no longer be sure of Andrew or Giovanni. Was she to love or fear them? But worse than that was the thought of Andrew marrying another woman and there was nothing she could do to stop him.

CHAPTER 36

Giovanni was hell bent on locating Andrew and had called in every available resource, including his Compare, Carl Cusanelli from New York. Carl's reputation preceded him, particularly in Chicago, where upon his last visit having discovered that his grandson had been disloyal to the Maratinzano family. Carl had personally put a bullet in his brain. He wasn't a man anyone wanted to cross and Chase was not happy about Carl being there.

"That guy gives me the heebee-geebees," Chase whispered to Big Mike when Carl entered the secret meeting room with Giovanni and an entourage of Giovanni's men from New York.

"Why?" Big Mike asked, unaware of his reputation.

"I'll fill you in later, but to sum it up, he operates with no mercy, so don't piss him off," Chase responded quietly.

Giovanni's men dispersed and formed a circle around the conference table with Giovanni and Carl standing at the head, directly opposite Chase and Big Mike, who were already seated. Noticing that everyone else was standing, Chase and Big Mike exchanged an uncomfortable glance and then scooted their chairs out from the table and rose.

Giovanni's eyes fell heavily on each member, as he brought them up to speed on what they knew. Speculation became fact in his speech, and Andrew was charged guilty without a trial. Chase wanted to speak up in his defense, to point out that they didn't have all of the facts yet, but doing so would be risking his own life. It would not have been unthinkable for Carl to put a bullet

through his brain right then and there; so Chase
bit his tongue.

Giovanni ordered his men to sit and once
they were all seated, he circled the table like a
shark, dictating what would transpire. The power
of his presence alone made all of them aware that
failure was intolerable. "Don Venturini has
conspired against me; against us," Giovanni
proclaimed. "He, being fully aware of the eminent
attack on His Eminence here in this city, has
chosen to allow it..." Giovanni stopped talking,
exhaled, drank in a deep breath and continued.
"To facilitate it!" He threw his fist into the air with
rage.

"With all due respect, sir," a man three
seats from Big Mike asked. "Why would Don
Venturini do this? What does he gain?"

Carl's gun was drawn and pointed at the
man before he even finished his sentence. The
man's face grew instantly ashen and Chase braced
for the worst. Carl neared the man and Giovanni
watched with darkened eyes. The room fell silent.
"You will not question the Capo di Tutti Capi!"
Carl growled, pushing the gun against the back of
the man's skull.

Out of the corner of his eye Chase saw Big
Mike's lips move, as if he were about to say
something, and reaching under the table, Chase
dug his fingers into Big Mike's leg; warning him
not to speak.

The man's hands trembled and his voice
shook as he said, "I me...mean no d..di..disrespect,
sir."

Giovanni raised his right palm into the air
and Carl withdrew the gun from the man's head.
"Let that be a lesson," Carl spat. "The Capo has
shown you mercy. I would have made an example
out of you."

"Grazie," the man muttered, lowering his eyes to the table.

Giovanni continued his speech as if nothing had transpired. The men were ordered to bring Andrew in at any and all cost. "I want him alive," Giovanni ordered. "You may kill the men who are helping him, but I want Don Venturini brought to me alive!" He growled with such intensity that Chase felt it vibrate right up his spinal column.

Giovanni nodded toward the door and one of his body guards opened the door and escorted Leo inside. Giovanni immediately draped his arm over Leo's shoulder and walked him toward the table to the end where Chase and Big Mike sat. "This is a member of the Venturini family. Leo the Lion." Giovanni spoke as if he were making a grand introduction. "Leo saved the life of my granddaughter and had the courage to confide in me and render proof concerning the blasphemous deeds of Don Venturini. Giovanni gave Leo's shoulder a squeeze. "He is a courageous lion indeed. He has knowledge of the inner workings of the Venturini family and their estates and will assist you in locating Don Venturini."

When the room finally cleared, Chase took a deep breath and stared blankly at Big Mike. "This is bad. Very bad."

"He sure painted Andrew as the devil," Big Mike mumbled. "You don't think Andrew is really going to let the Pope get murdered and Giovanni take the fall for it, do you?"

Chase shook his head. "Whoever is behind this operation is brilliant. "Freaky-ass brilliant," Chase mumbled allowed.

"Why do you say that?" Big Mike uttered.

"Killing the Pope on American soil would be bad enough, but making it look like a mob hit in Chicago is brilliant. While we should be coordinating our efforts, this rumor has divided our families, pitting one against the other, distracting us while the murderous plot steamrolls forward," Chase explained.

"So, you think the information wasn't leaked by accident?" Big Mike asked.

Chase shrugged. "All I know is that when the shit goes down, the world will be watching and they're gonna come after the mob families, starting with ..."

"The Capo," Big Mike interrupted and shook his head. "Who would benefit from taking out Giovanni?"

"A lot of people," Chase muttered. "Someone aspiring to be the next Capo? Someone who hates him, someone he's pissed off, which could be anyone."

"Let's say it all goes down like clockwork," Big Mike began, and started pacing around the table while he spoke. "The Pope is murdered and either a hit is put out on Giovanni and he's killed or the Feds come in and take him down, what happens then?"

Chase shrugged. "Beats me. It's unprecedented."

Big Mike narrowed his eyes. "They clean house."

"Who's they?"

"Whoever is behind this attack knows that the Feds will clean house. They won't just take down the Capo; they'll take down every Boss and Underboss here and in New York. They'll hit the families hard until they render them damn near non-existent," Big Mike explained. "And then, from the rubble..."

"A new leader will arise," Chase mumbled in an a-ha fashion.

They stared at each other for a brief moment, both of them mulling through what this meant. Just then, Leo popped his head in the room.

"Can I talk to you guys?" Leo asked, his eyes wide and his voice shaky.

Pulling a chair up next to Chase, Leo leaned in close and motioned for Big Mike to come in closer as well. Big Mike pulled a chair over and sat down. "The two Venturini guys stationed at the hospital to guard Angel's room," he began, his eyes darting back and forth between Big Mike and Chase. "They're with me."

"What does that mean?" Big Mike blurted.

"At the hospital, when those men showed up to kill Angel, the Venturini guys helped me take them out, get their shirts off and leave the message for you," Leo explained.

"About that," Chase said. "You never did tell me what the message meant."

"Pope Ignacio is the 266th Pope, which is what the 266 stands for," Leo explained.

"What about the upside down cross?" Chase posed.

"This particular Pope has been ridiculed for many things, one of which is that the back of his chair is adorned with an upside down cross. Don't you read the papers?"

Chase shook his head. "No time."

"I thought an upside down cross was a satanic symbol," Big Mike interjected.

"A lot of people think that, but it originally symbolized the Apostle Peter in the Bible, who was executed upside down on a cross. He actually asked to be hung upside down because he didn't feel worthy enough to be crucified in the same position as the Christ. So, the upside down cross is a sign of humility," Leo explained. Chase and

Big Mike stared blankly. "You guys didn't understand my message at all, did you?"

"It was a little over our heads," Big Mike said.

"Way-ass over our heads," Chase added. "We're used to messages like cuttin' somebody's dick off because they slept with another guy's wife. You know, straightforward stuff."

Leo cracked a smile and shook his head.

"So where are your guys now?" Big Mike asked.

"In hiding. They don't want nothin' to do with killing the Pope any more than I do," Leo uttered emphatically. "They're names are Lenny Getgher and Jacob Denalli. Lenny's a newbie and at first I didn't trust him, but it turns out he knows Don Venturini from his days on the force. He was an informant of some kind."

"So, he was a snitch," Big Mike grumbled.

"Listen," Leo said and leaned in closer. "I just talked to 'em and they said that one of the guys who came to kill Angel mentioned a name. It might be nothin' but I thought I better tell you."

"What's the name?" Chase asked, poising his fingers on his keyboard, ready to run a search.

"DiPietro," Leo said.

"Maybe it's the name of the guy who sent them to kill Angel?" Big Mike posed.

"Maybe," Chase quipped, opening search windows and entering in parameters.

"There's one more thing," Leo said, lowering his voice to a whisper. "Jason said that he heard a rumor that Angel was on sabbatical for an undisclosed period of time and that the Underboss was taking over the Maratinzano family."

Chase stopped typing and he and Big Mike stared at each other. This was weird. "There is no Underboss," Chase muttered.

"Did they say who the Underboss was?" Big Mike asked.

"I don't know his real name, but they call him the Snake."

When Leo left, Chase and Big Mike sat mulling over the new information. "I don't get it," Chase blurted. "Who would start that kind of wild-ass rumor?" He fidgeted in his seat. "I mean, unless you had a death wish."

Big Mike didn't respond. He sat frozen, his brows narrowed as if he were deep in thought. Chase kicked his chair. "Hey! I'm talking to you."

"I was just thinking..."

"I could see that," Chase quipped. "Care to share your deep-ass thoughts with the rest of the class?"

Big Mike stood up and moved toward the windows, overlooking the city. "If Andrew knew about the attack on the Pope and he knew that the fall out would be the death of every mafia family Boss, what would he do?"

Chase twirled a pencil between his fingers. "Lately there's no telling what crazy-ass thing he'll do."

Spinning around to face Chase, Big Mike strode back across the room toward the table. "No, what would the Andrew WE KNOW do?"

Chase looked up from his keyboard and met eyes with Big Mike. "He'd protect Angel," he muttered. "And the best way to do that would be to make sure everyone thought she was no longer around..."

"No longer a Boss," Big Mike interjected.

"He took her to save her," Chase uttered as the realization hit his mind.

"Because he might not be able to stop the attack on the Pope," Big Mike added.

"Now THAT sounds like Andrew!" Chase blurted.

"And it sounds like the Snake, too," Big Mike said. "Both of them willing to do whatever it takes to protect her."

"Damn straight!" Chase whooped.

"Now, if this is true," Big Mike began, "then we have a big problem."

"That's an understatement," Chase chided. "We have a super big-ass problem."

And they both knew what the problem was. Giovanni's team of twelve men, under the merciless leadership of Carl Cusanelli, were going to take Andrew and his men out.

"We've got to get to Andrew before they do," Big Mike blurted.

"How the hell are we gonna do that?" Chase moaned. "They've blocked me every step of the way. They've tampered with my surveillance, tapped into my security systems..." Chase shook his head. "For all I know they're watching us right now!"

"Find a way," Big Mike rebutted.

"It'll take a miracle!" Chase belted and just then Tony strode into the room winded and out of breath.

"It just hit me while I was driving," he panted. "So I came right over."

"I hope it's good news," Chase muttered.

Tony was beaming. "I know how we can find Angel."

Big Mike and Chase exchanged a curious glance. "How does the expression go? 'Ask and ye shall receive?'" Big Mike said with a grin.

CHAPTER 37

Olga couldn't figure out why she and Elsa hadn't been found, what with all of the surveillance cameras around the city, all of the tracking devices and Chase's affluence for locating people. She had been good at hiding in the past, but that was before the explosion of technology. Now, it just added to her feeling that something was terribly wrong.

Waddling back and forth, Olga paced in front of the motel window. "You seem disappointed that we're not being hunted," Elsa muttered.

"I'm not disappointed. I'm worried," Olga responded, wringing her hands together. "It feels like the calm before the storm."

"Did you ever think that maybe there are no monsters? That there is no storm? That maybe you've made this whole thing up in your head?" Elsa jawed.

"No," Olga snapped.

"Honey, I'm your friend, and as your friend it's my job to tell you the truth. You're crazy. You're off your rocker. You're one step away from the looney bin, and I...."

"Shut up!" Olga snipped. "A man came looking for you at the salon. He wasn't one of ours. So, who was he?" She leaned down in Elsa's face. "Who was he?" She demanded.

"I don't know what man you're talking about and even IF there was a man, so what?" Elsa rebutted. "I run a very reputable salon and sometimes men come in for a wash or a trim or even a manicure."

"Bah!" Olga snorted. "I don't believe you."

"It's true, there are several male clients who enjoy getting their nails cleaned and..."

"Merciful heavens, I'm not talking about manicures, Elsa!" Olga was exasperated. "I'm talking about the fact that you made me send my Angel to that school when you knew she would be in danger." Olga sank onto the bed, her shoulders slumping forward. "I trusted you. I considered you a friend, and I don't have many friends. They're hard to come by in our line of work...in our family."

"What line of work? YOU don't work. I don't think I've seen you work a day in your life," Elsa spat condescendingly and before she could say another word, Olga zapped her with the Taser.

"You bitch!" Olga sputtered. "I've worked hard all of my life to protect myself and to protect my Angel. And I won't let you or anyone take that away from me."

CHAPTER 38

A young man opened the door and appeared surprised to see Angel sitting on the floor in the dark. "Ms. Maratinzano?" He said and then reached over and flipped a light switch on the wall, causing the overhead light to illuminate the room. "Why are you sitting in the dark?" He asked but Angel didn't answer. She didn't even look up or make eye contact. What was the point? "I have food," he said as he carried in a tray and set it atop the bed. "There's some water and I can get you a soda or a glass of wine, coffee, anything you want." Angel didn't acknowledge his presence. "My name is Taelon. If you need anything just tap on the door."

When Taelon left, Angel moved to the bed to examine the food. It was a bowl of pasta Carbonara, two slices of Italian bread and oil and a side salad complete with a white linen napkin and a plastic white Spork. She rolled her eyes. It was obvious that Andrew didn't trust her with a real fork, not even a plastic one. *He's worried I'd use it to gauge poor Taelon's eyeballs out and escape,* she thought. *And I might.*

But escape to what? To where? To whom? Those were the real questions. Even if she could break free, she didn't know who to trust. Olga? Giovanni? Chase? Tony? *Good 'ole Tony, I can always trust him,* she thought. Winding up with Tony wouldn't be so bad. After all, he was the one she was planning to marry before her whole world turned upside down. If only there was a way to go back in time, back to before she learned of her mafia roots and her real identity, back to when ignorance truly was bliss.

Sitting cross-legged atop the bed, Angel dove into the pasta, wiping her plate clean with the remaining scraps of bread. There was no sense in going hungry. She passed on the salad. After all, what was the point in eating healthy and watching her weight if she was just going to be a prisoner? She wondered how long Andrew planned on keeping her captive and what would happen if the assassination attempt on the Pope was successful. Was Andrew right about the FBI and the rest of the world blaming Giovanni and conducting an all-out attack on the five families? Was it possible that Andrew was hiding her away under some guise of protecting her? Or was there another reason? The questions were driving her crazy.

Moving the tray to the floor, Angel lay down on the bed, careful not to put weight on her left shoulder, and fiddled with the silver cross that hung around her neck. Thoughts drifted in and out of her mind and she let them. There was no reason to focus on any one thing or try to make sense of the whole picture. Even if she could, she was powerless to do anything about it. She was locked in a room like a princess awaiting her knight in shining armor, only in this mob fairytale Prince Charming and her captor were one in the same.

CHAPTER 39

Tony slid the USB plug-in to Chase, who shook his head as he attached it to the port on his laptop. "Things keep getting wilder and wilder, man," Chase muttered.

"If Giovanni knew you put a tracking device in Angel's necklace, you would be a dead man," Big Mike whispered.

"Forget Giovanni," Chase quipped. "Angel's gonna have you by the balls when she finds out."

Tony winced. "How 'bout we keep this between us."

"All right," Chase snickered. "But one day I'm going to ask you for a favor in return," he said, rubbing his hand down his chin, giving his best Godfather impersonation.

"Watch it, Ace," Tony sneered.

"How long ago did you plant the bug?" Big Mike asked.

"I had it installed before I gave her the necklace, which was around the time that I asked her to marry me," Tony answered and Big Mike's mouth dropped open. "It's a long story. Everything's different now." Tony walked toward the windows and gazed down at the city.

"Yo, Romeo," Chase called out, "I need your password to access the device."

"CALCB," Tony answered. *Come A Little Closer Baby,* he mused with a quiet sigh.

"What's that stand for?" Chase asked, his fingers flying across the keys.

"None of your business," Tony chided. "Just find her."

The only sound in the room was that of Chase's fingers rapidly inputting data and trying to locate the tracking signal. "I see you've never used this device to track her," Chase noted.

"No, I haven't," Tony admitted. "For a long time she stopped wearing the necklace so there was no point. But when I heard the little boy from the school describe the silver cross around her neck and I remembered that she had it on the other night, it hit me that it might be worth a shot."

"A damn good shot," Chase excitedly sputtered. "We got her!" Bouncing his knees up and down in the chair, Chase narrowed the search until he was able to pinpoint Angel's exact location. He then used those coordinates to pull up an overheard view of the entire area, including a layout of the house, down to the very room in which Angel was sitting.

Big Mike and Tony watched over his shoulder. "Technology is a scary thing," Big Mike said, obviously intrigued by what Chase was able to do.

"I know, right?" Chase quipped. "I love this program. It's like Google Earth on freaky-ass steroids." He exclaimed, his fingers flying across the keys. "Watch this." Gnawing on the pencil between his teeth, he put the image on the big screen in front of them, dividing it into six sections. "Now that I know the coordinates, I can tap into any security surveillance and BAM!" The images appeared and Tony and Big Mike's eyes widened. They were looking at an old farmhouse, one frame showing an overhead, satellite view, another showing the land surrounding the property, and the other frames depicting the interior of the house. A small white dot represented the tracking device in Angel's necklace. "There she is," Chase proudly proclaimed.

"Holy shit," Big Mike uttered beneath his breath.

"I know, man. Impressive," Chase bragged.

175

"No," Big Mike rebutted, pointing at the screen. "Look at this room." Big Mike drew closer to the big screen and pointed.

Chase enhanced the picture. "Damn!" He blurted. "That's a helluva lot of weapons." Enhancing the picture again, Chase gasped, "He's got an M16A2, 5.56mm rifle."

"Yeah, Ace, and a handful of grenade launchers and handheld Uzi's," Tony said, pointing at the screen. "So what?"

"So... the M16A2 5.56mm rifle is a military grade weapon!" Chase exclaimed.

"Still not following?" Tony rebutted.

"It's not sold on the street," Chase explained. "There are a lot of M-16 models out there, but not the M16A2 5.56mm rifle."

"What's so special about it?" Big Mike asked.

Chase's eyes lit up like he was on cloud nine. There was nothing he enjoyed more than talking about weapons and this gun was one of his favorites. "It's lightweight, air-cooled, gas-operated, magazine-fed and can be shoulder or hip-fired," he explained excitedly. "It can fire automatic in three-round bursts or semiautomatic fire in a single shot." Plunking back into his chair, Chase began to key in data on his laptop. "The big deal is that you can't get it on the street, not even here in the crime capitol of the States," he explained. "And believe me, I've tried. None of my dealers can get their hands on one."

"So then how does Andrew have several of them?" Big Mike asked.

"They're government supplied," Chase quipped. "So either he's getting them through someone high up in DOD channels or he's got suppliers from the force."

"Chicago's finest doesn't carry M-16's," Tony objected. "They probably should, but they don't."

"That doesn't mean they don't have them or that they weren't shipped to them and confiscated by another group," Chase responded.

"I read about this," Big Mike interjected. "Just recently a bunch of police departments were suspended for losing weapons."

"Yeah, they were all part of the DOD Excessive Equipment 1033 program, which basically allows the Department of Defense to ship extra weaponry to police departments throughout the country," Chase explained. "Some of my contacts on the street have gotten some pretty sweet-ass items by paying off a cop or two," he said with a wink. "But no M-16A2's."

"So, why would Andrew need all of these guns?" Tony asked.

Chase shrugged. "It looks like he's anticipating something big going down."

"Well, then let's give him something big," Tony quipped, pulling the .45 from his waistband, checking the clip and shoving the gun back into his pants.

"I think you're gonna need a bigger gun," Big Mike teased.

"Trust me, my gun is plenty big, Ace," Tony said with a smirk. "Now, let's go get the girl."

CHAPTER 40

Thomas was beside himself and there was nothing Detta could do to calm him down. Sex didn't work and he was already liquored up. "They're gonna kill me," he slurred and then took a swig right from the whiskey bottle that was clutched tightly in his grip, slamming it onto her kitchen counter and knocking over her cup of coffee in the process. Detta rushed toward the paper towels and began to mob up the spill.

"Who's going to kill you?" She asked.

"The Diaglios," he leaned close and whispered into her ear. "I'm supposed to meet with them tomorrow and give them the jump drive, but I don't have the jump drive, so they're gonna blow my head off." Thomas whirled around and knocked over a glass that had been sitting on the edge of the counter next to the fruit bowl. It crashed to the floor but didn't break.

"Maybe you should sit down," Detta said, taking him by the arm and leading him into the family room, where he sank onto the couch and put his head between his knees. Thomas was beyond distraught and a part of Detta felt bad for him, but the truth was being rid of Thomas meant being free from this whole ordeal. Besides, she didn't know what to say to console him because she knew he was right. If he didn't show up with the jump drive, he would be killed.

"I'm a dead man," Thomas moaned and then abruptly raised his head. "Unless..." He stared at Detta with fiery eyes.

"Unless what?"

"YOU got us into this mess," Thomas slurred, rising from the couch and pointing at Detta. "YOU'RE gonna get us out of it!" He threw the whiskey bottle to the floor and took her by the shoulders. "You're going to pay a visit to Angel Maratinzano, get the jump drive back from her and bring it to me."

"You're crazy," Detta spat.

"Crazy like a fox," Thomas grinned and called Jack out of his room.

"Leave him out of this!" Detta yelled.

"Oh, no," Thomas slurred. "You, me and the kid are going for a ride." Thomas pulled a Glock from his waistband and shoved the barrel into Jack's ribcage. "You'll tell Angel Maratinzano that the kid has a school project on that jump drive and you need it back."

"Detta?" Jack said, fear rising in his voice.

"It's okay," Detta said softly.   "Just do what he says and everything will be okay."

Detta grabbed her purse and tan trench coat as Thomas nudged them outside. "You drive," he slurred.

"I don't have any gas in my car," Detta said.

Tossing her the keys to his red, Ford Mustang, Thomas pushed Jack into the backseat and climbed in next to him. "You put a scratch on my baby and I put a scratch on you, got it?" He stammered.

Detta's heart was beating fiercely as she started the car and pulled out of the mobile home park. She needed to come up with a plan and quick.

CHAPTER 41

Taelon tapped on the door and then nudged it open and carried in another tray of food. "I thought you might want a snack," he said, setting the tray at the foot of the bed.

"You know, if you keep bringing me food and keep me cramped up in this tiny room, I'm going to get fat," Angel retorted.

He smiled sheepishly. "I'll let the Boss know you're requesting bigger quarters."

"I'm not requesting a larger prison cell," Angel quipped. "I'm asking for my freedom." Taelon met her eyes and then quickly darted his away, which indicated to Angel that he felt conflicted or at the very least uncomfortable about being assigned to watch her. "Why you?" She asked.

"What do you mean?"

"Why were you assigned to babysit me?"

He shrugged his shoulders.

"You do know who I am, don't you?" Angel asked.

"Yes ma'am," he answered with a crocked grin. "Everyone knows who you are."

"And that's somehow amusing?" Angel spat and the smile quickly disappeared from Taelon's face.

"No, ma'am," he responded. "It's just that we all heard a lot about you for a long time and finally getting to meet you in person is, well, it's kinda cool."

Angel narrowed her eyes and stared at him. Though a little flattered by his response, she saw nothing cool or amusing about this whole situation. Crossing her arms and cocking her head to the side she eyeballed Taelon from his head to his feet and back to his eyes. He was young, probably in his early twenties and obviously new to the family, that was to say if he was even a Made member yet. Somehow she couldn't picture him hitting a mark. He had dark brown hair, light green eyes and a smile that surely made him a lady killer on the nightclub scene. He was over six feet tall and what he lacked in brawn, as he was more wiry than muscular, Angel thought he probably made up for in brains.

"Why are you staring at me like that?" Taelon quietly asked.

Drawing closer to him, Angel kept her eyes locked on his. "I was just sizing you up. Wondering why Andrew would assign someone like you to guard the granddaughter to the Capo di Tutti Capi." She circled behind him and he quickly turned to face her. "Wondering if you have any idea what my grandfather will do to you when he finds out you assisted in my kidnapping." She circled back toward the bed and slowly sat down. Angel felt gratified when she saw fear framing the edges of Taelon's eyes. If Andrew wanted a game of cat and mouse, Angel was more than willing to play. "You see, Taelon, I can tell just by looking at you that you're a newbie, probably not even Made."

Taelon's eyes widened.

"I can see fear in your eyes and hear your heart pounding. You've never killed anyone have you?" She didn't wait for him to answer because the answer was etched all over his face. "That's what I thought." Smiling and leaning forward, Angel took Taelon's left hand in hers. "Do you really think that you're going to be able to shoot me if I get up and walk out of this room?"

Taelon quickly withdrew his hand and moved it to the handle of the gun that was wedged in the back of his jeans. "Please don't make me do it," he stammered, taking two steps toward the door. "I don't want to, but I will."

Angel sank slowly back onto the bed. She had gained the information she wanted. She now knew he was left-handed and that his gun was tucked in the back left side of his pants. When sizing him up she hadn't seen any other weapons, which meant he probably didn't carry a back-up; a common mistake of a newbie.

"I'd like you to take the food away," Angel said softly, feigning retreat. "And I'd like you to give your Boss a message." Taelon skittishly grabbed the tray from the bed and then quickly moved toward the door. "Tell him that I will not eat nor drink anything until I am set free. Tell him that I won't accept hospitality from a man who doesn't have the decency to look me in the eye and tell me the truth." Taelon nodded his head up and down. "Oh, and Taelon?" Angel called out just as he was about to close the door.

He peeked at her through the crack.

"Tell him I said congratulations on his upcoming nuptials."

Taelon left without uttering a word. His mouth was half opened and his eyes wide, so she knew he'd go straight to Andrew and deliver her message. She felt a little guilty for manipulating him that way, but Andrew was the one dumb enough to send a newbie to guard her. Not only had she put the fear of God into the poor guy, but she felt confident that she could take his gun away from him when the time was right. She just needed to be patient.

Besides, she knew that refusing to eat or drink would eventually drive Andrew crazy, but not nearly as crazy as her knowing about his engagement. He would undoubtedly demand to

know how she had found out and that's when
Angel would make her move.

CHAPTER   42

Detta's hands were trembling as she approached the main doors to the Towers. Thomas remained in the car, holding Jack at gunpoint and threatening to kill him if she didn't return with the jump drive. She had a choice to make. If she ran, Jack would die but she would be free. If she entered the Towers, she was probably as good as dead.

Glancing back over her shoulder, Detta could see Jack's terrified face through the window. He wasn't her son. He was just one of the many foster kids that came in and out of her world; and the truth was she only joined the foster program so that she could reap the government benefits of monthly checks and food stamps. She didn't do it because she loved kids. In fact, she couldn't stand children, but she didn't believe they deserved to die.

She looked down at the car keys clutched tightly in her hand. Thomas was too drunk or too stupid to realize she hadn't left them in the car, so if she didn't return he was stuck. He was in no condition to drive anyway. This made the desire to run that much more tempting. Perhaps she could enter the main doors of the Towers and exit a back door without Thomas seeing her. This would at least give her a head start in case her plan failed.

Pressing the intercom button on the keypad to her right, Detta took a deep breath. "I need someone to help me. Please?" She said.

The door buzzed and Detta immediately pulled it open and stepped inside. A large bodyguard dressed all in black stepped toward her. "How can I assist you?"

Detta made herself sound breathless and appear distraught, which wasn't difficult

184

considering the current circumstances. "I was walking by and saw a man holding a child at gunpoint."

The bodyguard approached the doors and peered outside. "Where?"

"Parked on the street. They're in a red Mustang," Detta said. "I was too afraid to confront him myself and I don't have my cell phone to call the police. Maybe I could call them from here?"

"Not necessary, ma'am," the bodyguard uttered. "I'll handle it." The bodyguard immediately placed a call and then assured her that help was on the way.

Detta bit the inside of her cheek to keep from smiling. It was working. "Do you think I could sneak out a back door so the man doesn't see me and know that I turned him in?" Detta licked her lips and put on her best damsel in distress expression. "There are some real psychos out there and a woman can never be too careful. I mean, what if he took a picture of me and found out where I lived and..."

"No problem, ma'am. This way."

The bodyguard escorted her to the lower level, through the parking garage and out the back entrance of the Towers. "You'll get that boy out of the car, right?" Detta asked him. "I mean, you'll help him, right?"

"Yes, ma'am."

Detta thanked him and sauntered slowly across the street until she was certain he had gone back inside; then she headed toward the side of the building in a dead sprint. Ducking behind a row of bushes where she had a clear view of the Mustang, Detta pulled her cell phone from her coat pocket, opened the app and quietly waited.

She watched as two bodyguards emerged from the Towers with their guns drawn and approached the Mustang. She could hear Thomas hollering obscenities and the bodyguards demanding that he release Jack and step out of the car. The moment Jack was pulled from the backseat, Detta depressed the red detonator button on the app and the explosion lit up the night sky. She didn't stick around long enough to see if anyone survived. She was free.

CHAPTER 43

The explosion rattled the Towers and Giovanni's men flooded the bottom level of the building in anticipation of an attack. Chase, Big Mike, and Tony were in the secret meeting room, devising a plan to rescue Angel and warn Andrew of Giovanni's eminent confrontation when the explosion occurred. Chase immediately pulled up the surveillance feed from the exterior cameras circling the building. He zoomed in on the vehicle, taking freeze frame shots and enhancing them in an attempt to better ID the parties involved.

"We got one man, Caucasian, one woman, Caucasian, and one Caucasian, male child. Looks to be about twelve years old," Chase said aloud as his fingers raced across the keys, rapidly jumping from feed to feed to get different angles.

"What the hell happened?" Big Mike blurted.

"Looks like their car exploded. Damn shame too," Chase added. "It was a pretty sweet-ass Mustang, cherry red."

"Any survivors?" Tony asked.

Chase played back the surveillance feed as the explosion occurred. Thomas had been leaning against the side of the car and was blown to pieces, as was the bodyguard who had him at gunpoint. Chase grimaced at the image. The other bodyguard and Jack were several feet away from the car when it exploded and were thrown backwards into the middle of the street. They weren't moving, but it was possible that they could have survived. "I don't know," Chase responded. "The police and emergency vehicles are on their way now."

"This can't be random," Big Mike said.

"No shit, Ace," Tony quipped. "Explosions don't randomly happen right in front of well-known Mob buildings."

It was clear by his expression that Big Mike didn't appreciate Tony's sarcasm.

Chase was checking the different camera angles around the building when Leo rushed into the room with Caleb in tow. "What happened?" He panted. "We were on the penthouse patio and there was this huge explosion."

"Car bomb, we think," Big Mike said.

"You should take Caleb back upstairs, man," Chase said, glancing up from his keyboard long enough to give Caleb a friendly nod. "This is no place for a..."

"That's Ms. Palumbo," Caleb interrupted, pointing at the big screen.

Leo's eyes widened and he rushed toward the screen. "Detta?" He uttered softly.

"Detta, as in your crazy-ass-hacker sister, Detta?" Chase said to Leo.

Leo's mouth was hanging open as he stared at the surveillance feed. "I'm going to take your silence as a yes," Chase quipped.

"Yes, that's Detta Palumbo," Caleb said, still pointing at the screen.

Chase divided the big screen into six surveillance sections so they could see what transpired in and around the building during the time of the explosion. "There's Jack!" Caleb shrieked, pointing at the screen with Jack and Thomas in the car. "And there's Thomas." Caleb's face contorted into a ball of anger. "I hate Thomas! I hate him! I hate him!" Caleb jumped up and down screaming at the big screen.

"Somebody get this kid out of here!" Tony barked and Chase shut down the feed and rushed toward Caleb, who was red faced and sobbing.

"Come here 'lil bro," Chase said, scooping Caleb into his arms. "It'll be okay. We're gonna get Jack away from Thomas and bring Jack here to stay with you for a while. Would that be cool?"

Caleb was gasping air from crying so hard as Chase tried to console him. "Now, I need you to do me a huge favor? Can you help me?" Chase asked and Caleb widened his eyes and nodded his head up and down. "I need you to go to Angel's house upstairs and chill out there for a while so that I can go get Jack. Sound like a plan, 'lil man?" Chase held up his knuckles and Caleb gave him a bump. "All right!" Chase whooped.

Big Mike escorted Caleb back upstairs while Chase turned his attention to Leo. "What was Detta doing here?"

Leo shook his head. "I have no idea."

"Did you contact her?" Tony demanded.

"No!" Leo whirled around to face Chase and Tony. Digging his cell phone from his pocket, he slid it across the table toward Chase. "You can check my phone. I didn't contact her. I swear."

"Then how did she know you and Caleb were here?" Chase argued, taking the phone and filing through the numbers.

"Who's to say she knew anything?" Tony interjected. "We're assuming she was here because Leo and Caleb are here, but maybe she had another reason."

"Far-ass-fetched, if you ask me," Chase chided.

In that moment, Giovanni stormed into the room. "What is the meaning of this?" He demanded.

"I'm working on it," Chase said, reinstating the feed to the big screen.

"I want to be debriefed in twenty minutes; and I want answers!" Giovanni growled and then stormed from the room with two bodyguards on his heels.

Chase and Tony exchanged glances and Chase's fingers flew faster over the keys. From the various surveillance angles, he was able to piece together an overview of what took place, but he couldn't ascertain motive; and he knew that was the one piece of information Giovanni wanted.

Chase was obviously rattled and Tony paced behind him. "Have you explained to Giovanni that you don't believe Andrew is behind the attack on the Pope," he asked.

"I've tried," Chase remarked. "He won't listen. He says that they have acquired substantial evidence proving that Andrew not only has helped facilitate the attack, but has violated the Omerta."

"What evidence?"

Chase shrugged. "He won't say. Only that Carl presented him with proof." Chase shook his spikey haired head rapidly back and forth. "Whatever info they have has got to be big."

"Could it be solid?" Tony slid into the chair next to Chase. "You know I'm not a fan of Andrew, but something about this smells fishy."

"Something IS fishy," Chase retorted. "There's just so much stink I can't pinpoint where it's coming from."

"There's got to be something we're missing," Tony quipped, leaping up and pacing toward the windows. "Who are our key players?"

"I don't even know what wild-ass game we're playing!" Chase jawed.

"In a matter of days, most of our people have disappeared. Trig, Harry, the Snake, Angel, Olga... Am I missing anyone?" Tony turned to look at Chase and noticed something on the big screen. "Wait, pause that frame!" He blurted and then moved quickly toward the screen. "Look," he said, pointing to the top left frame. "She's making a phone call."

Chase enhanced the frame and brought it full center in the screen. It showed Detta, rising from her crouched position in the bushes and placing her cell phone next to her ear. "I'll be damned!" He whooped. "She IS making a call."

"Can you find out who she's calling?" Tony asked.

"It'd be a lot easier if I could call Sal and use the FBI database to run the numbers," Chase responded, wiggling in his seat and working three keyboards at the same time.

"Why can't you?"

"Sal's working for Andrew. He's blocked me at every path and has stopped responding to my attempts at contact," Chase huffed.

"That's it," Tony spat. "I've had enough of this cryptic bullshit." He stormed toward the door.

"Where are you going?" Chase blurted.

"To talk to Andrew and to get Angel back!"

"Whoa, tiger!" Chase leapt from his seat and jumped between Tony and the door.

Tony drew his .45 and placed the barrel against Chase's forehead. "You're not going to stop me, Ace."

Chase put his hands up. "I wouldn't think of it." He grinned and Tony lowered the gun. "But, if you're going to take off on some wild-ass, Lone Ranger mission, let's at least get you wired so I can help via remote."

A few minutes later Tony was outfitted with a state-of-the-art earpiece and a tiny camera with a microphone that fit into the front button on his shirt. "We'll be able to talk to each other and I'll be able to see everything that you see."

"Got it," Tony said.

"When you get near the property stop and make sure I'm with you and able to pull up your location before you go trying to shoot your way in," Chase reminded him.

"This isn't my first rodeo," Tony sneered.

"It's my job to make sure it isn't your last."

By the time Big Mike returned to the secret meeting room, Tony was gone and Chase was fast at work trying to find out who Detta called from the bushes.

"I heard two of Giovanni's men talking near the elevator," Big Mike began. "They said Carl told them he'll have Andrew's location by midnight tonight."

Chase stopped abruptly and turned to face Big Mike. "How?"

"Dunno." Big Mike shrugged.

"How could Carl possibly know where Andrew is? The only reason we found him was because of Angel's necklace." Chase frowned and then went back to work on his laptop.

"Maybe he's got someone on the inside?" Big Mike posed.

"This shit just keeps getting fishier and fishier," Chase moaned.

CHAPTER 44

"It's done," Detta said when her call was answered.

"And the drive?"

"I'm sure Angel Maratinzano has it, but I can't get to her," Detta explained.

"Andrew Venturini has a copy."

"How do you know?" Panic rose in Detta's throat.

"It doesn't matter. We'll have the information by tonight but we'll need you to decode the files."

"If I'm going to stay in this, I want Thomas's share of the money," Detta blurted.

The call disconnected.

CHAPTER 45

Angel pressed her ear to vent the moment she heard voices again coming from below. She could identify the Snake, Lisben, Andrew and Trig. If there was anyone else in the room they weren't speaking.

"How many times has he tried to call?" The Snake asked.

"Eight," Andrew responded. "He's trying to reach Sal as well and Sal's starting to get nervous."

"I'm telling you, man, we gotta bring Chase in. Let me fly over there and scoop him up. I'll get in and out and nobody will be the wiser," Trig snipped.

"You can't sneak up on someone in a chopper," the Snake rebutted.

"Besides, Chase is probably working for Giovanni and contacting him would lead us right into their trap," Lisben added. "I mean, they've got to be searching for Angel by now."

"I'm sure they are but there's no way they'll find us here," Andrew reassured. "This property is not linked to the Venturini family."

"I could contact Chase," the Snake interjected, "just to let him know that Angel's fine. Maybe then he would quit hounding you and Sal?"

"It's too risky," Andrew said. "I'm going to meet Madeline Brioschi, as planned, and find out what she knows, if anything," Andrew explained. "Snake, you keep working with Sal on deciphering the information from the jump drive, particularly the numerical patterns overlaid on the streets. We need to know if those are gunman coordinates or access codes to some form of security within the Pope's vehicle itself. Lisben, you keep working to find out which officers have been assigned to the Pope's security team, if they've received a bribe, and where they are to be positioned." There were shuffling sounds as if Andrew was making his way toward the door. "Also, find out exactly how many officers are assigned. I need to know how many men we're going to need."

"What about me?" Trig blurted. "What do you want me to do?"

"You're gonna fly me to the meet Madeline," Andrew answered and Angel could almost hear the smile spread across Trig's face. Trig loved to be in on the action.

CHAPTER 46

Detta checked into a dilapidated motel on the east side of town. She dialed the main line for Northwestern Memorial Hospital and asked if a twelve year old boy had been admitted earlier in the evening. She was put on hold and after forty seconds felt it was too risky to remain on the line and disconnected the call. For all she knew the police were tracing calls from anyone asking about the explosion and survivors. She couldn't help but wonder if Jack lived through the explosion. She hoped he did, but pushed the thoughts aside. If she dwelled on it, she'd start to feel guilty. *Focus on the money*, she told herself. If they agreed to give her Thomas's share, she'd have a full one-hundred thousand dollars. She would consider lending some to Leo, since she did promise him twenty-five thousand to not kill Nicholas, but that was moot now that Nicholas was already dead. All that was left to do now was sit tight and wait.

CHAPTER 47

Angel opened the cabinet beneath the bathroom sink then slammed the doors shut and grunted. There was nothing in the bathroom she could even remotely fashion into a weapon. There was a hand towel, a toothbrush, a small, white bar of soap like one you'd find in a hotel and a small tube of toothpaste. Her frustration level was growing and her patience had worn thin. Not only had Andrew not come to see her after receiving her message from Taelon, but he left to go meet his fiancée. Her blood boiled with a hot mixture of anger and jealousy. There was no way she was going to be held captive one more night. She was determined to get out and she no longer cared who might get hurt in the process.

Unrolling a piece of toilet paper from the roll, Angel wet the corner and wiped the smeared mascara from beneath her eyes, when an idea hit her. She removed the toilet paper from the holder, pulled the center rod free and dismantled it. Inside was a small metal spring. She quickly put the rod back together, minus the spring, placed the toilet paper back in its proper position and returned to the bedroom, where she began to work with the spring until she had one edge flattened straight. It was pointy and if used as a dagger, could be deadly. Angel practiced holding the spring in her right fist, allowing the point to show through between her index and middle fingers. One punch in the right spot and she could render Taelon inoperable, at least long enough to get his gun.

She sat down on the side of the bed feeling conflicted but hopeful. Taelon seemed like a nice guy and she didn't want to hurt him; but at the same time, she couldn't just sit still while a war was brewing between Giovanni and Andrew and the Pope's life was on the line. She wanted to look Giovanni in the face and ask him for the truth. Despite his power and reputation, he was her grandfather and he had always done what he believed to be best for her. Was he doing that now where Andrew was concerned? She desperately wanted answers, answers she would never get by remaining a captive.

With Trig and Andrew gone and the Snake and Lisben tending to their assigned duties, it was time to make her move. All she had to do was come up with a way to lure Taelon into her trap.

CHAPTER 48

Tony reached the outer road leading to the old farmhouse just as Trig lifted the chopper into the air. "That's got to be Trig!" Chase yelped into Tony's earpiece. "Follow the chopper!"

"I'm not following the chopper," Tony blurted. "I'm here to get Angel."

"Fine," Chase said. "I'll try to track the chopper via satellite."

Leaving his vehicle parked near the edge of the woods, Tony continued on foot, figuring it would draw less attention. He slid a .22 pistol into the ankle strap beneath his right pant leg, placed a .38 semiautomatic in the holster around his chest and a 9mm Beretta in the back of his waistband. The 9mm was for Angel. He assumed she was unarmed. He shoved several extra rounds in his pants pockets and then clutching his .45 tightly in his right hand, he twisted the silencer in place, crouched down and made his way through the trees.

The wood surrounding the house was thick with foliage and it wasn't easy to work his way quietly. Though he couldn't see anyone, he knew that they weren't there, so he tried not to snap twigs or crunch loudly on leaves. When he finally made it to the clearing, he stopped and stretched his back.

"Slowly pan so I can get a lay of the land," Chase said into the earpiece and Tony turned his body slightly from one side to the other.

The trees ended thirty yards from a two-story, old farmhouse, showing signs of weathering, with more white paint chipping from it than was left on it. A gravel road led to the house and a brick path from the driveway to the front door. There were a handful of vehicles parked in front of the house, so Tony decided to circle around to the back. There was a security camera mounted above both the front and rear door. "Cameras on both entrances," Tony whispered into the microphone.

"Circle to the north side," Chase said and Tony followed his instructions. "I'm showing an entrance there," he said. Tony stood up straight so Chase could see the north side of the house. "There!" Chase blurted. "Go through those cellar doors."

Tony wasn't keen on entering through the cellar. He felt it put him at a disadvantage because it limited his escape access. One way in and only one way out; he didn't like those odds, but slowly creaking open the cellar doors, he lowered himself onto the staircase and quietly closed the doors behind him. It was pitch black.

"Angel is on the second floor," Chase instructed through Tony's earpiece. "Or, at least her necklace is. It looks like your best bet is to go straight about thirty paces and there will be a staircase to your left. It'll put you on the first floor."

Using the light from his cell phone, he made his way across the cellar and found the staircase to his left, just as Chase had said. Inching upward, he tried to tread lightly to avoid squeaking floorboards, which was virtually impossible in such an old house. Each step rendered a squeak that made Tony halt and hold his breath. "I'm not showing any infrared signals near you, so you're clear to move faster," Chase told him and Tony picked up the pace. He finally arrived on the first floor and was almost to the next flight of stairs when Chase warned of someone approaching. Panicking, Tony dove into the nearest room, which happened to be a walk-in pantry that looked as if it were stockpiled with enough canned goods and bottled water to last a lifetime. "Is he preparing for Armageddon?" Tony whispered.

"Sure as shit looks like it," Chase quipped and then yelped into Tony's earpiece. "Holy, Mary, Mother of..."

"What the...?!" Tony exclaimed. "Can you refrain from yelling in my ear?"

"Someone just entered Angel's room," Chase said, this time a little quieter. "I can see the infrared signal. There's definitely someone standing in her doorway. Now they're moving closer.

"Closer to me or closer to her?" Tony whispered.

"Her. There's a confrontation. Somebody's got her!" Chase yelled into the ear piece. "They're grabbing her! She's in trouble!"

Tony didn't need to hear another word. He sprang from the pantry in a dead sprint, raced up the spiral staircase in a blind rage, and planted a bullet into the thigh of a man he met in the hallway. The man hit the floor and Tony stopped only to remove his gun and threaten to put the next bullet between his eyes if he made a sound.

"It's three doors down on your left," Chase spoke into his earpiece, and Tony charged forward.

The door was locked and, using brute force driven by angered adrenaline, Tony kicked through the lock on the door, forcefully swinging it open. He barged into the room with his gun drawn, shocked to see Angel whirl around and take aim at him. "Babe!" Tony gasped. "What are you doing?"

"Tony?!" She exclaimed, obviously surprised to see him. "I almost shot you!"

"Likewise," Tony uttered and then stepped toward Taelon. "Is this the asshole that attacked you?" Blood was steadily trickling down the side of

Taelon's neck and he was holding the bedspread tightly against it.

"No, I attacked him," Angel clarified.

"Holy shit!" Chase exclaimed. "These Maratinzano women never cease to amaze."

"I think I dug it in too deep. He needs a doctor," Angel said.

"Impressive, Babe," Tony said with a grin. "Now, let's get the hell out of here." Tony headed for the door, peering down the hall.

"I'm showing you all clear," Chase uttered into the earpiece. "But hurry."

Turning to Taelon, Angel bent down. "I'm sorry I had to stab you," she said, a twinge of guilt tugging at her.

"Ms. Maratinzano," Taelon whispered. "I know you could kill me for saying this but don't trust him."

"Who?" Angel asked.

"Someone's headed your way. Get out of there NOW!" Chase ordered.

"We gotta go NOW, Babe!" Tony barked.

"Who, Taelon? Who can't I trust?" Angel touched his arm and searched his eyes for revelation.

"Your grandfather," he labored.

Before she could respond, Tony fired two shots into a man approaching the room, took Angel by the arm and pulled her down the hallway. "Get us out of here," he muttered to Chase.

"Turn around and go the other way! You've got three men coming up the staircase behind you. MOVE!" Chase yelled.

Shoving Angel into a room to the right, Tony took out the first man to enter the hallway, sending the other two diving for cover. "Get us out of here!" Tony hollered again.

"Go out of the room, head right about ten paces and take a doorway to your right. It's a back staircase that leads to the kitchen below," Chase instructed.

Stepping out first, Tony fired two warning shots down the hallway where he knew two men were hiding. Then, shoving Angel ahead of him, they raced several paces down the hall and thrust open the staircase door. Tony nudged Angel through, immediately spinning around to take aim at anyone on their tail. "They retreated," Chase said. "They're gathering below you in the kitchen."

"How many?" Tony asked.

"One...two...three... six," Chase counted. "Six in total."

"Is there another way out?" Tony questioned.

"Not unless you want to jump from a second story window," Chase quipped.

"Wouldn't be the first time," Tony chided.

"Where do we go?" Angel whispered, but before Tony could answer the Snake's voice came booming up the staircase from below.

"Don't shoot, Tony. It's me. Snake."

"I don't want to kill you, Sean, but you know I'll do whatever it takes," he warned.

Angel's heart was beating so hard it felt as if it would pound right out of her chest. Getting in the middle of a shoot-out between Tony and the Snake hadn't been part of her escape plan. In fact, she had hoped to quietly incapacitate Taelon, which she did, steal his gun, which she did, and then sneak out of the house unnoticed. She might have pulled it off had Tony not come barging in.

"I'm unarmed," the Snake hollered up the steps. "And I'm coming up to talk to you."

"Like hell you are," Tony growled, and aimed his gun down the staircase.

"Hold your fire!" The Snake yelled and raised his hands above his head, revealing he had no weapon. "I can help you, but you've got to trust me," he said in a hushed tone. "Give me your weapons, as if you've surrendered," he whispered. "I promise to give them back to you once we are in a secure location."

"You smokin' somethin', Ace?" Tony retorted.

"You're surrounded, Tony," Chase said into the earpiece. "There are three men in the hallway just outside the door and two more down below the Snake on the staircase. Take the deal."

"No way!" Tony barked.

"Take the deal or you're a dead man!" Chase hollered and Tony cursed aloud.

Angel knew by the look on Tony's face that they were trapped. She handed her gun to the Snake and then crossed her arms. "I thought I could trust you," she said.

"You can," the Snake mouthed and then took the .45, .38 and 9mm from Tony.

"Taelon needs medical attention," Angel blurted.

"Shot?" The Snake asked.

"I stabbed him in the neck," she admitted and the Snake contorted his face into a grimace. "I'm pretty sure I missed the artery, but he still needs a doctor."

The Snake immediately turned to the two men below him on the staircase and instructed them to go and find Taelon; and then he led Angel and Tony at gunpoint down the staircase and into the kitchen. Angel stopped abruptly, feeling an angry surge of adrenaline when she met eyes with Lisben.

"We meet again, Ms. Maratinzano," Lisben said.

"Oh, hell no," Tony gasped and then turned toward the Snake. "What are you doing with him? I offered to take this piece of trash out last time he screwed us over."

"Andrew seems to think he holds value," the Snake retorted, his disgust toward Lisben evident.

"If I remember correctly, Stidda found him valuable, too," Tony sneered, taking a step toward Lisben, who immediately threw his palms in the air as if to motion for Tony to calm down.

"Listen, that was different, I didn't have a choice. They were going to kill me," Lisben pleaded.

Angel watched intently as Tony's eyes darkened and his jaw tensed. "Too bad they didn't," he chided. "It would have saved me the trouble." In one fluid motion, and before Angel knew what he was doing, Tony grabbed the .22 from his ankle holster and shoved the barrel against Lisben's forehead.

"Wait!" Lisben cried out. "I swear I'm trying to help now. Let me make up for my past mistakes. Please." His eyes were round and veins were protruding from his neck. "Please," he begged. "Snake, tell him I'm helping Andrew stop the Pope's assassination."

Tony glanced over his shoulder at the Snake, who cocked his head to the side and shrugged. "Supposedly he's supplying Andrew with the names of the Chicago PD who are believed to be a part of the assassination."

"How are you getting access to that information?" Tony asked, pushing Lisben down into a wooden chair and keeping the gun against his head.

"I've been on the Force a long time and I know a lot of people. I can get into their database and get the names of the cops assigned to the Pope's security detail," Lisben explained.

"So can any hacker," Tony quipped. "Why is Andrew REALLY keeping you around?"

"You've got visitors," Chase spoke into Tony's earpiece. "Two men are carrying a third man down the main staircase and three more are coming from the doorway to your left."

Angel saw Tony's eyes dart toward the door and her heartbeat quickened. She lunged toward the Snake. "Give me a gun," she uttered, but he took a step back from her.

"I'm sorry, Angel. I can't," he said and she couldn't believe he was refusing to help her.

"Sean?" She whispered, but he ignored her plea and didn't even make eye contact with her.

"If you leave this house, you're as good as dead," the Snake blurted, raising the .45 and taking aim at Tony. "Put your weapon down," he ordered.

A sickening grin spread across Lisben's face. "I hear more men coming and you only have one little .22 pistol. Are you going to use it to kill me before the Snake can get a shot off or try to shoot your way out of here?" He made a clicking sound with his lips. "You can't possibly do both. What a predicament."

"Lower your gun, Tony," the Snake repeated. "You don't have all of the facts."

"Neither do you," Tony rebutted.

"Giovanni is a part of the conspiracy to murder the Pope. If you return Angel to him, she will be assumed guilty by association and taken down," the Snake hollered.

"What?!" Chase yelled into the earpiece. "What evidence does he have to support this?"

"Ow," Tony winced. "Stop screaming in my ear!"

"Sorry," Chase muttered.

The Snake smirked. "Tell Chase I say hi."

"Is that why you've named yourself Underboss of the Maratinzano family?" Tony asked.

"Yes," the Snake answered. "To protect Angel. If she isn't in a position of power during the assassination attempt than she cannot be held accountable."

Three men barged into the kitchen through the door to Tony's left with their guns drawn, each taking aim at him. Angel's heart felt like it was going to beat right out of her chest. "And where did you get this information?" Tony yelled to the Snake. "From this piece of shit?" He pushed the barrel of his gun harder against Lisben's head.

"Lisben brought his suspicions to Andrew," the Snake said. "Andrew confirmed them."

"How?" Chase squawked in the earpiece.

"How did he confirm them?" Tony asked.

"Giovanni arranged a marriage between Andrew and a woman named Madeline Brioschi. He told Andrew that his goal was to merge the families. After everything that happened with Stidda and the CoBroGas attack, the Venturini's were in a weak position and this marriage would strengthen their presence. In return for Andrew's cooperation, he would groom him to become the next Capo di Tutti Capi."

"What?!" Chase exclaimed.

"Andrew found out that the Brioschi woman is the sister of Nicholas Diaglio, the man Angel shot and killed at East Side Junior High. We believe he was looking for the jump drive that the little boy gave to Angel."

"The jump drive that has the schematics and codes that will be used to kill the Pope," Chase interjected, though only Tony could hear him.

"Olga sent Angel to the school in the first place and we don't know if this was coincidence or if she was acting on an order from Giovanni to retrieve the drive," the Snake added and silence fell over the room. Even Chase sat quiet, as if in a state of shock.

"Wait a second," Angel interjected, "if Olga was obeying an order from Giovanni, why would she Taser Harry and his other guards to get away? Why would she run?"

"Maybe she's not running," Chase responded and Tony repeated what he said. "Maybe she's doing exactly what she was instructed to do?"

"However it went down, we're speculating that Giovanni may have cut a deal with the Diaglio family, allowing them to murder the Pope on American soil if they promised to leave him out of it," the Snake explained.

"IF he did cut that deal then surely he would have negotiated to leave Angel out of it too," Tony added.

"He would never cut a deal like this!" Angel raged.

"Maybe not," the Snake rebutted, "but if he did, then he'd most likely have had to agree to SOMEONE taking the blame; whether it would be all of the other bosses or the man-to-become-the-new-Capo."

Andrew? Angel couldn't wrap her head around the idea that Giovanni would set Andrew up in such a sinister way. Even if he were capable of this manner of cunning, she did not believe him capable of having any part in murdering His Eminence.

"Why kill the Pope?" Tony asked. "What does anyone gain?"

"We know the Diaglio family laundered money through the Vatican for years. When the new Pope put an end to it, he refused to return the money that was currently in the Catholic Church's possession. Not only did he not return the money, he donated the funds to a Catholic sponsored charity in the name of the church," the Snake explained.

"That's a damn-ass harsh move," Chase spat.

"So, the Pope took credit for the donation and it pissed the Diaglio's off?" Tony murmured.

"On top of that, he cast them out of the church altogether, stating that Mafioso could not be Catholic and a true Catholic could never be Mafioso," the Snake added.

"So, the Diaglio's want revenge," Angel stated.

"Why not just kill him while he's at home one night? Why kill him here?" Tony posed.

"If it happens on American soil it will be considered a worldwide act of terrorism," Chase blurted.

"It will cause a distraction," Harry said as he entered the kitchen with his gun drawn. "One so big that it will consume media headlines and the world will focus only on justice here in Chicago."

"But, even if Giovanni cut a deal, won't he, as head of all Mafia families, still take the blame in the eyes of the media, the government and the general public?" Tony asked.

"One would think so unless he is nowhere near Chicago at the time and there is no evidence to link him to the assassin," Harry eluded.

"The timing doesn't look good," Chase uttered into the earpiece. "Let me guess, Andrew and this Brioschi woman are supposed to marry before the Pope is killed?"

Tony repeated Chase's question aloud.

"Yes," the Snake answered. "They will be wed by the Justice of the Peace first thing Tuesday morning."

"Damn, I hate it when I'm right," Chase moaned. "It's a trap and Giovanni knows it, that's why he's getting out of dodge." Chase's fingers moved quickly over the keyboard. "I'm pulling up his flight record and it looks like he is scheduled to return to New York tomorrow evening." Tony repeated what Chase had said.

"If Andrew and the Brioschi woman wed and Giovanni publically releases the fact that Andrew is being groomed to be the next Capo, who do you think will take the fall for the hit on the Pope?" The Snake asked.

"Andrew," Chase, Tony and Angel all said in unison, but Angel still didn't believe it. He wouldn't set Andrew up to be murdered, would he? *No. He wouldn't.* Giovanni knew how much Angel cared for Andrew, then again, why would he force him to marry someone else, knowing it would crush Angel?

"Madeline Diaglio-Brioschi-Venturini will become the devastated widow, will do penance for her husband's sins, will seek out the new Pope and re-establish the Diaglio's long history of money laundering through the Vatican and set up God knows what here in the States," the Snake explained. "At least, that's the theory under which we're operating right now."

"That's why they chose Chicago," Chase uttered. "The Holy Name Cathedral is the seat of the Roman Catholic Archdiocese of Chicago, and one of the largest Roman Catholic dioceses in the United States."

"What does that mean?" Tony blurted and both Chase and the Snake started to speak at the same time. Tony held his hand up. "Wait a second, I'm talking to Chase. What does that mean?" He repeated.

"It means if you wanted to establish a solid-ass relationship with the Catholic higher-ups in the States, you'd do it right here in Chicago," Chase explained.

Tony abruptly lowered his gun and Angel saw Lisben breathe a sigh of relief.

"Everyone stand down," the Snake ordered and the three men to the left of Tony and the two men who had carried Taelon to the kitchen and laid him on the floor, lowered their weapons.

"These accusations are huge," Tony said, turning to face the Snake. "I want to see all of the evidence."

"Sal has intercepted phone records between the Diaglio family and Giovanni's estate. There's also a trail of money changing hands between Giovanni's bank in New York and the Diaglio's bank in Italy," the Snake explained.

"Tell the Snake to tell Sal that he can communicate with me," Chase blurted and Tony repeated his request.

"Done," the Snake said.

"So, what is our next move?" Tony asked.

"You take me home," Angel blurted. "That's your next move, remember?"

The Snake and Tony exchanged glances. "I'm sorry, Babe, but I don't think that's such a good idea," Tony said and anger ignited in her belly. She couldn't believe Tony was suddenly on their side.

"You'll pay for this," Angel huffed. "Giovanni will find you and he will kill anyone who has helped hold me here against my will!"

"Let me talk to the Boss lady," Chase said through the earpiece and Tony reluctantly removed the piece from his ear and handed it to Angel.

"Chase wants to talk to you."

Placing the piece in her ear, Angel blurted, "What?"

"I'll get you the evidence you need to either confront Giovanni for wrongdoing or prove his innocence to everyone, but you gotta make me one promise. I know better than to ask you to promise to keep your wild-ass there, so promise me that IF you leave, you'll contact me so that I know you're safe. Deal?"

"Deal," Angel said softly.

"There's one more thing. Giovanni is sending a team to take Andrew and his men out. He wants Andrew alive but everyone else is expendable, even the Snake," Chase said and Angel relayed the message.

"I was expendable the moment I let you walk into that school," the Snake muttered.

"How does he know where to find us?" Harry asked.

"Carl Cusanelli is supposed to obtain the coordinates to your location sometime tonight," Chase explained. "How and from who? I don't know."

"Carl's here in Chicago?" Angel was shocked. Giovanni must really be in a tizzy to call and ask Carl to come.

"He flew in this morning with an entourage of Maratinzano men," Chase responded and Angel relayed the message. "Suffice to say he's pissed, like crazy-ass pissed," Chase muttered and Angel could sense fear in his voice.

"Watch your back," she told him.

"That's an understatement," Chase quipped. "Oh, and tell the Snake I said it might be a good idea to dig out some of those M16A2's from the weapon's room on the north side of the house. Tell him to save one for me." She relayed the message and then handed the ear piece back to Tony.

Just then the Snake turned toward Tony. "Wait a second, how did YOU find us?" He puzzled.

"Let's just say it was an act of God," Tony shrugged and Angel narrowed her brow.

"Oh, brother," Chase muttered into the ear piece.

"An act of God?" The Snake repeated.

"Yeah," Tony said. "Let's just call it Divine Intervention."

"You're going to hell, man," Chase blurted and Tony grinned while Angel glared at him with a skeptical eye.

CHAPTER 49

Trig set the chopper down on the landing pad just outside the Venturini primary estate in the city. The expansive estate sat on three acres of land and was surrounded by a wrought iron, electric fence, secured with beautiful red brick pillars. Met by several of his bodyguards, Andrew and Trig were immediately escorted inside. "Your guest has just arrived, sir," one of his bodyguards said, as they entered through the back door.

Andrew rushed toward the foyer and peered out of the window at the black stretch limousine that had pulled up in front of his home. "Escort them to the library," Andrew instructed. "Tell them I've been detained and will join them shortly."

With Trig on his heels, Andrew raced down the hallway and into the security room, where a man sat, viewing several monitors. "Don Venturini," the man rose upon seeing Andrew.

"Relax, Pete," Andrew said, patting his shoulder and pushing by him. "Pete, this is Trig. Trig, this is an old friend and one of the best security guys on the street, Pete Bellasco." Pete looked like he could have been a bouncer at one of the hottest nightclubs in Chicago. He was big, linebacker big, bald and pierced in places that looked painful to be pierced.

"What can I do for you?" Pete asked.

"Pull up the security cameras on the library, and then get Sal on the line," Andrew ordered. "I want him to run ID recognition on my would-be wife."

"You don't think she's who she says she is?" Pete asked, as he brought up the feed from the library.

"Just a safety precaution," Andrew uttered beneath his breath.

When the image of Madeline Brioschi appeared on the screen, Trig's jaw fell open. "Damn, she's smokin'," he muttered. "You are one lucky SOB." He held his fist up to give Andrew a bump, but Andrew just rolled his eyes.

"Let's not forget that she might be a terrorist," Andrew said.

"I'd still like to hit that," Trig uttered. "Damn."

Out of the corner of his eye, Andrew saw Pete's lips curl upward. "Not you, too," Andrew moaned. "Seriously, don't encourage him."

"Sorry, boss," Pete said, clearing his throat.

Madeline sat on the brown leather couch in the library, crossed her left ankle behind her right ankle and set her hands daintily on her lap. She was wearing a black, form fitting dress and her auburn hair cascaded over her shoulders. A diamond pear-shaped pendant hung around her neck, matching the diamonds that dangled from each of her lobes. She had olive skin, full lips and bright blue eyes, the kind that easily distract even the most trained bodyguard. She was either the epitome of beauty or a serpent in disguise. Andrew's job was to determine which.

Seated next to her was the Brioschi family Consigliere named Serco Mertesca. He had accompanied her to the States for the purpose of handling the marital agreement between the families. Giovanni and the Brioschi Boss had already discussed the terms. Serco's job was merely to see that those terms were met.

"She checks out," Sal said when Andrew answered his cell phone. "That is indeed Madeline Brioschi and the man with her is Serco Mertesca, Consigliere to the Brioschi family."

Andrew exhaled. A part of him had hoped to learn that they were imposters and he could simply go in with guns blazing and put an end to this whole thing. "Thanks, Sal," Andrew murmured.

"These aren't people you want to mess with," Sal warned. "The Brioschi family is one of the most ruthless in Italy, second only to the Diaglios. They're known for their cruelty. Whatever you're doing, be careful."

Andrew disconnected the call and turned to Trig and Pete. "I'm going to need a diversion."

Leaping out of his chair, Trig threw his dreadlocks over his shoulder and pulled a Glock from his waistband. "I'm on it!" He whooped and Pete and Andrew looked at him and then at one another and smirked. "What?" Trig eyed them. "What's so funny?"

Pete chuckled. "Nothing."

"What?" Trig demanded. "You want a diversion, I'll give you one. I'll storm into that room and..."

"And you'll be dead in under a second," Andrew interrupted.

"Have a little faith, bro," Trig quipped.

"I have faith," Andrew rebutted. "But I also play the odds and if you barge in there waving a Glock in Serco Mertesca's face, the odds aren't in your favor."

Trig holstered the gun into his waistband. "Fine. You got a better plan?"

Andrew inhaled slowly. "Yeah, I do," he exhaled. "Pete, I'm going to need you to take Serco on a tour of the Venturini estates."

"Which one?" Pete asked.

"All of them."

"All of them?" Pete's eyebrows jetted higher. "We can't see all of them in a day. We'll be stuck in traffic for hours."

"You can if you're traveling by helicopter," Andrew said and a smile filled Trig's face.

"Right on, bro, I'm tracking with you," Trig said, clapping his hands together.

Pete stood up. "Do you think he'll leave Madeline alone?" He scrunched up his face in an outward display of doubt.

"I'll handle that part," Andrew retorted. "It's only fitting that two people should have some alone time before they are expected to wed."

"Try before you buy. That's my motto," Trig jeered. "You gotta know that all of the parts are in working condition." Trig gawked at Madeline on the monitor screen. "Not that I see anything on that woman that ain't working. I mean, that right there is damn fine specimen!"

Andrew reached over and turned off the screen. "Are you done?"

"I could be, if you'd turn the monitor back on," Trig quipped. "Give a brother a break."

Clearing his throat and moving Trig toward the door, Andrew instructed him to get the chopper ready and wait. He and Pete then headed down the hall toward the Library. As Andrew stepped inside, Serco and Madeline immediately rose.

"Don Venturini," Serco said, extending his hand. "Thank you for your hospitality."

"Serco Mertesca," Andrew retorted, shaking his hand. "Thank you for accompanying Ms. Brioschi." He then turned toward her with his hand outstretched. "Andrew Venturini," he uttered in a softer, less aggressive tone than he had taken with Serco.

"Madeline Brioschi," she responded, giving his hand a gentle shake, her hand lingering in his to the point that it teetered on awkward.

Releasing her hand and turning his attention back to Serco, Andrew requested to

speak with him privately; and he and Serco
stepped into the hallway. Andrew acknowledged
that he understood Serco accompanied Madeline to
make sure that everything went smoothly, and that
all of the agreed upon parameters were met. "But,
I'd like to request a few hours alone," Andrew
explained. "Surely, man-to-man, you can
understand this?"

Serco looked as if he were trying not to
smile. "Madeline is a beautiful woman," he said.
"And you are to be wed very soon."

"Yes," Andrew interjected. "I would like to
at least have one meal with her before our
nuptials."

Serco pondered his request and then spoke.
"I see no reason why you should not be allowed a
few private hours to get to know one another," he
admitted and Andrew fought to conceal his glee.
His plan was working, which was exciting
considering Plan B was to incapacitate Serco with
a heavy dose of Seroquel, which would
undoubtedly be something to which the Brioschi
family would take offense.

"Grazie," Andrew said, placing his hand on
Serco's shoulder. "In anticipation of acquiring
your blessing, I have arranged a tour of the
Venturini estates for you. I understand that part
of the agreement is that, upon their arrival to the
States, the Brioschi family will commandeer one of
my estates."

"Yes, that is the agreement, though the
family was not planning on making their move to
the States for several months," he retorted but
Andrew ignored him and continued maneuvering
him down the hall and toward the back door.

"I will have my men give you a quick tour
while I escort Madeline to a late supper and then
we will meet back here," Andrew said quickly as

they approached Pete, who was standing at the back door. "Pete," Andrew continued so that Serco didn't have an opportunity to object. "This is Serco Mertesca, Consigliere to the Brioschi family."

Following Andrew's hurried example, Pete quickly opened the door and ushered them outside. "It is an honor to make your acquaintance," Pete said.

"Please give him a complete tour of the Venturini estates and take him to Culleta's on 11th Street," Andrew instructed, moving them toward the chopper. Culleta's was one of the oldest Italian restaurants in the city, known for the best food and the slowest service. "Order the special," he told Pete.

"Yes, sir," Pete said and opened the chopper door for Serco, who turned toward Andrew as if to say something, but Andrew didn't give him the chance.

Shaking his hand, Andrew uttered, "Grazie, again. I will not forget this." Then he immediately turned and rushed back toward the house. He didn't want to linger and give Serco the opportunity to change his mind. His plan had worked even better than he had imagined in his mind and he didn't want to look the proverbial gift horse in the mouth; especially in lieu of the fact that he might have to kill this particular gift horse later. Now, all he needed to do was woo Madeline into giving him information that would help him take down whoever was behind the attack on the Pope.

CHAPTER 50

Olga waddled down the motel corridor carrying two Cokes, a variety of mini chip bags and candy bars. As she passed the door just before her room, she heard a woman's voice. It was loud and raspy with emotion, and Olga stopped to listen. *There is nothing more exciting than eavesdropping on a lover's quarrel,* Olga thought as she leaned closer to the door.

"I told you I want Thomas's share of the money!" The woman screamed and when no one answered, Olga quickly realized she was eavesdropping on a telephone conversation. "I won't help you until I get the money I was promised," the woman clucked. "Bring it to me tonight. East Moon Motel, room 137. Be here at 9:00pm sharp and don't show up without my money!" Olga heard the woman exhale and then just as she was about to take a step forward, the door to room 137 thrust open and the woman ran smack into Olga, knocking a can of Coke right out of her arms. The Coke hit the pavement, exploded and shot soda all over Olga's legs.

"Merciful Heavens!" Olga gasped.

"Oh my goodness," the woman sighed. "I'm so sorry." She bent down to retrieve the can of soda, but it was leaking so badly that there was no point in picking it up. "I will replace it," the woman said, searching her pockets for change.

"That's okay," Olga said. "It's bad for me anyway." She saw tears welling up in the woman's eyes. "Is everything okay?" Olga asked. "I couldn't help overhearing your quarrel."

"Yes," the woman forced a smile and then deflated. "No," she admitted. "Someone owes me money and I don't know if he'll pay me and without that money I have nothing."

"Oh, sweetie," Olga wailed, shuffling the snacks and remaining soda can into one arm and looping the other arm into the woman's. "Why, you look like an independent, strong woman to me. You remind me a lot of my great niece. Beautiful. Independent. You don't need to depend on any man to get by." She patted her arm and smiled. "Things are going to work out. I can feel it. Now, don't you worry."

Drying her eyes, the woman sheepishly smiled. "Thank you," she murmured and gave Olga a hug. "I needed to hear that."

"Now you put a smile on that pretty face and don't let anyone take it away from you," Olga said. "Especially not a man," she whispered.

The woman started to walk away and then turned back around. "By the way, my name's Detta."

"I'm Olga," Olga responded. "It's been a pleasure meeting you."

"Maybe we'll bump into each other again," Detta said.

"I would like that," Olga replied and made a mental note to eavesdrop on Detta's room at 9:00pm tonight, to see if her male visitor shows and make sure everything goes smoothly. *Even an independent and strong lady can use a little back up now and again,* she told herself.

CHAPTER 51

Angel was not happy about remaining a prisoner in the Venturini hide-out, although at least now she could move around freely. At her request, the Snake led her and Tony down the cellar staircase and into a surveillance room, where they could maintain contact with Chase more easily.

The room resembled a bomb shelter with bunk beds lining one wall, enough to sleep eight comfortably and shelves filled with medical supplies and boxes of ammunition covered another wall. Long tables filled with computer monitors and surveillance equipment lined the remaining two walls. The Snake sat down at one of the tables and began working his fingers across the keys.

"You have any idea what you're doing there, Ace?" Tony teased.

"Yep," the Snake quipped. "You can't spend years in the military without picking up a thing or two." His fingers didn't move as rapidly as Chase's did, but whatever he was doing was working because images began to appear on the many screens.

"Tell him to create an uplink to me," Chase blurted into Tony's ear and Tony jumped as if startled, then groaned, pulled the ear piece from his ear and handed it to the Snake.

"He wants you to link to something," Tony said with a shrug.

The Snake placed the ear piece in his right ear and followed Chase's instructions. A few minutes later, Chase's face appeared on one of the monitors.

"Hey there, Boss Lady," Chase whooped. "Nice work, Snake."

Angel was glad to see Chase. She felt more
secure knowing that he was working behind the
scenes, and seeing him made her feel more
confident that they were going to get to the bottom
of whatever was happening. With Sal and Chase
working together, they should be able to gather the
information needed to stop the assassination
attempt on the Pope and end this nightmare once
and for all. She was also hoping that Chase would
discover evidence to support her belief that
Giovanni knew nothing of the attack. Angel
needed validation of his innocence. There was no
question that Giovanni had been ruthless in the
past, but she could not believe that he would
participate in an attack on His Eminence or any
member of the clergy. There were unspoken rules
and understandings among the Family and killing
the Pope was definitely a violation of those rules.

Chase and the Snake worked on creating
uplinks to Sal so that the exchange of information
would be seamless. "Sal, can you see me?" Chase
uttered and then, like magic, Sal's face popped
onto the monitor next to the one Chase's face was
on.

"Crystal clear," he answered. "I'm patching
into the Venturini estate. Andrew's getting ready
to interrogate Madeline Brioschi and needs me to
monitor their situation."

"Patch us in," the Snake said.

"Give me a minute and you should see the
uplink," Sal answered.

Angel stared at the monitor, unsure of
whether or not she wanted to watch Andrew with
his soon-to-be-wife. What if she was beautiful?
What if he fell in love with her? What if this meant
that she and Andrew really were over? That was a
reality that was too harsh to face, at least right
now. She glanced sideways at Tony and felt that

familiar twinge of confusion. How could she love two men so differently but so intensely that she couldn't imagine life without either one of them? It was wrong and unfair. She couldn't bear the thought of Andrew marrying someone else, no more than she could stomach the idea of Tony sharing his bed with another woman. Eventually, she knew she was going to have to let one of them go; but not today. *Please, God, not today and not like this,* she silently prayed as she waited for the uplink to go live.

CHAPTER 52

Entering the library, Andrew ordered his body guard to remain outside the room. As he closed the door behind him, Madeline immediately rose from the couch with a look of concern etched across her face.

"Where is Serco?" She asked.

"He is embarking on a tour of all of my estates," Andrew answered with a smile, gesturing for Madeline to sit back down and then joining her on the couch. "I thought you and I needed a little time to get to know each other. We are supposed to be wed and I'd like to at least feel as if I know a little bit about you. I'm sure you agree."

Madeline lowered her gaze and nodded. "What would you like to know?" Her Italian accent was thick.

Just then, the surveillance uplink went live and Chase, Sal, Angel, the Snake and Tony were all able to eavesdrop on their conversation from their various locations. Angel neared the monitor.

"Damn!" Chase blurted. "That is one fine-looking lady."

"Wow," the Snake muttered.

"She's hotter than..." Tony started and then noticed the scowl on Angel's face and quickly stopped talking.

The moment Angel saw Madeline's beauty, the butterflies that had been flitting around in her stomach dropped dead, causing a wave of nausea. How could a man resist a woman as beautiful as Madeline Brioschi? How could she ever compete with that? Angel's shoulders slumped forward and only one thought popped into her head. *Game over.*

Draping his right arm over the back of the couch, Andrew turned his body to face Madeline and smiled warmly. "Let's start with your name," he said. "Are you named after anyone?"

"My grandmother's name was Madeline," she spoke softly. "My mother said I resemble her."

"And your middle name?" Andrew asked.

"Maria," she said and he quickly repeated it, as if he was somehow intrigued by her name or maybe he was simply trying to commit it to memory.

"Do you have siblings?" Andrew posed and Madeline shifted her legs, uncrossing and re-crossing them as if she were nervous.

"A brother," she said softly. "But we are estranged."

"I'm sorry to hear that," Andrew added. "I had hoped to meet all of your family."

Madeline fiddled nervously with her fingers. "Is this your first trip to the States?" Andrew asked.

"Yes, it is," she answered and Sal, who's face filled the monitor to Angel's left, shook his head and frowned.

"That's a lie," he blurted. "According to my records, Madeline Maria Diaglio has traveled to the States three times prior to this trip. Once in 2005. Once in 2009, and one time last year," Sal explained.

"Why would she lie about coming to this country?" Tony posed and Angel shrugged.

"Sal, can you find out if she has any other aliases?" Chase pondered.

"I'm running her through our database as we speak," Sal responded.

Andrew lightly dragged his fingertips across Madeline's shoulder and she glanced toward him, as if surprised by his touch. "Do you want to know anything about me?" He asked.

A smile lit Madeline's eyes, and Angel didn't
know if it was because he had touched her or
because she believed the interrogation was over;
whatever the reason, she appeared suddenly more
relaxed. "Yes," she said. "I heard about the
murder of your father and brothers. I offer my
condolences for your loss."

"Thank you," Andrew nodded.

"Losing loved ones is difficult," she said as
she placed her hand on his thigh, giving it a tender
squeeze. "It can make a person feel as if there is
no more reason to live, wouldn't you agree?"

"I think there is always reason to keep on
living," Andrew responded.

There was a faraway look in Madeline's eyes
and Andrew scooted closer to her. "Penny?"

Confusion shown on her face. "I do not
have any money with me," she confessed and
Andrew grinned.

"It's an expression. A penny for your
thoughts?" He explained and Angel felt a twinge of
jealousy. That's what he used to say to her when
they were working together at Tetterbaum's pub.

"Ah," she nodded. "I am sorry. My English
is not so good."

"You were thinking of someone?" Andrew
pried.

"No, it is nothing," she said quickly. "Tell
me more about you. Who is Andrew Venturini?"

Angel leaned toward the screen to hear his
answer. *Good question*, she thought. *Who IS
Andrew Venturini?* As of late, she no longer felt
that she knew the answer.

Andrew was eerily quiet, as if he, himself,
didn't know how to answer the question. Madeline
appeared pleased by his silence. "You are cop in
your heart," Madeline said and placed her hand
against his chest. "But because you have lost your

family, you now become head of this family and give up what is in your heart?"

Taking her hand from his chest, Andrew lowered it to the couch and released it. Madeline quickly placed her hand back into her lap and glazed at the floor. "I have made you uncomfortable," she muttered.

"Yes," Andrew said bluntly, rose from the couch and walked across the room, leaning his arm against one of the tall, mahogany bookcases. "You appear to know a lot about me and I find myself at a disadvantage."

Madeline rose and walked toward him. "You want to search me?" She asked, raising her arms above her head. "Ask of me anything."

"I'd like to search her," Chase interjected and the Snake and Tony laughed. Angel rolled her eyes, then directed her attention back to the screen. It was addicting, like watching a soap opera.

Madeline placed her hand against Andrew's chest. "I want to know if there is room for me in here?" She said and without hesitation, Andrew gripped her long, auburn hair, tugged her head backwards and pulled her into a deep, passionate kiss. Madeline didn't fight him, but appeared to melt into his arms, and Angel knew that feeling. Andrew had a kiss that could make any woman's toes curl.

Releasing her, Andrew gazed downward. "Does it feel like there is room for you in my heart?" He asked with a warm smile.

"Si," she uttered breathlessly. "It does."

"Good," Andrew said and brushed a piece of hair from her face.

Angel couldn't describe the surreal feeling of watching Andrew with another woman, other than to say that it broke her. Watching him hold

Madeline the way he had once held her. Watching
him caress her hair made her feel as if she might
vomit. She couldn't breathe and at the same time,
she couldn't bring herself to look away from the
monitor.

"Babe?" Tony said, but Angel didn't hear
him or if she did it didn't register in her mind that
he was talking to her. "BABE!" He repeated, a little
louder.

"What?!" Angel blurted, suddenly startled.

"Are you okay?" Tony asked, reaching over
and wiping her cheeks. Angel had been so
enthralled in watching Andrew and Madeline that
she hadn't noticed the tears that had spilled from
her eyes and were now running down her face.

The Snake glanced up at her with a certain
softness in his eyes. Without uttering a word, she
knew that he knew her heart was breaking over
Andrew; but she didn't want to hurt Tony by
making it so obvious.

"I'm fine," she said, pulling back from
Tony's touch and pushing her shoulders back.
"I'm not feeling very well," she lied, rubbing her
shoulder for dramatic effect. "I didn't take any
pain pills this morning."

"I'll get you some," Tony said and
immediately left the room.

Once Tony was gone, the Snake turned
toward Angel. "You know he's doing what he needs
to do to make her trust him," he said and Angel
nodded. The Snake stood up and took her hands
in his. "Ms. Maratinzano, everything Andrew has
said and done the past few days has been in an
effort to protect you."

"I know," she whispered, tears filling her
eyes again. "He'd make me think he hates me and
marry a stranger before he'd put my life in danger."

"Exactly," the Snake agreed. "That's how much he loves you."

"That isn't love, Sean," Angel blurted and wiped a stray tear with the back of her hand. "He's a coward," she spat, her jaw tightening. "When you love someone you fight for them, despite the danger. You have faith that if you hold on long enough or tight enough that things have a way of working out. You don't do what he's done..." her voice tapered off.

"Ms. Maratinzano," the Snake squeezed her hands. "Maybe he believes he doesn't have a choice?"

Angel pulled her hands away. "There's always a choice." Moving quickly around the Snake and leaning toward the monitor that held the uplink to Chase, Angel swallowed hard and then spoke. "I'm coming home now," she said matter-of-factly.

"Boss lady, I don't think that's a good idea," Chase rebutted.

"I wasn't asking your permission," Angel barked. "I'll be home soon and when I get there I expect to be outfitted with the equipment I will need to find Olga."

"Ms. Maratinzano..." the Snake began but Angel whirled toward him and held up her hand in front of his face.

"I don't want to hear it," she quipped.

"But..." he tried again.

"If I were you, I'd shut my mouth," she interrupted him. "You assisted the Venturini Boss in kidnapping me and then you conspired to overthrow my position as head of this family. I'd hate to have to give that information to my grandfather," she sneered. "I can't imagine how he might respond. Can you?" The Snake lowered his arms and exhaled slowly, in an outward display of

defeat. "Now, give me a gun," she ordered. The
Snake pulled a 9mm from the back of his
waistband and handed it over. Guilt washed over
her, as she knew she was transferring her anger
toward Andrew onto the Snake. He didn't deserve
it and she hated threatening him, but it was the
only play she had. He wasn't going to allow her to
leave any other way.

With the gun clutched tightly in her grip,
Angel stormed from the room, across the cellar and
up the staircase that led to the kitchen. She was
on a mission to find Tony and ask him to drive her
home. If he refused, she would force Taelon to
help her; that is, if he had stopped bleeding.

Upon hearing voices at the top of the steps,
Angel stopped abruptly and peered through a small
crack in the door. She saw Lisben sitting at the
oval-shaped, oak kitchen table. He was leaning
forward with his elbows on the table and speaking
in a low voice. She couldn't see who was seated
across from him, other than his forearms and
hands; but she could hear him.

"We have the information back," Lisben
said and reached into his pocket, retrieving a jump
drive. He slid it across the table to the other man.
"I copied all of the files Andrew had uploaded from
the original drive."

"So, we need the girl to unencrypt it for
us?" The man asked. Angel noted that he sounded
younger than Lisben and spoke with an accent;
one she guessed was Italian.

Lisben grinned. "That's the beauty of it.
The files I copied were already decoded. Ironically,
Andrew did the work for us."

"I'll deliver this right away and then we're
done? We're good to go?" The man asked and
Lisben nodded.

"There is one more thing," Lisben said, holding up his index finger. "I want to add to the plan and your expertise is needed." Lisben leaned closer to the other man. "Andrew has a weak spot for Angel Maratinzano. His judgment, where she is concerned, is poor; and that's where your skills are required." Lisben glanced over his shoulder, as if to make sure they were alone. "She is in the way and we need you to rid us of this... complication."

"You want me to take out a Boss?" The man sounded shocked by the request. "You know who she is, right?"

Lisben nodded slowly.

"Are you crazy?" The man uttered. "I hit the Capo's granddaughter and I'm a dead man."

Lisben sat up a little straighter and folded his hands on the table. "You're not understanding," he whispered. "She needs to meet with a terrible accident."

Angel couldn't believe what she was hearing. Why would Lisben want her dead? What did he have to gain from her death?

"Listen," Lisben spat, leaning across the table. "That bitch has foiled our plans more than once. She gets in Andrew's head, disturbs his thoughts. While she is alive Andrew will never marry Madeline Brioschi, but with her dead, he'll acquiesce and the rest is in the bag." A sinister grin crossed Lisben's face and Angel felt her temperature rise.

Clutching the gun, she fought the urge to storm through the door and put a bullet right through his brain. *That's what should have been done after he betrayed us to Stidda anyway,* she justified; but then a twinge of guilt stopped her. When had she become someone who easily justified murder? Moral reasons aside, rushing in was too risky because she had to assume that both

Lisben and the man across from him were armed. Even if she shot Lisben, what would stop the other man from taking her out? *Besides,* she thought, *I need answers and Lisben might be the only one who can provide them.*

"Does the Boss know of this new plan?" The man asked.

"I like to think of it as a pleasant surprise for him. An eye for an eye, so to speak. Think of the reward you'll receive for going above and beyond," Lisben said with a grin. Silence fell between them and Angel could only imagine how the man's mind must have been swimming. Being asked to kill the Capo's granddaughter was not something to be taken lightly. "Are we going to have a problem?" Lisben chided, staring with deadly intensity.

"What's your time frame?" The man asked.

"Immediate." Lisben's wrinkles stretched as his grin grew bigger. Pulling a white envelope from the interior pocket of his gray suit jacket, Lisben slid it across the table. "This is half," he said. "You'll get the other half when the job is done."

Angel watched as the man extended his right hand and Lisben shook it. She noted he had a tattoo on the inside of his right wrist that looked like a capitol D with a cross in the center. Hearing the squeaking sound of chairs scooting across linoleum Angel surmised that both men were now standing. Their meeting was over and her heart was racing as she tried to determine her next move. Should she blast through the door right now and try to catch them both off guard? Could she take them both down before either one could get a shot off? Should she lay low until the hired hitter left and then barrel in and confront Lisben?

Her palm was sweaty as she tightened her grip on the 9mm.

Lisben stood and he and the other man shook hands. "I don't need to remind you what's riding on this," Lisben warned. "Do this job and you'll be rewarded beyond your wildest dreams. Fail and you won't live long enough to have another dream."

Angel stayed hidden until Lisben escorted the man from the kitchen to the foyer and out of the front door, and then she made a dash through the door, across the kitchen and up the staircase that led to the second floor. She needed to find Tony, which surprisingly didn't take long. He was in the master bedroom, first room on the left at the top of the steps, searching through drawers.

"Babe," Tony gasped when he saw her. "I'm still trying to find some pain killers for you. You'd think someone would have a friggin' aspirin, but ..."

"I need to tell you something," Angel blurted, cutting his sentence short.

Tony sank onto the corner of the king sized bed. "I know, Babe," he said with a sigh. "You still have feelings for Andrew and what happened the other night was ..."

"No," Angel blurted and Tony leapt up.

"No?" He exclaimed.

"No. I mean, yes. Yes and no. I don't know!" Angel moaned and Tony sank back onto the bed. "What I mean is, no, that wasn't what I was going to say." She went on to tell him about the conversation between Lisben and the other man and Tony's face turned red with anger. Before she had even finished, Tony leapt from the bed and stormed from the room, his .45 readied and clutched in his fist.

234

Lisben was just entering the front door when Tony reached the foyer with Angel hot on his heels. Taking aim at Lisben's head, Tony snarled. "You've got one chance to give me the name of the hitter, Ace!"

A smirk spread across Lisben's lips. "My, my, you do have that Andriachini temper, don't you? Just like your father." Lisben folded his hands in front of his body. "You know, me and your dad go way back."

"I don't give a shit about your relationship with my dad," Tony quipped. "I want the name of the hitter."

"I don't know what you're talking about," Lisben lied.

"I heard you," Angel interjected. "In the kitchen. I heard your whole plan to take me out."

Lisben lunged forward in a desperate attempt to distract Tony while retrieving his weapon from his chest holster, but it didn't work. The moment Lisben moved, Tony fired a shot into his right thigh. Lisben yelped in pain and fell to the floor, gripping his leg.

"This is your last chance. I want the name!" Tony yelled.

"You'll never stop it," Lisben laughed. "The hit's already been commissioned."

"Give me the name!" Tony hollered, raising his gun and taking aim.

"Go to hell," Lisben growled.

"You first," Tony snipped and fired a second shot right through Lisben's forehead.

Angel gasped as his body flipped backwards and blood began to pool around him. Despite the number of people she had seen shot and killed, it still made her knees buckle.

Having heard the gunshots, the Snake, Harry and several other Venturini men rushed into the foyer with their guns drawn. "What the hell happened?" The Snake blurted.

"I took out the trash," Tony quipped.

"He commissioned a hit on me," Angel panted. "I heard the whole thing."

The Snake harnessed his gun. "He had it coming, but Andrew's gonna be pissed."

"Wouldn't be the first time I pissed Andrew off," Tony rebutted.

The Snake gave Angel a sideways glance and exhaled. "I have a feeling it won't be the last."

"You're probably right about that, Ace," Tony said, stepping over Lisben's body and patting the Snake on the shoulder as he went by. "Now, at the lady's request, I'm taking her home. With a target on her head, she'll be safer at the Towers. You can't protect her here and neither can I."

The Snake begrudgingly nodded. "Did you see the hitter?" He asked Angel.

"No. I only saw his hands and a tattoo on his wrist," she said as Tony led her toward the cellar door.

Before the Snake could ask any more questions, Tony had dragged Angel outside and into the trees. The gentle breeze from earlier had now become a howling wind that whipped her hair into her face. Looping her fingers around it to form a makeshift pony tail, Angel ran behind Tony, using his girth as a wind shield. By the time they made it back to his SUV, she was shivering and happy to hop into the front seat to get out of the wind.

"There's a storm brewin'," Tony muttered as he climbed behind the wheel.

"That's an understatement," Angel remarked, only she wasn't talking about the weather. There seemed to be a storm brewing in every corner of her world. "I've got to find Olga," she said out of the blue.

"We'll find her, Babe," Tony said, reaching across the seat and giving her knee a gentle squeeze. "Don't worry."

Tony placed the key into the ignition and turned it but nothing happened. He cranked it again. The engine still didn't turn over, but instead made a loud popping sound. Angel saw his eyes widen with fear and then everything warped into slow motion. Tony pointed at Angel and screamed, "Get out of the car!" She saw his lips moving but the meaning of his words didn't immediately register in her mind. There was a millisecond of lapse. Then, lifting the door handle, Angel thrust open the passenger door and leapt from the car just as the force of the explosion hurled her forward, into the trees. The sound alone made her cover her ears with both palms for fear her skull would crack wide open.

"Tony!" She cried, but her ears were ringing so loudly that she couldn't even hear the sound of her own voice, much less hear any response from him. Her shoulder was throbbing and the fall had knocked the wind out of her, but she was in one piece. Disoriented and dizzy, but alive. Standing up wasn't an option, as her equilibrium had been compromised by the blast, so Angel began crawling through the trees, the leaves crunching beneath her knees. She knew she needed to distance herself from the vehicle in case there was another explosion, but she wanted to circle the flaming SUV to find Tony.

Smoke billowed into the air as she rounded the back of the car; the gravel from the road digging into her palms. "Tony!" She cried out a second time, coughing from the smoke. *Please be okay,* she silently willed him. Before she could reach the other side of the SUV, she felt herself being lifted from the ground and turned to see the Snake, his arms cradling her. "Tony," she uttered and pointed toward the other side of the car.

"I've got him!" Harry hollered.

Rushing Angel back through the trees and toward the house, the Snake instructed several men to help Harry retrieve Tony. "I want pictures of the bomb," he ordered.

Once inside, Angel's head continued pounding and it was difficult for her to hear, but she was able to sit up without feeling too nauseated or dizzy. The Snake placed her in one of the kitchen chairs and began shining the light from his cell phone in each of her pupils. "I want to get you to a hospital," he said but Angel shook her head.

"How is Tony?" She uttered.

"Harry's taking care of him. They'll be here soon."

Angel's breathing was labored, partly from smoke inhalation, partly from exhaustion and partly from the weight of her own emotions. "Sean," she whispered and the Snake sat down next to her and leaned in close. "I want to go home."

The Snake studied her face, obviously torn between her request and Andrew's agenda.

"I'm not safe here," she uttered. "I know you don't think I'll be safe with Giovanni but..."

The Snake held his finger up, cutting her sentence short, and then placed his cell phone to his ear. "Trig," he spoke into the phone. "Change in plans. I need you to bring the chopper right away and take Angel back to the Towers."

"I'm playing tour director for this Serco dude right now," Trig retorted.

"Tell him you've got to run an errand and you'll be right back," the Snake argued.

"Did you clear this with Andrew?" Trig asked.

"No, and we're not going to tell him until she's back in the Towers, safe and sound."

"I don't know if this cats down with that," Trig groaned.

"Somebody just tried to blow Angel to smithereens!" The Snake's voice elevated. "She's not safe here, so get over here and take her home."

"Andrew's gonna be pissed, bro," Trig warned.

"He's gonna be pissed anyway," the Snake chided and disconnected the call.

"Thank you," Angel said, just as Harry and two other men escorted Tony into the kitchen.

Tony was a little worse for wear, but considering the bomb had gone off on the driver's side, he looked considerably well. Angel could tell his head was hurting by the way he squinted his eyes and pressed his palms against his ears. He appeared to be dazed.

"He was unconscious when we found him," Harry explained. "Blew him about fifteen yards from the car." They all looked at Tony. "But I don't think anything's broken." Harry slid a cell phone across the kitchen table toward the Snake. "I got pics of the bomb."

At the sound of the chopper whirring above, the Snake escorted Tony and Angel outside. Tony climbed into the back of the chopper and then the Snake lifted Angel in. "Thank you," Angel told him, brushing her fingers gently across his cheek. "Be careful," she said.

"You, too," he said, taking her fingertips in his hand and giving them a tender squeeze. "Watch your back. I'll be in touch thru Chase."

Closing the chopper door, he patted the side and then watched as Trig lifted them into the air.

Angel waved, then turned and leaned her head against Tony's shoulder. She immediately felt something warm and sticky against her face, and reaching up to wipe it, quickly realized it was blood. Angel gasped and sat up straighter, staring at the side of Tony's head and the trickle of blood that was coming from the inside of his ear. "Trig!" Angel yelled. "Take us to Northwestern Memorial Hospital! Hurry!"

CHAPTER 53

After dropping Tony at the hospital, Trig high-tailed it back to where he had left Pete and Serco. Pete was none too happy about Trig flying off without an explanation, but Serco appeared to be enjoying his tour of the Venturini properties, so Pete didn't tell Andrew about Trig's disappearance. He assumed Trig would return, which he did, so no harm was done; although Pete's curiosity had been peaked.

Angel checked Tony into the hospital, then borrowed a cell phone from a gentlemen in the waiting area and called the Andriachini estate, asking them to send someone to Northwestern Memorial to stay with Tony until he was released. Next, she sneaked back into the emergency area where Tony was lying in bed, bent over him and planted a soft kiss against his forehead.

"It feels like my skull is in a thousand pieces," he moaned and Angel knew the feeling. The blast had left her head throbbing and a shrill din piercing her ears. It was worse for Tony because he had been closer to the bomb.

"I know," she said. "They'll get you fixed up." Tony reached up and touched her face.

"Don't leave, Babe," he uttered.

Angel sighed. A part of her wanted to stay, but she knew Tony would be okay and they were running out of time. She needed answers and she needed to get with Chase to figure out a way to stop the assassination attempt on the Pope. More than that, there was an assassin after her and Lord only knew where he was right now. Was he the one who planted the car bomb? If so, had he been watching the entire time and knew she survived it? Had he followed her to the hospital?

Angel glanced nervously over her shoulder. She never saw the face of the hit man which meant that he could be anyone at all. Staying with Tony would only put his life in danger...again. "I have to go," she whispered. "I'll check in on you later. I promise."

"Babe?" Tony grabbed her hand and Angel leaned closer. "Take the gun out of my waistband." He rolled over onto his left side and Angel pulled a .45 from his jeans and slid it into the back of her pants, draping her shirt over it. "Shoot first. Ask later," he said and gave her a wink.

Angel nodded. "When they release you, come to the Towers."

"You can count on it," he muttered, forcing a smile, but Angel could see the concern that clouded his eyes.

Leaving the hospital, Angel walked two blocks, gazing periodically over her shoulder to make sure she wasn't being followed. She then hailed a cab to the Towers.

The cabbie was an Armenian man with dark skin, dark eyes and a crocked smile. He had pictures of his children taped to the dashboard and Angel was swept away by the images. Flashes of her own childhood filled her mind, followed by images of the students at East Side Junior High School huddled together in the back of the classroom and finally, the memory of sweet, innocent Caleb. *Caleb.* Would she ever see him again? Did he really believe that she was an angel? An angel with a gun? She smiled at the notion.

"Do you have one?" The cabbie asked.

"I'm sorry?" Angel answered, having no idea what he was talking about.

"A bracelet that tracks your steps." He held up his wrist to reveal the black rubber band around it. "Since I got mine I've been healthier, you know, like making myself get out and walk around between rides." He smiled at her through the rear view mirror. "How one bracelet can track sleep and steps is amazing to me. What will they come up with next?" He shook his head. "Though it's sort of weird thinking that all of my personal information is out there somewhere in space." He waved his arms upward to indicate space.

Angel smiled. He was obviously very excited about his Fitbit, just like Olga had been when she got hers. All of a sudden the cabbie's words triggered a thought. If the Fitbit used satellite technology, would Chase be able to trace it? Could he use it to find Olga? Angel's pulse quickened with excitement and she leaned forward and asked the cabbie to hurry.

As soon as the cab stopped, Angel leaped out, rushed inside, ordering the guard at the front door to pay the cabbie. "And tip him well!" Angel hollered over her shoulder as she headed for the elevator.

"Ms. Maratinzano!" the guard at the elevator gasped. "Giovanni will be glad to see YOU."

Angel nodded and quickly punched in the code to take the elevator to the secret meeting room. She knew that that was where she would find Chase. "Tell my grandfather where I am and tell him I am requesting a meeting immediately, she told the guard as she exited the elevator.

As she rushed into the secret meeting room, Chase's eyes bulged and he almost fell over backwards when he saw her. "Boss Lady!" He shrieked. "What the hell are you doing here?"

"Tell Big Mike to get here now and get me Chito," Angel barked. "And Monahan, and anyone else we know we can trust."

In a matter of minutes, Big Mike raced into the room, a smile spreading across his face when he saw Angel. "Damn, we've been worried about you!" He said and threw his arms around her in a big bear hug. That was Big Mike. Scary as hell outwardly but a big 'ole teddy bear on the inside. Angel laughed and it felt really good. She couldn't imagine him hugging any other Mafia Boss, but then again, she wasn't a normal Boss. She was re-writing the rules daily and the truth was, she didn't mind a hug or two along the way. While caught in his embrace, she gazed over his shoulder and couldn't believe her eyes. There, standing in the doorway, was Caleb. Pulling away from Big Mike, she rushed toward Caleb, who was also running to meet her with his arms wide open. He leapt into her embrace and squeezed around her neck so tightly that she felt like she might choke; but she didn't care. The joy she felt upon seeing him was indescribable. She lifted him up and spun him around, closing her eyes and holding on tightly. It was surreal. It was unlike any feeling she had ever experienced. It was love. Unadulterated. Unconditional. Abounding. Love.

"I thought you would NEVER come home!" Caleb blurted. "What took you so long? Did you have a sleepover?"

Angel laughed. His glistening eyes were so sweet, so innocent and curious. "Yes," she giggled. "I had a sleepover, but if I would have known YOU were here I'd have come home right away." She darted her eyes to Chase as if to say, *you should have told me!* Chase raised his arms and shrugged his shoulders.

"I've been playing with your cats," Caleb said excitedly. "I think Moe really likes me, but...," he paused and leaned in close, whispering in her ear. "I'm sort of scared of Midnight."

"Lots of people are scared of Midnight, but he won't hurt you," Angel said. "Now, how did you get here?"

"Uncle Leo brought me," Caleb said and slid from Angel's arms, pointing to the door where Leo stood sheepishly.

Angel's eyes widened. "Leo the Lion," she mumbled. "Uncle Leo?"

"Well, he's not my REAL uncle because I'm a foster kid, like I told you, but he's Detta's brother, which makes him my foster uncle." Caleb tugged at Angel's arm until she bent down and then he whispered in her ear. "He's really nice to me. He's not like Detta."

Leo stepped through the doorway. "Ms. Maratinzano," he acknowledged, tipping his head. He then turned his attention to Caleb. "Buddy, why don't you go back upstairs for a while?"

"NO!" Caleb screamed and wrapped himself around Angel's leg. "I'm not leaving my angel."

Angel was shocked and as she glanced around the room she could see that everyone was awed by his reaction. They could orchestrate hits, fight Stidda, take down traitors and flush out infiltrators but none of them had any experience dealing with a child. Chase tried to coax Caleb off of Angel but nothing worked. Big Mike threatened to forcibly remove him but it only made Caleb hold her tighter, with white knuckled fingers of determination.

Caleb sat on Angel's lap while they waited for Monahan and Chito to arrive. Monahan was the Messaggero, the liaison between the families in the States and those in Italy. Angel hoped he would have helpful information about the Brioschi and Diaglio families; anything that would explain why Giovanni chose the Brioschis to merge with the Venturinis. Chito was head of a local Chicago

gang called the Cobras. He and Big Mike had a
history. He also knew Trig and had a proven track
record of helping the family. Despite the fact that
most Made members were full-blooded Italian,
Angel considered offering Chito the opportunity to
take the Omerta and become a Made member of
the family, but she felt it was pre-mature. If he
proved himself one more time, she'd consider
officially bringing him in.

While they waited, Chase worked diligently
to track Olga's Fitbit.

Giovanni strode forcefully into the room
with two body guards in tow. "Michelangela!" He
gasped.

She immediately jumped to her feet, with
Caleb clutching around her like a little
chimpanzee. "Grandfather!" She said and he took
her by the shoulders and kissed each of her
cheeks. She winced but didn't pull away.

"What is the expression? You are a sight
for my sore eyes," he uttered and Angel smiled.

"I know the feeling," she said.

Distracted by Caleb, Giovanni stepped
back. "What is the meaning of this?" He pointed
to the boy.

Angel gave a shrug.

Caleb peeked at Giovanni. "She's MY
angel," he said, with his brows narrowed.

A softness lit Giovanni's face. "Ah, I see,"
he muttered.

Angel mouthed to him. *He won't let go.*

"I cannot blame him," Giovanni said. "With
the way you've been disappearing as of late, I'm
tempted to hold on and not let go either." Giovanni
gave Angel a wink and then ushered her back to
the chair in which she had been sitting prior to his
entrance.

"I will tell you what, Caleb," Giovanni said softly. "How about you sit on one side of Angel and I will sit on the other side?"

"We'll share her?" Caleb asked.

"Si, yes, we will share her," Giovanni answered.

A hesitant Caleb slid from her arms into the chair next to her, but kept his hand in hers. Leo sat on the other side of Caleb and Big Mike, Chito, Monahan and Chase sat across the table.

"Grandfather," Angel began. "There is much we need to discuss, but first, we need to figure out how to stop the assassination of the Pope."

"Agreed," Giovanni said.

During the course of the next two hours, Monahan shared backstory on the Diaglio family and their connection to the Brioschi family and the Vatican. They already knew about the Diaglio's money laundering through the Vatican, but what they didn't know was that the Brioschi family and the Diaglio's were arch enemies. "They make the Montagues and Capulets look like best friends," Monahan expounded. He went on to explain that the Diaglio's had single-handedly diminished the Brioschi line to the point of potential extinction. "Aside from one son, there were no male heirs left to continue the legacy," Monahan explained. "Under the guise of making amends, the Diaglio Boss offered his daughter's hand in marriage to the one remaining Brioschi son."

"Madeline," Angel uttered aloud.

"Yes," Monahan responded. "Madeline Diaglio married Mario Brioschi and it was thought that the families had called a cease fire and were going to merge their resources."

"That did not happen," Giovanni huffed, folding his hands atop the table. "Mario was gunned down shortly after their nuptials."

"Who killed him?" Chase asked.

"The Diaglio family," Monahan answered and continued to explain that although the Diaglio family was the most deadly, the Brioschi family was the wealthiest. "The Diaglio's had the power of reputation but lacked the financial backing, while the Brioschi's had the money but were running out of heirs to carry on their legacy."

"How did killing Mario help the Diaglio's?" Angel posed.

"The Brioschi family Will stipulated that everything went to Mario, and when Mario died, everything went to his wife," Monahan explained.

"But that wouldn't come to fruition until Mario's parents had passed, right?" Big Mike interjected. "The Will for the son doesn't supersede the father's life span."

Monahan took out his phone and pulled up an article. He slid it over to Chase, who input the address into his laptop and brought up the article on the big screen. They all turned to see the headline that read: Brioschi Boss Beheaded in Bathtub

"When did this occur?!" Giovanni pound his fist on the table, making little Caleb jump.

"This is today's headline," Monahan answered. "Keeping in mind they are seven hours ahead of us."

"Holy..." Chase uttered but his voice faded before he finished his sentence.

"Madeline Brioschi now owns everything," Monahan explained. "Making the Diaglio family the wealthiest, most powerful mafia presence in Italy and all of Europe."

"This is an outrage!" Giovanni growled. "Who is responsible?"

"The Diagli..." Monahan began but Giovanni was on his feet and cut him off.

"Si, si, the Diaglios, I know." He slammed his palms down on the table. "I want to know WHO ordered the hit. Specifically, WHO!" Giovanni's face had turned bright red and fire lit his eyes.

Chase's fingers flew across the keyboard. He was uploading the article and sending the information they had just learned to Sal, requesting his help on locating leads to track down whoever ordered the Brioschi hit.

"Sir, our contacts over there are working on it," Monahan replied.

"BAH!" Giovanni sank back into his chair and rubbed his hands over his jowls. "Everyone is working on it, working on it, but I get no answers. All I get is working on it!"

Monahan went on to explain what they already knew, that Nicholas Diaglio was in the States working on setting up the assassination attempt on the Pope with the help of Detta Palumbo. "We know Nicholas is dead, but we're still searching for Detta," Monahan added.

"Us, too," Chase quipped. "She blew up a car and one of our guys right outside the building, made a phone call from the bushes and then disappeared into the night. Poof, into wild-ass thin air, like everybody else," Chase huffed.

Angel inhaled and then exhaled slowly. She dreaded bringing up the next topic, but there was no denying that the two were linked and she needed to know how and why. "Giovanni," she began, her palms growing sweaty. "You arranged a marriage between Andrew Venturini and Madeline Brioschi." The moment the words fell from her lips, Giovanni's face grew pale. Angel knew instantly that he had not made the connection in his mind. She could see that until this very moment he hadn't realized that Madeline Diaglio and Madeline Brioschi were one in the same. Though his surprise was evident, something about it didn't set well with Angel. The Snake's words replayed in her mind, *"You don't get to be Capo by being stupid."* Angel stared at him, trying to connect the dots. This was Giovanni. Guarded, non-trusting, Giovanni. If he had arranged a marriage, he would have known everything about the individuals involved. He would leave nothing to chance. No surprises, that was what he had always taught her. She gawked at him. "You didn't make the arrangements, did you?"

Giovanni shook his head. "No, I did not make the arrangements. I simply gave Don Venturini an incentive to consider the request."

"By promising to make him the next Capo?" Angel asked.

"Si," Giovanni nodded. "The Brioschi family and the Venturini family were in need of re-building. By coming together, they could flourish and in the next five to ten years, Don Venturini could be ready to take a leadership position." Giovanni held his chin high. "It would prove beneficial to everyone involved."

"Everyone?" Angel muttered beneath her breath.

"Michelangela, personal matters will not be discussed in a public setting," Giovanni growled and Angel felt anger rising in her gut.

"You had no right to force him to marry someone else!" Angel blurted, despite his warning that they were not going to discuss it now.

"I did not force him," Giovanni retorted. "I presented the offer and he chose to accept it."

Angel swallowed the lump that was trying to lodge itself into the back of her throat. His words stung her heart. Andrew chose to marry someone else for the betterment of his family name. Could she blame him? *YES!* Not only could she, but she did blame him. She blamed Giovanni for presenting the idea and she blamed Andrew for agreeing to it.

"It was business. It was not personal," Giovanni stated.

"Is there anything more personal than your business?" Angel rebutted, both of them staring at the table in front of them.

CHAPTER 54

Chase brought the Snake up to speed on the information Monahan had given them and the Snake agreed to relay the information to Andrew as soon as he returned from his date with Madeline.

"Where does Giovanni stand?" The Snake asked.

"On what?" Chase posed.

"Me. Andrew. Everything."

"I don't know, man. If I were you I'd keep my ass hidden for a while, just to be on the safe side," Chase replied. "Keep the line open and watch your back."

"Roger that," the Snake exhaled and disconnected the call.

CHAPTER 55

It's was 9:00pm sharp when Olga heard a
solid knock on the room next door. She peered out
of her peep hole to see if she could catch a glimpse
of Detta's male caller, but the vortex of the peep
hole angle didn't stretch far enough. Frustrated,
she rushed toward the wall and planted her ear
against it.

"What are you doing NOW?" Elsa clucked.
"I swear, Olga, you need to keep your big fat nose
out of other people's business for a change."

"Sshhhh!" Olga waved her hand in the air
to hush Elsa.

"Don't you shush me!" Elsa snapped.

"You either shut your trap or I'll Taser your
boney ass again!" Olga rebutted.

"Fine." Elsa pursed her lips together. "But
just so you know, when this is all over, you and I
are no longer friends."

Olga rolled her eyes and pressed her ear
harder against the wall.

"Do you have my money?" She heard Detta
ask.

Thata girl! Get right down to business, Olga
thought.

"Yes, but I need you to unencrypt the files
first," the man said.

Olga heard the sound of computer keys
clicking and clacking and she guessed that Detta
must have been pulling up information on a
computer.

"You give me the money and then, after you
have left and I arrive safely to an undisclosed
location, I will text you the codes that you need to
open the files."

The man laughed in a low, raspy tone.
"They said you were smart," he clucked. "You've

caught me in a good mood so I'll play along. You have one hour to send me the codes. If you are one minute late, your brother dies."

"My brother?" You don't even know my brother."

The man pulled up a picture on his phone and spun it around to show her, and Olga heard Detta gasp through the wall. "Where is he? What have you done to him?"

He must really have her brother, Olga thought.

"Nothing...yet," the man hissed. "And I won't have to if you prove you are loyal. You see, loyalty is everything and must be proven over and over again. It cannot be taken for granted. One cannot operate under a fake pretense of loyalty because when push comes to shove, and it always does, the disloyal will die. You are not disloyal are you, Ms. Palumbo?"

Olga pulled her ear from the wall. "I know that man," she whispered more to herself than to Elsa. "I know that low voice. I've heard that loyalty speech," she uttered beneath her breath. Olga felt her pulse quicken as a terrible realization rushed over her. Detta was in trouble, big trouble, way-over-her-head sort of trouble. This man wasn't a lover who owed her money. This man was a ruthless killer.

"Merciful Heavens!" Olga gasped and pulled herself from the wall. "We've got to do something." She rung her hands together.

"Oh, here we go again with your delusions," Elsa moaned. "You need to be medicated. You're off your rocker."

"Shut up!" Olga snapped and placed her ear back against the wall.

"How do I know you're loyal to your brother? How do I know you're loyal enough to your brother to send me the codes on time?" Olga could hear him take a deep breath and exhale loudly. "You see my dilemma, don't you?"

Detta whimpered and Olga tried not to imagine what he was going to do to her.

"You're asking me to take a risk and in my line of work, well, let's just say it's my job to eliminate risk," he clamored. "Let's just cut to the chase. You give me the codes right now and I'll kill you quickly and painlessly or I can torture you and then go kill your brother slowly."

Detta sniveled. "What are you doing? Don't come near me."

"Merciful Heavens! He's going to kill her!" Olga rushed toward her purse, retrieved her Taser and fired it up.

"Where are you going?" Elsa burst.

"I know that man next door and I know that he's gonna kill that young woman if I don't do something about it..."

"You're crazier than the half-witted, drunk, old coot I used to be married to," Elsa spat.

"I don't care what you think of me. I've got to save that woman," Olga uttered and quickly cut the tape from Elsa's ankles.

"What are you doing?" Elsa squirmed.

"I'm freeing you," Olga blurted.

"Why?" Elsa kicked her legs free. "I mean, why now?"

Olga stood up straighter and took a deep breath. "Because I might not live through the next few minutes and I don't want to leave you taped up in here where it might be days before someone finds you." Elsa's face softened. "Even though you are a cranky old bitch," Olga added and Elsa pursed her lips together and narrowed her eyes.

"Humph! Just when I was thinking about liking you again," Elsa blurted and crossed her arms.

"Seriously, now," Olga said, nearing the motel room door. "If he takes me out I need you to do me a favor. Get in contact with Michelangela Maratinzano and tell her that it was one of Giovanni's men that hit me."

"Michelangela Maratinzano?" Elsa's eyes widened. "The mafia boss? Why on earth would I contact a mob boss?"

"Because she's my niece, my Angel..." Olga swung open the motel door and waddled down to the next door, room 137. "Holy, Mary, Mother of God, protect me now as I enter the valley of the shadow of death," she said and made the sign of the cross over her body. Placing her ear against the door, she could hear Detta crying and felt anger rising inside of her. She knew what Giovanni was capable of ordering and she knew that his men would have no difficulty in following through. It was up to her to put an end to this here and now, even if it meant she would not survive or that she would be forced to spend the rest of her days in hiding. Just as Olga lifted her hand to knock on the door, it thrust open and the base of a man's palm hit her with such intensity that it drove Olga's nose upward into her forehead, thrusting her body backwards onto the pavement. The Taser fell from her grip and the man stepped over the top of her, got into a car and sped from the lot.

Hearing the commotion, Elsa opened the motel room door and peered out, astonished to see Olga lying on her back with blood running down from her nose and pooling into the crevice of her neck. "Oh, my!" Elsa shrieked. "Help!" She ran toward Olga and bent over her. "Help! Someone help!"

When the police and ambulance arrived, Elsa told them to check room 137 and explained that Olga was attempting to save a woman she thought might be in danger. Even the paramedics winced when they opened the motel room door and beheld what the mystery man had left behind. Detta's wrists were deeply sliced and she lie dead in a pool of blood.

"We're going to need a statement," the police said to Elsa, whose mind was swimming. "What were you and your friend doing at the motel?" The policeman asked, but Elsa didn't answer. "How did you know about the woman in room 137?" Elsa wasn't paying attention. She was preoccupied watching the paramedics place Olga on a gurney and lift her into the ambulance. "Ma'am, did you see what happened?"

Elsa shook her head to indicate that she hadn't.

"Is there any information you can give us that would help us track down who did this?"

Elsa stared at the Officer and then uttered softly, "no."

CHAPTER 56

Angel tucked Caleb into Sophia's bed and stayed with him until he had fallen asleep. She then crept quietly from the room and into the kitchen to make some hot tea. She was startled to find Giovanni sitting in his arm chair in the family room.

"Grandfather?" Angel called out upon entering the living room.

"Si, it is me," he answered quietly.

"Would you like some tea?" She asked, approaching him and setting her cup on the coffee table.

"No, grazie. Even decaffeinated tea will keep me up half of the night."

Angel sank into the couch across from his chair and studied his face. "What is troubling you?"

"Bah, nothing," he said, waving his hand in front of his face.

"Liar," Angel said with a smirk and this caught his attention. No one dared call the Capo di Tutti Capi a liar, or any name for that matter; no one except Angel. She raised her eyebrows as if to taunt him in a what-are-you-gonna-do-about-it manner. And this made him smile.

"Michelangela..." he said with a sigh. "Always a handful."

"I'll take that as a compliment, grandfather."

"It was meant as such." He folded his hands atop his lap and gazed at her. "You and I need to have a, how do you say it, heart to heart conversation. Cuore a Cuore," he said in Italian and touched his hand to his heart.

Angel took a sip of her tea and returned the cup to the table.

"I feel a responsibility to protect you. Since your father is not here to make the tough decisions, I feel as though the burden falls to me."

"The burden?" Angel repeated. "Did you really just call me a burden?"

"Ah, women, you take everything so literally," Giovanni said with a sigh and a shake of his head.

"Well, help me out here, how am I supposed to take that comment? If I'm not literally a burden, am I figuratively a burden? Emotionally a burden? Mentally a burden? Physically a burden?"

"At this moment you are all of the above!" Giovanni blurted, throwing his hands into the air. "You will not even allow me to explain."

Angel shook her head and leaned back on the couch, crossing her arms over her chest. "Fine. Explain."

Giovanni opened his mouth to speak just as the Penthouse door burst open and Chase raced into the room. "Angel!" He hollered, making a beeline for her bedroom. "Boss lady!"

Angel jumped to her feet. "Sshhh! You'll wake Caleb!" Angel scolded.

Chase whirled around and headed toward the family room. "There you are!" He blurted excitedly. "I traced the Fitbit."

"You did?" Angel's eyes widened.

"What is a Fitbit?" Giovanni questioned and Chase and Angel exchanged a glance, both questioning whether or not they should explain that the Fitbit was linked to Olga.

"Where is it?" Angel asked, momentarily ignoring his question.

"Northwestern Memorial," Chase replied and Angel's heart sank. "You must have left it there," Chase lied.

"What is this Fitbit?" Giovanni posed again, this time with a more forceful inflection.

"It's like a pedometer only it tracks steps, calories, sleep patterns..." Chase's voice faded as he saw Giovanni's expression.

"You have been searching for a pedometer instead of searching for Olga and Andrew and the Snake?" Giovanni's eyes darkened.

"I asked him to find it," Angel interjected. "Andrew gave it to me and it has sentimental value," she lied.

"I see," Giovanni nodded. "Instead of diamonds, he gives you a step counter. That is but one more reason he is not the man for my granddaughter," he spat and then shook his head. "On that note, I am going to bed. Michelangela, we will talk, you and I, in the morning."

Angel could see that Giovanni was disappointed that their conversation had been interrupted, but finding Olga took precedence. She told him goodnight and kissed him on the cheek. "Ti amo nonno," she whispered in his ear.

"And I love you," he uttered gruffly. Once Giovanni had left the Penthouse, she turned to Chase. "Let me get my shoes and we'll go."

On the way to the hospital Chase informed Angel that upon tracking the Fitbit to Northwestern Memorial he had called and asked if Olga had been admitted as a patient. "She's in ICU," he said. He didn't know what had happened and they wouldn't give him any more information about her condition. "I had to lie and tell them I was immediate family to even get that much info," he told Angel, whose grip on the Tank steering wheel tightened as she further depressed the gas pedal.

Before leaving the Tank both Chase and Angel checked the clips on their guns and Chase stuffed his jacket pockets with extra rounds. Angel slipped into a Kevlar vest and then pulled a black cashmere sweater over the top of it, all the while complaining that it stretched out her best sweaters.

"Andrew would be proud," Chase teased and Angel rolled her eyes.

"Shut up and put your vest on," she ordered. "We don't know what we're walking into." And that was the truth. They had no idea how or why Olga wound up in ICU. Was it natural causes or had someone put a hit out on her? If the latter, was the killer coming back to finish the job? On top of that, Angel knew that there was a hitter on her tail and on the off chance that he had been stalking her this whole time, she had to be ready for a fight. Alhough her 9mm was wedged into the back of her waistband, she retrieved a .22 pistol from a duffel bag in the back of the Tank and slid it into the front of her waistband, covering it with her sweater. Tonight having a back-up gun felt like a good idea.

They entered the hospital and immediately made their way to ICU, where Angel stopped at the front desk to speak with the nurse and Chase took a defensive stance, scanning the area for possible threats. Angel's heart sank when she was asked for identification and unable to provide proof that Olga was her aunt. "I'm sorry, but the rules are immediate family only," the nurse repeated, gesturing toward a sign on the window which indicated as much. "If you can't prove you are family, I can't let you in."

From behind her came a small, high-pitched voice and Angel whirled around to see Elsa, looking more frail than usual. Her red hair was mussed and her boney wrists had red marks and duct tape residue. "Elsa?" Angel gasped.

"I can vouch for her," Elsa told the nurse. "She is Olga's family."

The nurse eyed Elsa and Angel up and down and then shook her head. "All right, but only because of her condition," she muttered and buzzed them through the door.

Elsa walked through and Angel held open the door and turned to Chase. "Aren't you coming?"

"They won't let me in," Chase mouthed.

"Of course you can come in," Angel said loud enough for the nurse to hear. "You're my husband."

Chase's face lit up with surprise and then he stuck his chin out and strutted through the door, draping his arm around Angel's shoulder in an overly dramatized display of manliness. "Knock it off," Angel whispered as the nurse led them to Olga's room.

"What?" Chase teased. "I just wanna do you right...be the man of your dreams...the guy who rocks your world."

"Don't make me shoot you," Angel rebutted and Chase removed his arm from her shoulder.

"I see how it is," he quipped. "Wedding band goes on and you go from funky-ass frisky to freaky-ass frigid."

The teasing stopped abruptly when they turned the corner into Olga's room. In fact, it felt like time stood still. Angel had never seen Olga like this. Her knees buckled and she gripped onto Chase for support. Over half of Olga's face was bandaged and the visible skin was black and purple in color. A lump instantly lodged in Angel's throat so that when she tried to utter the words, "What happened?" only a squeak came out.

"I think you should sit down," the nurse said and motioned toward a chair in the corner. "You fainting won't do her any good."

"What's her condition and prognosis?" Chase asked, after he lowered Angel into the chair.

"She has a broken nose and contusions on the face and the back of the head. Because of the rapid swelling of the brain, we're treating her as a TBI patient, which is why she's in ICU. We've run a CT scan and an MRI and started a dose of Mannitol to try to remove some of the fluid from the brain. We're waiting for Dr. Grossman to arrive as we speak. Once he looks at her, we'll have a better idea of what we need to do to treat the cerebral edema."

"What does that mean?" Angel lifted her gaze from Olga and made eye contact with the nurse.

"It means the doctor will let us know if the Mannitol is enough or if we need to prep for surgery," she replied and then attached the clipboard onto the bed and turned toward the door.

"Will she wake up?" Angel asked and the nurse turned back around.

"Sweetie, it's better if she isn't awake. We've got her sedated to keep her calm and pain-free. You don't want her coherent through this process," the nurse explained and then left the room.

Angel moved to the side of the bed and slid her hand beneath Olga's. Her fingertips were cold and it sent a shiver up Angel's spine. Seeing Olga like this was almost more than her heart could bear. She gently squeezed her fingers. "I don't know if you can hear me, but I'm here, Olga, and you're going to be okay," Angel whispered to her. "You have to be okay because I need you." Tears dripped from Angel's chin as she bent down and kissed Olga's fingertips. "I love you."

Chase turned toward Elsa. "Are you Thelma or Louise?"

"I'm sorry?" Elsa replied, confusion etched on her face.

"Never mind," Chase said. "Inside joke."

Releasing Olga's hand, Angel turned toward Elsa. "What happened to her?" The color drained from Elsa's face and fear flashed in her eyes.

"I didn't see anything. I just found her this way," Elsa sputtered and it was obvious that she was lying. Angel motioned for Chase to close the door, which he did, and Elsa's hands immediately began to tremble. "Please," she begged. "Please don't hurt me. I swear I had nothing to do with this."

"Judging by your reaction you obviously know who I am," Angel said.

"No, I don't know anything," Elsa lied.

"Really?" Angel neared her, took her by the wrist and raised her arm into the air. "What's this?" She asked, pointing to the duct tape residue. Before Elsa could say anything, Angel continued. "It's tape residue and I'll bet you have it on your ankles too." Elsa's eyes were wide with fear. "Let me give you some advice. I'm going to ask you one more time and unless you want to end up sharing a room in ICU with my aunt, I expect the truth!" Elsa was trembling so much so that compassion tugged at Angel's heart. She didn't want to frighten the poor woman to death; but she needed the truth. "What happened to my aunt?"

When Elsa finally started speaking the floodgate opened. She recanted every detail of the experience from the moment that Olga showed up at the hair salon to the moment that she found her lying in a pool of blood outside of the motel room

door. Elsa broke into violent sobs. "If you could
have seen what he did to that poor woman in room
137." Angel grimaced at the thought. "Olga tried
to save her. All she wanted to do was save her and
I accused her of lying...no, worse, I called her
crazy," she cried.

"Do you have any idea who did this to her?"
Angel asked and Elsa peered up at her with teary,
terror-stricken eyes.

"I saw him," she muttered almost inaudibly.
"I saw him get into his car and drive away." Angel
pulled a chair over for Elsa, who sank down into it,
weeping. "I didn't tell the police because...well...if
everything Olga had said was true...if she was
mafia and he was mafia...then, what if the police
were in on it?" Elsa's bloodshot eyes sought
Angel's for understanding of her predicament. "I
didn't know if I should trust them or not?" She
wept.

"You did the right thing," Angel consoled
her. "Don't be afraid, Elsa. You did the right
thing." Angel turned to Chase. "Get a hold of the
Snake and tell him to find Andrew and get him
down here. I need his police influence on this."

"I'm on it," Chase said, retrieving his cell
phone from his jacket pocket.

"Then get Trig and Big Mike and tell them I
want Elsa escorted to the Towers and protected,"
Angel ordered and then turned to Elsa. "You'll be
safe there until we can get to the bottom of this."
Elsa nodded. "Do you have any reason to believe
that this man knows who you are or that you saw
him?"

Elsa shook her head. "No, I don't believe
so."

By the time the Snake, Andrew and
Madeline had arrived, Elsa had already been
escorted to the Towers. Angel met them in the ICU

lobby and was shocked when Andrew and Madeline exited the elevator holding hands. *Why would he bring HER along?!*

After making awkward introductions, Angel requested to speak with Andrew alone, at which time the Snake accompanied Madeline to a seat in the lobby while Andrew flashed his old detective badge at the nurse's station and he and Angel were escorted to Olga's room. He outwardly grimaced upon seeing Olga.

"I'm so sorry, Sweetheart," he uttered, and reached for her hand, but Angel moved away.

"How could you bring her here?" Angel demanded. "How could you?!"

Andrew dropped his chin to his chest and exhaled. "I didn't have a choice."

"Bullshit!" Angel barked. "There is always a choice!" Angel yelled and then quickly lowered her voice. "We don't even know if she can be trusted."

"I know that she can be trusted," Andrew remarked.

"No, Andrew, you don't even know the whole story. You're in bed with the enemy and you don't even care! What happened to you?" Angel shook her head. "Where is the man that cared about truth and justice and doing the right thing?"

"I AM doing the right thing," Andrew rebutted. "The right thing for my family. I'm walking in my father's footsteps, protecting our legacy. Isn't that what we were born to do? Isn't that what's expected of us?"

"Who ARE you?" Angel blurted. "What the hell happened to you?"

"The only thing different is that I'm no longer putting YOU first," Andrew chided. "And as far as the question of what happened... I got married tonight. THAT'S what happened." He held

266

up his left hand to display the gold wedding band on his finger and it felt like a dagger was driven right through her heart.

"Get out," Angel said softly.

"What? No congratulations?" Andrew taunted.

"Get out!" Angel yelled. "Get out of this room and get the hell out of my life!"

Andrew stared at her, as if he were shocked by her reaction. "Angel..." he began but she turned her back toward him.

"I hate you," she said quietly.

"Angel..." he began again.

"Get out," she seethed. "I never want to look at you again. You are dead to me."

Even she couldn't believe the words that had spilled from her lips. It was over. Forever.

CHAPTER 57

"Nonno?" Angel said when Giovanni answered his phone.

"Michelangela, what is wrong? It is the middle of the night," he grunted.

"I need you," she cried. "I'm at Northwestern Memorial with Olga and I need you to come here."

"You have found Lucia?" Surprise rang out in his voice. "Is she okay?"

"No. I don't know. Just come, please. We're in ICU."

"Sarà bene, nipote," he uttered. "I am on my way."

Angel didn't know exactly what he had said in Italian, but she knew he would make everything better. Somehow he would fix this. He had to. As she sank into the chair next to Olga's bed, Angel took her hand, buried her face in Olga's arm and wept.

CHAPTER 58

Andrew and Madeline were in the lobby when her cell phone buzzed. "It is probably Serco, checking on my whereabouts," she explained to Andrew. "I better take this before he sends a search party after me." Stepping away from Andrew, Madeline lifted the phone to her ear. "Si?" She answered.

"We have the drive and the codes," the man said.

"Si, that is good news," Madeline replied.

"But we were unable to get the location of Don Venturini's hideout. Our inside contact is not responding and assumed dead. We need this information. Proceeding without knowing exactly what Andrew Venturini is planning is too risky. We need to dismantle his operation tonight. Get this information from him."

"Si, I understand," Madeline uttered and disconnected the call. As she approached Andrew, she forced a smile and looped her arm into his.

"Is everything okay with Serco?" Andrew asked.

"Si. He is over-protective," she lied. "I told him I would see him in the morning."

"And he was okay with that?" Andrew questioned.

"Si. He knows I am with my new husband." She ran her finger down the side of Andrew's cheek and over his lips. "Even Serco understands the need for, how do you say, newlyweds, to be alone."

"I like the sound of that," Andrew uttered with a smile.

"I was thinking that we could go somewhere where no one will find us. Like a hideout. Is there a Venturini property that is unknown to everyone else?" She brushed her lips tenderly against his.

"No, unfortunately all of the Venturini estates are well-known properties."

Madeline pouted. "Is there no place where we can enjoy one another without interruption?"

Andrew smiled. "I have a place," he said and escorted her out of the hospital.

CHAPTER 59

It was 2:00am when Giovanni and his entourage arrived at Northwestern Memorial. Carl and four body guards escorted Giovanni to the ICU, while two other men took flanking positions near the elevator doors. Everyone coming and going would be under the watchful eye of Maratinzano Mafia security.

Angel looked up as a nurse entered Olga's room. "There are two men outside who claim they are family."

Poking her head out of the door, Angel saw Giovanni and Carl through the glass in the door. "You can let them in," she said.

As soon as they entered Olga's room, Angel rushed to Giovanni and buried herself in his arms. He held her tightly against him. "Shhhh, mi nipote, everything will be okay," he consoled, although Angel could hear a crack of concern in his voice.

"Michelangela, I am so sorry," Carl uttered quietly. "Was she in an accident?"

Angel shook her head. "She was assaulted."

"We will find the man who has done this," Carl growled.

Giovanni stepped toward Olga's bedside and took her hand. "What hell has befallen you, sister?" He planted a tender kiss on her hand. "I will not rest until this action has been avenged. You have my word," he uttered.

"Has she regained consciousness?" Carl asked.

"No," Angel replied. "They are keeping her sedated, trying to reduce swelling on her brain. We're waiting for a doctor to review her tests and tell us whether they need to do surgery to relieve the pressure."

"Did anyone see what happened?" Carl questioned.

"Yes," Angel answered excitedly. "We actually have someone who can identify the man." Giovanni's face lit up and Carl took a step closer.

"Who?" Carl asked.

"Olga's friend who was with her at the time."

"Was she wounded as well?" Giovanni asked. "Is she here?"

Angel shook her head. "No, she found Olga and the other woman after the attack."

"Another woman was attacked?" Giovanni repeated.

"Detta Palumbo," Angel said and Giovanni's eyebrows lifted higher on his head. It was obvious that he had made the connection. "Where is Detta now?"

"Dead," Angel replied. "She was staying in the same motel where Olga was hiding out. Olga tried to save her from the man she was meeting, but she didn't get there in time." Angel wrapped her arm in Giovanni's and leaned her head on his shoulder. "Elsa said Olga told her that she knew the man and that if something happened to her, she was to contact me."

"So, we are to assume that Olga knew her life was in danger," Giovanni uttered.

"Yes," Angel said.

"And that she knows her assailant by name," Giovanni added.

"Probably," Angel answered.

"Does her friend, Elsa, know the assailant by name?" Carl asked.

Angel shook her head. "No. She only knows what he looks like."

"Where is Elsa now?" Giovanni asked.

"I sent her to the Towers with Trig and Big Mike. I thought she would be safer there," Angel explained.

"Very good," Giovanni uttered. "We will speak with her upon our return."

"Giovanni, perhaps I should return to the Towers and handle things there while you and Angel stay here with Lucia," Carl interjected. "There is nothing I can do to assist you here."

"Si, si." Giovanni nodded. "Grazi, friend."

Before Carl left he promised to check in with Giovanni and Angel in the morning to see how Olga was doing and to send them a change of clothing and breakfast. "I will continue my search for Andrew," he said to Giovanni.

"Don't bother," Angel blurted.

"Why not?" Carl responded. "If he is somehow behind the conspiracy against His Eminence, we must do what we can to stop him."

"He's not behind the plot against the Pope," Angel spat. "Besides, he and Madeline Brioschi got married tonight."

"Tonight?" Giovanni gasped. "They were not scheduled to be wed until Tuesday morning."

"Well, I guess they were so smitten with each other that they just couldn't wait that long," Angel spewed.

"How did you come by this information?" Giovanni questioned.

"Andrew was here, showing off his shiny wedding band." Tears welled in her eyes but Angel fought them away. She refused to allow herself to cry over him. "He even had the audacity to bring Madeline here with him."

Carl left and Angel and Giovanni spent the next hour watching over Olga and waiting for Dr. Grossman to arrive.

CHAPTER 60

Chase had flown back from the hospital with Trig, Elsa, Big Mike and the Snake. They escorted Elsa to the Penthouse to wait for Angel and then met in the secret meeting room, where Chase was reviewing the schematic designs for the Pope's arrival into the city. Now that he and Sal were on the same team, he felt confident that they could stop the assassination attempt.

"Things are falling apart," Big Mike shrugged. "Olga's fighting for her life. Andrew married that Diaglio chick. Angel's devastated. The Pope's about to get whacked and we can't do anything about it."

"Andrew married her already?" Chase blurted. "Holy shit! Why would he do a stupid-ass thing like that?"

"I'd have married her," Trig interjected. "Have you seen that woman? Damn!"

"She's smokin'-ass hot, but I didn't think he was really going to marry her," Chase rebutted.

"None of us did," Big Mike added.

"I did," the Snake said. "I knew he'd marry her." They all gawked at him. "He's trying to gain her trust and get information. He had to marry her."

"I'm pretty sure Angel's not going to see it that way," Chase rebutted.

"How Angel does or doesn't see it is irrelevant to the bigger picture," the Snake said. "It's not about her right now, it's about saving the Pope. That's all Andrew is focused on."

Chase shook his head. "I get it, man, but, uh, that don't make it any wild-ass easier to swallow."

The Snake slid his cell phone across the table toward Chase. "Can you upload these pics for me?"

Chase connected the phone and began retrieving the data. "What are we looking at?"

"Photos I took of Nicholas Diaglio after Angel shot him at the school and photos of the bomb placed in Tony's car," the Snake answered.

Chase pulled up the pictures one-by-one, analyzing his clothing, shoes and weapon. "I don't even know what we're looking for," Chase moaned.

"Anything," the Snake muttered. "Everything."

Chase advanced to the next photo, which was a close-up of Nicholas Diaglio lying dead. He zoomed in and immediately noticed a small tattoo on the side of his neck. It was difficult to make-out through all of the blood, but it looked like a capitol D with a cross in the center.

"What does that mark mean?" The Snake asked.

"Could be a Diaglio family crest," Chase said.

"It ain't a local gang symbol, I can tell you that," Trig added.

The Snake leapt to his feet, grabbed his cell from the table and dialed Angel. When she confirmed that the tattoo she had seen on the hitter's wrist was a capitol D with a cross in the center, the Snake dialed Sal and requested a worldwide search. He then dialed Monahan, uploaded him a picture of the tattoo and asked him to check with his contacts overseas. "It has to mean something," the Snake blurted.

CHAPTER 61

Angel was carrying two cups of coffee back to the ICU when her cell phone vibrated in her pocket. Setting down the coffee in the lobby, she retrieved her phone and noticed there was no caller ID associated with the number. She answered tentatively, surprised to hear a familiar voice on the other end.

"Ms. Maratinzano, it's Taelon. Do you remember me?" Taelon sounded nervous.

"Of course I remember you. How's the neck?" Angel asked.

"It's okay," he said. "Can we meet?"

Angel was surprised by the question.

"Um... I'm wrapped up in something right now," Angel stalled. "What is this regarding?"

"Turn around," Taelon said and Angel spun around to see him standing near the elevator next to Giovanni's body guards. He disconnected the call and took two steps toward her. "No, it can't wait," he said face-to-face.

"Mr. Maratinzano, you want us to get rid of him?" One of the body guards asked, stepping forward and taking Taelon by the arm.

Angel lowered her phone from her ear and exhaled. "No, he's okay," she told the guard, who released Taelon's arm and stepped back to his position in front of the elevator doors. "What are doing here?" She asked him.

"I need to talk to you, privately." He motioned her toward a row of chairs against the far wall. "I could have contacted your people, but I don't know that they would have taken my call. The way I see it, you owe me," he explained, rubbing his hand over his bandaged neck.

Angel rolled her eyes. "I've apologized for the neck. Okay, you have five minutes."

Taelon lifted his phone and swiped open a program she didn't recognize. "I've been running my own decoding program on the information we retrieved from the jump drive."

"Okaaay," Angel mumbled. "Sal and Chase are already deco..."

"I know," he interrupted. "They don't have this program."

"How do you know?"

"Because I wrote this program. I created it," he replied and leaned closer so he could hold the phone where both of them could see what was on the screen. "The files we pulled from the drive are multi-dimensional images, each one layered on top of another and encoded."

"We already know that," Angel said.

"The program Sal and Chase are using decodes each layer separately, but it can't decode the whole. It can't look dimensionally into the image as a whole." Taelon's eyes searched Angel's face for a glimmer of understanding.

"So, we're not seeing the whole picture?" She asked.

"Look," he said and swiped his finger across the screen, revealing an image of the schematic design that Angel had not seen before. "See the numbers right there in the center of the design?" Angel nodded. "I believe that's a date and time reference."

Angel took the phone from his hand and looked closer. "Right. It references Tuesday morning. We already know that the Pope is arriving Tuesday."

Taelon shook his head. "I think it's time stamped in Italian."

"It doesn't matter whether it's in English or Itali..." Angel stopped as the relevance of what he said sank into her brain. The language wasn't in

Italian, the time was. Italy was seven hours ahead of Chicago.

"Do you have any other evidence to support this hunch?" Angel asked, trying not to appear skeptical but having a hard time believing that this young man could stumble upon information both Sal and Chase would have missed.

Taelon shook his head and stood up. "I thought you were different." He started to walk away and then turned around. "Ms. Maratinzano, if I'm wrong there's no harm done, but if I'm right then the Pope dies in a few hours and the Diaglio family wins." Angel stared blankly. "I told Don Venturini but he insisted I tell you."

Taelon threw up his hands and started to walk away when Angel leapt up. "Wait a minute! Andrew sent you to me with this information?" Her jaw tightened as a well of mixed emotion sprung up inside of her.

"Yeah, but ..."

"Stay here," Angel ordered and dialed Chase. She told Chase about her conversation with Taelon and could hear the skepticism in his tone. "I think you should at least take a look at it," Angel said and then handed the phone to Taelon. "He wants to talk to you."

Taking the phone from Angel, Taelon began to explain his findings to Chase, while Angel carried the coffee to Giovanni and informed him of what was going on. When she returned, Taelon was sitting in the lobby waiting for her. "Some guy named Trig is going to pick me up in the chopper," he told Angel.

Just then, Giovanni stuck his head into the lobby. "Michelangela, the doctor said they are going to prep Lucia for surgery. A decompressive craniotomy."

"Okay, I'll be right there," Angel said.

Stepping into the lobby, Giovanni took a deep breath. "Go to Chase and do what you can do to stop the threat against His Eminence. I will tend to matters here."

"I'm not leaving you..." Angel began but Giovanni cut her sentence short.

"That is not a request, Michelangela," he spoke sharply. "There is a bigger picture and your aunt would want you to go."

Angel hugged him and made him promise to call her the moment Olga was out of surgery.

As they flew over the city, Angel couldn't help but wonder why Andrew sent Taelon to her. She couldn't escape the feeling that there was a specific reason and that the timing of everything, including him moving up his nuptials, was somehow relevant. She just couldn't fit the pieces together and she hoped Chase and Sal would be able to help.

Once inside the secret meeting room, Chase uploaded the program from Taelon's phone and then forwarded the file to Sal. "I've never seen anything like this," he told Taelon. "How long have you been programming?"

Taelon shrugged. "As long as I can remember. I used to create my own games when I was a kid."

Chase's fingers worked their magic across the keys and Angel paced back and forth in front of the windows, waiting for his feedback and waiting to hear from Giovanni as to Olga's condition. The sun was beginning to rise and the secret meeting room was beginning to fill with men who had been called in for the mission of protecting the Pope. Trig, Monahan, the Snake, Big Mike, Chito, Leo the Lion, Chase and Taelon gathered around the table. Tony, who had been released from the hospital earlier and diagnosed with a concussion, text Angel that he was in route to the Towers; and Harry was on his way from the Venturini hide out.

When everyone arrived, Angel gave Chase a nod to proceed and he began to explain the new information Taelon's program had uncovered.

"We believe this new evidence confirms that the attack against the Pope will commence today, not Tuesday morning," Chase explained, placing the diagram on the big screen. "What we're looking at here is the entry route. The Pope will come down Chicago Avenue to State Street and stop at the Holy Name Cathedral on the corner of State and Superior."

"What are the red dots?" Trig asked.

"We think they mark the locations of the Pope's security team," Chase answered.

"They mark the position of the police officers hired to secure the Pope's route," Andrew said upon entering the room with three men on his heels. Angel immediately recognized two of the men from the hospital and Leo went over to greet them.

"I've taken great personal risk coming here but I believe the only way to stop this attack is to pool our resources, share what we know and work together," Andrew explained. "Despite what Giovanni may have told some of you about me, I am not conspiring to assassinate His Eminence. On that note, I'd like to introduce you to three of my most trusted colleagues. Jacob Denalli, Lenny Getgher, and Pete Bellasco."

The room grew quiet.

"Before my internal Chicago PD contact was abruptly cut off, we learned that twelve officers had been commissioned as extra-security for the Pope during his travel to the Holy Name Cathedral. Each officer received twenty-five thousand dollars deposited directly into their bank accounts. Our guy was killed before we were able to pinpoint from where the money came." Andrew glared at Tony.

"If you're referring to Lisben, I'm not sorry," Tony chided. "He was a traitor and an arrogant asshole, not to mention the fact that he put a hit out on Angel and that hitter is still at large."

Andrew appeared genuinely surprised by this news. "Where did you get this information?"

"I over-heard Lisben talking to the hitter at your hide out just before Tony killed him," Angel blurted.

"And just before my car mysteriously blew up," Tony added and it was obvious by his expression that Andrew knew nothing about what had happened. "This is all news to you, Ace? Where the hell have you been?"

"Getting married," Angel sneered. "He was getting married."

You could have heard a pin drop in the room for several seconds and the tension between Angel and Andrew was no secret to anyone.

Finally, Chase broke the ice, directing the conversation back to business. "Andrew, do you know who the commissioned officers are? Have they been commissioned to protect the Pope or help in the attack?"

"If I may speak to that," Pete interjected. "Sal has run background checks on each one and we have been conducting surveillance the past several days. None of these men give me any reason to believe they pose a threat to His Eminence."

"So, if the cops aren't being paid off to help with the attack, who is?" Chase questioned.

Pete asked to borrow one of Chase's laptops and, sitting down next to him, began pulling up financial records from the Vatican bank. "The twelve transactions of twenty-five thousand each are traceable back to the Vatican bank, which at first look confirms that the Pope has paid a pretty penny to beef up his security here." Chase glanced over his shoulder as Pete continued. "However, when we dig deeper, we find that the transactions originated at the New York Bank & Trust, were sent to the Vatican Bank and were then distributed to the twelve officers."

"If the money originated here in the States, why send it to the Vatican just to send it back to the States?" Chase asked.

Pete shrugged. "Someone wants it to appear that the money was paid by the Vatican, when it really wasn't." Pete took a deep breath. "That's odd enough, but this latest transaction is the one that doesn't set well with me," Pete said, pointing to the screen. "The transfer was made yesterday."

"Two million dollars paid from the Vatican Bank to the New York Bank & Trust," Chase read aloud. "That's a big-ass wad of dough."

"Yeah, with no traceable connection to property, loans or charity," Pete uttered, shaking his head. He went on to explain that he and Sal had run the account through their database and come up empty handed. "It has to belong to someone, but I'll be damned if I can find out who," Pete said.

Taelon neared the computer and hunching over Pete's shoulder, he squinted at the screen. "I have an idea," Taelon said quietly. "This program is only pulling from the public parameters of what's on the banking site, so you're not seeing the multi-leveled customer tracking information that links the worldwide databases and transactions together."

Pete gave Chase a dumbfounded look and then slid out of the chair. "Go for it," he said to Taelon.

"It'll take some time to write the program, but I can find out where the two million dollars went," Taelon said.

Gnawing on her fingernail, Angel stared out the window overlooking the city. She was worried about Olga, worried they couldn't stop the attack on the Pope, and just plain worried. When Andrew crept up behind her and placed his hand on her shoulder, Angel pulled away.

"I can't stick around what with Giovanni and Carl after my head," he said.

"Nobody's asking you to stick around," Angel rebutted and crossed her arms.

"I know you don't understand and I'm sorry," Andrew whispered quietly and before she could turn around, not that she was going to, he was gone.

CHAPTER 62

Leaving all of the men in the secret meeting room, Angel went to the Penthouse to check on Caleb. As the elevator door opened and she stepped out, she saw the stairwell door closing. Angel rushed toward the door but by the time she got there and thrust it open, there was no one in the stairwell. An uneasiness swept over her. "Caleb?" She called down the stairwell. "Is that you?"

Her first thought was that Caleb had awoken and came searching for her. Her second thought was that someone had sneaked into the Penthouse. Pulling her 9mm from her waistband, Angel approached the Penthouse door. Upon entering she was relieved to find Caleb sound asleep on the couch and the television blaring cartoon network. She turned off the T.V. and then stood for a moment just gazing at him. He looked so peaceful curled into a little ball. She placed a throw pillow beneath his head and then gazed around the room for a blanket. Remembering the old quilt that was kept at the foot of Olga's bed, Angel walked down the hallway to retrieve it. A sense of sadness swept over her as she passed Sophia's bedroom door. She missed her mother and with everything going on, she wished more than ever that she was there with her. Elsa had stayed the night in Olga's room and Angel tapped lightly on her door. When she didn't answer, Angel quietly slipped inside and retrieved the quilt, which had fallen from the edge of the bed to the floor. She sneaked out of the room but as she turned to quietly close the door, she stopped dead in her tracks. Angel's heart rate quickened, she dropped the quilt and rushed back toward the bed. Grabbing Elsa's wrist, she felt for a pulse, but there was nothing. Elsa's skin was a gaunt shade of green and gray and her eyes were wide open. *NO! No, no, no, no!*

Upon getting her call, the Snake grabbed Pete and hurried to the Penthouse, where they analyzed Elsa's body. "It was probably a heart attack," Pete surmised.

"Sshh," Angel reprimanded. "I don't want to wake Caleb. The last thing he needs is to wake up and find a dead body in the house."

"We can move her down to the lobby and have the paramedics pick her up there," Pete whispered. "That way the boy never has to know."

Pete took one side of the bed and the Snake took the other. They took hold of the sheets from beneath Elsa, pulled them taut and began to lift her from the bed. "Hold up!" The Snake blurted. "Lay her back down."

They did and the Snake reached behind Elsa's head and retrieved a tiny clear cap, the kind that fits on the tip of a syringe. He had seen it roll behind her when they had lifted her.

"What is it?" Angel asked.

The Snake tossed it to Pete. "Did Elsa have any reason to self-medicate?" The Snake asked but Angel didn't know. He lifted her shirt and analyzed the skin on her belly; and then he and Pete rolled her over and analyzed the skin on her buttocks. They searched her wrists, her shoulders and her fingertips.

"What are you looking for?" Angel questioned.

"If Elsa gave herself regular injections, for say diabetes or something of that nature, we would be able to see it," the Snake explained. "And she'd have given herself a shot probably in her stomach, which is the easiest place, maybe an upper arm, for someone very skilled..." his voice tapered off as he turned Elsa's head to the side and noticed the mark in her neck. He shot Pete a glance and Pete moved to the other side of the bed to get a closer look.

"We've got a homicide," Pete uttered.

"What?!" Angel exclaimed. "Someone murdered her? Here? While the door was guarded and Caleb was sleeping down the hall?" All of sudden the most horrifying thought occurred to Angel and she darted from the room, down the hall and into the family room where Caleb lie still on the sofa. "No, no, no, no," she muttered as she hit her knees, slid her arms beneath Caleb and lifted him against her. His body was limp, like a rag doll. Angel rocked him against her. "NO!" She screamed and the Snake raced into the room.

"Lay him down!" The Snake ordered but Angel wasn't listening. She was lost in terror and emotion and rage. "Lay him down, Angel!" The Snake yelled and snatched Caleb from her arms. Pushing his fingers against the boy's neck, the Snake exhaled loudly and then turned Caleb's neck side to side. "He's alive, but he's been sedated," the Snake said and pointed to a tiny mark on Caleb's neck. Angel couldn't stop her body from trembling. Tears poured from her eyes, her hands shook and she felt as if she might vomit. Pulling him into her arms, Angel kissed his head over and over and rocked him.

"You're alive," she whispered. "You're alive."

CHAPTER 63

Upon learning that Olga had weathered the surgery well and the pressure and fluid on her brain was decreasing, Angel could now focus on finding Elsa's killer. She brought in a doctor to examine Caleb and he confirmed that the dose of Seroquel Caleb had been given would not cause permanent damage. This was good news, though it did not minimize the rage she felt toward whoever had done it. They had no way of knowing how Caleb's body would react to the drug and could have ended up killing him, just as they had killed Elsa.

The Towers were on lock down and every man was being questioned. Angel was determined to find Elsa's killer and she was convinced that whoever killed her was the same man who assaulted Olga. It stood to reason that he killed her because he must have known that Elsa could identify him.

Chase called a closed door meeting with Angel, Taelon and the Snake to discuss what Taelon's new program had uncovered. With Caleb being heavily guarded by Leo and Big Mike, Angel joined the three men in the secret meeting room. "We've got a problem," Chase blurted the moment she walked in.

"Several problems at last count," Angel chided sarcastically. "To which one are you referring?"

"Andrew," he said and the smile left Angel's face.

Chase gave Taelon a go-ahead nod and Taelon sent the image on his computer to the big screen in the front of the room. He then stood up and took a deep breath as he approached the image. "What we're looking at are hundreds of thousands of transactions between the Vatican Bank and the New York Bank & Trust," he began. "As we narrow the parameters to a two million dollar transaction date stamped yesterday, we have just one trail." He clicked some keys to isolate the transaction and all of the other data fell away. "The transaction has been encoded seven times along its journey. It started in a Brioschi account in Italy, was moved to an account at the Vatican Bank then leapt across the pond to the New York Bank & Trust where it was split into four, $500,000 chunks and dispersed."

Chase piped in and explained that one chunk was sent back to the Vatican bank, another deposited in a Venturini account here in Chicago, a third deposited into Nicholas Diaglio's account in Chicago and the fourth into the Maratinzano account in New York.

"What?" Angel gasped. "Why would someone pay Giovanni $500,000?"

"To look the other way?" The Snake shrugged.

"To set up a hit," Chase added.

"To arrange a marriage," Taelon posed.

"The other good question is why would someone pay Andrew $500,000?" Chase asked and Angel's heart sank. She couldn't refute the fact that the lump sum of money made him look guilty, but something else was heavy on her mind; something she hadn't told anyone. The night Andrew kidnapped her from the pub, he had drugged her with Seroquel, the same drug found in Caleb's system. Was it possible that Andrew was the one who killed Elsa? After all, he was in the Towers. He had access to the Penthouse. And he whispered "I'm sorry" before he left. Angel assumed that he was apologizing for running off and eloping, but what if his apology was preemptive? What if he was apologizing in advance for killing Elsa? Angel tried to shake the thought from her mind, but it kept creeping back in. The most horrifying thought was that if he did kill Elsa, it meant he was also the one who had assaulted Olga; and as angry as she was at him, she couldn't bring herself to believe he had become a monster.

"Chase, have you been able to pull up the surveillance feed from the stairway around the time of Elsa's murder?" Angel asked.

Chase shook his head and she could see frustration on his face. "Somebody tampered with it. I've run through the whole damn feed, twice! It shows no one entering and no one exiting."

"Who would have the capability of tampering with our internal security system?" Angel asked.

"I thought I was the only all-powerful one," Chase snipped. "But Sal got into our system before, so obviously there are others as freaky-ass brilliant as me." He grinned.

If Sal had tampered with the system before, was it possible that Andrew had asked him to do it again so he could slip into the Penthouse unseen and murder Elsa? Angel tried to shake the thought from her head, but it kept coming back.

"Don't worry, Ms. Maratinzano, we're re-encoding all of the security uplinks so nobody will be able to hijack the system again," Taelon added.

Angel nodded but her heart sank. They were no closer to finding Elsa's killer and Andrew was beginning to look more and more guilty.

CHAPTER 64

"Are you alone?" He asked when Madeline answered her cell.

"Si, for now, but he will be back soon."

"The foundation is laid. The money is in the accounts."

"And the eye witness?"

"Dead. There are no more loose ends," he said. "Everything is back on schedule. Everyone is searching for shooters and studying entry routes. By the time they figure anything out, it will be too late."

"Excellent," Madeline remarked.

"Now, you need to do your part," he said.

"Si," she answered softly. "I will have him there, right where he needs to be."

CHAPTER 65

Time was running out. If the schematics were indicative of a date and time stamp in Italian time, then the Pope would be heading down State Street in less than two hours. Angel's stomach was churning because something still didn't feel right. Everything was pointing to Giovanni and Andrew as the people involved in plotting or, at the very least, ignoring an assassination attempt on the Pope, which was out of character for both men. She kept mulling over the details in her head. The money. The marriage. The timing. The money. The marriage. The timing.

Her men were loading into SUV's and heading out to their assigned positions when Angel thought to call Giovanni and check on Olga one more time. When he answered she was happy to learn that Olga was continuing to progress and that the doctors were hopeful that she would regain consciousness within the next several hours. "Carl and I will take good care of her," he assured Angel and then reminded her to keep him informed of any new information that they gathered.

Angel hadn't told him that they believed the assassination attempt was going to happen a day sooner. It was better that he didn't know, so he could focus on Olga and not worry about anything else.

As the SUV's pulled away Angel returned to the secret meeting room to follow along on video surveillance. Tony, Pete and the Snake were heading up three factions of four men each and were fitted with two-way earbuds, a microphone and a camera unit. While Chase monitored their progress, Angel stared at the schematic designs on the laptop. She was looking at the multi-dimensional image from Taelon's program and noted that it was so detailed that it felt as if she could spiral down right into the middle of the image. "Chase?"

"Yeah, Boss Lady?" He replied, twirling a pencil between his fingers.

"What would happen if we projected this image outwardly?" She turned toward him and swore she could actually see the wheels spinning in his brain.

"That's a wild-ass idea," he quipped excitedly. "It would be like making the dimensions one step deeper, like bringing the picture to life around us."

Angel shrugged. That was what she had envisioned but didn't know if it was technologically viable.

Moments later, Chase had hooked up a projection unit and activated the external display. "I've never done this with a multi-dimensional image, but let's see what happens."

The image didn't just project onto the wall, it filled the floor and the ceiling as well. It was as if it were designed to be projected and fill an entire space. "Holy, Mary, Mother of..." Chase stopped abruptly when Angel called out his name.

"Chase," she gasped. "The red dots are no longer dots. They look like bunches of numbers, sort of mashed together..."

"Coordinates?" Chase muttered aloud but more to himself than to her. He studied the numbers, his eyes darting from sequence to sequence. Finally, he yelped, "They're triggers! They're timed triggers!" He fumbled with the small microphone on his laptop. "Keep our men back!" Chase yelled into the microphone.

"No need to yell," the Snake retorted, obviously annoyed by Chase's voice that had boomed through his ear piece.

"Sorry. The red dots are timed triggers, leading to an explosion. I think."

"You think?" Pete quipped. "You wanna take a moment and figure out if there's a bomb or you want us to just walk around until one of us blows up?"

"We're trying to decipher this shit as fast as we can," Chase rebutted.

"Roger, that, we're holding position on the exterior of the Pope's route," the Snake confirmed and Angel saw Chase breathe a sigh of relief.

"Hold that position until you hear from me," Chase added.

"Lower your volume, Ace," Tony interjected through his ear piece. "You almost made me shoot myself in the foot."

He then dialed Taelon. "Get your ass up here, bro," Chase squawked into the phone. "You gotta see this!"

Moments later Taelon stood next to Chase and Angel in the center of the multi-dimensional image.

"What are we looking for boys?" Angel asked.

"First of all, the twelve triggers have to lead to something. My guess is that there will be an explosive device located near the end of the route," Chase explained. "Look for something that denotes a specific location."

They searched the entire diagram and were unable to find any other red markings to indicate a pending explosion.

Angel paced in front of the windows, replaying all of the information in her mind. Nicholas Diaglio, Madeline Diaglio-Brioschi's

brother, hired Detta Palumbo to hack into the
Vatican system, gain information and create the
multi-dimensional image they were looking at right
now; all for the purpose of assassinating the Pope,
whom the Diaglio's hated for his anti-mafia stance.
The Brioschi Boss was recently murdered, leaving
Madeline the sole heir of the Brioschi fortune.
Now, Madeline has money but no respected family
presence. Giovanni arranged for her to marry
Andrew, promising him the next Capo position,
which would give the Brioschi-Venturini name bi-
continental power. These felt like disjointed facts
with a missing piece that would hold them all
together.

One question kept returning to Angel's
mind. Why would Madeline want to join her family
with the Venturini's? Andrew himself had said
that the family had grown weak and many
members left after his father's death. What did the
Venturini name offer a woman like Madeline?
There had to be more to the story.

Angel turned on a dime. "Can you pull up
a copy of the marriage certificate between Andrew
and Madeline?"

Chase scrunched up his face as if to
indicate that it was an odd request, but he didn't
object. His fingers flew across the keys until he
had found the records of the county clerk, and
retrieved the license. Angel read it aloud. "Andrew
Venturini and Madeline Diaglio." She looked at
Chase. "She used her maiden name. She didn't
use the Brioschi name."

"So?" Chase shrugged.

"So their union isn't about building the
Venturini family or saving the Brioschi name. It's
about empowering the Diaglios."

"I thought they were already one of the
most powerful families in Italy," Chase said.

"Remember what Monahan told us? The Diaglios are the biggest family but the Brioschis are the richest." Angel gnawed on her fingernail as she tried to put the pieces together. "Kill the Pope on American soil, put the blame on the mob here and let the cards fall," Angel muttered beneath her breath.

"Say what?" Chase clucked.

"I was just thinking aloud," Angel replied as she returned to the table and sat down next to Chase. "Kill the Pope on American soil and let the mob here take the blame," she repeated. "That's the plan, right?"

"As far as we know," Chase answered.

"Who wins?" Angel posed.

"Depends," Taelon piped in. "Depends on the motive." Taelon sat down on the other side of Chase. "If you want the Pope dead, then you're siding with the Diaglios and if he dies, you win. On the other hand, if your motive is to take down the American mafia, or take over control of the mob here in the States, you have to go a lot further to win. You have to bring the Pope to Chicago, kill him on foreign soil and frame someone in particular to take the blame. Then, when they fall you have to be ready to rise."

Angel and Chase exchanged glances and then looked back at Taelon. "What if we're dealing with both of those scenarios?" Chase posed. "What if it wasn't the Diaglios who set this plan in motion at all? What if someone from here, knowing how upset the Diaglios were with the new Pope, used them to arrange this whole thing?"

Angel shook her head. "How? It would take someone with very powerful connections to pull something like this off."

Just then, the pieces began falling into place and Angel felt her pulse quicken.

"Oh...my...." her voice faded before she could finish the sentence.

"I've seen that look before, Boss Lady. What is going on in that crazy-ass skull of yours?" Chase quipped.

"The CoBroGas attack," she uttered in monotone. "They tried to take us all out with the CoBroGas attack and they failed." She stood up slowly. "It was revenge, or it was supposed to be, but when it backfired they had to come up with something better."

"I'm not tracking with you," Chase muttered.

Angel whirled around to face Chase. "We never found out who was behind the CoBroGas attack. Remember? All we found was a monetary trail from the New York Bank & Trust to an account we later assumed was one of Stidda's."

"And..." Chase taunted.

"What if the same person who tried to take our families out in the gas attack is trying again now?" Chase gave her a skeptical glare. "Don't you think it's coincidental that the money transfers in both situations are going through the same New York bank?"

"Angel, hundreds of thousands of people use that bank," Chase rebutted.

She knew it was a long-shot and she knew Chase was right to play devil's advocate, but it was irritating nonetheless. She grunted in frustration and went back to pacing. Moments later she blurted, "Why would Giovanni arrange a marriage between Andrew and Madeline?"

Chase shrugged. "Because everyone knows he didn't want you to marry Andrew, so he married him off to someone else."

Angel shook her head. That was true but not the answer she was looking for. "I don't think

he arranged it. Someone else did. That's why
Giovanni was utterly shocked when we told him
that Madeline Brioschi's maiden name was
Diaglio," she explained. "Giovanni would never
have done business with a family like the Diaglios."

"So, who did?" Taelon asked. "Who
arranged it?"

Angel shook her head and exhaled. "I don't
know."

Chase got out of his seat and took Angel by
the shoulders. "Listen, Boss Lady, I know Andrew
hurt you and I'd like to cold-cock the son-of-a-
bitch upside the head, but you have to let this go."
His eyes were filled with compassion as he gazed at
her. "I'll tell you what," he said, moving back to
his chair and sticking a pencil behind his ear. "I'll
run a search on Madeline's cell phone and see if
she's been in contact with anyone we know. I
doubt we're gonna find any wild-ass connections,
but it won't hurt to have a look." His fingers
danced across the keys and Angel felt hopeful that
he would find a tidbit of evidence to point them in
the right direction.

CHAPTER 66

"Are you ready to go?" Madeline entered the bedroom where Andrew was seated on the end of the bed.

"Yes," he answered, sliding a .45 into his chest holster.

"Darling, you shouldn't take a gun when you are going to meet a man of peace." Madeline said.

"There are people in this world who, no matter how blessed they are, cannot embrace peace and fight to destroy it at every turn," Andrew uttered, standing and sliding his arms into his charcoal, gray sport coat; and then pulling it over his shoulders.

"And you are going to stop all of the bad people in the world," she said and then smiled and kissed him on the cheek. "You will be my hero, Andrew Venturini."

"Will I?" He eyed her.

"You already are, my love," she said without missing a beat. "That is why I couldn't wait a moment longer to become your wife." She nuzzled her face into the nape of his neck and planted a kiss on his skin. "Let's come back here and make-love all night long."

From the doorway, Serco cleared his throat. "The car is ready," he informed them. "You don't want to keep His Eminence waiting."

"How is it again that you were able to schedule a private meeting with Pope Ignacio on such short notice?" Andrew questioned.

"Our fathers knew one another well," Serco said in a tone laced with pride. "Ignacio and I practically grew up as brothers. When he heard that I was in the city, he almost demanded we meet," he explained as they walked toward the front door.

"Are you uneasy about meeting him? Serco asked. "Because, though he is the Pope, he is just a man like you and me, putting on his trousers one leg at a time."

"No, I'm not uneasy," Andrew replied. "A little nervous, maybe," he admitted. After all, it's the Pope. "When you mentioned we were getting a private audience with him, I just assumed it would be after his speech tomorrow."

"Si," Serco nodded. "When he found out that Madeline had married an ex-Special Detective on the Chicago police force, he insisted I bring you to him at once," he explained. "Your reputation precedes you and I have a hunch he might want your advice on addressing the crowd tomorrow."

"From how many people does His Eminence seek advice?" Madeline gleamed. "I am so proud of you, my husband."

Serco got into the front seat with the limo driver and Andrew slid into the back next to Madeline. The uneasiness he had felt for days lay heavily upon his shoulders. He didn't trust Madeline though try as he may, and he had tried, he could find no evidence against her. She was linked to no murders, no money laundering, no tax evasion, no drug smuggling, nothing at all. She was squeaky clean and it looked as if her only flaw was being born into a family as ruthless as the Diaglios. Faulting her for that would be like faulting Angel for being the granddaughter to Giovanni and Salvatore. It didn't make sense. The truth was that from the moment he met Madeline, she had treated him with nothing but respect, kindness and affection. He didn't love her but arranged marriages were not built upon love, and who was to say that he could not grow to love her in time? He was given an offer he felt he could not refuse for the sake of his family and it was his obligation to uphold his word. There was no going back and Andrew understood that breaking one's word to the Capo di Tutti Capi was breaking ones very own neck. If, or until, he had proof that his bride was linked to the alleged assassination attempt on the Pope, he had to play the role of doting newlywed. Besides, perhaps meeting with His Eminence would allow Andrew the opportunity to subtly warn him about the rumored threats, or suggest extra precautions. Placing Madeline's hand in his, he gave her fingers a tender squeeze. "I'm excited," he admitted. "I've never met the Pope."

"My love, I think he will be blown away by you," Madeline leaned close and uttered, while brushing her lips softly against his. "Completely blown away."

CHAPTER 67

Tony, the Snake and Pete all had the schematic designs uploaded to their phones, showing the twelve red dots along the Pope's entrance route. Pete and his men were assigned to the first four dots, the Snake and his men were assigned to the next four dots and Tony and his men to the last four dots.

"Chase, man, we're in position here," Tony said through the mic and earpiece.

"Us, too," Pete added and the Snake followed suit.

"Roger, that," Chase answered. "Scan your areas for anything that looks out of the ordinary. These triggers can be small. Attached to trash cans, street signs, lights..."

"We're basically looking for a needle in a haystack?" Tony groaned.

"Yeah, basically," Chase retorted. "Don't make your presence obvious. We don't know who is watching. Let me know if you find anything."

Taelon had been quietly tapping away at the keyboard and startled both Chase and Angel when he leapt to his feet and yelled, "Viola!" A projected image filled the room again, but this time it looked to be all numbers.

"What is it?" Angel asked.

"I wanted to see if the triggers were numerically encoded, and guess what? They are," Taelon said excitedly.

"Holy shit!" Chase barked.

"I know, right?" Taelon agreed. "Pretty cool."

"No, man, not cool," Chase rebutted, his eyes widening. "If the triggers are encoded with a numerical sequence, that means they are set to automatically advance when their particular code

301

comes into range, which means the final explosive trigger is automatically set to blow. Even if we could find it in time, the chances of us being able to deactivate it are crazy-ass slim...as in not a frickin' chance in hell!" Chase blurted. He quickly video conferenced Sal and showed him what they were looking at; hoping Sal, with his years of FBI training and experience, would know what to do.

"Pull your men out," Sal muttered.

"That's it?" Taelon interjected. "That's all you've got?"

"Pull your men out or they're dead where they stand," Sal repeated. "I've seen similar technology and our best men were useless to deactivate it."

"It's satellite driven," Chase said. "Isn't there a way to track it and shut it down?"

Sal shook his head. "It's probably Russian designed and these new-fangled bombs with satellite detonators are impossible to locate. Some can be as small as the tip of a pin and blow up an entire tank." Sal looked weary and concerned as he moved closer to the camera, his face filling the screen. "I'll do what I can, but if you don't pull your guys out of there, they're dead." Sal disconnected the call.

"Get them out of there," Angel muttered and Chase immediately took the microphone and began ordering Tony, the Snake and Pete to pull out, but none of them were responding. "Do you copy?" Chase stammered into the microphone. "Tony, Snake, Pete, do you copy?" Flipping the big screen to show the three surveillance cameras on each man, they could see that the men were fine, moving about the street and surrounding area, trying to appear nonchalant while searching for a trigger.

"Why can't they hear you?" Angel asked.

"I don't know," Chase murmured, checking the connection and trying to reach them again. He tried their cell phones but each one went straight to voicemail, as if they weren't even ringing. He text but every text shown an error message stating that the message was undelivered. "Something's wrong," Chase murmured. "Something's blocking the signal."

"Something or someone?" Taelon chided.

Chase pulled up satellite feed of the entire area, narrowing the parameters to State Street. Suddenly they saw twelve police officers walking in formation down State Street, one by one dropping out of line and standing along the side of the street.

Taelon's fingers flew across the keyboard as he retrieved satellite data of their coordinates. "They're marking the trigger coordinates," Taelon observed aloud.

"Holy shit!" Chase barked. "They're the triggers! The cops are the actual triggers!"

"What does that mean?" Angel blurted, but Chase didn't answer. Instead, he ordered Taelon to run a satellite based trace, locating the cell phone numbers on each of the twelve cops.

"Compare their numbers to the ones in the dot positions on the schematic," he hollered and Angel had never seen two man's fingers move with such immediacy and precision. Side-by-side they worked the keyboards as if they were playing harmonious instruments.

"I got 'em," Taelon blurted. "They match! All twelve match! They're the triggers!"

"Now, let's go out on a limb and assume that our mystery assassin is consistent and that the final trigger that will cause the explosion is also a cell phone number," Chase muttered more to

303

himself than anyone else. "Whose phone would it be?"

"There are thousands of people in the surrounding area. In the middle of the city, how the hell are we going to locate a phone when we don't even know what number we're looking for?" Angel wailed.

"I can do it!" Taelon blurted. "I can write a program to gather the cell phone data of everyone within a fifteen mile radius of the Holy Name Cathedral. We can run those numbers against all of the numbers on the schematic and see if there's a match." His fingers flew across the keyboard as he spoke and it was evident that he wasn't waiting for permission.

"We won't have time," Chase chided.

"I can do it!" Taelon gritted, never looking up from the computer.

Angel turned to Chase and put her hand on his shoulder. "While you do this, I'm going to go and get our guys out of there."

"No! It isn't safe. I'll go," Chase objected.

"We need you here," Angel argued. "I can't do this technology stuff."

"Listen, Boss Lady, I don't know when that explosion is going to go off or exactly where it's gonna blow. They've somehow scrambled frequencies so the minute you get close to State Street I'm going to lose contact with you." Chase's eyes were lit with concern.

"We don't have a choice," Angel told him. "I'm not sitting here and watching twelve of my guys die when I could have done something to save them. I may not be able to save the Pope, but I'm not quitting on my men."

Angel exited the room with purpose and made a beeline to the garage level and her Tank, where she slipped into a Kevlar vest and made certain her 9mm was readied. She had just pulled out of the garage when Chase rang the phone inside of the Tank.

"You know the search I was running on Madeline's cell phone?"

"Yes..."

"I wanted to let you know it's clean. She hasn't been in contact with anyone from the Diaglio family. In fact, the only person she's been in contact with since she arrived in the States is Carl Cusanelli."

"Huh," Angel mumbled. "I guess they were working out marriage details but I'd have thought he would have been discussing those things with the Brioschi Consigliere and not directly with Madeline."

"Dunno," Chase replied. "But she's clean."

Damn. I was hoping to have found a justifiable reason not to like her; that is, one other than pure jealousy," Angel thought to herself.

Disconnecting the call, she couldn't escape the nagging feeling that something wasn't right. Why would Carl and Madeline be talking? She dialed Chase back.

"How many times have they spoken?" She blurted the moment he answered.

"Three or four," Chase answered.

"For how long?"

"What?" He quipped, his tone showing obvious annoyance by the questions.

"What was the duration of their calls?" Angel replied. "Ten minutes? Thirty minutes?"

"Man, you are an obsessive one, aren't you?" He teased and pulled the data back up on his screen. "Each call was less than one minute. Can I get back to work now?"

"Yes." Angel exhaled and disconnected the call.

Less than one minute, she repeated Chase's words in her mind. *What can two people discuss in under a minute?*

Red flags were waving in her gut. Something was wrong with this connection between Madeline and Carl. Was Carl the one who convinced Giovanni to arrange a marriage between Andrew and Madeline? Did he not realize Madeline was a Diaglio or did he know and intentionally hide the information from Giovanni? If so, why? Why would he want to do business with the Diaglio family, knowing that it would taint Giovanni's name and jeopardize the Maratinzano family integrity? Or was that his goal, to taint Giovanni's name? Angel shook the thought from her mind. Carl was a lifelong friend, almost a brother to Giovanni. He had been by his side longer than Angel had been alive. She had witnessed him gun down his own grandson for traitorous actions against the family. It was unthinkable that he would do anything to put the family in jeopardy. Still, what reason would he have to be in direct contact with Madeline?

Thoughts popped sporadically in and out of her mind as she drove. The New York Bank & Trust. The money transfers. The marriage. The timing. The CoBroGas attack. Where was Carl during the attack? Angel recalled that she had phoned him in New York and he had offered to come to Chicago, but she told him to stay there and handle things for Giovanni. Come to think of it, as his Compare Carl handles all of the finances for Giovanni. He has for years. Could Carl have been the one to set this whole thing in motion? But why?

Angel dialed Chase back from the car phone. "Did you ever find out who Detta phoned from the bushes that night?"

"No," Chase replied. "After she was found dead, the search seemed irrelevant."

"Can you do it now?"

"I'm at your wild-ass beck and call, Boss Lady," Chase sarcastically teased. "I mean, it's not like I'm trying to find and stop a bomb or anything."

Ignoring his sarcasm, she disconnected the call and reconnected with her thoughts.

Elsa had told Angel that the night Olga was attacked she had said something about knowing the man who was in Detta's room. Elsa also alluded to the fact that she thought Olga was afraid of him. What if the man in Detta's motel room that night was Carl? All of a sudden Angel's pulse quickened as a terrifying truth hit her. While standing in Olga's hospital room, she had told Giovanni and Carl about Elsa seeing the man who assaulted Olga, and told them that she had moved Elsa to the Towers for protection. Carl left the hospital shortly thereafter. Was it possible that he went straight to the Towers to kill Elsa? Angel started to pant as panic engulfed her. Carl was at the hospital right now with Giovanni and Olga. What if Olga awakens and identifies him as Detta's killer? What will Carl do to her?

Dialing Chase, she explained her theory and told him to contact Giovanni's body guards at the hospital and move them from the elevator to Olga's room. "Don't tell them our theory..."

"YOUR theory," Chase interrupted. "This all sounds a bit like hyped-up, weird-ass, grasping-at-straws to me."

"Just tell them that we have reason to believe that they may be in danger and we need to beef up security. Tell them to be discreet. If Carl is guilty, I don't want him getting jumpy and thinking that we might be onto him," she explained.

She then dialed the only other person she thought would help her, Tony's father.

"Don Andriachini, this is Angel Maratinzano," she hurriedly spoke when he answered.

"Michelangela, I heard you were on some sort of sabbatical," he said.

"I'm back and I need your help," Angel blurted. "It's a matter of life or death and it could win you big time favor with Giovanni."

"I'm listening," Don Andriachini uttered and Angel told him her theory about Carl.

"I need manpower at the hospital right away," Angel said. "I'll owe you whatever you ask in return. You have my word."

"You have my men," he said and disconnected the call.

She was almost to the top of State Street but traffic was slowing down to a crawl. Her cell phone was rendered inoperable, which she knew meant she was nearing the path of the triggering mechanisms. Pulling the Tank to the side of the street, Angel jumped out and took off in a dead sprint. She could get to her men faster on foot. Besides, she only had to tell one and then they would spread the word to each other quickly. She saw Chito first and breathlessly instructed him to tell the others to pull back. "Get everyone you can off of the street and away from the Cathedral," she panted.

Chito took off running toward the other men and Angel could see the ripple effect beginning. She had made it in time.

When the Snake heard Angel was in the area, he began searching until he found her. "Ms.

Maratinzano, we've got to get you out of here now," he grunted. "We've lost contact with Chase."

Angel appreciated his desire to protect her, but now that she had warned her men to pull back, she wanted to find a way to warn the Pope. "All communication is being scrambled or blocked somehow. Chase said that the numerical data from the officer's cell phones are working as the triggers. If we turn off their cell phones, will it stop the bomb?"

The Snake's face drained of color. "No," he uttered. "If they're using a satellite multi-triggering device that they have linked to the cell numbers themselves, then they only needed a moment to lock into position. The phones are irrelevant now."

"Is there any way to stop the bomb?" Angel asked and he shook his head.

"Not without knowing what the final trigger is." He threw up his hands. "The best we can do now is try to clear the streets and get as many people out of the blast zone as possible."

"Assuming the blast zone is the Cathedral," Angel said wryly. The truth was they were operating solely on speculation. They didn't really know if there was a bomb or where it might explode.

"If the goal is to kill the Pope and the Pope is inside the Cathedral, than I'd say assuming the bomb is in the church is the best hunch we have to go on," he replied.

They worked their way up and down the street, trying to move people away from the Holy Name Cathedral, which was no easy task, as it is one of the most famous tourist attractions in the city. Finally, the Snake made Angel promise to get into the Tank and leave. "I'm going to go and find the officers that were here and tell them there's a bomb," the Snake panted.

"What if they don't believe you?" Angel asked.

"Then I'll tell them I set the bomb and you'll just have to come and bail my ass out of jail later," he replied with a sideways grin.

She didn't like the notion of him getting arrested, but couldn't deny that it was a great idea. The cops would have to take a bomb threat seriously, which meant they would evacuate the Cathedral and adjoining streets.

The Snake sprinted back up State Street to find the officers but they were already gone.

Heading back to the Tank, Angel saw a black stretch limousine pull up next to the Cathedral. *Is that the Pope?* She wondered, ducking behind the side of a parked car and peering over the hood. She would have been admittedly surprised if His Eminence was transported in such an obvious, eye-catching manner and dropped off in front of the church, in plain view; but stranger things had happened. She watched closely, deciding that if the Pope did indeed exit the vehicle, she was going to have to make a scene, threaten him or do whatever it took to get him back into the limousine and away from the Cathedral.

I just might end up in jail too, she thought. One of Olga's favorite expressions played in her mind...*better to be judged by twelve than carried by six.*

Before she could play out too many what-if scenarios in her mind, Serco Mertesca exited the passenger side of the limo, walked around the rear of the car to the sidewalk and opened the back door. Seconds later, Andrew emerged from the backseat, followed by Madeline, who looped her arm in his and rubbed her hand up the side of his bicep. He gave her fingertips a squeeze and she gazed up at him and smiled.

I'd like to slap the smile right off her face, Angel muttered in the quiet of her mind as her jealousy quickly became a distraction. *I can't believe he married her! Just out of the blue...BAM...married her! Who does that?!*

She watched as Serco led them to the main entrance, where he was greeted by a clergyman wearing a white robe with a golden sash. As soon as they entered, Angel darted across the street, up the sidewalk and toward the doors, praying they hadn't been locked after their entrance. She was about to reach for the handle when the door in front of her thrust open, pushing Angel behind it. Serco stepped out, holding the door open for Madeline, and then they hurried down the sidewalk and into the limousine.

Why are they leaving without Andrew? Angel thought and then a horrible possibility struck her. Chase had surmised that the final trigger was another cell phone. *What if the trigger is Andrew's phone!* Throwing open the door, Angel dashed inside with her 9mm drawn and crashed directly into two clergymen who were attempting to lock the door. One took her gun while the other grabbed her arms and pulled them tightly behind her back. Angel winced from the pain in her shoulder.

"Andrew!" She hollered and her voice echoed through the cathedral ceiling. "Andrew!" She hollered again, this time even louder.

"Scream all you'd like. Andrew isn't coming to your rescue," one of the clergyman said.

"Where is he?" Angel demanded. "I saw him come inside. What did you do to him?"

The men dragged her down the center aisle of the church and into a room that jetted off from behind the pulpit. Shoving her forcefully through the doorway, Angel tripped over the bodies of two Papal security men and fell at Andrew's feet.

"Angel?" He exclaimed. "What are you doing here?"

"Give me your phone!" She demanded.

Andrew looked puzzled but searched his pockets. "I guess I don't have it with me," he muttered, seemingly stumped, as he always carried his phone. "What's going on?"

Angel was confused. She had been so certain that Andrew's phone was the trigger. Glancing around the room she saw the bodies of four men, the two she had fallen over and two more that had been dragged into the corner of the room.

"Where is Pope Ignacio?" Angel asked.

"They took him," Andrew said, helping Angel to her feet.

"Don't you worry, the Pope is fine. In fact, he's preparing for his big speech," the clergyman with the gun clucked. He was a young man with sandy brown hair and light green eyes. He had dark pink lips and feminine mannerisms and Angel immediately noticed the tattoo on his wrist. It was the same marking she had seen on the man commissioned to kill her.

"You don't have to do this," Angel panted.

"That's not true," he hissed. "What's true is that you don't have to be here."

"If you don't need her, then let her go," Andrew interjected. "I'll stay."

A smile spread slowly across the man's face. "Ahh, Andrew Venturini, always a hero." He chuckled to himself and then pursed his pink lips together. Turning his attention back to Angel, he flipped his sandy hair to one side and said, "You thought Andrew's phone would trigger the explosion, didn't you?"

"What is he talking about?" Andrew asked Angel.

"Long story," Angel muttered.

"I've been a bit out of the loop so maybe you could fill me in?" Andrew said to the clergyman.

"Oh, right, right, right, right. You've been on your honeymoon," he sing-song-ed, wiggling his hips from side to side and raising his eyebrows.

"Yes, I did," Angel muttered. "I did think Andrew's phone was the trigger."

"You were close!" He brought his two hands together as if to applaud. "Andrew's phone will dial the number to the cell that will then trigger the blast," he said with raised eyebrows. "That way, when the smoke clears and the police trace the call, they'll find out that Pope Ignacio was murdered by none other than American Mob Boss, Andrew Venturini."

"No one's gonna buy that," Andrew muttered.

"But wait, there's more," he said with sickening glee. "What's that you say? Haven't you heard? The Capo di Tutti Capi funded the assassination of the Pope!" He laughed out loud.

"No one will believe that," Angel spat.

"Honey, all they have to do is follow the money trail."

He paraded back and forth across the room and Angel could tell by the way he pranced about that he was either gay or no stranger to women's high heels. She tried to size up his physique beneath the robe. Was he stronger than he looked? Surely, Andrew could take him down with one punch, but would taking him down stop the explosion? If he didn't have Andrew's phone, it will all be for naught.

"Sure is a shame to have to destroy a Cathedral of this grandeur. It almost looks like it belongs in Italia," he clamored, while shimming his shoulders and gazing up at the ornate paintings on the ceiling.

"Where is Andrew's phone?" Angel asked.

"Why, his lovely wife has it," he answered without missing a beat. "Isn't she to die for?" He said and then giggled to himself. "Literally, right?"

Andrew stared at him, motionless and seemingly emotionless. Angel couldn't tell what was going through his mind or if he was completely void of thought.

"Where did the other guy go?" Angel asked.

"Curious minds want to know," the clergyman chuckled. "I bet he's getting the Pope ready for his speech. We get to hear it first. Isn't that exciting!" He pulled open the door and ordered them at gunpoint to walk onto the pulpit. "Before you get any ideas, Mr. Muscles," he said to Andrew, "keep walking and sit in the first pew."

Angel and Andrew stepped down from the pulpit and sat in the front pew. "When it's time, follow my lead," Andrew said softly. Angel had no idea what he was planning.

The flamboyant clergyman eyed Angel. "You weren't part of the deal," he said to her. "But I don't see how killing you can hurt the results. We'll look at it like a bonus." He raised his eyebrows and grinned.

Just then Pope Ignacio was led at gunpoint to the pulpit by the other man dressed in a clergyman's robe. He, too, shared the same tattoo. The Pope stepped to the pulpit in stoic fashion. Angel scanned the room for more men, more bodies, something they could use as a weapon and something that looked like a bomb. She kept replaying the details in her mind. Each trigger

314

linked numerically to the next, and the final one would cause the explosion. That meant that there had to be a bomb somewhere. She remembered Sal explaining that the bomb could be the size of a pin head and still blow up a tank.

"We want to hear your speech," the clergyman chided, while sitting down in a cushioned folding chair and excitedly wiggling his hips back and forth. The other clergyman took a seat on the pulpit steps, in close proximity to the Pope.

"I will deliver my speech tomorrow afternoon," Pope Ignacio rebutted.

"Noooooo, you won't," the clergyman burst. "Unless you plan on sharing the big pulpit in the sky with Saint Peter," he whispered and pointed upward.

"I'd like to hear your speech," Angel said softly.

"Oh, how sweet," the clergyman mocked and drew a little tear drop on his cheek with the barrel of one of the guns. "Hey, guess what?" He said to Pope Ignacio. "I bet your sermon is gonna be a blast." He burst out laughing. "You get it? A BLAST?!"

CHAPTER 68

As soon as the Snake could get his phone to work, he dialed Chase, and upon finding out that Angel had not returned to the Towers as promised, cursed aloud and spun a U-turn, heading back toward the Cathedral.

"Tony hasn't come back yet either," Chase said.

"He's with me," the Snake replied. "We're heading back to the Cathedral."

"Guys, we haven't been able to confirm the last trigger or locate the explosive device. I need eyes inside the church. Your cameras are still live even though our ability to communicate gets locked up," he explained.

"We're on it, Ace," Tony responded. "You'll have your eyes in the church."

"Be careful," Chase said.

"Roger, that," the Snake replied.

"Oh, and if you see Angel, tell her she was right. Detta called Carl from the bushes the night of the car bombing and talked to him again the day she died," Chase explained. "She's got some weird-ass instincts."

"Roger, that," the Snake said and disconnected the call.

CHAPTER 69

"Since it appears eminent that this is my final earthly sermon, do you have any requests?" Pope Ignacio asked and Angel found it amazing that he appeared so peaceful in the face of death. "Or, I can perform a marriage ceremony if you would like to be wed?"

"He's already married," Angel replied.

"Yes, but I'm going to have it annulled," Andrew responded.

"Don't do anything on my account," Angel snipped.

"Oh, you can't have a marriage annulled," the feminine clergyman stated emphatically. "No, sir, it's until death do you part. That's why the wedding band is a circle to symbolize that the marriage can't be broken. It's a mind-blowing ride and only death can incinerate those nuptials."

Andrew took Angel's hand in his and she forcefully withdrew it. "Don't touch me!" She spat and Andrew leapt to his feet.

"Here we go again! Don't touch me. Don't look at me. Don't love me. That's all I ever hear from you!" Andrew ranted, waving his arms in the air in a way that was completely out of character. "You're always pointing a finger at me, pointing out what I do wrong, or what I don't do right! Always nagging, bitching, moaning..."

All of a sudden, while she was watching Andrew carry on in such dramatic fashion, clarity erupted and she understood what he was doing. He was picking a fight and he wanted her to fight back. He needed a good, old fashion fist fight. Angel leapt to her feet and slapped Andrew clean across the face.

Without missing a beat, Andrew slapped her back, a hard, stinging slap on her cheek. Pope

Ignacio gasped and for a split-second she saw regret in Andrew's eyes, but he covered it quickly. She grunted and lunged at him, pushing him backwards.

"Now you two stop this!" The clergyman, who had been sitting on the pulpit steps, leapt up and ordered.

"That's right, stop this right now!" The other clergyman fussed and held up his gun as if he were trying to decide at which one of them to take aim.

"Is that all you've got?" Andrew hollered, pushing Angel backwards.

With a high pitched shriek, she dove toward him, grabbing his legs and knocking him to the ground. Her chin cracked against his kneecap and she felt something hard dig into her ribcage. It was a gun located in his left ankle holster. Angel glanced up at Andrew and she knew in that moment exactly what she needed to do. Gripping her chin with her left hand, Angel feigned sobs, accusing Andrew of breaking her jaw and crushing her heart. Her wails echoed throughout the church and Andrew, as if on cue, sat up, thereby drawing his left ankle under her where it couldn't be seen. He took her face between his palms, wiping her tears and feigning sympathy, in what appeared to be a tender moment; while Angel used her right hand to release the gun from his ankle holster. One gun. Two armed bad guys. Angel had a choice to make. In one fluid motion, she pushed Andrew backwards, raised the gun and fired two shots into the chest of the clergyman who stood behind Andrew, next to the pulpit stairs. Then turning she fired at the feminine clergyman who was behind her, but he managed to get off a shot that soared into her back. She felt a hot impact strip her of breath and force her body

318

forward. Andrew grabbed the gun from her hand and fired two more shots. She heard the clergyman's body fall, but she was unable to move.

Sliding his legs out from under her, Andrew left Angel face down and pulled up her sweater. "Talk to me, Sweetheart," he ordered. "Talk to me!"

"It burns," she moaned.

"We've got to get the vest off," he said aloud, rolling her over, pulling her sweater completely off and quickly unfastening the vest. He then flipped her back over to assess the damage. There was a big, red, hot mark, but the skin hadn't been broken. "Thank God you were wearing a vest," he uttered, rolling her back over and lifting her into his arms. "Thank God," he sighed.

Andrew sat Angel down in the front pew and laid her sweater and the Kevlar vest next to her. He then went to the pulpit to check on the Pope, who was kneeling behind the podium in prayer. "Your Eminence?" Andrew said. "We have reason to believe there is a bomb in the church and we need to get you out of here."

Pope Ignacio opened his eyes and Andrew helped him stand. Upon seeing the bodies of the clergymen, he gasped and then regained composure. When his eyes traveled to Angel sitting in the front pew wearing only her bra, the Pope asked, "Is she all right?"

"She will be," Andrew said and led the Pope from the pulpit, down the center aisle, stopping to pick up the guns from the clergyman and to help Angel get her sweater back on.

"What do we do now?" Pope Ignacio asked. "Wait for la Polizia?"

"Not here," Andrew barked. "A bomb could go off at any second."

They were hurrying through the front doors when the Snake pulled up to the curb and Tony leapt out. "Get in! Get in!" Tony hollered, opening the back door and hoisting Angel and the Pope inside, while Andrew climbed in the other side. The Snake sped away from the Cathedral and they all braced for impact, expecting to see an explosion at any moment; but nothing happened.

As soon as they were far enough from the Cathedral, the Snake tried to dial Chase, but the phone wouldn't work. "We called from this same spot last time and there was no interference," the Snake remarked.

"Maybe it's your phone, let me try," Tony said, but his phone didn't work either.

Angel tried hers too, but it didn't work.

"What's going on?" Andrew asked.

Angel's whole body hurt and her mind was racing. They should be away from the trigger and away from the bomb so logically their phones should be working. Unless...

Leaning forward, Angel put her hand on the Snake's shoulder. "If the satellite block is effective only on phones and other communication devices that are in certain proximity to the trigger, could it mean that the bomb is in this car?"

The Snake pulled to the side of the street. "What the hell are you doing, Ace?" Tony belted. "We've got the damn Pope in the car!" He turned and peered over the seat. "No disrespect Father," he uttered and then turned back toward the Snake. "We can't just sit here and wait for someone to try to take him out."

"If the triggering mechanism is in this car and we drive it to the Towers..." The Snake didn't finish his sentence. He didn't have to. Everyone knew what it meant. They were still in danger and until they could find the device, they couldn't go home and endanger everyone else.

320

"Drive to the downtown precinct," Andrew said. "I can get some guys from the bomb squad to get to the bottom of this."

"Sal said even his best men were powerless against this type of technology," Angel told him.

"Anywhere we go, we endanger the people around us. Not to mention the fact that one of you may blow sky high at any second," the Snake seethed. "We've got to think."

"Well, pull into that parking garage so we're at least off of the main street," Tony said and the Snake maneuvered into the first level of the garage.

"We need to search the Pope," Tony uttered matter of factly, stepped from the car and yanked open the back door. "Your Eminence, if you wouldn't mind stepping out of the vehicle and stripping down?"

Pope Ignacio's eyebrows rose slightly and he stared at Tony like a deer in headlights.

"You can't ask the Pope to take off his clothes in public," Andrew muttered.

"It's nothing personal, Father, really," Tony told the Pope and then turned to Andrew. "I don't see that we have a choice. You got a better idea?"

Andrew got out of the car and asked the Pope to stand and raise his arms above his head. He then proceeded to pat him down.

"We're going to hell," the Snake mumbled beneath his breath.

After patting him down, Andrew turned to Tony and Angel. "I didn't feel anything," he said.

"Maybe we need to do a cavity search," Tony suggested.

"Are you out of your mind?" Andrew gawked.

"We're definitely going to hell," the Snake muttered.

"Do you want to blow up or do you want to endure a little uncomfortable fondling for the sake of safety?" Tony remarked. "Father, we're gonna have to ask you to bend over."

"Tony!" Angel gasped.

"What, Babe? I'm trying to get to the bottom of this," Tony said and then smirked. "Oh, no pun intended, Father."

The Pope looked as if he were stunned into silence, Andrew looked completely shocked and the Snake laid his head against the steering wheel in what appeared to be utter dismay. Angel bit the inside of her cheek to keep from grinning and she suddenly found herself thankful that Chase couldn't hear what they were saying. His comments, of which he would have had many, would have brought on hysterics.

"Wait," Angel said. "There's got to be a logical explanation...something we're missing." She paced by the side of the car, replaying the events in her mind from the moment she saw Andrew, Madeline and Serco enter the Cathedral. "Andrew, why were you meeting with Pope Ignacio today?"

"He asked for a private meeting with me," Andrew replied.

"That is not a true statement," Pope Ignacio rebutted. "It is you who asked to review my speech to see that it was acceptable."

"What?" Andrew growled.

"So, you were set up to be together," Angel commented. "You thought he asked to meet with you and he thought you requested an audience with him." She gnawed on her bottom lip. "The bomb might be somewhere on you, Andrew."

"Why would you think that?" He scoffed.

"Because they obviously went to great lengths to get the two of you together," she replied.

"The plan wasn't for the Pope to assassinate a mafia Boss; it was for the Pope to be killed and the mob to take the blame."

"What plan?" Pope Ignacio gasped.

"It's a long story, Father," the Snake responded.

"All right, Ace, arms over your head," Tony said and began patting Andrew down. He ran his hand over his crotch. "Nope, don't feel anything substantial there," he taunted and Andrew glared angrily at him.

Angel stepped away from the car, her mind swimming with scenarios, questions, thoughts, flashes of images and conversations. Her shoulder hurt. Her back ached and it was difficult to take a full breath, but she couldn't escape the feeling that the answer was right in front of her. She whirled around to face Andrew and blurted, "Why did you marry Madeline earlier than planned?"

Andrew shrugged. "She had thought the wedding was going to be a day earlier and I didn't want to disappoint her."

"Just like the Pope was arriving a day earlier than we thought," Angel uttered aloud but mainly to herself.

"I didn't feel anything worthy of taking a look," Tony quipped and stepped away from Andrew.

Angel's mind began to flash back to what the clergyman had said about marriage being an unbreakable bond until death do you part. It seemed so obvious and yet so easy to miss. "What time is it?" Angel blurted and the Snake lifted his head from the steering wheel and looked at the clock on the dashboard.

"11:59," he responded.

Twelve officers. Twelve triggers. Twelve numbers on a clock making it a perfect circle ...

just like a wedding band. Complete. Whole.
Round. Angel dove toward Andrew. "Your band!"
She shrieked. "Take off your band!"

"Babe?" Tony gawked at her. "Is this some
sort of jealous rage?" Angel ignored his remark
and stepped closer to Andrew.

"Take off your ring," she said calmly. "If I'm
wrong then I'm just a crazy person and we've lost
nothing, but...if...I'm right..."

Andrew twisted the ring from his finger and
tossed it across the garage. Nothing happened. *I
guess I was just crazy,* she told herself, grunting
frustration.

"I really thought..." She shook her head
and turned to climb into the car just as the clock
on the dashboard changed to 12:00pm and the
explosion jolted the ground with such force that it
lifted their SUV into the air. Angel dove toward
Pope Ignacio, knocking him backwards and saving
him from being crushed by the car which landed
on its side a mere inches from her legs. Tony and
Andrew were both thrown backwards, away from
the car and the Snake was trapped inside,
uninjured and dangling by his seatbelt.

The moment the explosion commenced
communications were back on line and Chase
began muttering into their ear pieces. "Everybody
okay? Are you alive?" He yelped excitedly.

"Yeah," Tony answered groggily. "We're
gonna need another car and something to cut the
Snake down."

Aside from ringing ears and mild head
trauma, they had all survived the blast.

With his hands on his hips, Andrew
meandered slowly away from the car, as if in
shock. Angel thought to follow, but became
distracted by Tony, who had draped his arm

324

around her shoulder. "How did you know the bomb was in the ring, Babe?" Tony asked.

"Just a hunch," she whispered, but felt that it was so much more. It was like tiny clues had magically aligned in her brain to form the image of a golden band; the indestructible circle that the clergyman had described. As if, in that precise moment, the dots were Divinely connected.

Back at the Towers, the Pope was given a private suite where he was able to notify the remainder of his security team of his whereabouts. His team was then allowed to join him. Angel ordered the men at the hospital to bring Giovanni and Carl back to the Towers immediately. "Leave four guards stationed with Olga," she told them. She also spoke to the nurse in charge and instructed her to call the moment Olga was awake and coherent.

Sal put out a level red security alert on Serco Mertesca and Madeline Brioschi and assured Angel that they would be unable to leave the country unnoticed.

Now came the hard part...confronting Carl and finding out just how much Giovanni knew about Carl's actions.

CHAPTER 70

While Giovanni and Carl filed into the secret meeting room and took a seat at the table, Angel, the Snake and Tony stood on the other side behind Chase and his laptop. Two of Giovanni's body guards took flanking positions by the door. Everyone else had been asked to leave the room because Angel knew that this particular conversation was not going to be pleasant.

"Grandfather," Angel began softly, stopping to collect her thoughts. This was a lose-lose situation. Either Giovanni was a part of the plot against the Pope or he was about to find out that his best friend and trusted Compare had been a traitor to him. "There is no good way to begin," she said. "First, we have evidence to support the fact that Andrew Venturini was not involved in a plot against His Eminence."

"We would like to see that evidence," Carl noted. "We have taped conversations alluding to the fact that Don Venturini was working with Nicholas Diaglio."

"That's bogus," Chase interjected. "You have only a one-sided conversation where Don Venturini says the name Diaglio. I've heard the recording and it proves nothing." Carl opened his mouth to speak but Chase continued over the top of him. "We have also contacted the caller to whom Don Venturini was speaking at the time and he corroborates Don Venturini's claim that he..."

"Andrew hired Sal to dig up any dirt on his future-wife, Madeline Brioschi," Angel interrupted Chase and he gawked at her. "Sal found out that Madeline's maiden name was Diaglio and he called Andrew and told him." She directed her attention to Chase and said, "This isn't a trial. We don't have to be that formal."

Chase raised his eyebrows. "What she said," he quipped.

Giovanni eyed Angel, running his hand along his jowls. "Is all of this about Andrew's marriage?" He asked.

"I wish it was," Angel muttered.

"Then, Michelangela, what are we doing here?" He questioned.

"Sir, we have substantial evidence that Carl Cusanelli has been misusing Maratinzano funds to plot against the family," Chase said.

"What?!" Giovanni and Carl barked simultaneously.

Chase gave Taelon a nod, but Taelon's eyes were wide with fear and he appeared frozen in his chair. Slowly shaking his head to indicate that he was unable to do his part, Chase took over. "Public speaking isn't one of Taelon's talents," Chase quipped, "but programming is, and he developed a program to track the money in and out of your many accounts for the past twenty-four months; especially any transactions that were encoded."

Giovanni narrowed his brows and Angel could tell he was angry. She surmised that he was probably feeling violated. After all, his money was no one's business but his. "The only reason we looked into your finances is because we had evidence of monetary transactions between the Diaglio family and your bank account," Angel added.

Shock sparked Giovanni's eyes. "I have never conducted business with the Diaglios!" Giovanni roared.

"See, that's what we thought," Chase pointed at Giovanni. "That confused, shocked-ass expression right there was what we thought we'd see because we looked like that a few short hours ago when we thought you were actually in on this whole thing..." his voice tapered off. "Not that we ever really thought you were guilty... I mean, it may have crossed our minds for a split-second but...I'll shut up now."

"That's a good idea, Ace," Tony remarked.

Angel handed Giovanni copies of the transactions from the past two years. "You can review these later," she said. "The point is, Carl used Maratinzano money to fund the attack against the Pope and to try and make it look like you had paid Andrew to murder the Pope."

"This is ridiculous!" Carl blurted and leapt to his feet, causing Tony to instinctively draw his weapon. "Your granddaughter is crazy!"

"Crazy like a wild-ass fox," Chase added. "Sir, her instincts have been dead-on," he said to Giovanni and Angel saw a momentary glimmer of pride in his eyes before his anger darkened them.

"Ridiculous!" Carl uttered.

"I'd pipe down if I were you, Ace," Tony chided.

"There's more," Angel said. "We have evidence that Carl paid off the people who stole the CoBroGas, shipped it to Chicago and used it to attack all of us at Tetterbaum's the night of our grand re-opening."

"This sounds like one of Lucia's conspiracy theories. You know how she is. You know how her mind is deteriorating," he said to Giovanni. "All of you young people don't know Lucia the way Giovanni and I do. We know better than to believe her ranting." Carl took a step toward the door. "This is a waste of our valuable time."

"Sit down!" Tony barked.

"Olga's mind is not deteriorating and the proof we have didn't come from her," Angel raised her voice. "You were sloppy or maybe just ignorant of our technological capabilities." Angel met eyes with Giovanni. "Please, grandfather, you need to hear this."

Giovanni folded his hands atop the table. "Come and sit down, Carl. We will hear them out." Carl strode slowly back to his seat.

"Grazie," Angel said softly. "We have evidence to support that Carl hired Nicholas Diaglio to plan the Pope's assassination. He then coordinated with Lisben to hire twelve police officers to unknowingly assist in the attack, paying them each twenty-five thousand dollars with transactions that ultimately led to your bank account."

"Ludicrous!" Carl steamed and leapt to his feet again. "Giovanni, are you really going to entertain this level of delusion?"

Angel raised her voice. "You knew the Diaglio's hated Pope Ignacio for his new policy against the mafia and you used that knowledge to your advantage. They wanted the Pope dead and you wanted..." Angel stopped abruptly. What she was about to say didn't sound right, and yet, she knew that it was accurate. "You wanted the rest of us dead. The CoBroGas attack failed and so you came up with a new plan."

"You're as crazy as your aunt!" Carl seethed.

"Is she?" Andrew had entered the room unnoticed while Angel was yelling. "I have a signed affidavit from the Archdiocese of the Holy Name Cathedral that says you contacted him and recommended that they invite Pope Ignacio to Chicago."

"That is not a crime," Carl hissed.

"The Archdiocese says you gave him one million dollars to make it happen," Andrew noted.

"Bah!" Carl spat. "These accusations are ridiculous. I made a donation to the church. I do not control the Archdiocese."

Chase lit the big screen with a banking transaction showing a one million dollar donation from Giovanni's account at the New York Bank & Trust to the Holy Name Cathedral in Chicago. "The one million came from the Maratinzano account, so legally you didn't make the donation, Giovanni did," Chase explained.

"Which is exactly how you wanted it to appear," Angel added. "So that after the Pope was assassinated, the FBI would follow the money trail leading to Giovanni."

"Your grandfather is a generous man," Carl said calmly. "He donates to the church regularly. This was no different."

"Whether the money was a donation or a bribe, we have proof that you conspired against His Eminence and purposefully constructed a money trail that would frame Giovanni and Don Venturini," Angel blurted forcefully.

"Michelangela, while I am distressed over the amount that was donated without my knowing, Carl has my utmost financial trust. These accusations are undeserving," Giovanni reprimanded.

"Fine. You don't want to talk about money, then let's talk about people," she blurted, glaring at Carl. "You hired Nicholas Diaglio to implement the assassination. He hired Detta Palumbo to hack into the Vatican security system and retrieve detailed data on the Pope's planned visit to Chicago. Detta put the information on a jump drive that one of her foster kids inadvertently took to school, thinking it was a school project." Angel paced around the table. "That's where I came in." Her blood was pumping now as adrenaline raged through her veins. "Your plan might have worked had Elsa not asked Olga to invite me to speak to her granddaughter's classroom that morning. It might have worked had I not killed Nicholas at East Side Junior High and unknowingly confiscated the jump drive detailing your plan," Angel taunted.

"Ridiculous." Carl shook his head. "You sound as crazy as your aunt."

Angel didn't acknowledge his remarks. Instead, she kept going. "Despite that, you sent men to the hospital to kill me and recover the drive; but they failed because Andrew and the Snake were one step ahead of you. So, worried about what they may or may not know, you convinced Giovanni that Andrew was conspiring against him and you came to Chicago with an entourage of men to take Andrew down."

"Rubbish!" Carl spat. "You have quite an imagination."

"But taking him down was never the real plan, was it?" Angel didn't pause long enough for him to answer. "That's why, even when you planned to attack the other night, it never came to fruition."

"I never learned of his location," Carl retorted.

"You knew it all along because you had Lisben on the inside, uploading information to you," Andrew interjected.

Chase's fingers flew across the keys until data displayed on the big screen, detailing the upload links between Lisben and Carl's email. "I love our friends in the FBI," Chase muttered with a grin.

"These emails are forgeries. I am being set up!" Carl seethed, slamming both hands against the table.

"No!" Angel barked. "Andrew was the one who was set up!" She had hit her boiling point and fought to control the all-consuming rage she felt. "YOU arranged the marriage between Madeline and Andrew knowing damn good and well that she was a Diaglio!" Angel's jaw tightened and her teeth clenched together.

"I arranged that marriage with Giovanni's blessing, as he did not want a Maratinzano and a Venturini to wed," Carl said with a cunning glare.

"BULLSHIT!" Angel screamed.

"Michelangela! That is enough!" Giovanni rose to his feet, glaring at her.

"You're right, grandfather, it is enough. Enough lies," she panted and looking toward the door, gave the body guards a nod. They immediately opened the door wide enough for Harry to enter, pushing Olga in a wheelchair.

"Lucia!" Giovanni gasped with surprise, moving toward her with open arms and kissing her tenderly on her forehead.

Angel stared at Carl the whole time, watching to see if the color would start to drain from his face; but he sat staunch, his hands folded atop the table and his chin pointed into the air.

Olga's nose was still bandaged, her eyes were black and blue and a bandage, from where they had performed the surgery to release pressure in the brain, circled her head. An IV bag hung from a rod attached to her wheelchair and it was evident that she was in no condition to have left the hospital. Giovanni didn't know it, but an ambulance was waiting downstairs to take her immediately back to ICU. Laboring to lift her arm, she tugged at Giovanni's hand, pulling him downward toward her until her lips were next to his ear.

332

"It...was...Carl," Olga whispered with great effort and Giovanni pulled back to meet her eyes. She nodded her head slowly and Angel saw Giovanni's back straighten, his jaw tense.

"What theatrics are these!" Giovanni growled, but Olga tugged at his fingertips a second time.

"Per l'anima della nostra amata madre, io te lo guiro... era Carl," she whispered in Italian and Angel saw a tear travel down her bruised skin. Giovanni stood straight but did not turn around.

Andrew called the paramedics from the hallway and they wheeled Olga from the room. Giovanni kept his eyes on Olga until she had gone and the doors were closed. He didn't even turn around when Angel began to speak.
"Grandfather," she said softly. "Carl murdered Detta Palumbo at the East Moon Motel and almost killed Olga when she tried to intervene. He then sneaked into the Penthouse, murdered Elsa because she could identify him and drugged little Caleb to cover his tracks."

"That is a lie!" Carl seethed. "Your sister and your granddaughter are conspiring against me!"

Giovanni turned to face them but didn't utter a sound.

Your sister is causing problems in the family AGAIN!" Carl scathed. "You should have taken care of her a long time ago. I told you."

Giovanni's eyes pierced through Angel, but she held his gaze. She was determined not to cower in fear, but to speak the truth even if he didn't believe her.

"Carl met with Serco Mertesca to arrange the details of the role Andrew would play in the Pope's assassination. Once Detta was dead, Carl communicated directly with Madeline to ensure the plan was executed smoothly," Angel continued.

"These are lies!" Carl spat.

"She's not lying," Taelon blurted and seemed to have surprised even himself when he spoke. "Um, with all due respect, Capo, sir, Angel is not lying." Taelon moved to the laptop next to Chase and danced his fingers across the keys, retrieving data and putting it on the big screen. "I can prove it," Taelon said. "I took all of the data from the cell numbers associated with Nicholas Diaglio, Detta Palumbo, the guy named Thomas, who blew up in the car bomb, Serco Mertesca, Madeline Diaglio-Brioschi-Venturini, and Carl Cusanelli..." Taelon took a deep breath. "I can prove that Carl has been in contact with each of these people."

For the first time, Angel saw a glimmer of fear in Carl's eyes.

"Is there anything you'd like to confess, Carl?" Angel taunted.

"Bah!" He spat arrogantly.

Angel turned toward Chase and said, "Okay, continue."

With the tap of a few keys, Chase placed a video on the big screen. "This is footage from the security cameras just outside of the East Moon Motel," Chase explained and Carl leapt to his feet, like a ravenous dog and began screaming in Italian. The entire room was shocked, none more than Giovanni, who stood motionless, staring at his friend.

Angel breathed a sigh of relief. They had finally broken him. She hadn't been sure it would happen.

"Everything would have been perfect if it wasn't for ..." Carl began but Chase interrupted him.

"Those meddling kids," Chase said and everyone stared at him. "You know, from Scooby Doo?" His comment was met with blank stares and Chase quickly turned his attention back to his laptop.

"Your sister and your granddaughter have made a mockery of you," Carl scathed.

Tony narrowed his eyes and held his .45 steady. "I don't think you're in any position to be pointing fingers, Ace," he seethed.

"You have grown weak, old friend," Carl said to Giovanni, "and I have stepped in to fill the gap in your authority. Look what I have done for you. For you."

Giovanni's jowls were drawn tight and his teeth clenched, but he said nothing. Instead, he looked at Carl Cusanelli with a piercing stare that Angel thought powerful enough to stop his heart or cause his brain to explode.

"You didn't want your granddaughter to marry a Venturini so I fixed the problem. I gave him a wife," Carl explained. "I have fixed all of your problems despite what your family has taken from me! My son is dead because of your whore of a daughter-in-law!" Carl's face reddened as his voice rose with rage.

Did he just call my mother a whore? It took Angel a moment to process his words and then she blurted, "Did you just call my mother a whore?"

Carl's cold eyes darted to Andrew, to Tony and then back to Angel. "Like mother, like daughter," Carl sneered.

"That's it!" Tony cocked his head to the side and took aim. "Permission?" He hollered but Giovanni did not respond. "Permission?" Tony repeated.

"He won't grant permission because he knows I speak the truth," Carl seethed. "His son was weak and fell to the charms of a well-known mafia whore, who lured him from New York and ultimately got him killed. At least when she got pregnant he was smart enough not to marry her. Who knows if the baby was even his? And look at Michelangela, following in her mother's footsteps, spreading her legs for every mob man this side of town. She has taken lovers from three of the five families!"

Angel's face flushed. He wasn't wrong. Tony was an Andriachini. Andrew was a Venturini and Grayson, God rest his soul, was a Galante. She couldn't refute the fact that she had had lovers from three of the five mafia families, though she didn't appreciate it being broadcast to the masses.

"Permission!" Tony yelled, his grip on the .45 tightening.

Carl laughed. "His sister betrayed him and his granddaughter is a feeble disappointment. I am the only one who has been loyal. I am the one who has stood by him every step. I have fixed every problem. I have made no errors." He turned to face Giovanni. "I have covered your weaknesses. I have sacrificed for your family. I have been strong, fierce and committed. I have NEVER let you down!" He screamed.

Giovanni never took his eyes from Carl.

"You stand there judging me when I have made you what you are!" Carl scathed. "Without me, you would have been taken out a long time ago. Without me, you would be nothing!" Carl's face was dark red and veins were protruding from his neck. "Your family has failed you where I have not. They have endangered you where I have protected you. When will you face the truth? The people in this room are against you. I am the only one who is for you!"

Giovanni allowed his eyes to move slowly over the faces of those in the room, and though she tried, Angel could not read his thoughts. Was he actually listening to what Carl was saying? Was he silent because he believed Carl spoke truth? She met his gaze and felt as if she were staring into an abyss. There was no emotion behind his eyes, no twinkle of recognition and no feeling etched across his brow. It was as if she were looking into the face of a monster and for a brief moment fear crept up the back of her neck.

"You can't offer a rebuttal because you know I am right!" Carl taunted. "You can't say a word because you know everything I have said is true!" Carl laughed. "You have nothing! Look at what the Maratinzanos have become because you have let three harlots run the show, mocking your authority with their betrayal. You are weak, Giovanni and undeserving of the position you hold. Capo di Tutti Capi...HA!" He spit on the floor in Giovanni's direction. "Yes! I corroborated with the Diaglio family to kill Pope Ignacio and yes, I framed Andrew to take the fall for it; and yes, I conspired to leave a trail of money that would lead the FBI to you," he panted. "Because you took my family from me. My son was murdered because of you and my grandson saw me as pathetic because I served you. I am pathetic no longer! DiPietro would become the new Pope and I would become the rightful Capo di Tutti Capi."

"DiPietro?" Angel asked, but she didn't pursue it further because, out of the corner of her eye, she saw Chase nod with recognition. She made a mental note to ask him about it later.

Giovanni turned and moved slowly toward the door.

"Uccidere i traditori in questa sala e dimostra di avere le carte in regola per essere il

Capo di Tutti Capi!" Carl sneered in Italian and though Angel didn't know what he had said, she knew it was powerful enough to make Giovanni stop dead in his tracks. "Dovrai dimostrare degno, vecchio amico, o ammettere che sono deboli," Carl added and Angel glanced around the room, searching faces for some sort of translation. Andrew dropped his eyes to the floor. Giovanni stood staunch. Taelon's mouth fell open. Chase's fingers froze on the keyboard and his eyes bulged from their sockets. Tony's jaw clenched tighter and the Snake raised his gun toward Carl and stepped next to Tony.

"Permission?" The Snake blurted.

The tension in the room was palatable and the silence deafening. Whatever Carl had said, it rendered everyone motionless. The only sound was that of Carl's panting.

"Rispondere!" Carl yelled and Angel didn't need that word translated. She knew Carl was demanding a response from Giovanni. "Or are you too afraid to speak?!" He seethed.

Angel pulled her gaze from Carl to Giovanni, anticipating that he would turn around and give Carl a piece of his mind; hoping that he would defend himself with a verbal lashing of epic proportions. He did nothing. As the weight of silence grew heavier in the room, Angel pondered whether he might be waiting for her or someone else to come to his defense? Should she speak up against Carl?

She licked her lips and swallowed hard, preparing to speak, but just as she opened her mouth, Giovanni's gruff tone filled the air. He uttered only one word. "Autorizzazione." In English it means "Permission."

It was unclear as to who killed Carl. Tony and the Snake fired simultaneously and their two shots made one large hole in the center of Carl's forehead. As his body hit the floor, Giovanni and his bodyguards left the room. Angel turned toward the door but Giovanni never looked back.

CHAPTER 71

The next morning Angel awoke to find a note at the foot of her bed. It was hand written and it read:

Michelangela ~
I am returning to New York and I would ask of you a favor. Enclosed is a check which contains the amount of money Carl received from the Diaglio family. I consider the money dirty and want to wash my hands of it. Perhaps you can use it to right the wrong that has been done in my name. My heart is broken and remaining here is a reminder of the treachery before me. Please give Lucia my love. You, dear Michelangela, have made me proud. You are not what Carl had spoken of you. Remember that.
Tutto il mio amore, which means all of my love ~
G i o v a n n i

Angel held the letter to her chest and cried.

CHAPTER 72

Parading into the secret meeting room with a manila file folder tucked neatly beneath her arm and Chase on her heels, Angel dipped her head in a gesture of respect and asked Tony, Andrew, Big Mike and the Snake to be seated. Pope Ignacio was already sitting at the head of the table with a body guard on each side. The men, with the exception of Chase, exchanged a quick glance, one that indicated their curiosity. What did Angel have up her sleeve? She had kept them and everyone in the dark, including the Pope.

"Your Eminence," Angel began, "I apologize for my tardiness."

"As you were the one who saved my life yesterday, you are forgiven," Pope Ignacio uttered with a grin and Angel smiled back. She liked that he had a sense of humor. It made him seem approachable.

Placing the file folder atop the table in front of her and letting her fingers rest gently upon it, Angel sat down with a sigh. "It's been quite a crazy couple of days," she said quietly.

"That is an understatement," Pope Ignacio interjected and Angel smiled. It was an understatement indeed.

"When I was a little girl I dreamt of meeting the Pope, but never did I imagine it would be under these circumstances," she said and Pope Ignacio nodded in agreement. "This week has changed me," Angel confessed and fought a wave of emotion that threatened to undo her. "I experienced fear unlike I have felt it before. In looking back, I can see that for the first time in my life I felt afraid for strangers' lives as much as for my own or my loved ones. I saw the weak and the innocent preyed upon and it angered me."

"We call that righteous anger," Pope Ignacio said with a sparkle in his eye.

Angel stood up and slowly paced around the table and all eyes followed her. "From the moment the first gun shot rang through the halls of East Side Junior High, I knew I was there for a reason; and as the events of the past few days unfolded, I became more certain." Angel stopped pacing and turned to face Pope Ignacio. "Your Eminence, I believe we are in this very room together because we were meant to be here. I'll admit the manner in which we arrived at this point is unorthodox, but here we are nonetheless and I have a proposal for you."

The Pope's security detail leaned toward him, the man to his right whispered in his ear and Pope Ignacio raised his hand and nodded, indicating that he understood whatever the man had said. Rising slowly, the Pope stared at Angel, his brown eyes engaging in what felt like a piercing analysis of motive. As soon as they saw him stand, Pope Ignacio's security detail were on their feet. "If you are suggesting that since you have saved my life, I owe you a favor, you must know, Ms. Maratinzano, that though I am eternally grateful for your actions, I do not do business with the Mob."

Angel swallowed hard. "I am not making you an offer you cannot refuse. I am presenting you with an opportunity that I believe you will not want to refuse." Angel neared him. "Your Eminence, there is no question that you and I live in two different worlds, but our desire for peace is very much the same. What I am proposing is not a business venture; it is an act of community."

Pope Ignacio lowered himself back into his seat and his security detail followed his lead. "I am listening."

Angel opened the manila folder and over the course of the next hour, she laid out the details of her proposition, point by point; and the Pope appeared pleased with her idea.

"When Cardinal DiPietro convinced me to come to your city to beseech my constituents toward peace, I had hoped my speech would inspire gangs to put down their weapons and stop their violent ways. I now realize that this is my true reason for being here," he said and tapped his fingertips atop the manila folder. "This will do more good in this city than any speech I could have delivered here."

Angel smiled at the sparkle in the Pope's eyes. She felt fulfilled. Together they would use the money Giovanni referred to as 'dirty' and the money the mob tried to launder through the church, to implement a city-wide protection program that would focus on security in Chicago schools. Children like Caleb wouldn't have to be afraid of gunmen in their classrooms. Teachers could do their job without being afraid. Parents wouldn't have to fear taking their kids to school. Together, they would minimize violence one school at a time.

As the Pope and his security team rose to leave, Angel said, "There is one more thing you should know."

Pope Ignacio turned toward her. "What is that?"

"Cardinal DiPietro cannot be trusted," she said and saw a hint of surprise in the Pope's face. "We've provided specific details in the folder, but he runs a secret society, one that is in favor of increasing mob relations with the church. You can recognize members by a tattoo , a capitol D with a cross in the center. The Diaglios are members of the DiPietro sect and are very dangerous. We have

343

evidence that he assisted in this attack against you and that the Diaglio family are grooming him to be the next Pope. Please be careful."

"Grazie, Michelangela, I will look into this," he said softly. "May God bless you."

Angel escorted the Pope and his security team to the secret meeting room door to say goodbye. After they left, she turned back around and was surprised to see Chase, Tony, the Snake and Andrew on their feet, smiling and applauding her.

"Damn-ass impressive, if you ask me," Chase said.

"Awesome idea, Babe," Tony added.

"Giovanni will be proud," the Snake said.

"Only a Maratinzano chick would come up with the idea for the mob and the church to work together," Chase uttered. "Wild-ass women, these Maratinzanos!"

Angel laughed. It was an unconventional plan, but it felt right. "Remember," she told them, "this is a secret partnership. No one can know about the relationship between us and the Pope; otherwise we won't be able to make it work."

"Right on, Boss Lady!" Chase whooped. "Taelon is already setting up a secure account through which the project can be anonymously funded."

Andrew never said anything, but she saw approval in his eyes.

CHAPTER 73

Caleb joined Angel out on the Penthouse balcony. "Whatcha doing out here?" He asked, slipping his hand inside hers.

"Sometimes I like to come out here and think," she said.

"About what?"

Angel lifted him atop one of the wrought iron chairs so she could look him in the eye. "I was thinking that maybe you would like to move into the Towers."

"With you?!" He shrieked and threw his arms tightly around her neck.

"Well, not with me, exactly," she told him. "Your Uncle Leo would move into one of the condos a couple of floors down and you would stay with him."

"You know he's not my real uncle, right?" Caleb scrunched up his nose.

"I know," Angel said. "But he wants to take care of you." Angel studied his little face. "Would it be okay if you lived here with Leo?"

"I could come up here anytime I wanted? And see you and play with Midnight and Mo?"

"Absolutely," she said and tousled his blonde hair. "Anytime you wanted."

Caleb was so excited that he leapt down from the chair and raced inside to find Midnight and Mo and tell them the good news. Angel laughed aloud and it felt good. She couldn't fix the big problems of the world, but if she could do something to help one person in their moment of need, then life somehow made sense. Helping others brought meaning to the chaotic existence of mafia life, which was why she had worked so hard to locate Leo's wife, Margo, and reunite them at the Towers. She couldn't force Margo to stay, but by offering them a home, a steady income and the promise that Leo would not be asked to murder anyone in cold blood, Angel hoped Margo would have a change of heart. Besides, Caleb needed parents and Angel had an inkling that Leo and Margo were the right couple for the job.

All she needed now was for Olga to be released from the hospital and the world would feel right again. Olga was making progress and had been moved out of ICU, but the doctor wanted to keep her a little longer for observation. She hadn't told Olga about Caleb yet because she wanted it to be a homecoming surprise. Angel smiled as she envisioned how Olga would spoil Caleb rotten with homemade Cannoli and cinnamon pancakes. Maybe a child was just what Olga needed to get her mind off of the fact that Carl had murdered Elsa; and Caleb could definitely use a doting grandmother in his life.

Caleb would be a good influence on Giovanni too, and Angel hoped he wouldn't stay away from Chicago too long. She knew he needed time to come to terms with Carl's betrayal and his death. Time to heal. They all needed it. As much as she wanted to take his pain away, she couldn't. Her only option was to be patient, to pray for him and to love him from afar.

As she leaned against the railing and momentarily closed her eyes, a familiar voice came from behind. "Penny?" He said and Angel turned to find Andrew standing in the doorway.

"No," Angel answered quietly. "You can't give me a penny for my thoughts." The whole penny-for-your-thoughts expression now made her think of Madeline and that made her want to vomit.

Andrew pursed his lips together. "I see. Well, maybe I could share my thoughts?" He didn't wait for her to answer. "I lost who I was," he said matter of factly. "With my dad and my brothers gone, I felt torn between who I was and who I was expected to be."

Angel turned to face him.

"I met with Giovanni and I asked for your hand in marriage," Andrew admitted and even though she had overheard him and the Snake discussing it, she was surprised by his disclosure.

"I knew the answer before I ever met with him, but I figured it was worth a shot." He smiled sheepishly, ran his fingers through his hair and momentarily stared at the ground. Angel could see that this was difficult for him.

"I wish you would have talked to me," she said. "I wish I would have known what was going on."

He nodded with obvious regret. "I just shut down, Sweetheart. I turned off everything I felt and..." he stopped talking and exhaled. "And I started blindly following orders. I guess I thought detaching from everything would hurt less."

Angel didn't respond. She didn't know what to say. Regardless of how it all went down, in the end he had pushed her away and married another woman. Nothing was going to change that. They stood in silence for a moment and then Andrew took her face in his hands. "Please say something."

"I don't know what to say," she uttered.

"I never wanted to hurt you, Sweetheart," he said, running the back of his hand along her cheek.

She wiggled from his grip. "You said horrible things to me..."

"I thought it would be easier if you hated me," he defended.

"Easier on who?" Angel blurted.

"I thought if you thought I was a jerk, you'd stop loving me quicker and move on."

"I DO think you're a jerk!"

"I know," he said.

"And I HAVE moved on!" She gritted, though she knew that statement wasn't entirely true. Her heart was still uncomfortably trapped between him and Tony.

"I know. I know," he stammered.

"But that doesn't mean I stopped loving you," she said softly. "I need time. This has been too much."

Andrew told her that he understood and headed back toward the door. "Oh," he stopped walking and turned around. "I left an M16A2 in the meeting room for Chase." He smiled. "I heard he was admiring my collection."

"I'll let him know," Angel said. "I know he'll be excited."

He turned toward the door to leave and then abruptly turned back around again. "And, I located Jack."

"Caleb's brother, Jack?" Angel stammered. She had been praying that he had survived the explosion, but she didn't want to get her hopes up. Caleb had been asking about him, and Angel feared she was going to have to tell him that Jack had been killed. "He survived?"

Andrew grinned. "He was released from the hospital yesterday, back into foster care." Andrew reached into his pocket and retrieved a folded piece of paper and handed it to Angel. "Here's the case worker's contact information. She's expecting a call from you; and from what I hear he's been asking about Caleb."

Angel's eyes misted with emotion. This was so Andrew. Through all of the chaos and the heartache, Andrew managed to focus on what was important to her, even when she hadn't verbalized it. He knew what she needed. Clearing her throat, she uttered a heartfelt, "Thank you."

Andrew nodded and turned a third time to leave. At the edge of the doorway, he spun on his heels. "One more thing," he said, holding up his index finger. "Last thing, I promise." He grinned. "I spoke with Giovani this morning and stepped down as Boss of the Venturini family."

Angel was completely shocked. This was unprecedented. Bosses didn't step down, they died. Death was the only way out. "Why would you do that? Who will take over?"

Reaching into his jacket pocket he pulled out his Detective badge and held it up. "This is who I am," he said with a sparkle in his eye that Angel hadn't seen in months, and it made her feel suddenly overcome with excitement. "I gave a few names to Giovanni, guys I recommend. I'm sure he'll be contacting you and the other Bosses soon to set up a meeting."

"So, I guess this is a good time to tell you that I've asked Leo the Lion and Taelon to work for me?" She grinned sheepishly, knowing that trying to steal members from other families was taboo.

Andrew chuckled. "You seem to be breaking all of the rules. I'd recommend Pete Bellasco, too."

Angel felt the sudden urge to rush to his arms. She didn't know what would happen going forward, but for right now it didn't matter. Andrew was back. The Andrew she knew and loved was back and a weight was lifted. She ran to him and threw her arms around his neck. They embraced with the firm intent of two people who didn't want to let go. The feel of his arms wrapped tightly around her was a rush of healing, the fire of wanting and the calm of safety all rolled into one.

"I'm glad you're back," she whispered and planted a tender kiss on his neck. "I didn't like that other guy."

"I didn't either," he said with a smile, squeezing her a little tighter. "He was a real ass."

"You got that right, Ace." Tony's voice boomed from the doorway. "Except for the use of the past tense. Some might say you're still a real ass. Now, you wanna get your hands off my girl?"

"Oh, is this YOUR girl? I hadn't noticed," Andrew said with a smirk and wrapped his arms even tighter around Angel's waist, playfully lifting her feet off of the ground and swinging her around in a circle. Tony didn't catch on to what Andrew had said, but Angel knew the underlying meaning. *"I hadn't noticed"* meant he was choosing to forget about walking in and finding her and Tony in bed the morning after she had stolen his SUV. It was Andrew's way of forgiving her.

"Aren't you married?" Tony provoked.

"Annulled," Andrew retorted.

"I'd hate to have to splatter your brains all over the patio, Ace," Tony warned and Angel gave him a scolding glare.

"Don't you have somebody to cavity search or someplace to go?" Andrew teased.

"Yeah, I plan on conducting a long and fulfilling cavity search," he rebutted. "Why do you think I'm here?" Tony smirked and Andrew released Angel from his arms, his smile quickly fading.

"Tony!" Angel scolded. She didn't like him rubbing Andrew's nose in the fact that they had slept together. "I'm sorry," she muttered to Andrew.

"It's okay, Sweetheart. I made this bed. I can handle lying in it."

Parading over and draping his arm around Angel's shoulder, Tony grinned. "I don't care where you lie, Ace, as long as you're not lying in her bed."

"Worried?" Andrew chided and Angel felt Tony's back stiffen. "Because I think you look a little worried."

Tony guffawed. "After the way you treated her, it would take a miracle for you to ever wake up next to her again."

Angel gawked at both of them. How could they stand there talking about sleeping with her right in front of her? *Unbelieveable!* It was like witnessing a pissing contest. It was like watching two male dogs scamper around marking their territory.

Andrew pressed his lips together and slowly nodded. "You may be right," he uttered and made his way toward the door. Just as he was about to step through the glass door, he turned slowly to face them, keeping his gaze locked on Angel. "But lucky for me, miracles do happen and with a little... *Divine Intervention...*maybe they'll happen again."

Andrew winked at Angel and she felt her stomach flutter. Andrew was back.

351

ABOUT THE AUTHOR

S.R.Claridge, nominated for the 2010 Molly Award, 2013 Pushcart Prize, awarded 2014 Best Short Story Suspense and awarded the 2011 Rocky Mountain Fiction Writers Pen Award, writes full-time and lives in Colorado. She loves autumn, moonlight and Grey Goose martinis with bleu cheese olives. She believes Friday nights are for indulging in Mexican food and Margaritas and Sunday mornings warrant an extra-spicy Bloody Mary. Growing up in St. Louis, Missouri and earning her BA in Psychology from the University of Missouri, Columbia, S.R.Claridge is a mixture of mid-western family values and western wild nights. She loves Jesus, believes in the power of prayer, in the freedom of forgiveness and that life is a gift that should be enjoyed to the fullest. With a background in theatre, S.R.Claridge creates characters with dramatic flair and is known for her intense plot twists and engaging humor. She would rather walk dangerously where there is a view than sit in idle safety and let life pass her by. Her spirited outlook comes shining through in her novels, as she takes readers to the edge of their seats with bone-chilling suspense. ~

AUTHOR ACCLAIM

"The Just Call Me Angel series is suspense at its best."
- RipeReviews

"A unique series from a one-of-a-kind author."
- APEX Reviews

"Riveting!"
- TrueBlueEbookReview

"One thrilling moment after another!"
- CanadaReviews

"A best-seller candidate indeed."
- BookWatchMagazine

BOOKS BY S.R.CLARIDGE

Tetterbaum's Truth *(book 1 in the Just Call Me Angel series)*
Traitors Among Us *(book 2 in the Just Call Me Angel series)*
Russian Uprising *(book 3 in the Just Call Me Angel series)*
Death Trap *(book 4 in the Just Call Me Angel series)*
Loose Ends *(book 5 in the Just Call Me Angel series)*
Divine Intervention *(book 6 in the Just Call Me Angel series)*

Petals of Blood *(short story; Pushcart Prize Nomination 2013)*
Spouse in My House (short story a la stylings of Dr. Seuss)

The Candy Shop *(suspense thriller)*

House of Lies *(political cult suspense thriller)*

No Easy Way *(debut novel; nominated for The Molly Award from the HODRW 2010)*

S.R.Claridge has also ghostwritten over ten novels.